Katie Kingman

DOWN WITH THIS SHIP

Katie
Kingman

DOWN
WITH THIS
SHIP

Mendota Heights, Minnesota

First Edition
First Printing, 2021

Book design by Jake Nordby
Cover design by Jake Nordby
Cover images by Elina Li/Shutterstock, Natasha_Chetkova/ Shutterstock, NewFabrika/Shutterstock, tete_escape/ Shutterstock, DeskGraphic/Shutterstock, Shumilina Maria/ Shutterstock, AlemCoksa/Pixabay

Flux, an imprint of North Star Editions, Inc.

Library of Congress Cataloging-in-Publication Data (pending)
978-1-63583-067-5

Flux
North Star Editions, Inc.
2297 Waters Drive
Mendota Heights, MN 55120
www.fluxnow.com

Printed in Canada

To Allison and Brindy
The garden of my imagination would never
have grown without you there to water it

CHAPTER ONE

I've scribbled some of my best story ideas in my notebook, in the margins of my otherwise boring notes. Nothing fuels my brainstorming for fan fiction like the forty minutes of equations and algorithms I sat through this morning in Algebra, and thus was born this morning's light bulb: the best dang almost-kiss *The Space Game*'s fandom has ever seen. If I pull it off just right, my readers will be needing shipper CPR.

I can do it. I know I can. But first, I have to survive writing this little poem in Creative Writing.

I push my glasses farther up my nose. I really hope Mrs. Liu isn't going to ask us to read these aloud. Writing fanfic online is one thing. Reading my assignment in front of an audience is another. Just the thought that she might call on me has my heart pumping so hard I can feel it through my lucky mustard sweater.

Colin Clarke, seated right in front of me, angles forward, focusing on the school's worn-down Chromebook. He bends farther into his keyboard, the back of his chair scooting closer to my desk. Soon he'll be knocking against it. I groan. Audibly. Intentionally. I didn't work to get into Honors Creative Writing only to be stuck behind Mr. Aiming for Valedictorian, especially when he can't mind his own airspace.

My cursor blinks, waiting for a command. The first few stanzas

I've haphazardly written aren't nearly enough to impress Mrs. Liu . . . but maybe the fact that my blog is in the running for Best FanFic on Stumblr would?

Not that I would ever tell her.

I close my eyes and before I know it, the words are coming from my fingertips—flowing richer than our Vermont maple syrup during the first frost of the season.

"Colin," Damian Wiles, a few seats back, whispers. "Colin!"

"Quiet, Damian," Colin says, nodding in his buddy's direction. "I've got to finish this metaphor."

Damian leans forward, covering his Panic! At The Disco T-shirt. Sometimes he wears a *The Space Game* T-shirt, and I get super antsy. It's *my* show, but I don't want to talk about it in here. "Did you study for the AP Bio practice test?"

"I had the summer assignment done the first weekend of break." Colin looks past me and nods at Damian. They share a nerdy grin.

Woo-hoo. More academic achievements unlocked for the smartest guys at school. "Can you guys please shut up?" I cup my hands around my face, attempting to focus on my screen.

"And the Curve-Breaker is here to destroy us all again," Hailey LaFonte, a few seats over, whispers. The Curve-Breaker. That's what the whole school calls Colin. If he's in your class—no matter the subject—don't even hope for a curve on a test. He's an exceptional writer too, and he knows it.

"You know I will," he says.

"Let me read my poem first this time," Hailey asks him, her voice all singsongy. "I've been practicing iambic pentameter with my tutor."

Ugh. So many kids at this school, with their top-notch tutors and fancy college-preparedness classes, don't realize that all you need is another skilled writer to help you hone your craft. That's what Michaela, my bestie, helps me with. But the kids at this school throw around their money like nobody's business.

Hailey and I, and a few others, had a short-lived friendship in middle school, but we didn't see eye to eye on where the show was heading (i.e., my ship, *the* only ship, the *correct* ship), and that was the end. And when Hailey said she'd never see why Captain Worley was willing to send Pippa to her maniacal uncle, I was done with them. You have to recognize a good story to be my friend. Plots get uncomfortable. You have to see them through. When our group split, I started calling them the anti's and we've done nothing but grumble at each other since then.

"Did you study?" Colin asks me, peeking around my computer screen. He's got this little glimmer in his eye, one corner of his mouth tucked in.

"Did you miss it when I said shut up? I asked nicely," I whisper, unavoidable sarcasm slipping in as I angle the screen down. "You know I'm not in that class."

"Whoops," he says, teasing. "Guess I forgot."

I squint. "No, you didn't." Sometimes it seems like he's just looking for excuses to talk to me. He's been a jerk to me since we swapped papers back in freshman year and he broke the red-ink oath all peer editors take: no laughing at your partner's piece, and I decided that I was never going to work with Colin Clarke again. But fate's fickle—she keeps putting us in the same writing classes.

They go back to whispering and giggling to one another, and I cup my hands around my face again, hoping everyone else will disappear.

Maybe someday I'll tell them I'm the most widely read writer here. But then again, maybe not. Social suicide doesn't sound too great when I've got one more year in high school.

None of the kids at school—save for my brother, Will, and Michaela—have any idea who I am. *Spacer*, my blog, gets thousands of hits every month. My audience wouldn't even fit in this whole school. If my classmates knew, this little competition for top-of-the-class would be over. Hands down. But I've learned something. Writing fan fiction may get me a lot of readers, but in high school it isn't exactly a one-way ticket to respect.

I hear the talk about fan fiction. It's *smut for fangirls who can't get a boyfriend. Nothing but a waste of time.*

They're wrong. It's a hobby. It's escapism. It's cathartic. So I've learned to be careful. To write only when I'm sure no one can see my screen. When no one is peeking over my shoulder.

My classmates will never know, because my blog is my space-y, angsty secret.

Back to the poem. My cursor mocks me with its little blinky-blink. Gotta get through the day first. I stick my pen in my hair just above where the braid begins.

"Gonna read your poem aloud, Kole?" Damian asks. A few heads turn. Their gazes burn like my curling wand. "If you're done."

Ugh. Even Damian knows she's going to ask for read-alouds, one of Crystal Lake Prep's favorite torture methods. In a private school this competitive—one where acceptance to one of the Ivy Leagues is a goal for a lot of kids here—reading aloud is a big deal because you, number one, get the spotlight, and number two, get the admiration of the teacher. Nothing works better on them come letter of recommendation time than a kid who's been one of the best since August.

Well, leave that to the others. The Ivys aren't my endgame.

"Read your own, Damian," I say.

"Ten minutes to wrap it up, my little Apples. First person willing to read their poem to the class gets extra participation points for the week," Mrs. Liu says. She always calls us Apples—that's Crystal Lake Prep's mascot. She's been teaching Creative Writing for so long her hair has started to go gray with pencil lead, but she knows her stuff.

I lean forward, settling into Colin's shade, fingers dancing across the home row as I wrap up a stanza.

Colin leans backward. Again. Oh, what rhymes with *elephant*? Cause he's just about that tall. Not that he's huge, just tall, and his gray sweater matches an elephant's hide almost exactly. And he's kind of awkward in the tiny chair.

Oh! There it is. *Sycophant.* An SAT word, bound to show up in one of those writing passages. And a better idea for my last line.

Banging the final word on the keyboard, I hit print on the Google Docs menu. We only had fifteen minutes to write this little work of art, which is totally the point of the exercise, and I'm the first done. *Nice job.*

A quick reread and *print.*

I shut my Chromebook just as Colin does, and flip around to put it back in the cart. It takes just a second to slip trusty #19 into her little slot, and the printer, which I lovingly call Lavinia, buzzes to life. I reach for my piece, the soft, thin sheet warm from the lasers inside. I swear it's happy to meet our world of typos and exclamation points, red pens and em dashes. Maybe it's even proud to have my words on it.

"That's mine." Colin reaches around me, his cologne flooding my nostrils. He grazes the long braid that hangs down one of my shoulders and grabs the paper clean out of my hand. It slips through my fingers, leaving a little paper cut.

"Ah—" I start, glancing at the top. *Crap.* It *was* his. Which means *he* was the first one done. I grumble, "Thanks for the paper cut."

I shoot a nasty look at Lavinia. She did me dirty.

"I finished first." He narrows his eyes when he says *first*, staring from behind his thick-rimmed square glasses that just happen to look exactly like mine. They match the deep gray of his sweater and his cold robotic heart.

"Whatever," I say.

He glances at my hand and when he looks back at me, the sarcasm is gone. "And I'm sorry about the paper cut."

I pause, blinking three times. He's at his nicest when he has to pass back a paper and he grunts to get my attention, but if he's gonna try civility, I'll give it a half second too. "It's no big deal." I stick the soft spot between my thumb and forefinger in my mouth. It only stings a little, but I make it seem like it really hurts. Must be the little sister in me.

He glances at my mouth. "Me being the first one done is usually how it goes in this class, right?" Civility over. Back to sass.

Damian snickers and leans back in his chair to watch us. "A valiant effort. Very *Braveheart*."

"That movie's like eighty years old. And we all know *first* rarely means *better*." I reach for the bottom end of my braid. It lands just where my left elbow is. When Colin looks, I fold my arms and hug my sweater to my chest. He needs to be about three more feet away from me. I wave a few fingers in the air. "Now move along."

He runs a hand through his dark hair. It's grown too long around the ears. "It's cool. Just try not to take credit for my work again. Might start to get embarrassing for you if Mrs. Liu catches on." He smiles, one little mountain peak forming on his cheek.

"Not even, Colin."

"Take it easy. I'm just joking." Colin hits my shoulder with the paper as he reaches over. I catch a whiff of what must be his dad's cologne again. I crinkle my nose. It smells like freshly chopped Christmas trees and mint straight from a late summer garden. A little bit of dirt too.

God, he's the worst.

"Someday you'll beat him," Damian says, eyes on me. He slips a pencil through his overly gelled hair and it stays tucked behind his ear. "I have faith in you."

I shoot him a look. If I say anything, I admit I care. And I shouldn't care about being faster than Colin. I should not give the competition in here one more thought. But I'm not that person.

I try to rip my paper from Lavinia, the devious old dinosaur, just before she's ready to release the sheet, but her muscles strain against my tug. She makes one of those whirring sounds like she's choking, so I take my hand away. *I hit print first. You and I both know it.*

"So, you wanna know something?" Michaela snuck up behind me as I was preoccupied. She's been my bestie for the last few years, since before we broke from the anti's. Our group dissipated through the first season of *The Space Game*, when we started to disagree on content. It didn't matter all that much until we got so wrapped up in the story that lines were drawn. Enemies were made. And now, when we see the other girls, we just ignore them.

"What?" I turn to her. Michaela's a Black, bi goddess, with

super short hair, big brown eyes, and eyeliner that's always on point. Today her hair is a freshly dyed shade of hot pink. It brings out the undertones in her dark skin and makes her smile pop. "That writing under a time constraint is a terrible idea?"

"Eh, it's not so bad. This little poem is the best I can do, that's for sure." She shrugs.

"Then what's up?"

"K, now, don't be mad at me. It's just something I've noticed." She puts a hand on my arm, as though I'll need support for what she's about to say.

Lavinia finally spits out my paper and I snatch it. "Oh geez. I'm about to be mad, aren't I?" I urge her to the side. The others are starting to line up for their drafts, and I don't want them to over-hear. It might be something about *The Space Game*, or my blog, or Will—she's had a crush on my brother for years. Or, knowing Michaela, it might be what color she'll be painting her nails tonight.

She leans into my hair and cups her hand around my ear. "Seeing Colin be an ass to you, for like the third time this week, made me think of something."

I put my hand over my mouth and glance at Colin. Heat builds in my chest. "I've been an ass to him too. I can dish it." He's already at the podium, waiting for the rest of us to finish up. Whenever it's his turn to read aloud, he basks like a lizard in the sun. I can only hope to be that confident, as it would take a major personality reboot.

She gets a big, wide grin on her face and says in a singsongy voice, "I noticed. You guys have a *thing*."

"No, we don't. There's no *thing*," I answer too quickly. She better not be getting any weird ideas . . . he's pumped full of entitlement, like the rest of the junior class owes him praise. That's the only *thing* I'm thinking about Colin Clarke.

"You and Colin, I could totally see becoming something other than enemies," she whispers, her paper cupped around her mouth.

She's going to say it. I know it. She *ships* us. As in wants us in a relation*ship*.

My gaze sticks to him, perched at the podium with his paper ready. Just when I should break eye contact, Colin flashes one of those quick smiles in my direction. I taste my breakfast.

"Besides, your names sound really cute together. *Kole and Colin*," she whispers.

"Stop. Now," is all I can muster.

"We could call you *Kole-n*—no, that doesn't sound right." She smiles. He knows we're talking about him. "How about *Kol-Col*? I'm picturing adorable engagement photos with matching black-rimmed glasses and L.L. Bean boots. Some red plaid jackets and a golden retriever would only add to the cuteness."

"Shut up, Michaela," I say under my breath as heat rises to my cheeks. This is humiliating, even if our glasses do match. There's no way I'd ever date him. He's too cocky. Too smart. Too . . . tall. "I don't see myself that far in the future, unless I'm in Hollywood. Writing for the show."

"This is all down the road, naturally. And I'm talking about your second home. For now, we're going to have to call you guys something, because I'm totally starting to ship it."

My palm sweats around my paper. Colin, still on the other side of the room, flicks his hand at me in a tiny wave.

"All right, Apples. Let's listen to Colin's poem," Mrs. Liu says as everyone heads to their seats.

I swallow, taking my seat again. There will be no shipping here. None. Nada. Nilch. Especially not with me. Save that crap for online, not real life.

I climb out of my window onto the roof, turn on the star twinkle lights that run across the opening into my bedroom, spread out my ancient green blanket, and pop my knuckles. My cross-eyed cat, Cricket, gets comfortable between my legs. So many stars in the sky tonight, hardly a cloud to hide behind. Once I pop my earbuds in, I won't be able to hear the moving truck that's taken up residence in the driveway across the street, and I'll be able to tune out Will's inane dribbling on our court in the backyard. He should be heading inside soon.

I open the trusty hand-me-down laptop my parents gave me a few years ago. It'll help keep this early September night a little bit warmer, since it's often on the verge of overheating.

T-minus five months until *The Space Game* returns, if they stick to the same schedule they did last year. Everyone watches it. Heck, every teenager with Wi-Fi and a phone. Or a TV, but those are really just for parents. The show is about a group of space pirates who've been tasked with trying to bring down a powerful mogul and save their own butts. Not exactly what you would expect in space, but how often can you watch a ragtag group of heroes save the galaxy? This one's something different. And magical, especially if you add in a good slow-burn ship spurred on by a crap ton of forced proximity. God, I love it.

A few years ago, when Michaela and I started writing fanfic about the show, I kept going long after she bailed. I veered from canon after season one, but I try to pull in some of the ideas from the actual show as I go. You have to incorporate the canon to appease some readers, but mostly I do what I want, especially as it relates to the leading man—I live and breathe for el supremo space-angst case, quartermaster Byron Swift. I stan him so hard. I would get his name tattooed across my chest with little flowers that wrap over my collarbone if my parents would let me. And then, at a con, if I'm lucky enough to meet the actor someday, I'd have him sign my collarbone in bright red lipstick.

Tonight's *Spacer* entry starts with some hefty feels. It'll get the shippers, those who want a few of the characters to get together more than they want anything in their actual lives, really riled up. Especially when Byron leans into Pippa's hair, but no kiss follows—those are the best scenes. A number of us had hoped an actual kiss would happen in the season finale—the writers had only spent the last four seasons building up to this lip-lock, but no kiss came. Tonight I'm hoping to get those feels in there, the kind that keep my readers up late at night and counting down the days until the season premiere.

I tug a crocheted blanket around my shoulders and push my glasses farther up my nose as the laptop grunts to life. Google Chrome and the link to Stumblr load. A quick click and I'm logged in. Like so many nights on my roof, *The Space Game* is now mine.

Eighteen thousand-ish unique visitors are on the site right now. So, if about twenty-eight thousand people read last week's entry—the one where Pippa and Byron's brother, Benedick, were training in hand-to-hand combat—with what I'm hoping to accomplish tonight, there should be upwards of thirty thousand readers next week.

I close my eyes and swallow hard. That's a metric shit ton. The comments section will be lit up like the scoreboard at one of Will's basketball games after he's made a slam dunk.

Okay, maybe Mom is right. I do get a high off this. It *is* an obsession.

But, in my defense, the show can't be on *every* week of *every* year, so I had to start writing my stories. And then other superfans found them and they became *Spacer*. The rest is just numbers and code and internet magic. My stories burn through the show's canon like wildfire, and readers need to be fed, especially on hiatus, when the show's renewal hasn't been confirmed yet. I fill in the little blanks because, truth be told, *The Space Game* is a crappy show, but it's also the best show ever; it has the right mix of CGI, beautiful actors, gratuitous kissing, and terrible plot twists to keep us all glued to our beanbags.

I click *new entry*. All I have to do is let go and let my mind take over. Let my fingers walk across the keys and type together the next round of *The Space Game*'s story. My readers will like it. I've been on a streak of mostly good comments for three days now. One of my longest runs.

As the old computer loads a blank entry, I watch the little girls moving in across the street. They're cute little redheaded dolls, but the license plate on the truck in front of their house says Massachusetts. I groan. Mass-holes.

Oh, *Boston*. Hey . . . maybe what I'm about to write will come up at the con they're having in a few months. God, that would be unreal. It'd be a dream to get to go, but I don't think Mom would ever okay a trip. I'll stick to watching the livestreams closely like Michaela and I always do, with a glass of sparkling cider and a box of Hot Tamales.

Blank page loaded. Here goes. I shut my eyes. From up here, above the cold, quiet streets of Crystal Lake, it's safe to write the galaxy of *The Space Game*. Heck, when I'm on my roof and all I can see are the Vermont stars, their sparkles slip into my words faster than I can type, and I drown in their consonant constellations.

So, yeah, maybe I'm a bit obsessed.

I sit up straight—no need for a backache tomorrow. Time to get into Byron's head. I move to the right side of the page, past the bright red notification of potential doom, *542 new comments.* I shut my eyes. *Keep going. Don't click until you're done for the night.*

I wiggle my fingers, feeling for the home row. *No pressure, Kole. You're about to write the almost-kiss that will break the fandom.*

And, go.

SPACER 3.4

Posted by: ToTheStars
Sept. 6, 2019. 9:46

Pippa lifts her head, the raindrops sliding off her forehead, and moves her face so close to Byron's that he can smell those damn flowers again. "Did you see the Orwell comet? I've waited for it."

"I saw it," he whispers into her hair, the cold evaporating. Orwell's not due for another ten weeks or so. The light was probably from when her head hit the ground.

She closes her eyes and rests her head on his shoulder. Byron flinches at the contact, but then he shifts his head just a little closer. This attraction isn't something he's felt in a good long while, and that hair's too near his nose again. It's starting to itch beyond something he can scratch.

He clears his throat before he tries to speak.

"Shut up, Dipshit!"

I rip out my earbuds. Did I seriously just type what someone on the other side of the street was yelling? The girls down below are too loud if I can hear them from my rooftop *and* over the sound of the music pumping through my ears.

Slam. A box slides down the ramp leading out of the moving van across the street and Cricket makes a bumbling dash through the window and into my bedroom. *Asteroids.* She sliced a big fat scratch on my thigh. It stings through my jeans.

I tap my ring finger on the delete key over and over again until the last sentence is sent down to the depths of hell. The cursor slips back to just after the word *speak* and the little pixels stare at me, daring me to command them. My fingers flinch above the keys, my left eyebrow cocked. My wrist twitches.

No thoughts come. I was in a zone—words were flowing for the first time since Michaela made my stomach do flip-flops in Creative Writing yesterday.

Crash. I pop in my earbuds, clenching my eyes shut as another box meets the ground. So much for tonight's writing session. Sorry, cursor, sorry readers, sorry feels that won't be felt.

With these new neighbors, my nights will be less peaceful. And the swearing I keep hearing? Most of it is coming from the boy, who looks about my age. He's definitely taller than me, definitely cuter, and definitely cooler. Sandy-colored hair, kinda long-ish, and he's moving around the boxes like he's done this a million times. From up here, he vaguely resembles . . . Byron.

Hot dang.

Or the actor that plays him, at least.

And this guy's voice, even though the words are less than pretty, makes me turn my music down. If chocolate had a voice, it would be his.

The new family has literally been unloading stuff the entire evening. The brother's now carrying a dollhouse infinitely bigger than the one I had. He staggers, about to drop the thing, and at the last second catches it. Impressive.

"I'm not going to be your best friend anymore!" one of the little girls shouts as he stumbles. I smile. That always worked with Will too. Now we fight over whether or not he's cleaned his hair out of the sink.

Eyes back on the computer. It's 10:01 on a Friday night. If I have to finish this post tomorrow, that means less time to finish my short story, which means less time to make sure it's my best paper. And less time to overthink the fact that Best FanFic winners are being announced on Monday.

Sweat builds on my forehead, the rush of excitement hitting my belly—the same kind I get when a new episode begins.

If my screen name, *ToTheStars*, pops up, I very well may die on my roof. Stumblr is the number-one site for fan fiction. That means viewers upon viewers upon viewers if you're nominated by readers and the admins pick you. I've been dreaming of unlocking this achievement since I started *Spacer*, but back then it was a pipe dream. Now it's something even Mom could be proud of. Maybe it would make her consider me a *real writer*.

I let out a heavy sigh.

Maybe.

And Byron and Pippa *will* win Best Ship. There's no bigger one true pairing, or OTP, on the interwebs. This is my hill and I will die on it, sweaty and red-faced, clutching the asteroid prop I won on eBay. And, when they win, Stumblr will pick the best fan site. In years past, winners have had fan pages dedicated to *their* fan page. Traffic has skyrocketed. And the fan art that I've seen . . . it's the stuff that writers dream of when they go to sleep after draining their fingers of prepositions.

I take off my glasses and rub my eyes. I flip around, make sure my shirt stays in place over the tiny roll just under my belly button and above my jeans, and crawl back inside. After plugging in my junky laptop's charger, I unplug the twinkle lights. The golden halo outside the window disappears.

I plop on the bed, wiggle out of my pants, undo my braid, and grab my pillow. Cricket's less-than-graceful leap on the foot of my bed rocks the wooden frame.

Yeah, Monday's gonna be a day.

Stumblr: Best Ship 2019

Sept. 9, 2019. 4:00

Hello Stumblrs!

The days are long. The hours we squeeze in to write our little fan hearts out are short, but that doesn't stop us! And here at Stumblr we're proud to announce the winners of our yearly contest, Best Ship. There were 15 incredible ships, but only one could be named the best.

As you know, we've got over 10,000 users that post weekly chapters from their art and fiction blogs, and we'll be posting links to the best fan fiction blogs if your little heart craves more than what canon has to offer.

For those new to Stumblr, we're a place where writers go to express their love, to celebrate being a fan by making their show their own. Some of our blogs are pure rubbish, some are close but no cigar, but some are pretty darn great. A select few are gold. Silver. And, well, bronze . . . as you'll see below. So, with no more further ado, we're proud to announce the top three Best Ships of 2019!

1. Byron + Pippa, *The Space Game*

   Best FanFic: **ToTheStars**

   ToTheStars's version of *The Space Game*, and the girl torn between her duties as a daughter and her love for a space pirate, stole our hearts at first read. We just can't get their take on the show out of our heads. And, oh, the angst. Dare I say we've all got our favorite ships in the office, and we can't wait to see how the story wraps up! Pippa's got some tough choices ahead of her . . . Congrats to ToTheStars for taking first place!

2. Dingo + Sasha, *TrampStamps*

   Best FanFic: **SomeoneCalltheCops**

   If anyone can make a story about Godzilla's godson interesting, it's this guy! He brings a little Jane Austen to the familiar monster-attacks-a-city story, and we're so here for it. Unless, of course, he includes that mating scene he's always teasing us about. *shudder*

3. Maple + Fig, *Tree Diaries*

   Best FanFic: **NoNeedForAFilter**

   When it comes to saving a forest, we love seeing how Maple and Fig band together and keep the evil corporations from burning them down. NoNeedForAFilter makes our emotions run wild—and the tree puns? We're loving them!

All right, Stumblrs—there's your winners! If you remember, our winner last year, PutonDeodorant, was a guest at GamerCon and went on to write a web comic all his own. Put on your pants, winners, your lives are about to change! Just don't forget us tiny nuts over here at Stumblr when you get your movie deals.

CHAPTER TWO

ToTheStars *just won Best FanFic on Stumblr.*

I survive a day at school and come home to this? I . . . won? Is Mercury in retrograde again? Or is this some glitch in the system? All more likely possibilities than a whole lot of someones at Stumblr thinking my version is the best version of *The Space Game.*

My breath is coming in so hard I can feel my stomach in my hips. I sit up straight, my bed creaking.

This is a big deal. A very, very big deal.

My phone, on my desk, lights up. Notifications are coming in.

I see myself on a stage, roses and peonies and carnations thrown at my feet as my adoring fans scream their devotion at me. I'm in a long blue dress, glitter sparkling more than the stars out the front window of the *Snapdragon* as it rips through the galaxy. Nina Garcia, the actress who plays Pippa, stands at my side, clapping as she places a hand on my shoulder. And everyone else—they're looking at me. Waiting for me to say something.

Hang on. My heart races faster. Having people staring at me is not on my list of favorite things. I shut my eyes. It was a fun thought. *Okay, Kole. Get to work. Your fans need you.*

Spacer waits.

When blood pumps through my veins again, I scroll through the three entries I wrote since last season ended. I spin the wheel of my worn mouse over and over. This is where the new hits will begin. My heart thumps in my fingertips.

I pull my legs underneath me, bunching my purple quilt up and disturbing Cricket's mid-afternoon bath. The heat in my palms builds, the sweat rising to the surface and seeping through my skin. Soon my fingers will be slipping across the keys.

I close my eyes.

Any second now, the words will come.

Like, right now.

I open my eyes.

The words . . . they're not coming.

I skim through the first entry, and there, in the second-to-last line, is a big old typo. I close my eyes. It's the wrong *there*. In the swear word of my favorite space heroine, *feck me*.

I can fix it. It's fine. In the next few minutes, the hit count will go from the 30,000-ish that followed the rabbit hole to my site to a whole heck of a lot more. Tears pool under my eyes. I blink, trapping them. This is going to bring a lot of readers. A lot of judgment. A lot of people catching the occasional typo. But this is what I wanted, right? I gulp. Maybe I didn't think that far ahead. I just wanted to win. And now . . . I have.

I grab a handful of jelly beans from the bag next to me and toss a few into my mouth. Chewing on a green one, I lean my head against an old Paramore poster. One of the thumbtacks pushes into my shoulder, sharp and jagged, and I flip my braid around to cushion the pressure. Across the room, the late afternoon sun shines on my signed *Space Game* poster. I won it on eBay last year; best money I've ever spent, even if it wiped my savings out. Byron's furrowed brow stares back at me, with his trademark stoic expression. What a hunk.

Winning Best FanFic is something really freakin' awesome. And my ship, which is obviously the best, just made number one. I ball my fingers up in front of my face and let out a silent scream to the fangirl gods. Byron and Pippa deserve this. This is a victory to them, and my interpretation rides in the wake of *The Space Game*. That's effing phenomenal, *but* I just got linked to a whole lot of eyes. That's effing horrifying.

I pick at my right index finger, biting a hangnail until it stings. *Refresh*. The pixels stutter and do nothing. *Oh, asteroids. Spacer* is getting slower. The fans are coming. I click to the web builder, where the graph of unique visitors is rising up, up, up in real time. So many hits. Commenters with their cat-o'-nine-tails. Haters with their pitchforks.

But . . . new fans?

Possibly.

Refresh.

594,328 unique visitors on my site at this moment.

Refresh.

618,403.

I can't change a thing. It'll be too confusing. The words will stay as they are. I fold my arms over my knees. This is just me, an old laptop, Google Docs, and a red squiggly line I like to call Two Finger Tap. I must own the typos. This is just practice for the big leagues—when I'm writing for a real TV show. Like one of those cute Netflix rom-coms, or a dystopia on Hulu. Those shows where some fans like what you write and some want to burn it on the stairs of the courthouse. The divisive kind.

I take off my glasses and rub my eyes. Hopefully my mascara doesn't bleed and make big old ravenous raccoon circles.

"Kole! Mom's going to be home in twenty! Make dinner!" It's Will. He's in his room, yelling on the other side of the bathroom that crosses between our bedrooms. I'm sure he's just come in from the basketball court and is dripping sweat on the floor we both share. *Yuck.*

"Oh geez. Okay." I scoot the laptop over to my desk.

Will comes into my room, past my dresser and the heaping pile of laundry that sits on my desk chair. That's only *part* of the reason why I write on the roof. "What's new in the Kole-sphere?"

All right, first time saying it in real life. "Are you ready for this? I just won Best FanFic."

"Seriously? That competition that you were going on about the other day? The one you stood *no chance of winning*?" He mocks my voice, like some kind of a singsongy bird.

"That's it." I hear the disbelief in my own words—and then it happens before I can stop myself. I squee. A high-pitched, fangirly kind of sound—like the air that flies out of the bottom end of a balloon. Cricket looks at me like I've eaten one of her squeaky toys.

A moment passes. Cricket's eyes cross more the harder she stares.

Will clears his throat. "Wow, that's cool. All from your little space story?" He's got his basketball propped under one sweaty armpit. I crinkle my nose.

"Well, it's not *my* story. It's based on *The Space Game.*" The smile escaping my mouth is enough to make Will tease me until I'm six feet under.

He grunts. "That stupid show all the nerds watch? I guess Pippa's kinda hot."

"Whatever, you like it too. And you especially like Pippa. And

I'm not a nerd. There's a difference between a nerd and a geek. I'm the latter." Everyone knows that.

"I know, I'm just teasing." He stands above my bed, his shirt glued to his chest with sweat. Gross. Boys. Sportsball. "What can I say, you like what you like."

Brother-logic at its finest.

"Now a whole heck of a lot of people are going to be seeing it. My *Space Game* stuff." I say the last words slowly.

He shrugs. "That's cool. Did you get a Disney cruise or something? One million dollars?"

"No. Recognition is all—lots and lots of readers." I stand up and adjust my shorts since they ride up when I park it on my bed. "My stomach is flipping." Time to head to the kitchen. Mom might be mad that we didn't have dinner started already, but I got distracted by this most major news.

"Sounds like one of my games. It's not so bad to have eyes on you—you just learn to tune the other voices out. So, want to meet Noah? He's coming over."

Tune the other voices out . . . "Wait, who? Noah?"

Will bonks his basketball on my head, gently, but I push it away as we make our way into the bathroom. "The neighbor across the street, dumbass."

The noisy new neighbors. The Byron clone. "No—uh—not particularly." I don't usually do well when it comes to talking to attractive boys even when they don't bear an uncanny resemblance to my favorite leading man. This could actually be a disaster.

"He's cool. He plays basketball too. I'm going to start working on him to try out." Will starts bouncing his basketball on my side of the bathroom counter.

Joy. Another jock. You'd think somehow people would get tired of throwing something at the ground and catching it again and again and again, but apparently that's not the case. "Would you stop? My things, all over the counter, that you're about to knock off, weren't cheap." Moisturizer. Gap perfumes. Proactiv. Hot Tamales. Stuff I don't want sprayed all over the countertop when that ball misfires.

"Sure thing, *Nikole*. Anyway, he'll be here in like ten minutes. Might want to comb the braid you've had since eighth grade."

"Well, I'm glad you have yet another new member of the Will-Is-the-Greatest Club. And don't call me *Nikole*, dummy." That whole *captain-of-the-basketball-team* thing has made him so stupidly popular. "I'm sure Noah's very cool, but I'm not putting my hair down for just anyone, thank you very much." I pull the braid that hangs over my shoulder. It's practically to my elbow—thick and blonde, with layers of reddish brown in between.

"Hey Kole, did you know that it's cool to have more than one friend?" He heads out the door. I follow. He always teases me about Michaela.

"I have more friends, you know." So what if I only know them by their screen names?

"They only count if you've talked to them face-to-face in the last year."

"Lame," I say. There *used* to be more of those. I have no desire to find new ones since the great split in middle school. Usually disagreements over canon cause people to go bonkers online, but I guess I wasn't prepared for when it happened with my actual friends. Having to talk to people who don't care about your show like you do? That belittle you when it's your whole world? No thanks. Let the trolls lurk online; I'll leave them under the bridge in real life.

And Will knows how I feel about all this too, he just loves to "get me going," as Dad says.

"And I mean the kind whose eyes you can see. Not the kind you know from notifications."

"Lamer." I turn my voice up a few pitches to mock Mom. "Because I can *never practice for a job interview if I don't have one-on-one relationships in real life.* You sound like Mom. And, I'll gladly meet Noah. I'm sure he's a real peach. Speaking of ways to improve, if we're giving each other advice right now, I *can* show you where the shower is."

"That's called musk. All the girls go wild for a taste of it," he whispers behind me as we head down the staircase. He's smiling; I can hear it in his voice.

"Disgusting!" I yell.

"I'm betting Noah's here in under three minutes."

"Too soon." Oh, the gods couldn't be crueler. Now the noise will be both inside and out. "He's got sisters, right?"

"Yeah, twins. I met them. Sara and Molly. Tiny girls are a different kind of annoying. Far worse than the taller versions at school." He heads to the door, running a hand through his thick brown hair, the basketball still tucked under one arm. "And, you know, I'm really excited about your contest. That's really great. Maybe someday you'll be as good at writing as I am at basketball. And then maybe a boy will ask you out."

"Will! Stop!" That's not at all why I'm doing this. Not. At. All.

"Just kidding. But seriously though." He stops at the bottom of the stairs and yanks on my arm. "I'm proud of you."

I smile. Sometimes, he's a feckin' good big brother. "Thanks."

I turn to the kitchen—there's not a lot in the fridge, he knows it and I do since Mom's due for a trip to the store, but he will still stand in front of it for an hour hoping for something to appear before he decides to go turn on the Xbox and hunt for aliens instead of a snack.

Ding dong.

Asteroids. Neighbor-boy's arrived. I scrub my hands up, good and bubbly, and rinse them as Will heads for the door. I try not to look. Introductions are my least favorite part of being human.

"Hey, Noah," Will says.

"Hey," the neighbor-boy says.

"The court's in the back," Will says.

"Yeah, I caught a glance the other night. Looks like a nice spot," the neighbor-boy says. I glance down at my forearm; the hair follicles are tightening. Heat is rushing to my face. The actor that plays Byron, Caden Rodgers, deepens his voice so his lines sound like faraway thunder: soft, deep, and coming right at you. Neighbor-boy's voice sounds similar, even more than I remember from the other night. It courses through me like I took NyQuil and woke up tingling.

"It works," Will says. "I mean, like, for a backyard."

Whack. Whack. Slam. The dribbling begins as they enter the hall. Mom's going to be pissed when she sees skid marks.

"Noah, this is Kole. It's short for Nikole, but don't call her that unless you want to be punched."

Dear god. "Thanks, Will," I say, hoping Noah doesn't notice that my face is probably the same shade of red as the dish towel I was holding, or that I'm smiling so wide my cheeks have transformed into big fat apples. I put a hand out for him to shake.

"Hi," he says. He takes my hand with a firm grip. His fingers are soft. And long. And the veins pop out between the bones. And his arms . . . they're hard in all the right places, especially near the shoulders. "Nice to meet you." So very, very nice.

"You too." I pull my arm away, maybe too fast. I've been studying him too closely. He knows. He has to. But his arms are so similar to how I described Byron's arms in the second *Spacer* entry. Like . . . all kinds of hot. This is growing more embarrassing by the second. I look to the side and, when he turns to Will, sneak another glance.

Noah's hair is sandy brown; you can only see the true layers of colors this close up, and there are freckles scattered across his cheeks in little fairy kisses. It's kinda close to Byron. I mean, Byron's usually in deep space, so his freckles have faded since he left his home planet. Still, this Noah is a whole kind of adorable. Who'd have thought I'd like a Byron-ish face with freckles? And I don't have a Byron-Swift-type, per se. I'm open to others. I contain multitudes, for sure.

Will's not saying anything. Noah's not saying anything. I'm not even sure I'm breathing.

Oh. Dude. I *really* need to rip my eyes away. And wipe the smile off.

"What year are you?" I ask. *Also, I just won a really cool contest. It's kinda a big deal. Which means I'm kinda a big deal. You should probably like me.*

"Senior."

"Cool. I'm a junior." I shrug my shoulders when I say it. *Also, Noah, I've never been on a date. Only been kissed twice. That was due to a couple of weak moments in junior high during the eighth-grade carnival. I prefer to pretend they didn't happen, but you didn't ask, did you?*

This is ridiculous. He's just a boy. No different than

dumber-than-a-box-of-dum-dums Colin, even if our names do sound nice together. I fold my arms across my chest. Who knew soft hands could do such things to me?

"When do you start classes?" Will jumps up onto the counter-top, getting his butt all over it. Gross. Where are the Clorox Wipes?

"Next Monday. Dad said we are getting settled this week, so no homework until he gets things all figured out." Noah flicks his head to the side, making his hair fly and bounce back into place.

"Yeah, homework sucks." I reach for my braid and drag a hand down it. Maybe it is time for a trim? *Kole!* Be profound.

"Yeah," Will adds, trying to balance the basketball on a finger. "But that's why we play basketball. To keep our mind off college *this* and college *that*."

"I don't mind the work." Noah shrugs. Who just comes out and says that? "It doesn't take that long, or at least it didn't at my old school."

"Where did you go?" I ask. Our homework doesn't usually take that long—unless you're trying to outthink Colin.

"Massachusetts. I'm hoping that schools in Vermont aren't that different." Noah leans on the counter.

I glance over his collarbone. Hmm. Perfectly placed right there under his neck. Delightful. "No promises," I say.

"Will you make us some drinks?" Will asks. "Pretty please, oh sister, dear?"

Seriously? I roll my eyes at him. "Fine." But only for Noah. Because I just got really thirsty.

"Cool." Will looks to Noah and tosses the ball to him. Noah catches it without a second thought—barely even a glance. "Follow me." They shoot out the back door and the dribbling of the basketball doesn't even bother me. Just as Noah leaves, he turns around, realizing he forgot to close the door, and glances at me. I reach for my collarbone like I've got pearls to clutch.

Cool. So, so, so cool.

Will invited Noah to stay for dinner, which means I had to reapply my deodorant. I even snuck upstairs and put a cool compress on my forehead for a few minutes.

We made spaghetti and meatballs, the kind you zap in the microwave. No fancy rolling them out here. Not when Mom and Dad both work late.

I lift a fork to my mouth and some of the spaghetti rolls off my lips and back onto my dinner plate. Will chuckles under his breath as Mom takes a sip from her oversized wineglass.

"So, Noah, how old are your sisters?" She's staring at him with a goofy grin.

"Five. But they think they're thirteen."

I tuck in a corner of my mouth. He's so funny, sitting over there and sounding like a parent himself. I mean, that's hilarious because he's like eighteen, but I think he could easily pass for nineteen. Maybe even twenty? A meatball rolls away from my fork, and I set it down. This isn't working. Who could eat with someone like Noah here? I lean my head on my palm, elbow on the table.

Mom swallows a big mouthful of wine. "Oh, that's younger than I thought. Will they be starting first grade next week?"

I reach for another roll, but she puts a hand on my wrist, adding a shake of her head. Her eyes say one thing: *you've had enough.* I swallow. *How many is too many carbs?* became her favorite conversation when I turned twelve. There's nothing wrong with a size eleven. At least she has the decency to keep her thoughts to herself in front of Noah.

"Yeah." Noah pushes the hair from his forehead, and when he shoves a big spoonful of pasta into his mouth, it's perfectly rolled. Not a string drops. Unlike mine. "They're going to the little charter school at the end of Mulberry Street. Dad likes to keep them as close as possible. He always worries."

"Why do you think that is?" she asks. She's always been super nosy. I guess that comes with being a defense attorney. I give another mouthful of meatball a shot, but only when he's looking away.

Noah shrugs. "Because they don't have a mom anymore."

"Where did she go?" Will asks, shoveling a spoonful into his mouth. He doesn't seem to care what's worse: his table manners or his questions. My elbow slips and I'm accidentally just a little closer to Noah.

"Will!" Mom both whispers and yells at the same time.

Noah glances around the table for a moment, like he's not sure he should say what he's about to. "She passed away a year ago."

I bite my bottom lip. *Yikes.* Leave it to Will. In the silence, Noah doesn't look at anyone. He just stares at his fingers, locked around his glass of milk.

Crap. Here we are, first night with the new neighbor, and my brother's put him on the spot. This is why I stick to just Michaela. Keeping track of another's feelings, on top of my own, is a lot of work.

Ticktock goes the old clock in the corner. A car's headlights flash through the front window, shining its light on the interrogation room that's become our dining room. I wipe my mouth with a black napkin and stick it back on my lap. *Say something, Mom.*

She's staring into her wineglass. Probably calculating how many carbs I've already had.

This silence has to stop. I interject with the first thing that comes to mind. "I won a contest."

"A contest? At school?" Mom asks, her eyes as big as the salad bowl in the center of the table. "That's great, honey."

"No. I mean—it is great, but—" I shake my head and sit up straight, careful not to knock my fork into my lap. "Not a school one. An online one."

Mom looks into her lap and adjusts her napkin. She doesn't meet my eyes; instead she looks to her wine. After a second, she tucks a piece of shoulder-length blonde hair behind her ear. "An online one? I thought we'd agreed that you were going to take a break on your blog."

That was what you hoped, Mom. "I didn't. I can't."

A car door slams outside. Mom watches her glass. Dad comes in the front door, his scrubs all ruffled and the stethoscope still around his neck. "Hello, my loin-fruit!" he calls toward the dining room. "How's my favorite basketball star and the next Stephenie Meyer?"

I groan, rolling my eyes. He knows that calling us loin-fruit is the most disgusting way to refer to your children on the planet? What. The. Hell. Dad. And now is not the time to tease me. With any luck, Noah doesn't know what *Twilight* is . . . or a loin.

"Hi, Dad." Will speaks up as Dad tosses his briefcase onto the table in the hall. "Mom, all the school writing competitions are dominated by Colin and Hailey. They act like their shit don't stink."

Mom glares at him. "Language, Will."

"Sorry. I'm just sick of seeing their names on every winning list, every new scholarship award some rich donor has left the school.

But you should shake them off their thrones, Kole. Nab some of that free money." He gulps his milk and the glass is empty by the time I register that Noah now knows I have a blog.

Will and I are super fortunate—our parents make enough money to send us to a fancy prep school and on to a prestigious college—but I've never been quite sure what Mom will say if I actually tell her what I want to do after graduation. I worry that she may disown me if I take a gap year or five. Or if I decide that community college is where I need to be.

Mom turns to me. "You and Hailey used to get along so well. It's too bad that friendship went south."

"We're not making up. Ever." I rest my arms in front of me as Will muffles a burp. "Anyway, this contest has a much bigger scope than one at school. There's like 40 million active users on the site."

She clears her throat. "Is it something you can put on a resume?"

"Yeah, I think so." It's quick, but I catch it. The brush-off. I've grown used to seeing it cross her face. She tries to hide it, sometimes. I lean back and fold my arms over my chest.

Dad comes around my side of the table. "Don't give my Kolington a hard time. We can't all be writing about spaceships until the sun comes up." He kisses the top of my head and Mom gives him a death look.

Feck. Now Noah knows my blog is geeky.

Dad pulls up a chair. "I gave twenty-three shots today and only four kids cried. I think that's a new record." Dad winks at me. "Think they'll still need vaccines in space?"

I smile. Dad's consistently voted the best pediatric nurse in Vermont, so they're in good hands. It's sweet of him to make an effort to relate to me, but Mom certainly doesn't try. My world is online, so it's not real to her. And maybe Will, who doesn't diss it, but at the same time doesn't ask to see my work. That's its own kind of drag. But at least Will is excited for me.

She swirls her wine around the glass again. "That *will* be good to add to your resume. I'm sure of it. And then it can help with your applications. You're starting them next quarter, right? That's what we're shooting for?"

I nod, heat rising to my cheeks. According to Mom, writing is practice for my *real career*, whatever that turns out to be. You'd think winning a major contest like this would impress her. It doesn't. Nothing will. Unless I try my hand at dribbling. I tuck the hair that's wiggled free from my braid behind an ear and scoop at my spaghetti with the other hand. It's a ball. In a hoop.

"What's the contest?" Noah asks.

I clink the fork on my plate. Loudly. I'd almost forgotten he was here. "It's a blog thing." Oh, man. Do I do it? Do I say the words *fan fiction* to the coolest person I've ever met? I glance at him. Seriously. The planets need to find a way to revolve around him.

"What's it about?" He looks at me with those eyes. Byron's.

My cheeks grow hotter. What should I say? A romance-y, angsty space adventure? "It's about a show. Winning the contest just means I get traffic. It's not really a big thing. It's just—whatever." *Lies, lying, liar.* Stack 'em up one upon the other in a big ol' tower of buttermilk pancakes because the contest *is* a really big thing. But I don't know Noah yet. He might laugh.

Will jumps in. "It's about *The Space Game* and space pirates. It's not that bad. If you like clichés."

I glare at him. They're not clichés, they're tropes. Any good writer knows the difference.

Noah laughs. It's mildly dismissive. My left eye twitches. "I've seen ads for that show. But never watched. Space pirates *could* be neat."

Yes! Pirates *are* neat, in space or on the water. I've always thought so. I also think Noah's eyelashes got longer in the last few seconds. Wait—what if he's read *Spacer*?

I shake my head. If he hasn't watched the show, he hasn't found the blog. "Yeah, um, so I've always thought." Get it together, Kole. Mom is staring at me like I've grown another head.

"That's wonderful, Kole." Mom delicately rolls up her last teaspoon of pasta. "Even if it is *fan fiction*."

And like that, my fork drops onto my plate.

She spins her head in my direction, glancing at my dinner.

We lock eyes. There. She got what she wants. Me to stop eating. My appetite is gone.

"Space pirates are meh. I like vampires better," Will says. "Remember that part in *The Lost Boys* when that one dude's face—" Will starts to giggle, and Noah jumps right in. They point at each other, as though they've communicated telepathically, and before I know it, Noah's giggling too. He must remember that one part in that one movie when that one dude's face did the thing. I blocked it out. That movie was beyond creepy. Not the cute kind of vampire at all.

And now Dad's chiming in with the obnoxious laughter. "Noah, you have to be sure to come to some of our summer barbeques. They're legendary, and I make the best rib eyes. Bring your family. I declare that *The Lost Boys* will be the first feature presentation of summer 2020." He slams his glass on the table, and now the plans are set in stone.

"Roger," Mom whispers. "Don't mar the wood."

Dad sits super still, like he's scared Mom's going to look at him.

"Sure thing, Mr. Miller," Noah says, when the laughter fades from his voice.

I'm happy to have Noah come over next summer. Maybe by then, I'll have figured out how to talk to boys.

Mom's watching them, horrified. Poor thing. She tried so hard to instill manners in us. And now look at my brother. He's practically rolling on the ground with his new best friend—the one with the eyelashes that I haven't been staring at *at all* because every time he blinks they grow another inch.

Eyelashes. *Byron's.* Crap. I have a blog to get to. "Can I be excused?" I turn to Mom.

She sighs. "Yes, go ahead." She takes a swig from the wineglass and then swirls it around to watch the whirlpool. She knows full well I'll be on the roof in just a minute, earbuds in, and keyboard a'clickin'.

Maybe someday she'll ask to look at what I'm working on.

SPACER 3.5

Posted by: ToTheStars
Sept. 11, 2019. 10:08

Pippa stomps into the new world, the crew's eyes on her back.

They've abandoned her.

The last one to walk away while the starship's heavy door closes is Byron, his eyes locked on her as though she threw his old Shakespeare book into the waters around the ship. He runs his hand through his sandy hair as the door lowers. When it locks into place, she turns away.

It makes sense why Byron did this, but his betrayal lines her eyes with tears. She couldn't go against something her dad had commanded her to do. And certainly not if she had everything to lose, but Byron had made her a promise. The whole crew did when they formed their agreement: help her find her father's killer. But Byron was the only one she'd watched the stars with. The only one she'd sat in the silence with.

Her feet wobble on the uneven pavestones. She pulls the sweater closer, wishing it could gobble her up and spit her back into the sky.

Sept. 11, 2019

Comments Section:

TeamByron {Yuma, AZ}: Pippa seems like she's hott AF. Can we get some more info on her measurements? I need a clearer image in my head. Come on, ToTheStars, give us more visuallllsssssss. Maybe a drawing or two of Pippa in the moonlight? In some kind of thin lacy nightgowns

Anonymous19445 {HIDDEN}: this is the shittiest writing I've ever had the displeasure of reading. Something is off in Stumblr. how is this best fanfic

AntManWillSaveThem {Thanos's Butt, MARS}: Someone's read too much *Fifty Shades*. gag

PippasBaby {Bikini Bottom, ATLANTIS}: Loving this. Can't wait to see who she chooses

Anonymous29993 {HIDDEN}: IF Byron DIES WE RIOT

StripperTripper {Fresno, CA}: the last thing Cedric wants to do is leave her. Is Pippa really that dumb?

EatDrinkStumbl {THA}: OMG I NEED MORE PLEASE POST TONGIHT

YourTeacher {Bennington, VT}: The only way this prose would be purpler is if it actually managed to bruise your face. If you want to see real writing, head over to my page and see how it's done. Still salty this page nabbed the top spot. Mediocre story at best. And the writing is on par with a seventh grader.

MonstersExist {FRA}: Byron and Pippa own my soul!!!!!!!!!

Tatertots {Sunnydale, CA}: TEAM CEDRIC 4 LYFE

Anonymous 49920 {HIDDEN}: Byron+Pippa. I will die on this hill!!! Byron is daddy.

VoiceofReason {Sarasota, FL}: Cedric is the perfect example of a toxic boyfriend. Anyone who ships him and Pippa clearly doesn't care about Pippa's feelings. This is fact.

Tatertots {Sunnydale, CA}: NOT TRUE Cedric is trying to save Pippa irregardless of his feelings for her

VoiceofReason {Sarasota, FL}: OMG are you even reading the same story

Anonymous 49920 {HIDDEN}: when are we gonna know more about GEM, ToTheSTars?

CHAPTER THREE

Thirty-two minutes into Creative Writing and all I can think about are two things: french fries and the comments section of *Spacer*. I shouldn't have even taken a peek at it. It was enough to make me shut my laptop and consider deleting my work. And now Mrs. Liu wants to bring up this year's lit mag? Ugh. Just when I'm feeling like my writing is not even worth being snapped to ash by Thanos. What feckin' timing.

"I want to see every one of you submit something to the lit mag. You've all got the talent—there's no doubt about that—and this is a golden opportunity. Not just because your name will be splayed across the front, but because this is something that'll sit pretty on your resumes," Mrs. Liu says, hanging on to the podium like it's trying to run away. "I know a number of you are eyeing Ivy League schools. This is just one more mark for that checklist to get through the doors. And the best part is that it comes with a $1,000 prize, thanks to a rather generous grant from one of our alum. In senior year, if you make it in again, it jumps to $2,000."

Kids start glancing around at one another, all eyebrows raised and chins tucked in. They smell opportunity. I'll admit, it *is* enticing. I shoot a look at Michaela, and her eyes are as wide as ever.

I don't even know exactly what I'm doing after high school—but it's certainly not an Ivy. It'll be whatever route gets me to Hollywood's writing rooms fastest—which is probably a bus out of Vermont . . . which that prize money can definitely help with.

And *something for the resume* can be helpful. Something to make me seem like a legitimate writer. Not just a *fanfic writer.* And . . . maybe something Mom would approve of. Something with my actual name on it.

Only about three people from Honors Creative Writing make it into the infamous lit mag, so the best of the junior class. The rest of the pages end up going to seniors who've already taken Creative Writing and Journalism. They make it into the advanced section, like the golden and delicious apples they are, hardened by peer editing sessions that have left calluses on their previously unmarked skin. We're still sour apples in this class, barely ready to be plucked.

Still, I can try. The money would go a long way in community college, where I could learn screenwriting basics and not waste away in some lecture hall studying ancient jugs or yet another algebraic equation for how to find the diameter of a jigsaw puzzle.

Hailey sits up straighter. She started to emit gamma rays when Mrs. Liu started speaking. Today Hailey's hair is curled, resting just above her shoulders like the bottom of a waterslide. This girl's been thinking about Dartmouth since before she could hold a pencil. She's probably already drafted something to send in.

As the legend says, if you make it into the mag junior year, you're an elite, bound to have someone call you the next Suzanne Collins, of *The Hunger Games* fame. If you don't make it, you can forget an A in this class. You're left to boil with the Bs while the As get their names in print and a shiny gold star. And, if Mrs. Liu is to be believed, a first-class ticket to the Ivy Leagues. Every New

Englander's dream. Except for me. I just want to be a real TV writer someday, and fan fiction is practice.

Colin's sitting up higher in his chair now too. I could barely see the podium to begin with anyway. He raises his hand after tucking his pencil behind his ear. How there's room for that and the glasses, I just don't know.

"Yes, Colin?" Mrs. Liu says.

"Exactly how much of an edge does this give us?" His voice is so sweet it gives my ears hives. He rests his head on his palm as he waits for her response.

I lean back and pick at the bottom of my braid. Some of these split ends have begun to look like strands of DNA.

"The schools are competitive—that's no secret. But what they want is a well-rounded student. If you can show that you've got athletic talent, creative talent, and an entrepreneurial spirit, then you've got an edge. And, even if we're not talking Ivy League, there are scholarships open to those that make it in . . ."

Her voice slips out of my ears as she hands Colin a sign-up sheet. He hunches over as he signs the sheet, probably breaking his pencil tip in the process.

Entrepreneurial spirit . . . does having your own blog count? I mean, I went out of my way to start something, to stick to it, and now I'm getting recognition. I twist the bottom of the braid around my fingertips. I shouldn't have read the comments last night. People were downright nasty. Stupid, ignorant trolls. Writing *Spacer* was supposed to be my own little lullaby—but last night it was nowhere near soothing. It was . . . embarrassing? Some of the comments even make me question why I won too. I swallow.

The *ship* was what they said when the winners were announced.

The things we get invested in. Characters. Feelings. But they're easy. The writing—not so much. Not the setting. Not the sentences. Not the plot. That comes with planning. With practice and with real work.

The comments on my actual story? Flowery. Too much description. Lack of concise phrasing. *Over the top*. Sounds like a seventh grader. A *Star Trek* knockoff.

And that's just a taste. This is far worse than any critique I've gotten at school—teacher or otherwise.

Except for Colin. Freshman year English. He ripped my persuasive paper to shreds and I swore a blood oath that I'd hate him for the rest of my life. He called me a clown and drew a red-and-white tent in the margin because I was writing about the terrible treatment of circus animals. It was not my best work, but I was proud of where it was. I get that hating him over an editing snafu is a bit dramatic, but I almost let him kill my spirit that day. Then Dad and I talked and he said to brush it off and keep trying. But that day, I vowed to never swap with Colin again.

"So, who thinks they might be interested in submitting something?" Mrs. Liu raises her hand as though we need an example of what it looks like.

Hands fly up. Colin's first—he practically rips his blue sweater as he reaches for the sky. Everyone's hand but mine meets the air. I catch Mrs. Liu's eye as she angles her head around Colin to find me. I sink lower in my chair.

"No, Kole? Not something you're interested in?" Mrs. Liu asks. Twenty eyeballs land on me. Colin doesn't turn around.

My blood runs cold. "Um, maybe? I just need to think about it for a little bit."

"No harm in that. And there's nothing to lose!" She always has a way of trying to make something sound like it's a piece of cake.

"I'll be signing up. It would be an honor to be published under such an esteemed piece as the *Apple Literary Magazine*." Hailey turns to me, hand over her heart. Oh man. She's giving Colin a run for his money in the biggest douche category. Michaela, seated over Hailey's shoulder, rolls her eyes and puts her hand over her heart in a mocking show of camaraderie. I snicker.

I scrunch my nose at Hailey and quickly pop my shoulders when Mrs. Liu looks away. It's a nice way of saying *leave me the hell alone, you concealer-covered bullshitter.*

She breathes in quickly and looks away, appalled at my snark. Good. At least on my blog, I don't have to look the comments section in the eye. I spin my braid around my pointer finger until it's good and tight.

There's the trick. Blocking the comments section out, again, and doing what got me recognized in the first place—just good old writing for good old me. My biggest fan.

By the time I've taken six pages of notes on filler words, we've got five minutes left before lunch. My stomach is crying out for french fries. I reach for my backpack, tucked somewhere behind me, and when I look up, Colin has turned around. He's looking right at me. I freeze. The T. Rex has spotted me. If I don't move, he won't see me.

He flips his whole darn body around and straddles his wimpy plastic chair. Then he props his big arms up on the back and folds over into my space. "Why aren't you signing up, *Nikole*?"

I glare. He knows I hate being called that. I have to tell every single substitute teacher so. "Why do you care?"

"No need to be contentious." He glances to the ceiling. "Nice. My third SAT word for the day."

I lift my eyebrows. "You're counting your SAT words." Someone needs a girlfriend.

"Yes. So far I've used sanctimonious and laconic. Bet I can get to ten by the time school is out. So, back to the lit mag. There's only a few people in here who actually stand a chance of getting in the mag. I'm trying to figure out who the competition will be."

Sitting up straighter, I glance to the side of the room. "Do you consider me actual competition, Colin? Cause it sure didn't seem like it when you were slashing my papers and slathering them in red ink like something out of a horror movie."

He shrugs. "Editing is a ruthless game."

Okay, I was a little dramatic, again, but he's the worst peer editor to grace the halls of Crystal Lake Prep. It's not that I can't take criticism; I get the writing process. It was the smile he'd crack when he'd find a typo—the gloating. The laughter. Ugh. Not one person wanted to work with him, but I volunteered. Stupid mistake. I mumble, "That it is."

"You not entering makes it easy for me." He looks at my notepad and fusses with the little wire that's unraveled in the spine.

Colin Clarke just admitted that I'm his actual competition. My stomach growls. That means . . . he thinks I could nab his spot. I put a hand in front of my chin, lean a little forward, and pretend to be focused on last week's hangnail. "Maybe I will. I'll probably think about it tonight. You know, before I tackle another sonnet. As I do, sometimes, before bed. Lots of writers write those."

"It's cool. You don't have to enter. I'm not pressuring you." His voice gets kinda low, not at all like when he's talking to Mrs. Liu and the podium is his throne. He taps his finger on my notepad in some sort of rhythm. "Just curious."

Sure. I can play nice too. I reach for my orange pen, ready to stash it away. "I'll let you know next week what I decide. How about that?"

"Here." He reaches for the pen and pulls it from my fingers. Before I can say a word, he begins to write numbers on the back of my sparkly green notebook, the one that, up to this point, didn't have a mark anywhere but where it should: on the pages.

He writes seven numbers with his clunky, ugly, boy handwriting. There's little dashes. Between the digits. A phone number.

My eyes grow wide.

"Text me. I stay up late." He eyes me through those annoyingly square glasses before he grabs his own bag and stands up. "Who knows, you might need help. Sonnets are a cakewalk for me." He gets up, puts his backpack over one shoulder, and stands by Damian at the door. Damian looks over at me and nods.

I turn to Michaela, who is watching with her jaw open. She mouths, in slow, deliberate syllables, "I ship it."

If I could find my hands right now, I'd flip her off, but the bell rings and shakes my brain back to normal. I wait a minute, hoping I can stand when I move my legs. I shove my things into my L.L. Bean bag before Michaela can see the color in my face.

She's standing by me in an instant. "Kole—"

"Don't say it. I swear to god." My head is spinning. Nothing could have prepared me for this—not a million angsty moments between Byron and Pippa, no matter how beautifully the stars are shining through the front glass of the *Snapdragon*.

I can't learn a thing in here when I'm surrounded by this stupid competition, and now Colin wants to work his way into my nights?

Someone shoot me now.

SPACER 3.6

Posted by: ToTheStars
Sept. 14, 2019. 10:47

Santiago promised not to hurt Pippa. But he did. In no part of the seven skies is that okay.

Byron doesn't need an order from his captain, just a threat of his own. He raises his blaster to Santiago's head and puts his other hand out to help Pippa up. She winces before accepting, cradling her arm as she stands. Feck. She's both pissed and injured. The crew may be there now, but they were too late. They *let* this happen. He let this happen. Byron grits his teeth.

"Tell your man to remove his blaster from my face." Santiago's hands are raised, the knife still firmly gripped in one. Byron doesn't move, and he won't—unless Captain Worley commands him.

Byron's eyes go from Santiago to the captain as he hits the button on his blaster. The weapon hums. He pulls Pippa behind him and backs up to the stairs, his blaster never moving from the spot right between Santiago's eyes.

Worley motions for Benedick, Byron's brother, to draw his weapon, finally. Thank the gods. Threats only do half the job, even if Benedick makes for shitty backup.

"I know where Aster is," Santiago says, eyes on Benedick's knife.

Byron's blaster twitches.

Game changer.

I move the mouse to the *post* button. One click and this entry will go through the webs. I hover my cursor over the button, the autumn air growing colder by the second. Goose bumps line my arms under a heavy knit blanket. I hit *post* before my fingers are lost to frostbite and send a quick prayer to the stars. *Let them like it.*

Hey, at least I'm feeding my fans. Wild dogs on dead flesh—I can practically hear them coming for my corpse. That's more than the actual writers on *The Space Game* can say. We've had no news for six weeks now; nothing about guest stars, no passive-aggressive retweets, no hidden likes on Twitter.

My finger twitches about the comments from last night. One click and I can read them all. One click and I can rethink everything I just wrote. Or, one click and I can find those positive comments that must be in there somewhere, little Easter eggs spread through a field of manure.

No, Kole, be smart.

My stupid fingers move faster than I can convince them not to and I click on the red notification option. The screen moves to the last comment from last night, and I skim through.

Okay, actually, according to some of the comments, they don't all hate the ship. And by a few, I mean I've seen complaints about the romance element in 84-ish comments. Only 22 claim that Byron's a toxic jerk. The rest want to see Pippa end up with Cedric, a boring secondary character that I hardly even care enough about to include in my backstory. Plus, who loves a love triangle?

Still, that's a lot of math to keep track of. Heck, that's a lot of opinions that aren't mine to keep track of. I take off my glasses, set them on the scratchy roof tile next to my blanket, and rub my eyes. The goose bumps have crawled to my cheeks at this point. I glance across the street, as though I haven't wondered what Noah's been up to at least three times tonight, and wondered which bedroom is his, or when he's home.

Ping.

DefineSublime {Cleveland, OH}: I can't take this shit anymore. How did someone *actually* choose this as Best in Blog? I can link like ten other sites that tell a much better story than this.

Ouch. That one's harsher than most of the others.

Another comment illuminates my dashboard. I sit against the roof, the shingles pressing into my back like little jagged knives. Cricket inches closer to my legs. The commenters have found the latest installment of *Spacer*.

Ten new comments.

Pinching my cheeks and hoping for some warmth, I tug the long braid out from behind me and hang it over one shoulder. These guys are jerks. They're online so they think they can say whatever they want. That whole *we can't see each other so it's okay to be nasty* thing. But what's the point of trying to read if you hate something so much anyway? I should post that. Ask them to tell me, the esteemed author, to my computer screen, why they're compelled to keep reading.

Ping.

GoGnomes {Crystal Lake, VT}: It's painfully clear that whomever is writing this is an amateur. Did they literally google "clichés" to use in their story? Even the actual show isn't this bad. Love triangles. Hyperspace. It's like they just want to write stuff they found on the first page of Google about space . . .

Then why are you reading, jerk face? I should comment. *Well, yeah, because, once upon a time, this was just my story. My little baby, happy in its dark corner of the blog-o-sphere. And now you're all here. Feck off.*

The screen on my phone illuminates—fifteen minutes until Mom will yell at me to come inside. I click snooze, but my fingers linger. It would only take a few clicks to send a text about these douchebags. Maybe Michaela's up still. Or . . . maybe Colin's awake. Maybe he's working on his lit mag entry. Maybe he's wondering if I'll text him. I tap the green new-message icon with a lazy thumb, but the screen is as still as the night is cold.

I'll take that as fate. I shouldn't text him. He'll just annoy me at home and at school if I let his texts up here. This is my happy place—no use letting his meat-cleaver fingers up here too, even if he did catch me off guard today.

Cricket gets more comfortable against me, a big ball of warm in the autumn air, her purr the only sound in the silence. Maybe I liked my story better when it was just me and the roof, the keyboard and the twinkle lights.

I can't let the voices online take my story from me. As I roll the little ball on the mouse down the page, two familiar words catch me. A chill runs through my body. Location info is something I usually skim over, because who really cares, but this comment says Crystal Lake.

I live in Crystal Lake.

The goose bumps on my arm are so freaking tall the blanket stands up. There's no way my tiny little hole on the internet could have been discovered in this tiny little town, no effing way. I do a hasty sign of the cross, hoping the saints I used to pray to are listening, but if they are, they aren't talking.

Time to set the comments to mute. Again. And turn off the

location information. It does nothing but get in my head. And I don't want to know how close the sharks are. Like that one little fish says: I just have to keep swimming. They'll tire of my meat when I'm nothing but bones.

September 16th, 2019

Dear *ToTheStars*:

Hello! My name is Kasey, and I work for *The Space Game* Con-athon, one of the biggest conventions on the northern seaboard. This year our convention is scheduled for the first weekend in November. At this point, we've booked the three superstar powerhouses of the show: Nina Garcia, Caden Rodgers, and Ben Madan. We've got a number of supporting characters booked, and the executive producer, Seth Andelman!

So, why am I emailing you? Not only do our attendees want to see the actual stars of the show, but they'd like to see some fan-produced panels as well. They're interested in what goes into writing fan fiction, and many have said they'd love to hear from the person writing *Spacer* specifically! We thought we'd reach out to you and see if you might consider joining us this year.

A number of us behind the scenes at Con-athon, myself included, are fans of *Spacer*. We were reading long before *Best FanFic* discovered your blog. We were loving, shipping, and spreading the word about your story from the beginning. And now it would be our honor to host you on your very own panel at our convention.

We'd pay for your room and board, and you'd have an all-access pass to enjoy the con on your own before and after your panel. Oh, and we've included travel expenditures for a guardian, if needed, and one other guest.

So, please let me know if you're interested! If you'd like to chat on the phone, I'd be happy to answer any questions you may have.

Please be in touch!

Kasey Foster

Galaxy Conventions
Boston, MA

CHAPTER FOUR

The old dinosaur computer finally starts up, and this is how she greets me? An invitation to the most important con in *Space Game* fandom? If I hadn't already downed my hot chocolate, I would have spilled it all over myself.

This is the most incredible news I've been met with, well, ever. But something boils in the pit of my stomach, tightening my throat. This is another ball to juggle with hands that don't move as fast as things are happening.

Best FanFic.

A dreamy new neighbor.

The lit mag.

Colin's phone number.

How in the world has my blog become this massive *something* that people care about? My spoon falls into my bowl of Count Chocula as I put my hand to my mouth. This Kasey Foster said Caden Rodgers will be there. Caden-the-real-life-god-that-is-Byron-Swift will be within arm's reach of me. Arms that must've been sculpted by the gods.

If I go, I can tell him I worship his face.

Actually, I'm not going to start with that.

And Nina Garcia? The girl I've wanted to be since I was fourteen? I clutch the nape of my neck. We're not just talking about being at a con with these guys. We're talking about being a *part* of a con with these guys. A speaker on a panel.

But Mom will never allow it. Not in a million, gajillion years.

"Kole! Hurry up! You're going to make us late!" Will yells. He's at the front door, ready to lock up and grab his bike. "And I have to go grab N—"

I tune him out, wolfing down one more spoonful before shutting down my laptop and tugging on my sweater. Gotta survive the bike ride to school, then maybe I'll have some brain space to think about going to an actual con.

French fries. That's what I want. Maybe a hot dog. It *is* protein. My stomach growls at an embarrassingly loud volume while Hailey finishes reading her story at the podium. It was something about saving a cat from a raccoon fight. Entirely made-up, I'm sure, even though it's supposed to be a personal narrative.

"Who'd like to read their story next?" Mrs. Liu asks. I bet she thinks Hailey's story is crap. I mean, Mrs. Liu's example was about her grandmother immigrating here from Japan, so she's got to see a lack of quality in a story about a trash panda. Mrs. Liu scans the room.

I preoccupy myself with the wire that's come undone on my notebook. I play at it with my orange pen, the same one Colin used a few days ago. I glance at his back—he hasn't said a word to me. I sit up, knowing full well my glasses are beginning to slip down my nose. Liu's this close to calling on me and that's making my brow sweaty. Four people have already volunteered. Colin. Hailey. Paul.

James. I'm willing her to pick someone else, like some kind of Jedi mind trick, but her powers are honing in on me.

Maybe Michaela wants to read. I should look away, like I've got to check something in my day planner. I riffle through my backpack.

"Honestly, the silence leaves much to be desired, Apples. You should be proud to share your narratives. You have been working on them for weeks and they've been workshopped to death. There's nothing to fear in sharing. We're all here to grow."

Yeah, sure seems like the others in here are interested in growing their craft. They'd rather see who can get the loudest applause. Or the most scholarship money. I'd like to slink down in this chair and pretend that I can snake-slide to the door.

Colin leans back, practically into my face because our classroom seems to get smaller with each passing day, and raises his arms. He links his long fingers together behind his head. The veins begin to pop out in between his knuckles. Hey . . . Byron's do that too. Has Colin been working out?

"It's time we start taking some ownership over our writing voices." At this point, Mrs. Liu has a hand on her hip. She places a long, gangly finger on the podium. "Kole. Get up here with your story."

My mind goes blank. I shut my eyes. My heart is somewhere in my throat, clawing to get out and hide in a locker. "Do I have to?" I whisper, creeping lower. I can hide behind the mass in front of me that is Colin. In this instant, I'm thankful for his dark sweaters and his beefy shoulders. He is the moon between me and Liu, our own eclipse.

"You don't have to. But I'm asking you," Mrs. Liu says.

I pause, my feet prepped to kick the chair out from under me and head to the podium. I glance around the room. Eighteen eyes stare at me. Can't count Colin this time. My paper is heavy in my hands. I look at the first sentence, the big B+ at the top. I flip it over.

The others will be bored. They'll think my story's clichéd. *Purple-prosed.* Like the comments. But this is not *The Space Game.* It's something that happened when Will and I were ten—when he almost drowned in the creek in Vaughan Woods and I could only sit there, frozen, as Dad tried to get him out of a whirlpool. How I couldn't move when his face went under over and over again until the pond went still.

"Kole, I wouldn't be asking you to do it if I didn't think your story was one that the class needs to hear. Maybe even the whole school. It may be something for the lit mag."

I swallow. There she goes, beating that drum again. Michaela stares at me, beckoning me up there. Hailey looks at her fingernails. My feet don't move. My paper stays on my desk, face down with the big B+ at the top of it where no one can see. This secret lies between me and Mrs. Liu. It's not a stellar grade, but her words just now—*it's something the whole school needs to hear.* That's high praise from someone who's dedicated her life to writing.

Still, I can't do it. There are too many other voices. *It's painfully clear that whomever is writing this is an amateur. I can link like ten other sites that tell a much better story than this.* The words ring through my head, the high-pitched *ping* as they're uploaded a scream through my thoughts.

"Your story is about taking action in a moment of need—that's something we can all learn from." Mrs. Liu is really giving this her best shot.

I shake my head. "I can't. Not today."

She slow blinks at me, her head angled down and her eyes locked on my face. Her glasses rest low on her nose. She nods like maybe she gets it, but I've let her down. I've let someone's thoughts, many someones, enter into my mind no matter how much I tried to mute them.

I lay my head on my palm, allowing my elbow to slip off the edge of the desk. My head follows it downward and rests on the desk. I may not be able to take on the podium, but I can shut my eyes and hide in Colin's shadow.

Michaela has to think I'm a coward. The other eyes in here must agree. I may be hot stuff online but when it comes to real life, my words are B+. Barely above average. Just lame ideas and crappy sentences that Colin and Hailey wash out during revisions when they realize they can do a heck of a lot better.

By the time class is over I try to slink out of my seat before anyone says mum, but Colin turns around in his awkwardly small desk and his legs splay out into the walkway.

I look down. Just avoid his eyes.

"The podium a bit too far from your desk today?"

I glare. "Lay off, Colin."

He smirks, and then his face softens. "I was hoping you'd text." He leans into my desk again. Into my space. Any closer and our glasses will be touching. I thought for sure he'd smell like fish this close up, but instead his breath is minty; he's hiding gum in his cheek. Well, look who has an edge. Who would have thought? "If you ever want some feedback, I will swap with you. You don't have to pick Michaela every time."

I bite the inside of my lip. "I don't always pick Michaela."

"This year, I mean. Remember when Mr. Garrett put us together as freshmen? You don't always get a peer editor that challenges you. Half the students in freshman English were sticking commas in the middle of a prepositional phrase. Amateurs—they don't even know that semicolons are for more than smiley faces. And they have no opinion on the Oxford comma. But not you. You're different. You've got a knack for hunting down a comma splice." He takes my pen and spins it around between his fingers. "We could be a formidable team. You and I are on the same level."

Is there a time lord here? What version of reality am I in? "You're saying *you* want to swap with *me*."

"Might make it easier to share your work if you know it's been run through the ringer by an editor who knows what he's doing. I could help you own that podium, Kole, if you let me."

I narrow my eyes. This feels like Kylo Ren asking me to take over the universe with him. Over one million unique visitors are reading my blog. Do I need a Sith Lord on my team? But my work is not translating to real life. Still, it's Colin Clarke. "I'll stick to Michaela. At least when she critiques my work, I know it's not so she can fluff herself up by nitpicking. But thanks, Colin, for thinking I need you to get my work up to par."

He stares, his green eyes heavy, even through his glasses. "I was trying to help. That's all."

Maybe I was too mean. Maybe he meant it. I shrug. "Well, you have an odd way of trying." I stand and rush by Mrs. Liu as I storm out the door. She probably wants to talk to me, but I've got lunch to get to. No one gets in between me and french fries.

I rush past the lockers, my backpack hanging heavy on my

shoulders. Michaela's head bobs above the sea of students, headed straight toward me. I thought I could sneak out of Liu's room without facing her concern, but she found me.

"Hey!" Michaela says as we turn the corner to head to the cafeteria. "Did something go wrong in American History earlier? Why the attitude with Liu?"

"No." I slow blink. There's no avoiding what just happened. "I just really didn't want anyone to hear my story."

"It's awesome, Kole. Even Mrs. Liu knows it."

I watch my feet. "If a B+ is awesome, then yep. She knows it."

"It can still be a good story even with a mediocre grade." Michaela's got her bright pink hair piled high in a bun and the sun hits her nose piercing at just the right angle. It sends a sparkle off the tiny diamond as we walk under the skylight spanning the long hallway to the cafeteria. "So how many hits when you went to bed last night?"

"Sounds like you're talking about a video game." And I'm the one the troops are aiming for. "Maybe a million or so? I don't remember exactly. But it's more and more every time I log on." I suppose I should sound a little more excited. I mean, it wasn't that long ago that I won.

"Geez. And . . . the comments . . ." she trails off. "Who knew the world had so much room for such shitty opinions?"

It's a rhetorical question, but she's spot on. People and opinions—I thought this kind of drama was for Fox News. We slip through the door of the cafeteria, and I smell the sizzling saltiness. I'm this close to fries and my taste buds are on high alert. "I mean, yeah, the internet is an ugly place. Anonymity and all, but I doubt many of the anons have ever tried to write something."

Michaela loops her arm through my arm. "I know. I wish I could punch all the trolls across the keyboard for you, but all I have are my sparkling wit and clever puns. What should have been an accomplishment is out of control."

"Thanks." I lean my head on her shoulder. It's comforting to know that one person in all of this knows exactly what's going on.

Speaking of trolls, just as we pass through the cafeteria doors, I lock eyes with Raya, an Indian girl and one of the kids we used to hang out with before they became the anti's—as in anti-fanfic and anti-our ship. And we don't have time for that negativity—friends should be cool with each other's passions. She and Hailey sneer at Michaela and I. When we broke away from them, the tension between us never went away. In fact it got worse than I anticipated. Any time I see one of them, it's like I've just been teleported to Hoth—the air gets that icy. Michaela and I walk past them, nothing to say, nothing to see.

"Losers," Hailey says, all too loudly. Raya giggles.

"Ignore them," I say to Michaela. It may not be the only solution, but at least we're not feeding into the drama.

"Always," she responds.

We toss our bags like astronauts claiming the moon for our country on one of the empty tables in the cafeteria as kids pour in around us. "Hey, so did you catch that comment about Pippa's hair? I've always said her hair was dark brown. I mean, I double-checked that I never mentioned it was black. I didn't miss an error like that, right?"

"Yeah, I double-checked too. Even if you did, that can be fixed. Seriously, don't sweat it. The fact is they're reading it so they must like it."

But still I hear their words. *Flat characters. Clichés. Settings described like popsicle-stick puppet shows.* Those are the ones that sting, leaving little toothpick prints where my ideas live.

"Where's Will?" Michaela stands up and puffs out her chest like a pink-haired peacock.

"Again? Really?" Her crush is getting old. I'm fairly certain crushes are better in your head; you build them up until they're all daydreams and fuzzies, and then the real world flips them the wrong side out and you can no longer stand to be in the same room with the person. Unless they're Noah, of course. I can't imagine he's ever stepped a toe out of line. And I'm sure he can recognize a comma splice. Take that, Colin.

"He's over there. I can see his shimmer from here. Who's the guy with him? Is he being shadowed?"

Shadowed?

My thoughts roll to a stop. Wait one purple-prosed minute. I stand up, eyes skirting the line for fries, and spot my brother over by the soda machines.

Something in my chest leaps.

Noah is here, in my prep school, in all his glory. "It's Noah's first day."

I'm going to need the defibrillator in the gym.

He's wearing a crisp collared shirt in a shade of dark gray, not unlike the clouds before the rain comes pummeling down, and hot dang I've always loved a good downpour. His shirt's pulled out from his jeans, and he's got a backward hat on. Red Sox, but all you can see is the Sox logo. His sandy hair slips out of it, just a little, and he stands like this place is his very own basketball court and he's front and center.

"He *is* cute. Like you said." Michaela stares.

"Did I say that?" I lower myself back onto the bench, but this time I sit up a bit straighter. "I have no memory of this. And he's not handsome enough to tempt me."

"I heard it in your voice. Also, he's not as cute as Will."

"Gross. And also, that's not me saying it," I mumble, but I don't stop looking. He's exactly what a senior should be: filled out in the arms, a whole head taller than the freshmen, and looking like colleges are filling out applications for him instead of vice versa.

And I can be tempted. And Michaela knows it.

"I've known you long enough to know that when you say *he's not handsome enough to tempt me*, you are lying." Michaela pulls her phone out. "I also know that when you quote *Pride and Prejudice* it's because you're thinking about Mr. Darcy and that means you've got the hots for someone."

"Shut up, Michaela." Busted.

"I know how this goes. I've seen this Kole before."

"When?" I've never gone googly-eyed over a boy before. At least not seriously.

"James O'Heany. Ninth grade."

"That was over a weekend."

"Exactly. He quoted *High School Musical* and you thought you'd found your Troy."

"I blocked that out."

"And Max."

"Max was a smudge on an otherwise flawless record. And that wasn't serious." It's no big deal that Noah's here. I knew he was coming to my school. I also know that, out of all the kids here, I'm probably the only other student he's talked to besides Will. And I could have guessed he was going to be hanging out with my brother; those two have become frogs on the same log faster than I can say bromance.

"You know what's weird?" Michaela asks.

"What?"

"He kinda looks like Colin. Big shoulders, chiseled cheekbones. But Noah's shorter. And they're both total snacks, even if Colin is *barely tolerable*, as you've said. Which, I noted in my Kole's Crushes Journal, is another *Pride and Prejudice* reference."

I'll let that one slide. "Wait until you see Noah's eyes." I suck in my breath. "They're some kind of vortex."

"No, Kole." She's staring at me. "I've seen the end of this movie."

I'm going to have to punch her. "Don't."

"Noah's cute, but I still see you and Colin together. It's totally a Reylo thing. You just can't see it when you're the one steering the ship."

Then light the cannons because I will sink that ship faster than the *Titanic*. "I will find a way to kill you with your phone."

"Oh, stop it. You know you can't say stuff like that on school grounds. Someone will put you on a watch list. And I'm just having fun." She giggles, throwing her head back. She's loud. And drawing attention, even if her eyes are on her iPhone more than they are on me. "You should try it too."

"Stop it! People are looking."

"Let's go say hi." She jabs her phone into the back pocket of her jeans.

Before I can protest, she's headed to the line. Okay. Brave face. I'll be looking into Noah's eyes in just a few seconds, and I need to find some calm, cool place within me. Whenever I've thought about him, I've done nothing but start to get hot in odd places.

Will and Noah maneuver through the lunch bags and tables to the corner where all the jocks eat. Noah, oh joy, will fall in line as another one of them.

"Forget it. They got sucked up by the basketball brigade. Let's go get in line." Michaela pivots around.

"A far better plan."

Well, good for Noah. It's not so easy for everyone to make friends, but being an athlete slots you into a clique quickly. Must be nice to have others rework their social circles around you, as evidenced by the kids happily scooting over for him.

"I'm not hungry anymore." My stomach is rolling itself up in somersaults. I pull my braid over one shoulder and adjust my glasses to just the right spot.

"Just come with me anyway," she says.

We scoot our way through the backpacks and lunchboxes, messenger bags and laptop cases. They're a mess all over the floor, like the kids don't give a hoot about things getting stepped on. A voice rises above the others. "The *Snapdragon* isn't just old, she's ancient."

I glance behind me—it's a table of kids I've only ever seen in the gamers club after school. They're shuffling decks of Magic cards like card dealers in Vegas. Impressive, even if it's not my kind of geek. But they're young—freshmen. Yuck.

Did they just mention my starship from my show?

"That's not entirely accurate—" one says. Next to them a girl, with a mouthful of Oreos, punches him in the shoulder. "Ow!"

"Remember that one episode when Cedric met the critters from the Zoron moon?" she asks as he rubs his shoulder.

Hang on. *The Space Game*. My geek ears hone in on the sounds.

Another one chimes in, "Okay, but the space pirates are infinitely cooler. On *Spacer—*"

The blood in my face falls to my feet. *The ding on my website. Crystal Lake.*

"Come on!" Michaela grabs my sweater. I didn't even realize she'd come back for me—or that I'd stopped. I tag along, forcing my legs back into motion. I'm dragged over a series of strewn-about backpacks and the thought rattles through my brain.

A freshman said *Spacer.*

The back of the lunch line wraps around the cafeteria like a snake with a hundred students caught in its coil, all salivating for the same hot, salty french fries.

"Did you hear those kids? The gamers?" I ask.

"Yeah. They're loud as heck. Who didn't? They must be talking about *Critical Role.*"

"They were talking about *The Space Game*." A shiver rolls down my spine. "Then she said . . . *Spacer*." I can barely say it. The word, as it slips over my tongue, clogs my throat.

"Crap. I missed it." Michaela looks me square in the eye and cocks her head to the side like a little pink-haired puppy. "So someone in those more-than-a-million hits is sitting in this very cafeteria?"

A rim of salt water lines my bottom eyelids. "Yes." I can feel the blush rising to my cheeks and the heat surging to my face.

She looks at me like she wants to put a Band-Aid on my entire head. "So what if they're reading *Spacer*? No one knows it's yours. No one but a few of us. And the chances of them putting it together are slim."

I bite my lip. "I know I heard *Spacer* and Stumblr is right where gamers go. There's so much *Fortnite* smut and *Rick and Morty* gifs. The *Supernatural* fanfic is fantastic. And *Spacer's* been plastered across the home page for a week now."

"You're panicking over nothing. Either way, it's awesome."

The couple in front of us stops sucking face for about five seconds and steps forward. We're now about three steps from greasy goodness, but my head is too mixed about and my stomach is still following suit.

"Quit being paranoid. It's not like you invented *The Space Game*." Michaela reaches for a tray and hands it to me.

Paranoid. That's what I'm feeling. Something irrational. Something I can control. That's got to be it.

Breathe.

By the time I finally turned the twinkle lights out last night, just a few days after Kasey's email, I had 1.2 million hits on my blog.

Last night I was dumb. I unmuted the comments. Little turd stains that do nothing but leave skid marks on my story.

Clichés. Love triangles. Token characters. Red shirts. Grammatical mistakes. Insults stinging like tiny wasps from some corner of the globe where being nice doesn't translate to real life. Where usernames are nothing but shields to hide behind as you sling your mace at bloggers brave enough to put themselves on the battlefield.

And not to mention school: Colin's not-so-humble offer, homework's constant presence, and Liu's face when I refused to read my story.

It's too much. Even my metaphors are getting messy.

I need a brain break.

It's 10:00 on Saturday morning. Will's at the basketball court. My hair's in a ponytail, my athletic shorts (purchased by Mom when she thought clothes would get me excited for sports. Note: only worn once) are bunched up between my thighs. My sports bra is tight enough to cut off the circulation to my heart.

Dribbling. This is going to be my new thing. I'll ask Will to teach me how to bounce a ball up and down and up and down until the *whack* as it hits the ground stops bothering me and the rhythm becomes as natural as clicking keys on a keyboard.

No. No writing thoughts.

I hop down the stairs as the doorbell rings. I can see through the glazed glass that there's another basketball on the other side of that window.

Noah.

Asteroids.

I don't want Noah here. I want Will to teach me the basics without anyone else watching, not even Cricket. Last place I saw her was on the recliner, so I think I'm good there.

Ignore the bell. Will will never know.

"Let him in, Kole!" Will yells from the back door before he slams it closed.

I shut my eyes. No stealth here. I head to answer it knowing both my feet and my palms are getting sweaty. I open the door. This would be so much easier if direct sunlight made him less attractive.

"Hi, Noah." Force a smile. Be cool. Calm. Nonchalant. He means nothing to you. "Happy Saturday morning." I think I just became my mother.

"Hi, Kole." His mouth falls open as he sees my sneakers, neon green and pink, and my athletic shorts. They haven't ridden up too much since I last pulled them down, and the shoes are brand new still, even if they are from two Christmases ago. His eyes move quickly over my Columbia T-shirt, and then he glances up to my ponytail. It hangs a little askew, because I'm *trying new things*. No braid today. "Why are you dressed like this?"

I look to the side. "Because I'm going to play ball."

"Basketball, or, like, something else?"

"Yeah, duh. Basketball."

"Well, okay. It's just that when you say *play ball* it sounds like you're talking about baseball." He crinkles his eyes at me. Damn it. The lashes have grown.

"Yeah, um, I know." I turn and the ponytail flies off my shoulder. Noah shuts the front door as we head to the back, and I catch Cricket's eye. She can't be judging me for sounding like a moron, right?

Will's in the backyard taking a shot, and the basketball swooshes through the net. This can't be too difficult. I turn to Noah. "Do you like the teachers at Crystal Lake?"

"I like Mr. Hendrix, he's pretty cool. He's got this one tie that—" Noah stops when Will gives him the evil eye. I stay on the sideline.

"Do we have to talk about school right now? It's the effing weekend." Will retrieves the ball from the bushes lining the driveway. He dribbles. Maybe that's how we start.

Noah rushes to the middle of the court, right by one of the lines in the center or so, and bends his knees. He lifts his arms over his head and pauses, aiming for something on the backboard. I catch a peek at the lines in his forearms, the ones that show the tendons, the veins, and the other bits of boy that hide under the skin. Muscles. Lots. And the way Noah's hands curl around the ball, like they're bigger than I realized when we were eating spaghetti the other night—*umph*. Will smacks into me as he takes another ball from behind the bushes.

"Will!" I yell.

"Here, if you want to learn." He throws it at me and it hits me right in the left boob. That'll leave a mark. I'll add it to my list of annoyances to bring up later.

"You're an ass," I say, leaning over to get the ball from the gravel just as Noah takes the shot. He makes it.

"So you've said." Will stands right in front of me. "We'll start with one hand. You'll be ready to try two in about eight months."

Noah chuckles.

Will continues, snickering because he's impressed his new friend. "Throw the ball at the ground right in front of you and keep your hand out to push it back down when it snaps back up."

Easy. I take both hands and force the ball down, but it's been freshly pumped and it flies back into the air. I reach to bounce it back down again, but it slips out and slams into Will's face faster than I can move. There's a quick, deafening crack. He shoots backward, both hands reaching for his nose as blood slips in between his fingers.

"Will!" I run toward him, the ball getting lost in the bushes yet again. "I'm so sorry! I thought—I don't know. I thought I had it!" My hands are a flailing mess in front of my face.

He glares at me, furious as the blood gushes over his shirt. He groans and rushes inside. I whip around after him but he yells, "Stay outside!"

I stand at a loss. It can't be broken . . . right? I grit my teeth, turning to Noah, my hands over my mouth. What the heck did I just do?

Silence falls over the yard but for the door slam.

I feel bad. Truly. Deeply. Apparently, balls are unruly—who knew? I always worked hard to avoid them and actual human contact in PE last year. That's when I did some of my best brainstorming.

Will's nose is reason alone to give up on this endeavor. Maybe there's more to dribbling than I thought.

Noah comes up behind me but stays a few steps back. "Want to shoot while he's inside?"

Crap. "Please don't make me," I mumble under my breath.

"Isn't that why you're out here?"

No. It's to distract myself. But I don't dare tell him that. I shrug.

"Come on." He grabs my ponytail and gives it a gentle tug. It falls down my back warmer than before. "This way."

I turn around robot-like. Noah just touched me. His fingers in my hair like one of Liu's old romance novels. I stare, hoping the googly eyes aren't noticeable. "I might break your nose too. And I really, really don't want to do that." Master artists would have nothing left to paint if I hurt his face.

"It's still crooked from when Molly kicked me as a toddler any-way." He stands at the line in the center-ish of the court again. I'm still staring. His nose is straight as can be. This time he has to notice the googly eyes I'm tossing his way. "This is where you go for free throws. Let's start with that."

I don't want to try this. Not with him. With Will and Will only. I fold my arms across my chest. My boob hurts. I'm going to have a bruise the size of Canada.

"Watch what I do," he says, getting into some kind of position.

He sticks his butt back, and I swear I'm looking at a bottle of ranch with those pretty pictures on the label—two hills, in bright green shorts, perfect formation. Just the right amount of curve. He angles his arms up again.

Yeah, okay. I'll watch, but only if you insist, Noah-of-the-basketball-court.

He studies the hoop like it's a doughnut. I switch the foot I'm leaning on and stand up straighter. I need to tone it down. I'm studying *him* like *he's* a doughnut. Or a bottle of ranch. One that I want to dip a french fry into.

Kole!

I glance at the house, anything to break eye contact with his butt. I hope Will's okay. And I sure as heck hope he's not watching me watch Noah watch a basketball hoop. I'll never live it down.

"Keep watching," Noah says. "Look at my form."

"If you insist." I'm very good at following directions.

He flicks his wrists forward and the ball slips effortlessly through the air and into the net. It doesn't make a single sound as the net flies around it.

Wow. Too perfect. He turns to me with a tiny grin on his perfect face. He's got angles in his cheeks that look like mountain peaks and his hair's flopped over his forehead again. "See, nothing to it. Just a stance and a flick of the wrist."

Oh, great. He's hella good looking, but he's a big fat liar. There's always something to things that look easy. "I bet they say that about dribbling too."

He snickers and runs for the bushes where the ball has headed yet again.

"You try." He tosses the ball at me, and by some miracle I catch it with both hands. I go to the line, spread my legs apart, just barely, and look to the hoop. It's really, really far away. And really, really high.

He stands next to me, but not close enough to touch. I'm shaking. "Bend your knees."

Yep, okay.

"Spread your legs." I glance at him and prop my glasses back up on my nose before I look back at the hoop. I inch my legs apart.

"More." Now he folds his arms across his chest. Did he really just tell me to spread my legs *more*? I obey in what must be some kind of donkey mating dance.

"Better," he says. "Arms up, ball above your head. Put your hands like this." He puts his own out in front of his face as though he's making a shadow puppet. I try to focus, but there's too much looking. Looking at him. Looking at my hands. Looking at him look at my hands.

"Let me try," I say, hoping confidence can be something you can have and not know it. The glasses slip from my nose. Things are getting slick here.

"Not like that." He comes toward me and grabs my wrists. His fingers are cold still. Soft. And he smells of sap and wood chips, like he's been chopping down a maple tree this morning instead of sweating on a basketball court. "Like this." He adjusts my hands and I can feel them getting clammy. I know that's not just the humidity. *Please let him stop touching me, now and forever. Amen.*

"Okay, I think I got it," I squeak out. He steps away. Good. I need my air back.

"Now look at the basket and flick your wrists up and out."

Focus. It's a circle. With a net. I can get this thing in there. No problem. Just pretend it's all those commenters' faces I'm about to give bloody noses to.

Push. Flick. Jump. The ball gives a pathetic little leap from my hands and barely gets high enough to even bump the net.

"Feck!" I yell.

Noah laughs, a high-pitched wheeze, like he's trying to hide it. "What's feck?" he says.

"It's . . . nothing. And that was my first attempt," I say. Dang it. He heard me say a made-up word. That's embarrassing.

"You'll get it. Soon, maybe," he says between gasps. I stomp a foot and glance at the ball, bouncing its way to the bushes. It wants to hide from the game as much as I do.

"I kinda doubt it."

"It just takes practice. Like with anything else."

I go to the edge of the court and grab my ponytail. I pull it over a shoulder, where it feels just right, and begin to look at the tip. I miss my braid.

"Come on. It's just like writing that blog thing of yours. That's what you're up on the roof every night doing, right?" I can feel his eyes on me as I pull at a split end. "Is that show even any good?"

"Um, it's the best."

"You didn't learn the writing part overnight, right?"

I nod. "Right." Or at all, according to some.

"So try again." He offers the basketball to me, one-handed.

"Have you watched *The Space Game*?" I take the ball with both hands and hug it to my chest. I adjust my glasses as they slip from my nose.

"Nah, sci-fi is not my thing."

Okay, that's a bummer. "Too bad. It's a good show."

"Eh, I don't watch much TV." He tilts his head a little. "Unless it's a game."

"Like . . . a *Space Game*?" I tilt my head a little. I mean, he doesn't have to watch it, but I'll try to get anyone to at least give it a shot.

"Yeah, okay, maybe." He glances at me, but I don't think he's all that serious. "But I'll check out your blog. What's it called?"

Shit. I can't just run upstairs and lock myself in the bathroom. Will is in there still . . . but I got this. I may not be able to manage a basketball, but I can *kinda* write. "*Spacer*."

"And it's like, about a show?" Noah's eyes grow a little wider. "Must be good . . . ya know . . . for a fan fiction thing."

That's a really douchey thing to say. But, maybe he's just new to the idea. I smirk. "I think it's pretty good. And so does all of Stumblr. So, like, a legitimately good thing." I can't help but throw out some side-eye, because fanfic is fecking awesome.

"I'll check it out."

"It's fun." That's all it has to be—or should be—regardless of the asshats lurking online. Wait—did I just reveal my biggest, darkest secret to the cute guy I just met? I clench my eyes closed, but he's waiting on me to try and throw the ball again. "Listen, Noah, it's a pretty big secret. One that I'll die before I ever tell anyone about at school. So please, please, please don't tell anyone it's my site. Kay?"

He ponders for a hot second. "It's cool. Our secret. It's just a show, right?" He puts out a pinky, curled, the rest of his fingers in a fist. I stare at it. A pinky swear. I curl my finger and lock it with his, and our hands press together for a moment.

"Well, not to me. But it's cool."

"And I promise that I won't tell." He lets go and, within those few seconds, I'm pretty sure his name imprinted on my psyche.

I tilt my head. I have to make sure this goes nowhere. "Okay, so tell me one of your secrets so we're even."

He grins. "Ah, okay, um . . . I play Barbies with my sisters. And dress up—we have some bomb tea parties. High voices and everything. And some of it is on camera, so there's your blackmail fodder."

"Your secret's that you're a good brother?" That just doubled up the adorable.

"Yeah, okay, but videos like that can be deadly in high school." He lifts his eyebrows, suddenly serious.

Heck yes they can. "I get it. Reputation is whatever, but teasing sucks." I get enough of that from my old friends. This time, when I shoot the ball, it goes a little higher and a little closer to the net. But it's nowhere near close enough.

"See. You'll get there," he says from the sideline.

"Someday." I try again—ten more times until my arms decide they're done. There's sweat dripping down my brow and we've run out of conversation. We head inside for some drinks, and, judging by the trail of blood, I'm guessing that Will's still in the upstairs bathroom. That's where the first aid stuff is.

I grab some Kool-Aid for us, the grape kind, and Noah chugs it down like it's his first time tasting the good stuff. Some of it even trails down his chin, and he wipes it on his arm. When he puts the cup down, his lips are stained purple and I'm all but breathless.

He smiles. I almost choke on my own spit.

"What are your sisters like?" I ask when the world is no longer fuzzy. "Looked cute from above."

"Oh yeah. I remember seeing you on the roof. Molly's a bit of a drama queen, and Sara's a real smarty-pants. They're smart for five-year-olds, I'll give them that."

"They look sweet." With their curly mops of red hair and matching dresses—just like something out of a good horror movie.

"They're cool. You should come meet them." He reaches for the pitcher to help himself to some more. "They'll want to show you their ponies."

"Okay," I say, taking another gulp. In his house. Where he sleeps. And showers.

"Hey, jerks, I'm fine. Thanks for checking." Will's bounding down the stairs. His face is stained red and there's wadded Kleenex shoved up his nostrils like fat tampons.

"Oh, yay! I was just about to come check on you." I turn to him. It's a lie. I wasn't.

"Yeah. I can tell." He heads for the Kool-Aid himself. I catch the way he looks at me, like I've done something wrong. I know that look. It's like when Dad would build a fort with me instead of play catch with him.

Will's jealous.

Wow. Well, he doesn't get all the friends. Noah's nice. And cute. And helpful. I hate to get in the way of their bromance and all, but that doesn't mean Noah doesn't have time for both Miller kids. I know how to play at this game.

I stand up and flick the ponytail off my shoulder. "Hey, Noah, tell your dad that I'm looking to make some extra money. I'll come babysit the girls if he ever needs it." I shoot a look at Will.

"Really? That'd be great. Especially since I want to join the team and we'll be away at games here and there. I think they'll like you too."

Too? Did he just say too? Does that mean he likes me? Or that they'll like me on top of it? Mother of pearl, I have no idea how to navigate flirting.

"Really, Kole? Are you sure you're not still planning the lemonade stand? You've gotten so good at it. And you made ten bucks that one time." Will's voice is slick with sarcasm.

Noah snickers at Will. That's it. My brother's not a jerk. He's a dick. I narrow my eyes at him and put a hand on Noah's elbow. Fireworks shoot from my fingertips. "Just let me know. Anytime."

"Sure thing," he says, in a throaty kind of way. Good god, it's like Byron Swift is in my kitchen.

"I'll be upstairs if you guys need me. I've a blog to post. Over a million hits last night." I head toward the stairs, my ponytail bouncing behind me.

"See ya, Kole," Noah yells.

The dribbling starts almost immediately.

SPACER 3.7

Posted by: ToTheStars
Sept. 21, 2019. 10:11

Pippa looks to Byron, her eyes bigger than just moments before, but he doesn't have time to fall into them. Instead, he focuses on the waves beneath, the little time they have to prepare for the frigid waters.

He's got no blaster at his belt, no ire left in his fists. It's time to find some bravery in all this, even if it does mean abandoning this starship. They can survive the jump into the ocean. And when the starship knows what Byron's vengeance tastes like, they'll wish they killed him instead. And a jump is better than a fall, especially when Pippa's standing next to him. He puts a hand out for her to take, nods with his broken face, and smiles through the swelling. "Quite an adventure, eh, Scientist's Daughter?"

Adventure is one word for it. She grabs his hand, her fingers cold but soft from years of fancy creams, and they leap forward and into the air of Coracinus.

CHAPTER FIVE

I click *post* on the latest entry and raise the laptop above my lap, stretching my legs out over the thick, green blanket as my orange pen rolls a little farther down the sloped roof. Cricket looks at me, cross-eyed and ticked off because I dared to move.

The twinkle lights above my window frame make this pretty little yellow glow that helped me write some pretty little words tonight, and I feel better than I have about them since I won the contest. They just seem to jive together. I set the laptop down, take off my glasses, and rub my eyes before I blow off my fingertips like I shot a gun.

A great end to a great scene. Fans will like this one. They've got to be reading. The other commenters, the ones that seem to think that my writing exists only for them to critique it, can suck it.

But what are the other viewers thinking? They're unique visitors for Pete's sake, but they don't say a word. They must be thinking something. Maybe their silence is code for *this is okay and we'll keep coming back*.

Or maybe the quiet is code for *give it up, ToTheStars. You suck*.

Oh, God. What if Noah is on *Spacer* right now?

I scroll through the list of comments, paying attention to where they're posting from. Most in America. Some in Spain. The Philippines. South Korea. Canada. I zoom into the northeastern part of the United States.

Vermont.

My stomach falls. I click over to my dashboard and switch to the demographics. I can see the pings. I zoom in.

Eighteen hits from Crystal Lake.

That's as close as I can see—I can't tell from where exactly, but that's enough for *The Space Game* to be something of conversation in a town of about 9,000 people.

One I'm hoping for—Noah—and then there's Michaela, but the others?

I twist the wire of my earbuds between my fingertips. The conversation in the cafeteria. I didn't hear the gamers wrong. *Breathe, Kole.* Suck air in and out and count to ten.

This is fine. I am fine. I close my eyes and lean my head on my knees.

It could be them. My old friends. The anti's. They might be reading. They may know about the contest. And they might still hate it.

Maybe I need a good coach. Maybe Colin is right. Maybe joining him would make my writing stronger. But it's Colin-couldn't-be-cockier-Clarke. That would feel a little like Faustus selling his soul to the devil.

I run my thumb over the new message icon on my phone. This time, it shoots open. I grab the notebook where he wrote his phone number and flip it over. I save his number under *Probably Shouldn't Text Him* and type a message.

10:17 PM

Working on your lit mag piece? I hear the competition's steep this year.

And, *send.* A heat rises from my toes and almost settles my goose bumps back down under my skin. I run my hands up and down my leggings—Colin definitely shouldn't be causing anything on me to heat up.

When I raise my head, a light has turned on across the street in one of the upper windows. It's right in one of the peaks in the roof. Noah stands by the doorframe, looking at something on his phone. He runs his hands through his hair like he's trying to get it to that just-right angle (which it'll pop back to effortlessly), and then he comes to the window. I try to look away, but I can tell he sees me. He waves and I hear a tiny, "Hi, Kole."

I wave back. I can't stop the stupid smile that plasters itself across my face. He turns back to whatever he's focused on. Probably some of our oh-so-easy homework.

Or maybe he's checking out *Spacer*.

Yikes.

My phone lays hot and heavy in my hand. Oh man, Noah knows how to take my mind off a possible alliance with the enemy. Cricket rustles on her side of the blanket and meows rather loudly at me.

"Yeah, you're right," I say to her, beginning to pack up. "It's time to go in."

By the time I've put my glasses away, brushed my teeth, combed out my braid, and pseudo washed my face, my phone has lit up. Colin.

Probably Shouldn't Text Him

10:41 PM

Hey, Kole. I'm not worried about the others. Got any sonnets in your head tonight?

All right, Mr. Smarty-pants. Must have figured I'd be texting him at some point—he probably doesn't go handing out his number to everyone at school. And, oh geez, I hope he's not actually thinking I'm up writing sonnets. But no harm in stringing him along a little.

10:42 PM

I'm feeling a little inspired. Might even end up submitting this one. We'll see what the night brings . . .

> Probably Shouldn't Text Him
>
> *10:43 PM*
>
> *Let me hear it.*

Whoa. Not cool. This is called *teasing*. I can't just tell him it's a big old fib. I'll wait a few minutes. Let him stew.

10:46 PM

I don't want to lose the mojo. Maybe another time.

> Probably Shouldn't Text Him
>
> *10:46 PM*
>
> *Then show me after submissions, ok?*

10:48 PM

No promises. Night!

> Probably Shouldn't Text Him
>
> *10:48 PM*
>
> *Mrs. Liu will like whatever it is you're working on, I'm sure of it.*
>
> *You should read your next story to the class.*
>
> *Night.*

I should tell him that just because we've texted it doesn't mean I'm going to be giving him anything more than a cold shoulder and an even icier sneer at school tomorrow. And I should probably tell him it was a big old fib.

Cricket, stretched out at my side, offers a long, loud meow. She stares at me. One eye starts to wander. The other glares through my skull and into my soul. It's not possible, there's no way, but sometimes I think I can hear her thoughts.

Maybe Colin's not that bad.

"Yeah, well, Noah's a masterpiece. And he touched my hair, so shut up, you obese tub of jelly." I put my arm around her monstrous stomach and hug her close, because there's nothing better than spooning a purring cat.

Today we've moved Creative Writing to the computer lab. It's an awful place—the antique Apple computers move as fast as Water Street during rush hour, and we have to sit just like we do in class. Which means Michaela's on the other side of the room. And, since we're in rows now, Colin's next to me. His elbow is so close I swear his tentacles will reach out and grab the words right from my head.

I log into my Google account. Right at the tippy top is Kasey's email. The Con-athon. And there's Google's oh-so-friendly reminder, *received 7 days ago. Respond?*

Good lord, Google. That's a whole something I've got to figure out on a day that's not today.

I glance to the side. Colin's in a dark maroon sweater today, with tiny beige stripes. He's got a metal ring on one finger of his left hand and he pops his knuckles, tiny soldiers all in a row. I click past Kasey's email and over to Docs.

"Hey," I whisper, barely turning my head. "I didn't really write a sonnet last night." I did write a post though, and I'd call it mildly poetic.

"No shit," he whispers, an eyebrow cocked at me. "I knew you were lying."

Hmmmm. *Shit*'s not an SAT word. "Oh yeah? Well what were you doing?" I turn to him, and he's shaking his head. I catch the playful look even through his glasses. "Playing *Fortnite*?"

He cringes. "Never. I was annotating chapter three for AP Bio. And running through my SAT flashcards with my dad, yet again. An inactive brain is the first step to dementia, he says."

"Wow. That's really depressing. You guys know that's not how they test anymore, right?"

"Yeah, but my dad is old school—"

"Apples! Eyes up here." Mrs. Liu snaps her fingers and Colin and I turn.

Mrs. Liu assigns a found poem using a piece of literature of our choice, and of course I'm going with *The Scarlet Letter*. Not just because we're reading it in American Lit, and I'm neck-deep in Hawthorne's own purple prose, but because darn if Hester doesn't know how to own a look. Someday my balls will be as big as hers and commenters won't know what hit them.

I start to type, fingers flying over the keyboard. Something on the back of my neck prickles like someone is breathing down the collar of my sweater.

Him. Again.

"Kole," he whispers. He's not *that* close to me, thankfully, but it's too much to hear the sound of my name with his voice. "Do you want to swap when you're done? We can help each other."

I shut my eyes. Is today the day I sell my soul? Cricket said he might not be that bad. She's always been smarter than me. I turn to him. "Ask me at the end of class—no guarantees." I pop my earbuds in before he can respond, and look at my screen. He stares at the side of my face long enough for me to give him a side-glance, and then he resumes his hunt for the home row. I catch his groan over The Chainsmokers pumping through my earbuds. I'm not exactly sure what he thinks is in this for him.

Bzzzz. My phone vibrates.

Michaez

11:38 AM

I SHIP IT, seriously. I'm knitting sails. Ordering lumber.

She's staring at me from the other side of the room, eyes wide. She pops two big thumbs up before I look away.

11:38 AM

Have you even seen Noah

Michaez

11:39 AM

Yes. But matching LL Bean flannel. Glasses. Golden retrievers.

I have a plan.

I flip my phone over. Eff her plan. I type in my header, the heading, and make my way to the document. All I have to do is find some pretty bits and pieces of Hawthorne's words and slap them together. Our blocks are forty-ish minutes, and that means that I could easily find fifteen minutes to begin the next installment of *Spacer.* Mrs. Liu won't mind as long as I'm done.

After ten minutes, I whip the poem together and hit print.

Victory. I've beaten Colin at this game of print and win. I take a quick glance. He's pecking all over the keys like Mrs. Liu spread grain on the keyboard. I set my copy face down and just an inch too close to him. Maybe it'll tempt him to take a peek. Or to flinch. But he doesn't move an inch in my direction. I lean toward him, arms on the table. "I'm done. Maybe you need some help?" I ask in the sweetest voice I can muster. Feck, I won the class competition today, he should kiss my feet.

He narrows his eyes and glares, his focus barely on me. "I just need one more minute." He types out the word *traitor.*

"What book did you pick?" I put a hand on my paper. "I went with Hawthorne."

"Stop talking, Kole." He doesn't look at me as he slams one more sentence across his keyboard and hits the print icon. "There. *Count of Monte Cristo.* Longer than Hawthorne. More of a challenge." He leans back in his chair and puts his arms back behind his head. Ughhhh. Of course he has to try to be smarter than me.

"Yeah. Sure. You seem to like challenges." My eyes roll right to the roof. This maroon sweater just became my least favorite sweater of his.

"Always have. Why else would I be texting you?" He flashes me a look.

Heat rushes to my cheeks. I'm not a challenge. I mean, *challenging*, maybe sometimes. But he's in for it. I get up, knocking my knee on the bar that runs under the desk in front of me, and jump to the printer before he can move. I grab his newly printed poem and begin to skim the words. They're good. So good, I mouth the last few lines. When I look up, he's still staring at me. "Not bad. But not lit mag good."

"That's for original work." He tucks his hair behind his ear.

Yeah, okay. Be right, Colin. "Here." I hand him his draft and he rushes to reread it. I pick up mine and do the same thing. Okay, this isn't all bad. Maybe I can let him take a peek. When the silence gets weird, I put mine on his keyboard. He doesn't grab it.

"You can read it." I grab my braid and twist the end. See. I'm no challenge.

He picks the paper up and I pretend to clean my glasses on my own striped sweater. The world is a blurry watercolor.

"Yours was really good," I say. He takes a quick look at me and leans back in his chair.

It's totally fine that Colin's looking at my poem. Others critique my work all the time . . . but they're commenters. Faceless. *Just please don't let him laugh. Again.*

I put my glasses back on. Colin's totally nonchalant.

"Out with it." I rest my chin on my hand.

He clears his throat. "You captured Hawthorne."

Well, that's almost a compliment. "That's what I set out to do. So, is that a compliment?"

He stares. I stare.

"Yeah, it is." Colin looks at something behind me. I turn. "You've grown a lot."

His red ink and clown comments come back to me. I glance to the side. I shouldn't even care . . . but still. "You think so?"

"Yeah. I've always been a rough editor. Sorry."

I smile. At least he knows it. "And a jerk."

He tucks in a corner of his mouth. It's followed by a quick snicker.

"Dude. Let me see your poem." Damian snuck up, and he's reaching for Colin's draft. Such a good little fan. Today he's wearing his *Space Game* sweatshirt he got at a con a few years ago. He bragged about it all through third period and I had to put in my earbuds. Little does he know I've been invited to one now.

"Prepare to be impressed," Colin says as they share a douchey glance.

"Gotta be better than the crap I just came up with."

Colin swaps with Damian, then turns his attention toward his Drive.

They're distracted. Perfect. I mean . . . I usually just write at home, but I can use this time to get my latest draft up to speed. It helps to sleep on a draft before hitting submit, and I really need the time to prep entries now that so many anons are calling me out. And no one should notice; I can't be the only one with a stan account on Stumblr in this class. I log in, my hands easily finding the buttons that I need to do a quick reread. It shouldn't take long—so I'll just get the rough part finished. During tonight's roof session, I'll smooth it out before I let it go live.

Just as I get in the groove, I sense a presence.

"Whatcha working on, Kole? Doesn't look like Creative Writing," Damian asks. The embodiment of pure annoyance. "Some kind of side project?"

"You could say that," I answer, hoping it's enough to get him to leave. Damian ships my NOtp, or my no-true pairing, so I gotta get him off the scent. It's not that it's bad that we don't agree on the ships, but I don't see how any good can come of him seeing my site. My pulse quickens. I click a new tab so he doesn't get a good look. "See what Colin needs. Sharpen his pencil. Clean his earbuds. Rub his shoulders."

Colin chuckles.

"Don't be jealous, Kole. You know, I have a Stumblr page too." Damian's unfazed. "I put some of my music on there. Rap and stuff. I've even dipped my hand into fanfic once or twice. I have a couple hundred followers."

All right. Damian's a worm and obsessed with my show. He's gotta read other fanfic on the site. He's gotta know about *Spacer*.

"I'm sure it's awesome." I fold my fingers across my desk,

clenching my jaw. It's not too late. I can pretend it's my own no good, nothing special blog. "I just jump on every once in a while."

"Have you checked out the one that won—" He leans close into my monitor, eyeing my open tabs.

I put a hand over them, but his eyes have widened. "Stop being nosy!"

Colin's ears have perked up.

Damian leans in so close I can see his retainer. "Wait a second—there's no way you could be writing *Spa*—"

"Get lost, Damian. Like now." I minimize the whole browser. Heat rushes to my face. "This is just something I'm going to delete later today. Like, nothing important."

"No way, I recognize that background," he says, eyes lit like New Year's Eve. "I've been reading that blog since like, entry one. Used to be really good, but then it became about Byron and his abs. And now it's just gotten weird. Uninspired."

"The show is the one that's uninspired!" I slap my mouth closed. No, Kole, don't do this. He's not worth it. "Be gone." I speak louder than I mean to. My eyes sear craters into the monitor.

"Whatever. I mean, maybe it's something you should be proud of . . . if you were writing it the right way." Damian turns around and walks back to his seat, shoulders down and sneakers dragging. I catch his last words as he shuffles around the industrial desks in the lab. "And now I know your secret."

The right way.

Spoken like a true fanboy.

I put my fingers on my temples and rub. Why did I do it? Why did I try working on *Spacer* at school? It was something Pippa would have done in season one when silly mistakes were expected.

It's the comments. It's gotta be. I'm under the gun. They're making me doubt myself. But what's the worst a guy like Damian could do?

"What's he going on about?" Colin breathes in my direction. His eyes are ten times wider in his glasses, the green in them lighter than before.

"Nothing," I reiterate, hoping he's getting the message: leave me the eff alone.

My heart is pumping in my ears. My fingertips have grown cold.

I'll change the background of the blog; maybe I can try to trick him into thinking it was a coincidence. Still, my blood boils.

Colin taps my shoulder. "Hey. Ignore Damian. Ready for some notes?" He removes the top of his black ballpoint pen like he's unsheathing a sword. "It's a cute little poem. Truly."

I give him the evil eye and toss him my paper. It flits across his sweater and lands on his chest. I click my red pen, the one that leaves gooey globs in all the right places, and ready her for battle. He hands me his paper without a word.

I will make his poem bleed.

SPACER 3.8

Draft by: ToTheStars
Sept 26, 2019. 10:36

Bait.

The word rattles through Pippa's mind. Captain Worley has had a lot of ideas, but this is the worst. She gets to lure Uncle Santiago into a trap. Convince him to come to the Rocks and forget his vendetta. Hope that he'll see reason when there are blasters pointed at his head, and that there will be no more bloodshed.

It's a bad plan, but it's the only idea the crew has. Pippa, palms warm and fingers shaky, has to do it. No one else should have to die for her father's lies.

Worley continues, "The stations are *places of desperation.* Santiago must have connections on the *Sky Nymph.* Anyone with money and power does. And that's where we'll get him." He stares right at her as he says it, more gravel in his voice than the soils of Malva.

Regardless of Pippa's bounty being gone, she's still a well-known heiress, and that makes her a bull's-eye.

Dread builds in the pit of her stomach. There are other rovers out there, and they have many eyes.

CHAPTER SIX

It's an unusually warm day for late September in Vermont, so Michaela and I are sitting at a table at the Frosty Fisherman. Fall's laced its fingers around the branches of the maple tree above us, and it hangs over the sloped roof of the town's favorite ice cream joint. It's one of the last nights the Fisherman will be open, and we figured we'd better get our last fill of their butter-rum chocolate-dipped cone. We sit under a string of twinkle lights, crunching newly fallen leaves under our boots as we lick away the day's trouble.

Michaela's wolfing down the second scoop of her cone. "What did Colin end up having to say about your poem?"

"I don't know. I'll snag it from him when I see him after American Lit tomorrow." I wipe at the chocolate crusting around one corner of my mouth. "I read his poem though. It's okay. He can do better."

Her eyes light up. "Seriously?"

I nod. How does one push Mr. Future Valedictorian? "I just don't know how yet."

"Oh man. Sounds like the competition for the lit mag won't be too severe then. Maybe we should give it a shot. That money would go far. May even get me to the con too. Unless you decide you *are* going and I'm your plus-one."

"You can try. I'm consumed with *Spacer*. And I haven't even gotten back to Kasey yet about the con, so a plus-one is something I can't even think about yet."

"Seriously? Would you please get back to her?" Michaela practically yells. "It's our big chance!"

I roll my eyes, mostly at myself. "I haven't decided yet if I can summon the courage. I mean, it's a freaking panel. That's a lot of pressure."

"Then you better start reading your stuff out loud. Get over that speaking in front of a crowd thing, cause there's no way we're missing the Con-athon."

I cringe. She's right. I know it. It's a golden opportunity. "I'll figure it out when I have the headspace. Promise. If I don't have a new entry every few days or so, the comments section gets even nastier."

"They're eating up the story. But you really need more Cedric. I mean, Cedric stans are clamoring for it, even if he's our anti-ship."

I smile. As long as the hits continue, I'm okay with the criticism. At least, that's the courage I decided to have on the ride home from school today. This is the new, online-brave Kole. But tackling Creative Writing . . . that's . . . yikes. If only real life worked like a blog and I could choose when to log in and out.

My phone buzzes in my pocket, a swarm of bees in a little nest. "Hang on," I say to Michaela. Might be Colin—he might want to talk about our drafts.

"Someone expecting you?"

It's not Colin. "It's Will."

> *Broski*
> *7:34 PM*
> *Have you checked your grades today*

Crap. Have I checked my grades today? I did yesterday . . . but

I haven't been updated about any changes. Unless Ms. Peterson finally entered in our most recent Algebra test grades . . .

7:35 PM

No . . . why?

> *Broski*
>
> *7:35 PM*
>
> *Wait til I get home.*

7:36 PM

Ok, but I'm at the Fisherman. What's going on?

> *Broski*
>
> *7:36 PM*
>
> *Just promise you won't check.*

7:36 PM

Ok, weirdo.

My heart races. Doesn't he know that that's the worst possible thing to say to someone with through-the-roof anxiety? Ugh. I groan, audibly. Now I wish it had been Colin.

"What's he want? Probs wondering what I'm up to and where he can meet us," Michaela jokes, flipping her hair off her shoulder.

She wishes. "It's something about the school site. Made me promise not to check until I get home."

"What the heck?" Michaela furrows her brow and reaches for her own phone. "That's ominous. Let's head home. I can chuck the rest of this." She scrolls down her notifications, past the Snapchat and Instagram icons. "Oh shit, Kole."

My stomach sinks. Whatever it is, her look spells dread. "Don't tell me yet. Let me get home." I can't have an anxiety attack here. I've just had ice cream. I need these last few minutes of happiness.

She nods.

This can't be good. I take one final bite and we grab our trusty steeds—the matching lime-green beach cruisers we got for Christmas last year.

In fifteen minutes, we've skidded to a halt at my front door and thrown our bikes to the side. We dash around the house to the back. Will is there. Noah is there. Basketballs under their arms. As soon as they see us, they yank their sweaty tanks and wipe their foreheads. I only look at Noah for one second longer than necessary while he takes a long drink from his water bottle. One second is an improvement.

"Did you see?" Will asks.

"I told you I wouldn't look." I put my hands on my hips. "What's going on?"

I spot Noah gritting his teeth from over Will's shoulder. Will glances at him and they nod. Teenage boy for *go ahead*. Will hands me his phone after his fingers buzz a series of commands.

"I thought it would be taken down by now, but it's still there." Silence rests on the basketball court as I reach for the phone. "Just don't let it throw you, K?"

"Give it." I tune out his words. I barely even notice when Noah stands by my shoulder and Michaela scoots next to me.

Will's pulled up the journalism home page, the spot every Apple in Vermont goes to keep up with what's happening around campus. Not only does it link to where we check our grades and extracurricular info, but it's where they post the announcements. The school's heart. The wind picks up in what must be the first tornado to hit Vermont in a good long while, and I spy, right at the top of the page, a headline that sends a shiver through my bones.

The Apple Irregular

A Celebrity Among Us: Best FanFic Author a Crystal Lake Student

Posted by: Damian Wiles

Sept. 26, 2019

A few of us Apples hope to see our names officially published someday. We hope our legions of followers will gobble up our work and deem it award worthy. At least that's what some of us say in Creative Writing, though not all are lucky enough to make it into the esteemed class. And an even luckier few are fortunate enough to make it into the Lit Mag (submissions due in two weeks!). We all know that prize money is mine . . . but you can try!

What if I told you that somewhere among our school is a writer so well known that they have no need to worry about silly mortal things like the Lit Mag? You'd think I was lying. Heck, I'd think I was lying. I'm not.

Listen up, Apples. Big news on campus.

Heard of Stumblr? Heard of *shipping*? I bet you have, unless you pay no attention to pop culture.

So, here it is.

The very author of Stumblr's *Best FanFic* is a student at Crystal Lake. That means that Pippa's love affair with Byron, the winner of this year's most shippable couple, is the very brain workings of one of our own.

What? Damian, god of journalism, how can that be? How could someone of celebrity caliber walk among us?

It's hard to believe. I know it is. The estimated blog hits on *Spacer* per day are the kind of thing kids like us dream about. That's the stuff that Ivy League dreams are made of. But believe it or not, the author of *Spacer* is one of our very own.

But I'm not saying who it is. I won't tell you, even if you offer to buy me fries.

Let the author reveal themselves. Or, if you so choose, my fellow smart and attractive classmates, seek them out. Do what we do best and find the root of this gossip.

So, in case you've been living under a rock for the last couple of weeks, here's a link to *Spacer*. Don't forget to pick a ship, JUST MAKE SURE IT'S THE RIGHT ONE. (#TeamCedric)

Choose your side, Apples.

I cough in that awkward way when you're choking on nothing but air and spit. Will snags his phone as it slips from my hand.

What has Damian done?

"Kole?" he asks. "Should I make you sit or give you the Heimlich?"

When I can speak again, my voice squeaks. I close my eyes. "What do I do?"

"Who's Damian?" Noah asks.

"A worm in Creative Writing—follows Colin Clarke around like he wants to lick his face," Michaela answers.

Accurate. "Damian saw my blog a few days ago. I logged in. I didn't think, in a bazillion years, that anyone would recognize it. But he did, and I shot him down. Acted like it was nothing. He knew I was lying. Clearly." I put a hand to my throat. My voice was like a whisper.

"Why would he put the link on the website?" Michaela asks.

"It's a big story. He wants the attention." Will drags a hand over his forehead.

When the Journalism teacher sees, she'll delete it. I'm sure of it. "This will be gone soon, right? I mean, he's daring the school to find me—and my site's not school-related. Admin will take it down."

"But he's the fav in Journalism—Mrs. Brittain has to know he posted it?" Michaela's face drops. "Unless . . . she doesn't care? And he had her permission?"

"People will have seen it by then." Will begins to dribble the ball. "I'm sorry, Kole."

Logging in from school was the last thing in the world I should have done. I shut my eyes, forcing the tears back down.

"We saw it a half hour ago. There's nine hundred kids at school," Noah says all low and throaty over my shoulder. "Whether or not the blog is up by the time school starts tomorrow, the damage has been done."

People will be on the home page tonight; a ton probably already are. They have to log in to check their grades—their online classrooms—their athletics schedules. And they'll see his post. They have to click past it to get through to their homework.

"What's the worst thing that happens, Kole?" Michaela asks. "The anti's know, but what can they do? You don't have to say a word. You don't even have to post again. Let it blow over?"

"I'll delete it." I study her face. It's dramatic, yes, but if the whole school knows it's mine there will be questions. Judgment. Criticism. Water pools under my eyes. "Or deactivate it and make it go live when I get to . . . college or something."

College. I see Mom mouthing the word in slo-mo. Now the bus that was going to take me to Hollywood drives down the street,

leaving me in a leafy swirl as it takes someone else to the writers'
room of HBO's next big thing.

And I'm not in it.

"You can't. I mean, I haven't read it, but people love it, right?"
Noah says, taking a step toward me.

I tuck in a corner of my mouth, but Noah's sweet words aren't
enough to fix this. Will tosses the basketball off to the side of the
court and runs his hands through his hair. "Don't delete it. That's
your thing. We can't let Damian the Douche take it from you."

I nod slowly. Will is a good big brother. He knows what my blog
means to me. "Okay. At least not tonight. That's the only promise
I can make."

Noah folds his arms across his chest. "I'm going to need someone to point out this Damian tomorrow. I want to get a look at him."

I glance at Noah, knowing that in any other situation my heart
would be all aflutter. But not now. Too much is on the line. I take
off my glasses and pinch right in between my eyes. Fire rushes up
my legs, through my stomach, and lands somewhere in my throat.
Someone else at school is going to find out who I am. And they will
tell everyone.

Unless the anti's do it first.

That possibility bolts through my body; a full-throttle anxiety
attack is headed straight for me. I need to be alone before the wave
encompasses me and I can no longer stand.

I don't want to face them. Or anyone else.

"Thanks for trying. I'll see you all later." I can feel three sets
of eyes on me as I book it inside and up the stairs. I throw my coat
on my pile of laundry and flop on my bed. Cricket jolts awake and
dashes under my covers.

Great. I've even scared my cat.

Do I dare log in? Dare disturb the silence between me and the computer? The words Crystal Lake will be strewn across my dashboard more than any other location on that darn map. And if I look at the comments . . . do I dare see what anyone else actually thinks of my work? Will they use the comments section to guess who I am? To laugh at every typo and point out every dangling modifier?

They will. I know they will. Kids are cruel at Crystal Lake. Damian is proof. And Hailey. And Colin . . . what will he say when he finds out who I am?

Damian's ruined everything.

CHAPTER SEVEN

The link was not gone by morning. It was on the home page at 5:30. At 6:00. At 6:30. After the bike ride to school, it was still live. Apparently admin and the journalism teacher don't care. Or they don't know.

I couldn't find a scrape of inspiration to write last night, no matter how many fan videos I watched. No matter how many other Stumblr sites I lurked on. The promise to Will was the only thing that kept me from hitting control-A-delete on the whole darn blog. That, and Michaela loves my story. And Noah's maybe gonna check it out. I don't want to let them down.

I *won't* let them down.

And god, the con—Kasey. If I let Damian win, I'll be killing a future I've dreamed of since puberty.

I can't let him win, even if there's a ball of heavy heat in my chest aching to burst and splinter into little pieces.

The comments started the moment I walked through the front doors. During Algebra a teacher poked in and asked Ms. Peterson what that was all about on the home page. She said it was something the Journalism teacher has up her sleeve. A gaggle of girls whispered their guesses this morning. I turned my head the other way.

No one was considering me.

Now I pass through the B hallway before Art and there stands

Damian like he transmogrified into some kind of wraith. It appears he's enchanted the whole student body with some magical elixir, because they're staring at him with stars in their eyes. I stop dead in my tracks. He's dressed in head-to-toe black, his old *Firefly* shirt tucked into his jeans, and hair slicked back like an Elvis clone. It's almost enough to make me wish they forced uniforms on us here. But, at least today he's trying a new fandom. A big old belt buckle rests just at his hips, and across his face is a pair of aviator sunglasses. For once he's not in Colin's shadow, offering to carry his books.

Damian walks past the lockers. Even Bart Fletcher, one of the biggest jocks on campus, puts out a hand for Damian to slap. "I'm not telling, Bart, so don't ask." Damian cracks a big grin and nods his head.

"Come on, man!" Bart throws his hands up.

Seriously. It's like one of those ancient movies in the '80s. Like when we first got color film or something. After they've slapped each other on the back, Damian pulls back his hand and shakes it, pain etched across his face. Guess the high five was too rough for his taste. He can't hide that behind his glasses.

I'll run smack into him if I don't clear out of here. But the hall . . . it's a mess of kids. I could duck into the bathroom, make for a quick dash to safety, but there are too many of them. And a couple is making out in the doorway, all hands on butts and other areas.

Damian is a step from me when he stops. "Kole," he says, jerking his head up in a casual-cool hello.

"Douchebag," I say so only he can hear.

He smiles from ear to ear. "No hard feelings," he whispers before continuing on through the crowd. "Secrets are best spilt, eh, Scientist's Daughter?"

That mofo just used my own line on me. One of Byron's. I turn back to him, my fists balled up in the sleeves of my sweater, but he's disappeared into the nearby crowd. I grit my teeth before I say his name.

He stops and turns. "Make my ship set sail. Cedric and Pippa. Screw Byron."

"Or what?"

He sneers. "Or I tell everyone."

"That's your plan? You want me to write *your* ship into *my* canon?"

He nods and backs into the crowd.

My lip trembles. I've got it: an empty grave in the cemetery downtown. Hope no one sees me dragging his corpse. Someone runs into me, knocking my shoulder and making my glasses slip down my nose. I walk. Fast.

"Frankly, the writing is crap." Hailey, the bane of my existence, swirls a wooden spoon inside a massive yellow cooking bowl. The air in Culinary Arts is icier than normal today, with a side of purple batter, and my nerves are jumping out of my skin. "And I've never cared for science fiction. Why waste your time writing about things that don't exist?"

"It's based on that one show we used to be into," Raya says. "I've been reading *Spacer* for a few days now—"

Great. Now Hailey's caught wind of it. I try to stick a bit closer to the wall, but the bowl of spoons I'm carrying to the sink is making it hard to remain hidden.

"I don't have time for TV. Except for *Antique Roadshow* and

107

The Great British Baking Show." Hailey shakes her head but her hair doesn't move an inch. Girl doesn't know when to quit with the hair spray. "Don't waste your time on that nonsense. It won't get you to Dartmouth. Nor will it help prepare us for *The Great British Baking Show* auditions."

"You're right," Raya says, double blinking and more determined than before.

"Gag," I mutter under my breath as I throw a whole class's worth of spoons into the large, metal sink before me. They clang to the bottom loud enough to make a few of us cringe. Hailey, ever the drama queen, jumps an inch. Good. That'll shut her up. I still want to hear what Raya thinks.

"I highly doubt *The Space Game* would even want you watching it, Hailey," I say, loud enough for her to hear. "Stick to cupcakes."

"My marbleized raspberry cheesecake cupcakes will blow yours out of the water."

I roll my eyes. Like I care if she thinks her cupcakes are better than mine. "Taking Culinary three years in a row for an easy A is fool's play. Don't worry, I'm sure Dartmouth won't notice."

"Excuse me, Miss Nobody, but when you're auditioning for a baking show at seventeen, these classes do matter." She looks at Raya, and they share an obnoxiously loud giggle.

"You're not even British," I say under my breath. She whips around, her back toward me, and I seize the opportunity to flick a piece of batter at her white sweater. *Bingo.* It clings to a strand of her hair just where she can't see it. I hope it stays there all day.

"Who do you think wrote the last entry? Kole or the pink-haired girl—what's her name again?" Raya asks Hailey as they pull their cupcakes from the oven. "The one who thinks she's hot because she pierced her nose freshman year."

Michaela. Seriously? She has to be doing this on purpose. She's just playing it cool, like we didn't all hang out in middle school.

Hailey looks to the ceiling like she's caught a signal from a spaceship. I turn the faucet on with more force than I mean to, but that doesn't stop Hailey from speaking louder and glancing in my direction. "A reasonable guess. The stuff she's read in Creative Writing is subpar. And whoever it is clearly hasn't read *The Elements of Style* closely."

I begin to scrub the batter from the spoons so hard that half of them slip out of my hands. Even the rubber gloves between me and the water aren't enough to stop the heat from searing my skin.

I nudge my glasses higher with my forearm. Everywhere I've been today has had someone talking about *Spacer.* Hailey. Raya. The girls in the hall. The teachers. And Damian is now hotter than a lobster roll. This is some kind of parallel world nonsense—like something straight out of *The Space Game*, and I'm in the airlock.

How do I fix this? I scrub the spoons harder. Faster. The batter doesn't stand a chance. What would Byron do? He'd aim the hull of the *Snapdragon* right for the nearest asteroid and slam his hand on the blast button. He'd make Hailey stardust under his boot.

I need to be Byron. I need to take charge of my own starship by dethroning Hailey. And Damian. But in order to do that, I need to think smarter. Harder. Which means I need to make a deal with a couple of devils.

First step: the journalism teacher—see if I can get her to take the link down. See if she even cares.

Second step: Colin. Having compared our writing in the computer lab, maybe us working together isn't such a bad idea. He apologized for being a jerk. And he left me his feckin' phone number. On my trusty notebook. It was ballsy, and I'm not even that mad about it anymore. Maybe it just took the universe, and Liu, putting us next to each other for me to see it—like, we could make a good team. We can make each other better writers.

Ripping off the dripping rubber gloves, I flip around to the other side of the massive metal fridge where Mrs. Poissant can't see me. My phone is stashed in my back pocket, and I yank it free. I send the text before I have time to stop and second-guess it, even though I catch Hailey glance in my direction.

9:54 AM

Hey. Can you meet up? It'll only take a second.

Probably Shouldn't Text Him

9:54 AM

Hallway B in 10? I can ask Singh for a bathroom break . . .

I peek at Hailey. She's watching me. *Ugh.* I can't meet Colin yet—she'll alert Poissant to what I'm up to and a bathroom break will be impossible.

"These spoons need a better wash, but Nikole's too busy texting her *boyfriend*," Hailey says loud enough for Poissant to hear. I fecking hate her. Colin's not even a friend. He's a . . . means to an end. I'll make sure to hand her the half-pink blueberries next time we're tossing them into a stack o' pancakes. See to it that she gets the fake maple syrup instead of the stuff they made up the street at the orchard.

Back to Colin.

9:55 AM

Not yet. Meet me outside Journalism at 12:15.

> *Probably Shouldn't Text Him*
> *9:55 AM*
> *Why Journalism? Don't join. It's the worst.*

9:56 AM
I need something from Mrs. Brittain.

> *Probably Shouldn't Text Him*
> *9:56 AM*
> *Ok. Bring Peanut M&Ms. Trust me on this, Kole. It's the only way to get to her.*

M&M's? Strange.

I glance to the side. Hailey's watching with razor-sharp eyes. I glare at her, and she gets back to licking a spoon like Gollum gazing at the one true ring.

"What's his name, Kole?" she asks. "Is he cute?"

I turn my back to her. There are peanut M&M's in this fridge. We used them to make brownies a few classes ago. Swiping some should be easy, provided Gollum isn't watching.

9:58 AM
Ok. See you soon.

> *Probably Shouldn't Text Him*
> *9:58 AM*
> *See you soon.*

9:58 AM
And thanks.

The doors to Journalism aren't locked. No light streams through the sliver of a window on the side. I take my chance and yank the door open, hoping that somehow I'll be brave enough to get what I need.

I don't have Mrs. Brittain as a teacher, but rumor has it she's some kind of dementor. Only a projector light is on, and there's not a soul but her. She sits in one corner, bent over a batch of magazines. She's reading with a light and a magnifying glass, leaning over the table like she just had a sandwich of souls for lunch. She's so engrossed she doesn't hear it when I shut the door and step behind her.

"Mrs. Brittain?" I say, equal parts sorry and scared to break her from her news-ingesting trance.

"Who dares? It's lunch." She adjusts the glasses on her nose, much like I do when they're halfway down my face, and turns to look at me. She's in a knee-length fur coat, her white hair in a tight bun placed on the very top of her head.

"Hi. I'm Kole Miller. I was wondering if you could help with something? A favor, I guess." Crap, it just got cold in here.

"What do you need? A fancy invite to the Harvest Ball on the school's home page? Hoping that special someone will finally give you a chance? Those are booked for the next seven days." Her voice gets deeper halfway through, her breath snaking through the air between us.

I shake my head. The last thing I need is something *more* about me on the school home page. "No."

"A signature to get into my class next year, then? I don't give those out to just anyone, you know." Brittain stands up and comes to the front of her desk. She wraps one long leg around the other, waiting for me to break the silence.

"No, um, it's about the website."

"Come for an interview then?" Mrs. Brittain's shoulders bounce. "We're quite proud of it. Gatekeepers, that's what we call ourselves here. The funnel to all of Crystal Lake Prep's most important happenings."

I have to stop the urge to roll my eyes. "Did you see what was posted last night?"

"Naturally. I mean, what kind of mentor would I be if I didn't see what my students were uploading?"

My backpack just got heavier. I readjust my stance. "I was just wondering if you could change it."

She looks like I've just asked her to kill her cat. "Are you, Ms. Miller, aware that as of last night, we became the number one most visited high school home page in eastern Vermont?"

Great. She's concerned about hits. "I wasn't aware."

"No school site has garnered this kind of attention. But then, last night, my Damian had an announcement to make." Her eyes dart to the wall on the north side of the room. There's a framed picture of Damian before his braces came off, with the title *Reporter of the Month* across the top in big bubble letters. Across the bottom, it reads *12 months running*. After a deep sigh, she saunters to her podium, next to where I stand. "In other words, do you have any idea what this can do for our high school? To have the world know the writer of *Spacer* is in our midst?"

My eyes widen. *Spacer*.

And that means this . . . teacher . . . knows and doesn't care that it's on there. The silence slows my blood. It trickles through my veins.

"And why, again, are you here, Ms. Miller?" She squints.

"I was hoping there was something else we could put up."

"It's a silly science fiction site. Do you have some personal stake in it?" She begins to tap her too-long nails on the wood of the podium in rapid succession, *click click click.* "Some kind of *investment* you may have in this situation?"

The M&M's. The trick to Brittain.

I stick one hand in and wrap my fingers around the bag until the chocolate is probably melting. This ridiculous plan is never going to work, but it's all I have. I yank the candy out of my pocket and her eyes widen. I've found my wild card. And . . . it's all thanks to Colin.

"What are those?" she asks.

"A little something I was saving for later. In case I need a snack during seventh period." I take three steps toward the podium and pop one in my mouth. Brittain flinches. The package is crinkled and hot, a little ripped in one corner. That doesn't stop her. She's staring like it's the last bag on the whole planet, and I keep one finger placed right on top.

"If you won't do anything about the post, when's the next one going live?" I ask, trying to keep my mouth straight.

"It's not scheduled until next week. When they announce the picks for varsity basketball."

Of course. Will wants to make the team. And he's been trying to talk Noah into trying out. All right, here I go, guns a'blazing. "Yeah, big news, I guess. Those baskets and balls. But about last night's post—isn't it kinda invasive to try to out a writer like Damian is doing? And to try to get the whole school in on it?"

Brittain laughs. "Out a writer? How does one *truly* do that? We're dedicated to sniffing out the truth. And we've found it."

Great. She truly doesn't care. "I don't know. I think they'd probably like to be anonymous."

"Do you now?" Brittain taps those nails on the podium again, clickety-clack across all five fingers, eyeing me like she can see right through me. "The vending machines stopped stocking those forbidden fruit months ago, and here you are with them in my very classroom, asking me for a favor. How about this: you give me those chocolate delights, and I'll see to it the next post goes live tonight."

"Not tonight. By next period." Oh, lord, I'm pushing it.

"This afternoon, or no deal." She puts a hot pink, too-long nail on the bag. "The hits have slowed down anyway. Whomever wants to know about Damian's announcement already does. I'm afraid you're too late to make a difference, Ms. Miller."

"Fine. This afternoon then. Just get it off." I lay the bag on the podium. It's an offering, a sacrifice to the Journalism god. She grabs the M&M's out from under my finger and the bag rips even more.

"You've got a deal. Out of curiosity, have you read *Spacer*?" She pops three candies into her mouth.

"Well, yeah." Fudge.

"Do you watch *The Space Game*?"

I do roll my eyes this time. I mean, hello. "What teenager doesn't?"

"Then you know that it's a wildly popular show and that *Spacer* deserves all of the attention it gets, if that's your *thing*. Is it so wrong to want some of that clout on our site? To funnel that energy and encourage whomever is writing to be proud of it—maybe even consider coming forward?"

I put a hand to my braid and scratch behind my ear. Brittain doesn't know what it's like to enjoy something in the quiet and on the dark of your roof under a blanket with a big cat on your lap. And, once upon a time, it was about an audience of a few. But this is too much. "Yeah, it is wrong. You're setting the whole student body on one kid."

Brittain takes off her glasses and angles her gaze at me like I'm a bug under a microscope, wiggling and oozing life-goo all over the table. "Then that *one kid* better make their next move a damn good one."

By the time I get to the hallway where Colin and I agreed to meet, he's already there, his back to me. His shoulders are a whole head above me. He's in a royal-blue collared shirt, tucked into a pair of jeans, no sweater, and he leans against the deep-red lockers, his backpack high on his shoulders. His hands are in his pockets, but he's got a piece of paper slipped under one finger. He looks like someone from one of the Ivy League catalogs Mom places on my desk. I hope she isn't too disappointed when she sees them in the recycle bin.

I swipe the loose hair from my eyes and take a deep breath. "Hey Colin."

He turns around. "Kole."

No hello, then. I stop. Silence can be so very demanding. I better thank him—he's the reason I got the upper hand with Brittain. "Thanks for the tip about the M&M's."

He shrugs. "It was nothing. Something I learned freshman year."

"It saved my butt." Oh god. I said *butt* in front of Colin Clarke, most likely to be valedictorian, end up at Yale, and invent the next TikTok or something. My cheeks light themselves on fire.

But then he smirks. An almost smile. I narrow my eyes. Maybe Colin is just like the rest of us and enjoys a casual reference to butts, but he usually only smiles when Mrs. Liu cracks a joke about college admission scandals.

"So, what's going on? Decided you need help with those sonnets you were never writing to begin with?" he asks, a corner of his mouth placed precariously upward. Green, piercing eyes study my face. "The one you texted me about regardless?"

"I was writing something, but not sonnets, if you must know."

"And what was that?" He squints, tilting his head just a little.

"I'll never tell you, Mr. Valedictorian."

He smiles, shifting his stance. He likes that nickname.

Hang on.

Is this *flirting*?

Somewhere in the hallway, laughter. A distant piano begins to play the *Moonlight Sonata*. An ambulance skids past the windows on the north side of the hall, its siren blaring.

IS THIS FLIRTING WITH COLIN CLARKE?

My hands quiver to Beethoven's tune as the siren fades. This must be a wonderland where one lunch period can flip everything I've believed about high school upside down.

Exhibit A: the Journalism teacher is wack.

Exhibit B: me agreeing to work with the guy before me.

I swallow, hoping my voice doesn't sound like a mouse squeaking for a crumb. "I want to take you up on your offer to be partners. Let's swap our next drafts."

He adjusts his stance and crosses his arms. It pulls his shirt tight across his chest. I only look for .005 of a second. "And here I was thinking you still hated me."

"I do h—" *No, Kole. Start over. Be nice.* I glance around the hall, hoping for something to distract him from asking what changed my mind—one that could lead to me vomiting up the truth: that Damian has sent the whole school after me. That more than just my chance at the lit mag is up in the air; my online persona is at risk. But there's nothing in this hall to help me, just an old projector haphazardly pushed into a doorway and a few couples hiding between the lockers while they whisper sweet somethings. Farther down the hall, some kids are hanging yet another banner for the Harvest Ball. There's nothing to distract Colin's too-keen gaze through his too-cool glasses from reading my too-scared face. "Never mind. I just want to get better at this writing thing. I need help."

He tightens his mouth, taking the words in. I notice a tiny pink scar that runs from the top of his lip to the bottom of his nose. "I'm glad you've come around. I think we've got a lot to offer one another."

I can help *him*, I know that now, and he's agreed to help me, and selfish motivations are something I've never had a problem with. "Why do you say that?"

"I remember when we used to swap back in freshman year." He takes a step closer, like he's got a secret, and I lean against the locker to my side. "When I was *oh so mean*." He glances around and then clears his throat. "I was intimidated. So, yeah, I got mean."

"Yeah, you did. But to be fair, my writing was kinda crappy." I've really got to learn to take his apologies. Regardless, I'm sure those words from freshman year should be buried somewhere far below where worms are the only ones that can taste them. "That was forever ago anyway."

"Yeah, but it must mean something if I still remember what you were writing about, right?" He gives a little shrug. "Because it wasn't that bad."

This time I allow a tiny smile. "Maybe?"

"Definitely. You were good then. And now that I've read your found poem, you're really good. But I want to read your work now, not Hawthorne's blended-up prose for some random assignment."

He says that like the idea of a found poem makes him sick. Not the response I was expecting. But *he said my work was good.* And, shit, I still haven't read the notes he left me when we gave each other our poems back. They're shoved somewhere deep down in my backpack with the ghosts of Doritos past.

He continues, "I've been asking you to work with me because I want to be better. I want to learn from you. You're a far better writer than me, Kole. I want you to challenge me. Get me where I need to be for Yale."

My mouth falls open. I close it before he thinks I'm a mouth breather. His words. *You're the better writer.*

He shakes his head and clears his throat. "I said too much. Sorry."

He wants my help . . . and I came here for his. Well that's a tasty bit of irony. This time I definitely smile. "No, you didn't. That's why I came here too, right? I want to be better. So let's swap, from here on out."

He smiles back, a big grin. The kind that makes me want to look away, except I don't. I don't remember noticing that Colin has nice teeth, but then again, he's only smiling when he's giving me a hard time. "And I don't hate you. Or, not anymore. So don't say that, dumbass."

He sucks in his breath— I made his smile transform into a chuckle. I think I just won a challenge of some sort. The bell rings, breaking our eye contact. I rush off, leaving him standing against the lockers. The incoming rush of students envelops me. I fold my arms tight across my chest. I just called Colin Clarke a dumbass to his not-so-mean, not-so-slimy face.

Somehow, I feel like Pippa would be proud.

SPACER 3.9

Posted by: ToTheStars
Sept. 27, 2019. 8:58

Pippa looks around, lowering her eyes, and turns, her skirt twirling as she makes for the door.

Crap. Byron hit a soft spot. "Ms. Carlyle?" he says.

"Hmm?" She turns.

He clears his throat. "It's Byron. Call me Byron."

She looks at him through dark lashes, her eyes tired. "Okay, Byron." She whips around, hair falling over the other shoulder, and tiptoes down the stairs. A familiar scent whisks through the air—something he hasn't smelled in a good long while.

Hyacinths. Like the ones he used to rip to pieces in the fields.

"My gods," he whispers once the scientist's daughter is out of his command room.

Imagine that.

Flowers on the lonely deck of the *Snapdragon*.

CHAPTER EIGHT

Fridays are made for ham and pineapple pizza, sparkling cider, and the neon beanbags in the basement. For texting your best friend and making sure your brother invites his cute jock-friend-guy over to watch your show with you.

Noah's kinda my friend now too. I mean, we did play basketball together, we talked a lot, he touched my hair, I didn't break *his* nose, and we did some of that flirting thing.

Flirting. There's something I didn't think I'd try until like my twenties or something. When I'm mature. But I think I also did that today in the hall. It's hard to say—I've been talking to boys my whole life, Will's to thank for that, but when the guy I'm talking to appears cuter than he did a few days ago, and I add in a smile, some teasing, an ironic tone, a shuffling of feet . . . that makes it flirting, right?

Hang on. I'm thinking of Colin here. I pull the string on the beanbag. Man, these things are getting old. It breaks and pops back into my palm. *Flirting.*

Michaela scrolls through Netflix, buzzing past a million shows before she finds *The Space Game.* "Almost there. I think I saw it. Wait, I passed it."

Why's it so annoying when someone else has the remote? I would have had us there five seconds ago. "Geez, Michaela," I whine, sipping from the champagne flute in front of me. The bubbles fizz on my tongue in little fireworks. Finally, Michaela finds the right image: Pippa flanked by her parents, the *Snapdragon* behind her, and a field of stars. Perfect.

"When's Noah coming?"

"Any minute," I say. Might have been a good call to wait one second before answering, so as not to appear totally excited for his arrival.

Michaela giggles. "I call dibs on a seat by Will."

"Won't be an issue," I say, my eyes gazing at the screen until they enter a trance that'll hurt to break.

Yeah, Noah and I are friends. Totally. Why is this stuff, romance and friendship, birds and bees, easier to write than it is to figure out in real life? Simple things: a blog (with about 1.8 million too many followers). A show you love. Fifteen episodes a season. Four seasons broken down by forty-two short minutes.

I lean back and prop my legs, a little prickly since yesterday morning's shave, up on the coffee table. Pizza should be here any second. Boys should be here any second. And Michaela's on episode one.

"Did you hear anyone talking about *Spacer* today?" she asks.

I shake my head and break the trance. Ouch. "Yeah. Hailey and Raya. Kids in the hall. Even Brittain."

"I heard it eight times . . . and ten more if you include Twitter and Snap." Michaela nods. "Kinda cool to have our world made public? Maybe?"

"Not cool. They're going to find out it's me and I'll die. If adding Cedric into the story doesn't kill me before that."

"Is it still on the site?"

Crap. I haven't looked since school got out. Shivers race up my spine. Forcing a fist into the oversized, yellow bowl in front of me, I come back with a handful of popcorn. I shove it in my mouth with as much grace as a rabid dog—Mom wouldn't be proud—and then go back for another handful. It's okay to be unladylike. Noah's not here yet.

I've got to see if the basketball picks went live.

"I figured that if we watch two episodes every Friday night, not including the week of Christmas and New Year's, we'll be caught up when the premiere airs."

"If they start in mid-February again. That's a pretty big *if*," I nearly choke out. This is serious business. We don't want to skip a week, even by accident. "Hand me my bubbly, will you?" I say, in my best British accent. I reach a hand backward and Michaela slips my refilled champagne flute into it. Sparkling cider is truly the best, and it pairs nicely with movie-theater style popcorn.

I'm about to google the school site—see if Brittain followed through—when a stampede of bison named Will and Noah head down the staircase in front of us and enter the basement carrying more cider and three massive pizzas. Will and Noah, pizza and champagne. Noah's even got breadsticks. I can smell them from here.

I'm in love with him.

Heat rushes to my ears. THEM. I mean them. The breadsticks.

I really hope Noah isn't telepathic. I'd be so screwed.

Will raises the boxes, nearly losing his balance, and yells, "We got the goods!"

"Nice!" Michaela and I say in unison.

"I've got ep one ready," Michaela says before she takes the bottles from Noah. Will grabs a bright green beanbag he's had since the sixth grade and tosses it closer to the massive TV before us. Noah snags the blue one and tosses it halfway between mine and Will's so it's laying partially on both of ours, now in between my brother and me. That makes Michaela, on the orange one, closer to Will, and me closer to the slice of heaven that is Noah's forearm.

Oh, asteroids.

"The last one I saw was in like season three. Toward the middle. I remember an asteroid headed for the *Snapdragon*, and Pippa deciding they were going to hit it head on," Will says.

"Oh, that's later in the season, toward the end," Michaela corrects him.

OMG Michaela. That's not even right. "Episode four, season three. It's called 'Straight for Us.' It's the one when Sebastian decides he's going to destroy the *Snapdragon* because the starship will come for him if he doesn't get them first—when he was supposed to go to the Rocks? Like right before Aster comes in, you guys. Not the best episode, at least not until that one scene when the asteroid nearly cracks the windshield and the crew has to—" I glance around me. They're staring. "Never mind. We'll get there. We can just watch it."

"Oh my god, Kole." Will throws a piece of popcorn at my face, and it bounces off my glasses and into my champagne. *Plunk.* "Let me be the one to embarrass you tonight—you take the fun out of it when you do it yourself."

I toss more popcorn his way. I have to lean over Noah a little, but I don't mind a bit when he and Michaela laugh. "Laugh it up," I say. Dad's always said I'm a queen and I surround myself with court jesters. He used to be right—before we ditched the anti's—but how unfortunate now that his son happens to be one of the clowns I hang out with. "And I take back my apology for breaking your nose."

"Shut up," he whines, putting a hand to the bridge of his nose. It still looks rather tender.

Yeah, okay, that was harsh. "Okay, I don't really mean that."
He side-eyes me.

"What's the deal with the blog?" Noah asks while Michaela
hits the play button. "I jumped on a few days ago. There's so much
on there. It's like you've been doing it for ten years or something."

"It feels like that sometimes," I say, trying not to speak over the
montage of opening credits. I pull out my phone from in between
my knees. I want to focus on his questions, and his face and his
eyes and his lips, but there is a serious matter going on here. "Lots
of traffic. Lots of comments. But I'm hoping the link's not on the
home page anymore."

Noah's face falls, and he runs a finger through his hair, clearly
agitated. The lock plops back to its natural spot, right where his brain
meets his forehead. The place I'd kiss if given the chance. Before I
can consider how soft his lips must be, he looks to Will. "If Damian's
link isn't up anymore, does that mean the basketball picks are up?"

My heart picks up. The team . . .

"Coach said they were up next, so yeah, I guess."

"But if they're up early, I didn't get to try out," Noah says, his
brow knit into a million question marks. "I was supposed to meet
with him this week."

My mind goes blank.

"Check the page." Will doesn't break his staring contest with
the TV, especially when the group of assassins, the Sirens, are on
the screen. They'll be the big bad by the end of the season, but a
casual viewer like my brother doesn't know that yet. "Does Pippa
even know that the Sirens can crash the *Snapdragon* whenever they
want? All they have to do is sing?"

It hurts not to answer his question, especially when the answer is obvious, but I'll let Michaela get this one. She rambles in the distance as I unlock my phone. I need to make sure Brittain followed through . . . but that means basketball picks are up early, which means that Noah . . . won't have had a chance to make the team.

It might not be too late. Asteroids, let it not be too late.

On my green message icon there are three missed texts. *Colin.* I swipe them aside—I'll come back later—and get to Chrome. It only takes a second to pull up the school site.

I sit up. In my attempt to readjust my T-shirt (it's riding up a bit too much), the bowl of popcorn precariously jostles on my lap—careless, I'll admit. But rather than letting it fall, which I would have never done if we weren't in an emergency situation, Noah reaches over and steadies the bowl. When it's righted, he grabs a handful and I can feel the heat all the way from here. I raise my phone to my face hoping to block the blush, and it lights up like an airplane at night.

Damian's letter is gone. In its place is the varsity basketball team list.

The Apple Irregular

Crystal Lake Basketball Varsity Team: Fall 2019

Posted by: The Duffster

Sept. 27, 2019

Hello, Apples!

Coach McDuffy here! We're gearing up for a stellar basketball season this year. I've picked the ripest, most red-y (see what I did there? Haha!) juniors and seniors of this year's crop, and man, it's a good one. I know they'll do us at Crystal Lake proud when we take on the Norwich

Milkweeds at our first game in two weeks!

Without further ado, here's your varsity basketball team!

Jack Whitton

Todd Blake

Will Miller

Marshall Sawyer

Darnell Gray

Joshua Abraham

Anthony Barker

Johnny "Chubs" Falls

Garrett Lopez

Eric Guermill

Cody Bartlett

Justin White

If you see them in the halls, make sure to give them a big APPLE congrats! Boys, get ready for some killer passing drills and wall sits when we start next week. Can't let my apples get lumpy before I put them in the pie!

— Coach McDuffy

"Can I look?" Noah has his hand out to read the update.

My hands clam up. In my haste to get myself out of hot water, I threw Noah's chance at the team out the door. I didn't even consider what getting my blog off the home page would do to others. I suck in my bottom lip. It's going to crush him. Oh man. I'm the worst friend in the history of friends.

I hand him the phone, watching as his eyes rake down the list. Before he looks up, before I can see the red forming in his eyes, I take off my glasses, the world going fuzzy, and clean them on my old Red Sox shirt. It doesn't help. This is too messy and there's too much butter on my fingertips to make the lenses clear again. This mess won't come off without a little effort.

Hang on a minute.

Damian's the one who put me on blast. Noah didn't get on the team because *Damian's* post had to come down. He's the bad guy here. All of this is because of that slimy sea slug.

Damian. I need to salt his skin. Make him writhe under the acid of my revenge.

"There's no room for me on the team now. It's done," Noah says, his voice barely audible.

I swallow. I need a plan to deal with the dillweed of the century. I need a plan to get Noah back on the team. His finger slides up the broken screen of my phone as he scrolls through the list. "Someone's texting you."

"Don't worry about it. I'm sorry, Noah, about the team," I say. When he finally looks at me, he blinks a little too quickly. He raises his chocolate-chip eyes from the phone and blinks a few more times. God dang his eyes aren't semi-sweet; they're cavity-inducing. He tries to avoid my gaze, but I can see they've lost some of their shine. "Let me get you some sparkling cider."

"Nah. It's okay. I don't really feel like anything."

I glance at the TV. There's Byron, speaking over his shoulder to Coral. His brow is furrowed and arms are crossed at the helm of the *Snapdragon*, but I'm kinda not interested at the moment.

"Are the picks up? Please tell me Cockroach Cody didn't make this year," Will says, breaking his gaze with the cleavage on-screen. "I'm over his shit."

"They're up." Noah hands me the phone. It's warm from his touch when I grab it, like it's been sitting in the sun. "I didn't get a chance. Looks like it's already a done thing."

"Shit." Will pulls out his phone and pulls up the list. "Nah, man. I'll talk to coach. Get you on and Cody in the bleachers where he belongs. You can be an alternate or something. Coach will see you're better than at least three of these guys."

"Just make sure someone breaks a leg, Will." Michaela laughs. "Trip them. Coach will need Noah then."

She's only kinda kidding.

"Let's just keep watching. We'll deal with it on Monday." Will reaches for the remote and hits play again. Back to the boobs and babes. Ah, good old episode one. Nothing like the first: too much CGI, not enough plot, way more sex than necessary, and a whole lot of partial nudity. Sounds like a pilot. It would be great if more of this was about Byron, but his character doesn't get backstory for another few episodes.

I look back at my phone, while Michaela starts to laugh. Must be when Pippa trips, first time on the stardeck, and the crew laughs at her. I've seen it too many times for it to be funny anymore.

I open up my messages. Three new ones. All from Colin.

Probably Shouldn't Text Him
7:45 PM
I finished the draft you shared with me.
You sure you wrote this?

Colin winky faced me. Colin. Winky. Faced. Me.

7:49 PM
Yeah, I'm sure I did. Why? What's wrong with it?

Probably Shouldn't Text Him
7:50 PM
Not a thing. Honestly. I checked it for plagiarism myself. I don't really have any input for you, other than that you should read this on Monday. Mrs. Liu will be floored.

Colin *likes* my paper. What do I say to that?

7:51 PM
I'll see how I feel about it. That's kinda nerve-racking. But also? Plagiarize? What do you think I am. 🙂

"Hey, Kole," Noah whispers.

"Huh?" I glance at him for a second.

"How does hyperspace work?"

"Umm . . . that's a lot for a Friday night. Ask Mr. Sprinkle." I look back at my phone. I don't really have time to explain right now. And, truth be told, I don't really get it. I just use fancy words on *Spacer* and only until recently did one person ever notice: this stupid *GoGnomes* who keeps posting. Jerk.

"Sprinkle?" Noah nudges my arm. "Earth to Kole."

I shake my head to clear it from Colin's text. Oh yeah, he's new to the school. "Sorry, um, he's the physics teacher. I don't really get

it all myself, but the comments section didn't care until recently."
I glance at my phone again.

Probably Shouldn't Text Him

7:53 PM

I was just teasing about the plagiarism. All I meant is that your story is well done.

Did you see the link Damian posted to the school site?

Crap. Noah swipes his hand over my phone and I look up.

"I'm sorry." I'm being rude to the most gorgeous arms I've seen since *ever*.

"Screw the comments section," Noah says, smiling. Did I mention his eyes? "It's worthless. Just keep the audience guessing—that's what I try to do during a match. And your story is stellar. I read a whole entry." He reaches for the popcorn bowl and nearly snags it.

"Hey! That is *not* yours," I say, punching his arm. There—I snuck in a touch. Like hitting a wall of bricks. Another bruise, but this one aches in little pink vibrations. He acts like he's hurt, but he sneaks the popcorn bowl from my lap and I leap forward, stopping myself. I really shouldn't be offended over some popcorn, but sharing has always been one of my least favorite things. I grab a handful when he settles the bowl on his leg.

He shrugs, reaches for my sparkling cider, and downs the rest. Okay, sharing isn't so bad. I'm never washing this glass even if it's the last one before the zombies finally come and eat us all.

"That's not yours either." My eyes widen and my mouth salivates, but this time it's not for the food. Noah-of-the-basketball-field is making me rethink a lot of things.

"I know." He smiles, munching away. "I'll keep the bowl between us."

I'm starting to get this whole flirting thing. When he turns back to the show, the smile drains from his face. He begins to crack his knuckles, one by one, until his fingers must be sore.

Hang on. He read *an entry*. That's like . . . nothing.

But . . . he looked?

Still. He wasn't into it. The story or my writing. Or he would have kept going. I chew one piece of popcorn slowly, methodically.

He's not into my blog, and I'm not into his sport.

I look at the screen for a minute—Pippa's about to see her father's murder—then I look back at Noah. My show will always be #1, make no mistake, but somehow this Noah has managed to draw my attention, even if we don't share *things*. He's staring at the screen, but he seems a million miles away.

It's the team. It's got to be.

Damian's to blame.

And Damian is going down.

It's Monday, and Michaela and I walk into Creative Writing like we're ready for it to be Friday again. Bags dragging almost as heavily as our feet, faces tired from lack of sleep. I was writing a post until 2:00 a.m. last night, and we sent our last texts at 2:03 a.m. when I needed a little help with a synonym for *scowl*. It's hard writing antiheroes all the time. Really makes you up your vocab.

Part of why I couldn't sleep was because of what Colin said on Friday. That I should read my story aloud. My head spun in little messy tornadoes all night, mixing my thoughts into a storm of nerves. *Damian and his little contest. The comments section. Best FanFic. Noah. The basketball team. Kasey's unanswered email. Colin liking my words. Flirting. The lit mag.* I'm a jumbled, anxious mess, but feck it all—I'm feeling deliriously ballsy. Something about Colin's encouragement makes me want to try actually reading my story, even if Damian will be here. Today, I try the podium.

I glance over at Damian's seat. It's empty—but there's no way he's missing class. That kid's never missed a day of school. He and Hailey must be competing for some nonexistent attendance award. I look at her, clutching her paper, by Liu's desk. Lame. I know Hailey prints her essays on lavender-scented paper. They reek when she passes them down the row. I always plug my nose. She's restacking and stapling her paper, holding a hand to her chest and chuckling.

Colin comes through the doorway, no Damian at his heels, looking like he spent some time studying Tom Holland's look this weekend. His sweater's a deep burgundy, his glasses perfectly propped on his nose, and his backpack slung over his shoulder. Effortlessly casual. So Colin. Even his shoes are shined and his navy pants pressed. He nods his head at me, all quick-like, and I bite the top of my purple gel pen.

Heat rises to my cheeks. I ran my eyeballs up Colin's entire, six-foot frame, and he saw. What if he knows I think he looks like a snack?

Mortifying.

I gotta get these feels under control. Barely two days ago, I was salivating over Noah too. When did I become such a boy-crazy mess?

I uncap my pen and open my notebook. I'll add that question to the list of things to figure out later, along with Kasey's email. I'm going to get back to her. Soon. I told Cricket I had until Friday. She's very good at holding me accountable.

I tug my wheat-colored sweater closer to the one-degree-lighter wheat-colored shirt underneath. My clothing is at a low-risk level today—had to dress accordingly. Neutral colors in case sweat decides it's going to seep through my bra, undershirt, regular shirt, and sweater. I smooth down the braid on my right shoulder, tugging at the end. About ten minutes until Mrs. Liu asks for volunteers.

Colin takes the seat in front of me, like always, and grabs his notebook from his bag. He doesn't look at me. I pick at a split end. What does one do now? Speak? Maybe.

"Colin." I poke him with my pen. Smooth. Subtle.

He turns around, big shoulders and all. His legs block the tiny walkway between desks. "Hi, Kole."

"Hi, Colin."

He waits. I wait a second longer. "You didn't say a thing on the story I wrote. Not even a comma splice to point out? I thought you wanted to help each other?" I cross my arms over my notebook. I didn't mean to be quite so sarcastic, but I've never known him to have nothing to say.

He shrugs one shoulder. "There was nothing to edit. I told you I liked it." He cocks an eyebrow at me. "You've got a knack for historical fiction."

And, little does he know, sci-fi. "Nothing to add? What about that whole making each other better thing?" I cock an eyebrow right back at him. This is how people talk when they're trying to be confident. I'll follow his lead.

"If there's something to make better, then I'll make it better."

I press my lips together, mushing around the pink-lemonade chapstick I applied a few minutes ago. "I'm going to read it out loud."

"Nice. Then you *are* taking my feedback. It's really, really good."

He grins. "And, about the comments you left me, they were *insightful*. Truly." He looks at my notebook. "Thanks for them."

"No problem. I'm happy to help." What a relief. I thought for sure the few questions I left him would leave him hitting *reject* within a second.

"I rewrote it last night."

"Seriously?" Holy crap. A total rewrite?

The bell rings. Class is about to start. He flips around and sits up straight to get Mrs. Liu's undying attention. She's still busy shooting the shit with Hailey. I poke Colin with my pen again. He turns around and I catch a whiff of the forest.

"Where's Damian? Shouldn't he have been carrying your bag?"

He glances to the sides of the room. "Damian and I aren't seeing eye to eye on something right now, so we're taking a break."

Interesting. Neither are Damian and I. "Oh yeah? What's the problem?"

"You know that link he posted on the school site?"

My stomach falls. All too well, Colin. All too well. "I saw it. Briefly. I had other things to do. Stupid, really. What's *The Space Game*?"

"Some show."

I gulp down a smile. I hope he hasn't seen my folder. Or my lunchbox. Or the pins on the inside of my backpack.

"I think it's a dick move to try to get the whole school to find whoever's writing it. Damian's trying to be a writer too. He should know how pressure like that stunts creativity. Seems like it's nobody's business but the writer's, you know?"

I blink. Slowly. This is most unexpected. "I do know. And I

thought the same thing. Maybe it's just an art thing. Like, leave the artist alone. Let them decide when they want to be unfrocked."

"Exactly." He leans closer, like he wants to dish something juicy. "And that's what I told him. But he didn't budge. Said this little stunt will get Daisy to finally notice him. He thinks that if everyone's looking at him and talking about him, that'll make him hot shit and she'll finally give him a chance. Damian's always about wild schemes and grand gestures."

"And so you're not friends anymore?"

"We haven't talked since it went live. I won't be a part of this game he's playing."

I blink away my astonishment. *Colin gets it.* All I muster out is, "Wow."

He looks confused. "That's it? Wow? It's a big deal to send the whole student body after one person. You agree, right?"

"Yes. A thousand times, yes. What I mean is, no girl would ever go to a dance with a guy because he has some cool gossip." *And wow, Colin, you have a heart.* "I'm surprised that he thinks ruining someone is going to get him a date." I swallow. *Shit.* Does Colin know it's me writing *Spacer*?

"Exactly."

"Did he tell you who's writing the blog?"

"No. I don't want to know. Let the mystery stay. It's better that way. Makes for a richer story. Like Salinger, or Dickinson, or something." The fluorescent light reflects off his glasses like he made a wish on a comet a long time ago and it just came back around again.

"Or something . . ." Exactly like that. Reclusive geniuses. I . . . kinda like that. I smile. "You do know that I used to think you were an ass, right?"

The light's in his eyes now, an easy grin on his mouth. "It's been less than two weeks since we decided to be friends. That could still be true."

"Editors, not friends," I correct. "But, I just wanted to let you know that you've been upgraded to a jerkface. That's better than an ass."

"I'll take better-than-an-ass." He clears his throat and picks at the wire on my notebook. "So, when you read your story, if it'll help, you can look at me. Since you know I already like it. Maybe it'll help break your nerves?"

"Please. I'll be lucky if I can stay lucid." And if I have the guts at all to try to scan the room. That sounds like something worthy of a medal of valor.

"You're going to do great, Kole." He whips around and goes back to facing the whiteboard.

"Quick announcement, Apples!" Mrs. Liu's voice rings through the room, and we all settle in. "Don't forget that tickets for the Harvest Ball will go up on Friday. Get the early-bird prices before they're hiked up!"

My phone, not-so-cleverly hidden in the corner of my desk, lights up. It's Michaela.

Michaez

10:32 AM

You should ask Colin to go to the Ball with you

Spending time with Colin doesn't sound nearly as repulsive as it did a few weeks ago, but still. I flip the phone over. When I gave him the once-over this morning, his too-big shoulders didn't seem too big anymore. There's something to a perfect height-difference ratio in two characters. And his glasses do match mine. And his hair, so dark and . . . and . . . his babies are going to be beautiful.

I grimace. *Too far, Kole.*

But. Noah. Noah-of-the-basketball-field. Noah-of-the-shared-popcorn-bowl. And he didn't say a word when I fell asleep during episode two, even if it wasn't even 11:00 yet. I'm sure he said nothing if I was drooling, or if I began to snore.

My phone lights up. Again.

Michaez

10:32 AM

I'm telling you: matching LL Bean plaids. A golden retriever. You on your second series with Tor. Him writing his dissertation on douchebaggery. Think about it.

10:32 AM

I'm thinking how much I'm over this conversation

Liu's voice breaks through my thoughts and I pocket my phone. "On the docket today: historical fiction read-alouds. And then we'll begin to look at writing our final stories for the quarter." Mrs. Liu saunters up to the podium, glancing at our desks, looking for drafts. I've got mine, facedown. But today she's not going to call on me. I'm volunteering. "Anyone want to read theirs before I collect them?"

Hailey's hand flashes up in the corner of my vision. And then, through the door, comes the demon himself, Damian. Same dark shades. Same belt buckle. Same walk.

My spirit falls. I thought I'd get a day without Damian. I was wrong.

Colin groans and leans back into my space.

Same, Colin. Same.

Damian hands his late pass to Mrs. Liu and takes his seat over by Hailey. He puts his legs up on the chair in front of him, stretching out like a gazelle trying to impress the herd. Stupid, showy, shithead. He looks at Colin. Colin folds his arms across his chest and looks him straight in the eye. For an instant, they glare at one another. And the whole time, Hailey's hand sits in the air, hoping to catch Liu's eye.

Mrs. Liu asks again, missing Hailey, "Any volunteers?"

Hailey raises her hand higher. Damian raises his. Colin puts up one arm, lower than the others. And me—I raise my paper before the butterflies get to my throat.

Liu's eyes go big. "Kole! Come on up. What a great day this is! It felt particularly good this morning."

Oh geez. What have I done?

"What?" I hear Hailey whisper. "Her?"

Damian snickers. "I guess Kole's ready to shake things up. Wonder if she can write historical fiction?"

A couple guffaws follow his words.

I stand. *Deep breath.*

Mrs. Liu steps out from the podium and motions for me to come and claim it. She tiptoes back to her seat and I take six knee-shaking, ankle-twisting steps to the front of the room. When I turn around, all eyes are planted on me. I tug my braid a little, just for luck, and make sure it's in the right place.

Damian is the first one to catch my eye. He's taken his sunglasses off. *Why in this fresh hell did I look at him?* He begins to tap his pencil on the side of his desk. Each hit takes one minute, or so it seems. Hailey's jaw hangs open, her pink sweater a sickening shade of annoying. Michaela's smiling, flipping her hand for me to begin. I look at Colin. He looks back at me, expectant. I glance down at my story. It's something I wrote over the last few days, a little historical piece about the onset of the War in Afghanistan. Nothing special, but I like how it turned out. Different than *Spacer*. But as I look at my draft, the words mash together like overcooked macaroni. I can feel the heat in my cheeks, the water as it builds under my eyes.

I have to read. Can't back down now.

I begin, no intro, because it doesn't occur to me until halfway through the first sentence. My voice is tiny, and even I notice I'm reading too quickly. *"The day the soldiers came for my father I wore a pink tutu. It was my ballet recital, and his audition for the killing fields . . ."*

I glance up as I read, twice, when I remember that's something you do when reading for an audience. I would have looked to Michaela, but that would have made me snicker.

I look at the one who told me I could do this in the first place: Colin. He never looks away, even when the butterflies almost make me lose my place. When my cheeks are pinker than Hailey's sweater. When the applause makes me want to ugly-cry and thank them for letting me indulge myself in a story that pales when compared to the epic I've got online.

I remain in my seat the rest of class, avoiding anyone's gaze. Despite Damian's rather loud sigh, they liked my story.

When the bell rings, Colin rips out a sheet of paper from his notebook, folds it over, and hands it to me before he starts to methodically put his notebook in his backpack. The note's in messy, boy handwriting, and I turn my back to read it.

Your words are even more beautiful when I hear them in your voice.

The butterflies rustle up in my stomach again. It's almost too much—too sweet—but I don't feel my upchuck reflex kicking in. I shut my eyes . . . those words are lovely. And the butterflies—I need a can of Raid for them.

Michaela makes it to my desk before I can respond to him. "You read it! You really, really did!"

"I did!" I say, in a horrifyingly shrill voice. Michaela reaches for me and gives me a big hug.

"Mrs. Liu loved it. Hailey hated it. Damian hated it. Colin loved it." She whispers that last part because he's still packing up, but he's got his back to us. He hustles to put his things away. It feels . . . intentional.

Is he embarrassed?

"And no one had a thing to say after! Maybe the comments section in real life can be turned off. Who'd have thought?" I say through a smile. She puts a finger to her lips, reminding me to stay quiet. But this giddiness doesn't seem to be going away. Maybe the podium, and reading aloud, and Colin, aren't so bad.

Michaela giggles. "Come on. I'm buying the fries today."

We turn to leave, but Damian and Hailey are waiting, blocking us between the desks and the door. He licks his lips before he speaks. "Quite the story, Nikole."

Does everyone in this school know how much I hate that name? I glare, the grin ripped from my face by his presence in my air. "Get lost."

Colin turns toward us, watching. His face is stone.

"Me and Hailey want to talk to you."

"*Hailey and I*," Colin corrects him in that beautifully glib voice of his. Oh, how I now appreciate it. He thumps his backpack on his desk, noisier than usual.

"I have nothing to say to you, Damian." I bite my lip, hoping to appear tough.

"I didn't get to read my story today. That's never happened. When I want to read, I read. Always." Hailey narrows her eyes. Her hair is perfectly coiffed, per usual.

"Shame," I say, cocking my head. "Maybe Liu's grown tired of purple prose and run-on sentences."

Michaela snickers. "Or someone who thinks a word max is merely a suggestion. Four pages never means eight, Miss Verbose."

Hailey doesn't wait for the burn to set. "Or maybe she wants to give the less-desirables a chance for a change? But what do I care? Only makes our stuff sound better."

Damian puts a hand out to silence her. "Cool it, Hay. We just want to have a little chat with you, Kole. Meet us in the Journalism room tomorrow after school. Come alone."

"She's not going without me," Michaela says.

I put a hand out to silence her this time. If I meet him, I won't be able to see Noah in the hall before he walks with Will to basketball practice after school. The nod we exchange is what I most look forward to in my day, second only to fries. And now Damian wants to take that from me too?

I *have* to destroy him, not spend more time with him. "Not happening. I have somewhere I need to be."

"It'll happen, Kole, unless the words *control-A-delete* mean nothing to you." Damian waves his hand in front of him like he's wiping a slate clean. "Can you imagine what I can do with that simple little command? All that I can destroy? Like shooting an asteroid through a starship."

The muscles in my face go rigid. *Spacer.*

He puts out his pointer finger and his thumb. *"Pew pew."*

"You can't . . ." How the hell does he have that power? He can't log in to my blog. This numbnuts, no-good mouth-breather doesn't have my password. Unless . . . unless he's up to more than simply his little call to action. My skin prickles. "Fine. After school, tomorrow." I whip around and breeze past Colin, his face is locked on his Apple watch. I head out the door before Damian can say anything.

Michaela trails after me, her flats tapping the tile as fast as my heart. I didn't even notice if Colin overheard and put it together that I'm writing *Spacer*.

SPACER 3.10

Posted by: ToTheStars

Sept. 30, 2019. 11:09

Pippa glances out the window of her bunk, her eyes fuzzy from lack of sleep. She rubs them, stretches out her arms, and yawns. Somehow the late nights don't seem to hurt too much when they're spent at the front of the starship with a gruff quartermaster like Byron.

She may not have learned anything about her mother yet, but she's figured out that he isn't so tough. He just likes to think he is. He's always somewhere between a scowl and a head shake, but when he's under the spell of his old Shakespeare book, he's someone new. Someone kind. Patient. Pleasant. And, the two times he's smiled, he's become someone she wants to sit next to for a few minutes longer. And maybe that's ok?

Gods. This wasn't what she expected when she stepped onto this bucket of bolts. She hoped to find her family, but here she is, surrounded by people she'd like to get to know more. Maybe one a little more than the others.

What a trip this is proving to be.

And then there's Cedric. He's a possibility too.

There. I did it. I included Cedric as a crappy afterthought. Take that, crappy comments. My old computer is burning a hole in my thighs, but my blog is safe. 1.93 million people have been reading *Spacer*. Five hundred eighty-nine new comments alone were posted in the last twenty-four hours. This is positively, absolutely, unreal. I can't even read them all if I try.

Any confidence I gained from this afternoon feels like a distant memory. Never would have thought that baring my soul—even with Damian and Hailey's mocking—would turn out to be easier than enduring comments online.

Knock knock. "Kole?"

Cricket raises her head, ears cocked. I rip out my earbuds. She's the best alarm for when the parentals are close by. Mom's getting loud with the knocking—must figure I'm on the roof again. She catches me out here writing and she'll take my laptop for a week. Maybe even my phone this time too. I scuttle through the window, careful to make sure my laptop doesn't get knocked over, and adjust my clothes. Once again, my shorts have gotten comfortable just underneath the little french-fry roll I've been nurturing. I toss the laptop on the bed, the remaining jelly beans on my quilt bouncing.

"What's up?" I ask, reaching for the door to let her in. *Act cool, Kole.*

She hands me a paper slip once the door opens. "Noah's dad called. His name is John."

My stomach falls. "Okay?" I reach for the slip. Why in the world?

"He wants to know if you can watch the girls while he watches Noah's tryouts on Tuesday evening."

Tryouts? "Okay!"

She twitches her head at me. Maybe I was too chipper. But this means he might make the team after all . . . someone must have talked to McDuffy. Will maybe? This is interstellar. It's heart-pounding. It's intergalactically good. But watching his sisters . . . that'll cut into my writing time.

"Will said you offered?"

Oh, that's right. "I did. It was a bit ago. Guess I forgot?"

"Honey, that's so kind of you. It'll be nice to see you getting out of your room and away from the laptop a bit." She puts a hand on my shoulder. I know what that really means. *It'll be nice to see you doing something other than writing.* The words she doesn't say echo through my mind; a movie of all the times she has said them before. "You're just getting so grown up. It's the perfect way for you to get out there. Make some money. And Noah is, as I'm sure you've noticed, just adorable."

"I suppose," I mumble. She's one hundred percent correct. She leans in and I know *it* is coming. The hug. My arms robotically move into position and wrap awkwardly around her. It's not that I don't want to hug her. It's not that I don't love her. I have other ways of saying that—like hoping someday she'll give me the same look she gives Will when he walks on the court at his basketball games. She looks at him like her dreams are wrapped up in his, as much a part of him as they are of her. And it's . . . enviable.

"And Noah seems like a nice boy . . ." It's in the lilt of her voice. The way she angles her eyes. I know what she means now too. She means that he's cute and she wants me to think so too. Another step toward normal, away from the internet. Little does she know this is a battle I've already lost.

"Yeah. He's nice enough," I say. *Awkward.* "Can we not talk about this?"

"And he's cute too . . ."

"Noah is cool. But he's Will's new bestie." Not that that's curbed any attraction I have to him.

"Which is exactly why you should date him. Your brother has immaculate taste."

Yes, Mom, keep comparing us. That'll convince me. I groan and roll my eyes.

"Just consider it. I'm leaving in an hour to get Dad at the airport. Want to come?"

Perfect. More writing time. "No, I'll see him in the morning."

"All right." She turns and heads down the stairs, her voice dejected. "Call John back tonight, okay?"

"Yep!" I close the door and lean against the back of it. I push my glasses just a bit farther up my nose. Now I have to come out of my cave. I have to talk to new people. And I have to watch two red-headed monster children in Noah-of-the-basketball-field's house. What did I volunteer myself for? I push away from the door, but my braid gets caught on the hook and my head jerks backward. *Ouch.*

I'm gonna need a miracle.

CHAPTER NINE

'm pretty sure there's no worse class than American History. So many dates. So many names of people and countries and landmarks. Makes my head hurt. How can someone keep all these battles straight? There's just too many for the lumpy jello that is my brain.

But I guess if I can keep every asteroid in *Spacer*'s universe straight, then I can give American History a try, boring as it is.

I move my pen to the top corner of my notebook, a blue one this time, and begin to write *BYRON* in fancy, swirly letters. I drag them down the side of my notebook and add a few little leaves to the bottom of the *Y* and the top of the *B*. A work of art, that's what this is. Maybe they'll make these notes more fun to study.

I glance around me. If the other kids at this table weren't so dang close to me, I might do the same with Noah's name. Or maybe . . . nah. Too weird. Too . . . unlikely.

A pen tip swipes across my line of vision. Brian James is holding it, one of the other kids in this god-awful class. I share a table with him and a few others.

"Seriously? Team Byron?" he whispers. "That's so toxic."

I squint my eyes at him. "Like there's an option worthy of Pippa?"

"Cedric is far superior. At least he's smiled once since the show started. Byron doesn't even know how." He draws a line across the side of my page, right through Byron's name. I glare at him, my mouth hanging open, blood boiling. Brian clearly knows nothing about characterization. If I had the words for a curse, I'd make him promise his first child to me and I'd make it into one of those beauty pageant kids. Best revenge ever.

"Byron's seriousness is his *thing*," I whisper. "That's what makes him so good for Pippa. Pippa is a firecracker and Byron keeps her grounded."

"You're so wrong," he says. "Toxic masculinity at its finest."

"Are we even talking about the same show?" I raise my voice on that last bit, and it doesn't go unnoticed.

"Kole? Brian? Something you'd like to share with the class?" Mr. Reynaldo interjects. Crap. I'm lucky if he doesn't give me a detention for this afternoon, right when I'm supposed to be meeting Damian. "I bet you've picked up on some irresistible details about the Siege of Boston?"

"Sorry." I slink down in my chair and fold my arms across my chest. Stupid Brian doesn't say a word. Gotta be friends with Damian.

Brian drawing a line down my notebook doesn't do anything but make me want to write a better scene tonight. I'll be sure to name some red shirt *Brian* before I have him thrown out the airlock.

I tug at the bottom of my braid.

Allison, across the table, catches my eye. She holds up her notebook when Reynaldo turns his back and continues droning on about this siege-of-massive-importance. *Boring.* She flips the notebook around. *Team Byron*, it reads.

I put my hands out like *yes* and we both look at Brian. He shakes his head.

"More than half the student body disagrees," he whispers.

More than half? "That's like six hundred kids!" Okay, an exaggeration. But it's a lot, and they're all watching my show. And now I know some are reading *Spacer*.

Brian scribbles something on his notebook and flips it over quickly. It says, *Debate at lunch. Will finish after school. West side of the cafeteria. Be there to watch your ship sink.* He motions like a bomb is going off.

I shake my head. Stupid *Pipdrics*. They never know when they've lost. "Waste of time," I mumble.

"Do you even read *Spacer*?" Allison asks Brian. "The poll in the bathroom by the gym has Byron winning by a landslide. He's endgame. Duh."

"The poll in the bathroom?" WTF?

Allison looks at me like I've got three eyes. "*Spacer* Port. Where have you been?"

"Remind me to white it out," Brian whispers.

"Don't you dare!" I add too loudly. I've got to see this.

Reynaldo shoots us the evil eye. *Busted.* "Kole! Pick a new seat, take your stuff."

"Mr. Reynaldo—" I start.

"And you'll be in Ms. Singh's room for lunch detention."

My cheeks flush red as I grab my things. I can't even look Reynaldo in the eye as I stomp to the edge of the classroom, to a table with only one other kid.

I lay my head down, pushing my glasses into my face at an awkward angle. A poll in the bathroom? A debate? Is this a presidential election? My head gets heavier. I have to see this, but now I can't go at lunch. Feck this.

At least no one knows it's me—unless that's what Hailey and Damian want to discuss? A stomach cramp begins to clench my insides.

When I look up, a girl I don't recognize smiles at me, but it's not exactly nice. She moves aside her sweater, and there on her red T-shirt, in big black letters, is *The Space Game*'s logo. Underneath is some crappy fan art I've seen floating around Twitter. It's Pippa and Cedric from that one time they almost kissed when the *Snapdragon* lost all power and they thought they'd freeze to death. Season two, episode four.

I put my head back down.

Feck this shit.

The Journalism classroom appears empty when I walk through its door. It's dark. Again. You'd think Brittain would want some kind of a light, but this kind of reporting must be the kind that happens best in the dark.

"Damian?" I say, taking a few steps into the room. All that meets me are the humming of the computers and the distant sound of the cheerleading squad outside the windows that line the back of the room. I say this part a little louder, "Douche-nozzle?"

Lamplight flicks on in one corner, at the edge of Brittain's desk. Damian's hand is poised on the switch, and he's seated on a big rolly chair, with Hailey standing over his left shoulder. Her arms are crossed tight across her chest, her hair in perfect position. Big wow for the dramatic effect.

"You're such a creep. Do you even know that?" I can't hide the disdain, but I've got to see what the derp squad wants.

"Hello, Kole." He kicks a chair in my direction, and it rolls to my feet. "Have a seat."

I sit, slowly and razor straight. "What's this about? Did someone figure your little game out?"

He snickers. "Nah. Not yet. I think a severe lack of friends is what's made you so able to hide."

"Poor little Kole never recovered from when we ditched her. A tragic tale," Hailey says, a lilt in her voice.

I shake my head, grabbing the sleeves of my sweater and pulling them over my hands. "Not how I remember it—"

Hailey speaks over me. "At last count, seems like it's just you and Michaela. Guess you couldn't find more dweebs who like your show. And before you say it, your brother doesn't count. What do you think, Damian?"

"Sounds about right."

My chest tightens. I talk to people at school. There was a time when Damian would have been an acquaintance; we've been in the same classes since middle school when that thin, creepy mustache had just begun to form on his upper lip.

Hailey continues. "No one in this school would ever think of you as talented. A winner of a massive contest? The mousy little thing in Creative Writing? The one who's too busy staring at the Curve-Breaker like he's a piece of bacon and she skipped breakfast?"

My throat tightens, clever comebacks crawling up and evaporating before finding their way to my voice.

Damian throws his hands out in front of him. "Can we not bring Colin into this? He's pissed."

"Did you tell him?" Hailey asks, recrossing her arms.

Damian shakes his head. "He blocked my number. But he'll get over it."

I don't respond. I can't. Her words burn. *No one* would think of me writing *Spacer*. Not a soul. I'm too tiny, too much a part of the wall and not enough of the podium. Too much a backdrop in someone else's life.

And the part about Colin—I've done nothing but hate him until very recently. I try to say something—to tell them they're wrong—but my voice is still caught in the back of my throat.

Hailey rolls her eyes.

"You surprised us all yesterday, Kole. Reading aloud takes major balls." Damian sneers, tapping his hand on his thigh.

I suck in my bottom lip and swallow. *Come on, voice. We got this.* "I don't have time for this. I have a wildly successful blog to get to. So what do you want?" It's a feeble attempt at acting like they aren't getting to me.

Damian begins to fumble with something. A light comes on from a cell phone and illuminates his face. He looks like some form of Frankenstein's creature, slightly shadowed, his body hidden in the darkness.

"Yeah, about that blog. Keep at it, for now, but stop sidelining Cedric," Damian says.

For now? My pulse beats in my temples. "What are you saying?"

He scrolls through. "This comments section . . . are you sure you can really call any of these people fans?"

I swallow. He's browsing my page, reading the comments, and shaking his head. A sick grin is slathered across his face. "Please get to your lame point."

"'This is the shittiest version of *The Space Game* I've ever read.

Are you seriously suggesting that Byron's shuttle ship would be able to withstand getting that close to a sun? Even with a shield? Have you no respect for the laws of physics?'"

I swallow. Another critic.

"And terraforming is an intense process. Even when imagined. You can't just drop that phrase like it's an answer to all things world-building. Like, crack open a genre book, Kole. See if you can learn something from hard science fiction. This shit is just space angst, that's all."

I bite my bottom lip, eyes on the Grumpy Cat poster on the wall.

"Any of those comments particularly nasty today?" Hailey asks.

No. No. No. I don't want to hear them. They rattle through me till my fingers twitch.

He scrolls and scrolls and scrolls. "Here's a good one. 'This blog has gotten worse with every flick of Pippa's beautiful dark mane. Maybe it's time to wrap this crap story up?' And I like this one, 'All *Spacer* does is bait us. I'm done.'"

"There's good ones in there," I say. "I've seen them." I swallow, hoping to gather some courage. They may hate it, but these A-holes sure seem to know my site well. "Why are you even here, Hailey? Are you still stuck in middle school?"

She shakes her head. "Like I care about your lame musings. The show was over almost immediately after it began. But you two dorks couldn't see it."

"Please. We walked away from you. You couldn't see the poten-tial in what we were doing. And the only reason I think you're here is because you're jealous that people like what I write."

Hailey purses her lips together. White lines the edge of her lips. "Not Liu."

"Oh, she does." Or at least she did today.

Damian sits up straighter. "Do yourself a favor, Kole. You want your crappy story to continue, study Asimov. Read Dick. Watch *Lost in Space*. *Battlestar Galactica*. *The Martian*. Heck, you could get something from *Galaxy Quest*. I think it's still on Netflix. Learn a thing or two before writing about something you so clearly know nothing about."

Words spill out of my mouth, and my voice shakes. "Here's the problem with what you are, Damian. Fanboys think they know the exact way to tell a story, except they're not the one telling it. They're doing nothing but sitting before their screens leaving nasty comments about pseudoscience and techno-garble. But they keep watching and reading and replying. They contribute nothing to the discourse but emptiness."

Damian leans forward, the flashlight shaking as he squirms.

"What the heck, Damian. Read dick?" Hailey giggles. "How do you even do that?"

"As in Philip K. You're so out of your element."

Feck. He doesn't even care about what I said. I sit up, arms and legs crossed, jutting my chin out. "I'm familiar with the canon. I know sci-fi. But they've got *one* way of doing things that doesn't establish every rule for every universe. And it's not my story, dip-shit. It's fan fiction. You're aware of that, right? I'm doing exactly what I should—building on *The Space Game*'s world because I can. Because I'm a fan."

Damian continues, barely looking at me. "Here's a good one: 'she doesn't even get *The Space Game*.' You sure you're actually a fan?"

I blink more than necessary.

They can't be right.

They can't.

"You see, Kole, Damian's agreed to keep your secret." Hailey pauses. "And I will too. If you do a few little things for us."

Good. He's keeping mum. It's hard enough having the whole internet reading my site. If the whole school catches wind it's me, I won't be able to hide from my critics. I'll literally be walking among them.

But what the feck does *a few little things* mean? My bottom lip quivers. "What is it you want?" I look at him and then Hailey. Back again.

"Number one: don't read your stories aloud anymore. Hailey, elaborate." Damian snaps his finger.

Hailey comes around to one of the computer tables and rests a hip on it. "Once was enough. Let's pretend yesterday didn't happen, that your little story was just a fluke. You're back to mousy, silent Kole from here on out. And you're going to write something for me. Something good enough to get me into the lit mag."

For real? They're blackmailing me? I laugh, unable to stop it before it escapes my mouth. "That's the dumbest thing I've ever heard."

"Damian." Hailey snaps her fingers.

"Think it would take much to hack your little blog?" He scrolls through the phone. "I've got friends in the coding club. We can break in."

My laughter disappears. "Wait, what? You're not—"

"Wouldn't be too hard. Let's hope it doesn't come to that."

Hailey puts a hand on his phone. "We can completely change your story, mock the show, destroy everything you've worked for. We can piss off your fans; no one will believe it if you tell them it's not you. The internet is brutal. Or maybe we should save ourselves the trouble and just delete the whole thing." Hailey flits her fingers in the air dismissively.

I'll back it up. Move the blog somewhere else.

But I'll lose my domain. My followers. The story I've poured my lifeblood into.

And . . . will Kasey still want the writer of *Spacer* at the con if she doesn't like the story? If they mock the show or the fans or the special effects or whatever else and she thinks it's me?

I'll be *cancelled*. *Spacer* will be cancelled.

"Then what's the deal?" I ask Hailey.

"Agree to our terms. Number three is up to Damian, his own cross to bear." She puts a hand over her chest.

Vomit.

Damian gets up, the rolly chair making an obnoxiously loud groan as it rises from under him, and comes to me. "Kole, this is hard for me. I know what we're doing here is . . . wrong . . . but we're just making sure this happens the right way for all of us. You keep *Spacer* and your quiet corner of class where you can hide behind Colin. Hailey gets into the lit mag, which gets her into the Ivy of her choice, and now, here's what I want." He rubs his hands together in front of me.

"Say it." My face is a stone, my voice frozen.

"I'd like to ask you to the Harvest Ball."

I swallow a laugh. "What the hell, Damian? You're kidding, right?"

He sneers. "No, I'm not kidding. What, you going with Colin or something?"

"Not hardly." The thought of going to the ball hasn't even

crossed my radar. It's in less than two weeks, but who has time to consider that?

"Then what's the problem?"

"You're the problem, Damian. I don't want to go to a dance. Not with you, not with a dead raccoon. No one."

"Fine. Then I'll talk to the coding club. Maybe spill the beans on who you are."

Blood runs through my veins again, hot and heavy.

It's just a stupid dance. One night.

Spacer is worth it.

"No. Don't." I stand up. "I'll stay quiet in Creative Writing. I'll write a poem. I'll go with you to the stupid Harvest Ball, though I have no idea why in the seven circles of hell you'd want to go with me."

"It's not like that. God. Disgusting." Damian rolls his eyes and shakes his head. "*You're* going with *me* so I can get Daisy's attention. She'll be there with your brother. I'm going to dance like I'm in a K-pop band, and I need a partner. That'll get my little flower glancing at me."

The. Fuck. Will didn't tell me that she asked him? And Damian wants me to help him make another girl notice him? All this . . . and he expects me to dance? "You're trying to impress Daisy Bringas? Did you take *Gatsby* just a little too far, Damian?"

Hailey erupts in laughter.

"Laugh it up." Damian eyes her. "Yeah. It's a little Gatsby, a little green-light-ish. But it doesn't matter. I'm in love with Daisy, but your brother asked her before I got a chance to. So, I need someone to help her notice me instead of Will."

Spacer. All the late nights writing. The blood, sweat, and tears I've poured into my story. The readers who have enjoyed it. My brother. Michaela. Other faceless fans who've followed me since before *Best FanFic*. Since before my blog blew up in the fandom's face.

Most of all, it's the only thing I've felt truly good at. Like something I could use to level up and become a real writer. Make Mom proud. But if I don't agree to these things, it's over.

"There's one more thing, *ToTheStars*." Damian's face warps into a Joker smile. "I need you to take my ship seriously. Which means you're taking the story in a new direction. What you tried last entry was . . . lame. Endgame is now Cedric. Make it real. Make it good."

I shut my eyes, but I doubt they can tell in the darkness. *If it gets my blog back. If it gets my blog back. If it gets my blog back.* "If I do this, when does it end?"

"After I get the prize money that I've no doubt will be mine," Hailey chimes in.

"I'll consider lightening up after Daisy agrees to go on a date with me." Damian puts his hand out for me to shake. "We have a deal?"

They're taking everything.

But it won't last forever.

I'll talk to Michaela. To Will. Find a way to stop them. I accept his hand, give it a weak shake, and wipe my own on my jeans. I'll be scrubbing it raw later. "We have a deal."

"Then it's done. No more reading aloud and wooing Liu's socks off. A piece for Hailey. A date for me. And *Spacer* takes my creative direction."

"And Kole? *Spacer* is still your secret, it's just ours too now. One step out of line and Damian blasts you," Hailey adds.

I don't say a word. I turn and walk out of the classroom, one last glance at Damian's picture on the wall. If I had a dart, I'd hit him smack in the nose. By the time I get to the door, tears are flowing.

I run through the hall, past the lockers and trash cans, past kids from student council hanging yet another Harvest Ball banner, past the empty cafeteria and the all-too-quiet main office. I bound down the stairs after throwing open the double doors, Scarlett O'Hara-style, and then nearly fall over someone sitting on the steps. I don't turn to apologize; I don't stop to readjust my braid and fix my glasses. To wipe the sweat that's lining my brow or dry my tears on my gray sweater. I just need to get home, to hide under my covers and cry into Cricket's chub pocket.

Next hurdle: unlock my bike without falling apart on the pavement.

"Kole!"

I come to a stop on the grass, almost having made it to the bike rack. My insides twist themselves further. It's not Michaela. I'm supposed to fill her in on my little meeting as soon as she's done with her shift at Renny's.

I know the voice. I know the shoulders. Too well. But I don't want him to see me crying, so I keep my back to him and wipe the tears and snot all over my sleeve. It's okay; it can be washed.

"Not now, Colin," I garble out, sniffling like a toddler.

"I overheard the meeting in Creative Writing—I thought I'd hang around, see what Damian wanted."

"Just go away." I shut my eyes. Of course he did.

"Come on. It seems like he's being an ass to everyone lately. What did he say to you?"

I keep my back to him and run a finger across my forehead to get the hair off my brow, then I swipe under my eyes. My mascara is a mess. I drag my sleeve along my nose one last time and take a deep breath. I can't keep my back to him forever, but there's no way I can tell him what just happened.

I *could* try trusting him. I turn around, hands wadded up in the sleeves of my sweater, and look him dead in the eye. He looks over my face.

"What the hell happened in there?" he asks. "Do you need me to get someone? The counselor or the vice principal or something?"

The counselor? I could try that . . . I could seek help. But how much help was Mrs. Brittain? I can solve this on my own. "No, I don't need anyone to interfere. I just need to go home. It'll be fine in the morning. Cooler heads and all." Lies on my tongue that taste like salt water.

It won't be fine until after the Harvest Ball.

"Come on, Kole. Something's wrong."

My eyes begin to well again. "It's fine. It's all fine."

He steps closer and reaches for my elbow, stopping just before he touches me. "Is this okay?"

I look at his fingers and nod. He pulls me to the tree where the few kids still hanging about can't hear us. We both stand under the centuries-old maple tree that frames the front of Crystal Lake Prep. It hangs above like a storm cloud, its puffs yellow and orange, red and brown.

"Then why are you upset?" He takes in my face like he knows something.

I don't say a thing, just stand here sniveling. Why, oh why, was I dumb enough to log in on campus? "I really, really don't want to talk about it."

He looks at his feet and nods. "Did you know there was nearly a food fight at lunch today over that thing Damian posted?"

My eyes widen. An attempt at changing the subject. I guess Colin hasn't figured out that it's the same topic, even with that big brain of his. "On the west side?"

"Yeah. How'd you know?" he asks, concerned. "I didn't see you there."

"I was in detention."

"Really? Kole Miller in detention?" He smiles in disbelief, his eyes getting a devilish twinkle.

Crap. I'd almost forgotten to stress over how in the heck I'm going to explain that to my parents. "Yes. Thanks a lot, Mr. Reynaldo. I'm mortified."

He snickers. "That's rough. The debate kept going after school, on the south lawn. Something about a boat—I dunno. It sunk or something? Officer Beans had to break it up and make everyone go home. It was quite the show. Two guys just started throwing fries at each other, and soon they were throwing punches."

Okay, that makes me smile. "It's not a boat. It's about shipping." Imagine that. A fight over *Spacer*. "I would have liked to have seen that," I say. I wonder which ship won? I wonder who sits on my side, the RMS *Pipron*? Would have been nice to know who else sees reason in this school, since it feels like I'm one of the only ones. Or who would waste fries like that.

"Okay, but who cares about shipping? We don't even have a port here." He wrinkles his brow, confused as ever.

I start to smile. This boy doesn't know what shipping is. "Oh my god."

"What?"

"Mr. I-Own-The-Podium, you're so clueless." And it's kinda . . . adorable. "It's not that kind of shipping. It's about characters. Like, they want them together, as in, in a relationship. And there's two different ships in *The Space Game*. That's what they're fighting over."

"That's the stupidest thing I've ever heard of."

"Okay, but it's not." It's actually quite important. "People get invested in this stuff. It's more exciting than learning about wars that happened ages ago, or how to figure out the circumference of a pineapple. And maybe even on some days, it's more entertaining than debating the Oxford comma."

"Nothing's more entertaining than grammar. Or more important than school." He cringes. "But I guess that could be fun in some strange parallel universe."

"You're impossible, Colin Clarke. There's more to life than the Ivys, you know." I turn to walk to the bike rack, and he follows me like a little doggy.

"Tell my parents that." I hear the resentment in his voice as he sticks his hands in his pockets. Maybe I'm not the only one whose parents give them a feck of a time.

"Why didn't you get sent home?"

He shrugs, lowering his brow and shaking his head. "No way was I part of it. A suspension on my record would ruin a chance at Yale."

"Of course." Insert eye roll. Colin Clarke will always be Colin Clarke, even if he's not triggering my upchuck reflex any more.

"And, I wasn't a part of that. I was waiting. Wondering how things went with Damian."

"Back to that." Oh great. I start to unlock my bike. How in the heck am I going to avoid it this time?

"Back to that," he repeats as my lock clicks open. I can feel his eyes, a not-so-bad shade of green behind his glasses.

Stall. That's what I'll do. Ask him about Creative Writing tomorrow. Get the fox off the scent. "Did you get your script done for tomorrow?"

"Yeah. I shared with you at lunch. Can you look at it tonight? I could use some help with the format."

He's such a nerd. Who would have thought. "I'll get to it, promise." As I swing a leg over my bike, Colin steps back a foot or so. "See you later," I add. If my bike were a motorcycle, I would rev the engine.

"Hang on." He puts a hand on the handlebar of my bike. It's a little close to my finger. Like, maybe too close. Uncomfortably close. Almost touching. I need to stop staring at it. Danger, Kole Miller.

I look at his face, lips firm. *Please don't ask me about Damian. Not again.* I'll have to get uncharacteristically bitchy.

"You don't have to tell me about Damian." He shrugs. "I know when to back off. But I want to ask you about something else."

"The script?"

"No, Kole, not the script. You going to the—"

The Space Game's theme sounds loudly around us, a busy mix of what should sound like flying among the stars and angst. It's my phone, and though the theme is perfection, I could die of embarrassment. My cheeks burn as I whip around my backpack. I grab my phone and mute the theme. "Sorry. Will's calling. What were you going to say?"

He takes a little step back, and his eyes narrow. "They were playing that song at the tables earlier."

I try to sound like he must be mistaken. "Seriously? So weird, those kids." Wow. They were really going for it. I've got to check my Snapchat. Someone must have made it into a story. "What even is that show?"

"Don't lie, Kole. You know all about it. I can tell because you get this little dimple whenever I talk about it. And your eyes get brighter, almost like you're about to smile." This time he grins. I sneak a peek at his teeth. They sparkle like starlight as it slips across the front of the *Snapdragon*.

Wait. He just called me out . . . and I don't mind, even if I am blushing. Again. "I totally know all about it. Listen, I've got to go. I'll get back to you about your script tonight." I slip my phone into my back pocket and push my bike off into the grass. I've pedaled to the corner before I remember that I probably should have let him ask me what he wanted to.

CHAPTER TEN

Thirty minutes later and I come huffing through the front door. Will never picked up when I called him back—I get the sense from his texts that it was kinda urgent. Would have been nice if he'd said what it was about in the first place.

"Kole! About time you're home! I thought you'd completely forgotten about your babysitting job." Mom bounds down the hall, her slippers pounding on the wood. "Will's been trying to get a hold of you for the last half hour."

I groan. Shit. I'm watching Noah's sisters tonight. Which means not only did my tear-stained, blotchy face get seen by Colin, but now I have to face Noah the God, King of the Cafeteria, on his own turf. At this point my stomach's forgotten how to twist itself up; it only knows how to groan and squeal in obnoxiously loud ways.

Mom looks over my face. "Do you want me to call and cancel? Tell them you're not feeling well?"

"No. I've got it. It's fine."

"Really? You look so tired. Have you been up late writing again? You really need to give it a rest during the school year."

"No, Mom—"

"Or is it American History? I can see the stress in your face. Is another test coming? Or is it about the detention you got? I know how it makes you break out on your chin." She reaches for it, and I slap her hand away.

My stomach falls. Yeah, the whole send-an-email-home-when-you-get-a-detention. Yay. "Yes, I'm so very aware." But, oh, how I love reminders.

"Principal Whitehead and I had a talk today. He assured me that the detention does not go on your record. Detentions are a ridiculous punishment, but I know the behavior he explained is over, as I assured him. You understand that, right? The effect multiple detentions can have on your academic reputation?" She keeps looking over my face.

"I get it." I pick at my chin a little and she swats my hand away.

"Have you been sneaking sugary snacks again?"

"Mom! Not the time." I glance at my phone. I've got to be at Noah's in twenty minutes. Barely enough time to wash my face, slather some coverup on the zits sprinkled nicely across my chin, and hope my oily skin can play it cool until I can get to bed and wash it again. I hope I can squeeze some time for mascara in there and a re-braiding of my hair. "But I do need to ask you about something, just not now." I have to tell Mom about the con one of these days.

"What is it?" she asks.

"Later!" I yell. Not now. Anytime but now.

Oh, and somehow, I need to check my blog too. And Colin's draft. Ughhhh. And I gotta get back to Kasey's email *if* I'm given permission.

Half an hour later and I take the steps up Noah's walkway two at a time, stopping at the front door. The brass knocker stares into my soul. Noah's dad, John, seemed okay on the phone. But he's not the one I'm worried about. It's the red-headed monster children I remember from the night they moved in.

I'm sure that was just a rough night. I lift my hand to knock, but the door swings open and slams into the wall.

I'm met with big brown eyes, freckles sprinkled across alabaster skin, and the kind of smile that tells me she's had too much chocolate already. I can see it all over her gums. "Hi! I'm Molly! I like unicorns but you can't play with mine!"

"Okay, Molly. I'm Kole." I put my hand down for her to shake, but she gives me a high five. Okay, first awkward greeting out of the way.

"Dad! Kole is here!" In the back of the foyer, the other girl stands with her back against the wall, eyeing me. "Your glasses are nerdy."

Wow. I take them off and tuck them into the top of my shirt, thinking better of it when the room goes from clear to foggy in less than a second. It's going to be a long night.

"Hi, Kole. Welcome." John comes out from the kitchen, wiping chocolate onto a dishrag. "We've got to go, but the girls know the routine. I've written it on the fridge too. Bedtime is at eight. They've just had brownies. Help yourself." He dashes back into the kitchen, clearly in a rush. I have no idea where Noah is. "They're pretty mature—they can help with the essentials. Bed's at eight!"

"Okay, thanks." I walk into the living room, where the girls have spread out just about every single Hatchimal a kid can have. There are a few headless ones on the ground too, like they've recently been shoved into an oven and baked within an inch of their lives.

"Want to play?" Molly asks. She bends over the dark wood coffee table, her knees half lost in the long carpet fibers. This rug looks inviting.

"I'd love to." I sit cross-legged, happy to have a minute to rest.

"Bye Daddy!" Sara yells. She comes running to me after the door slams. Guess it's me and the girls now. Noah must already be at school.

"Here, Kole, this one is you." Sara hands me a Littlest Pet Shop kitten, its head half crushed and the electric blue hair in a pile on the ground. "I'll be right back."

"She squished that one," Molly says, pointing out what seems to be quite clear. "Wanted it to feel death."

I swallow. This is definitely above my pay grade.

When Sara walks back in, she's got a Sharpie in one hand and rips the kitten from me. When she hands it back, it's got a pair of glasses on its face.

"It's not pretty, so I named it after you. *Kole*, like the stuff Santa leaves when you're bad." Sara smiles, her mouth lined in dark chocolate.

My skin gets goose bumps. I hold the kitten by the tail and look at its fuzzy body. Wow. I'll be writing a demonic little girl into *Spacer* because holy shit is this giving me some ideas.

"I think you're pretty," Molly says. "And so does Noah."

I drop the kitten into my lap and the head bounces off. It rolls across the floor, right to Sara's feet. Great. Now I've been decapitated by a five-year-old and she's staring right back at me.

But, also, Noah . . . thinks I'm pretty?

Sara begins to hum a little ditty, quick and high.

Noah who dribbles the basketball like an all-star and never misses a shot? Noah who walks through the cafeteria and doesn't flinch at the eyes that stick to his face? Noah who wears a shirt like it's been made with his exact torso in mind?

My heart jumps. I sit a little straighter and make sure my shirt is covering my lower back. I can feel it sticking out of my jeans.

This is something. Truly, something.

"That's so nice. Thanks, Molly. I think you two are adorable too." I stare at Sara.

She squints her eyes at me and puts the cap on the Sharpie.

"Molly's not the smart twin." Sara kicks the kitten's head and it rolls under the coffee table.

I need to get control of this situation really quick. I jump up, ushering them to the stairs. "Come on, girls, show me your bedrooms. Do you have any Betty Spaghettys? Those were my favorite when I was little."

Sara's eyes light up. "I've got one with purple hair! Race you up the stairs! Try not to trip!" She makes a mad dash, her sister following after.

I lug myself up and head to the banister, moving far too slowly to trip. I should have charged John fifteen dollars an hour. Too bad I settled for twelve dollars, but hey, maybe I'll get a glance at Noah's bedroom.

"Kole," Byron whispers, his face hovering just beyond what I can reach. The sprawling hull of the *Snapdragon* is silent tonight, and the windows around us show nothing but the black—and the stars—stretching for light-years. I mumble something I don't even understand and crack an eye open, slipping out of the haze of dreamland. "Wake up. We're home."

Noah.

"Noah?!" Not Byron. But just as lovely. I shoot up, hoping I wasn't drooling. I adjust my shirt, my braid, my glasses. "How did it go?"

"I made the team!" His hair is slicked back, probably from sweat, but I don't mind, and he's wearing a ratty old Frost Heaves shirt. Guess he was the one fan before the team got nixed. "Will got McDuffy to reconsider when he showed him my stats from last year. I got to try out *and* he put me on the roster. I won't get to do every game, but I'm going to see if I can change his mind." He jumps up, mimicking shooting a basketball. I should know, I know how to do that now.

"Seriously? That's amazing!" I stand up and do a little cheer with my hands. That's the closest I'll ever get to pom-poms.

The stars in his eyes are so big. I don't think he even notices that I made an ass of myself and fell asleep on his sofa pretty much the second I got the girls to finally calm down.

John comes in from the hall, the same goofy grin plastered across his face. "I'm so glad McDuffy reconsidered. Seems like he's a good coach."

"Yeah, even said I could come to practice tomorrow."

"Perfect. As long as you stay on top of your grades." John points a finger at Noah and Noah rolls his eyes, but the grin stays plastered across his face. It's quite adorable, actually, the way he acts like his dad is giving him a hard time when he so clearly isn't. "Kole, how much do I owe ya? Twelve dollars times three hours, that's thirty-six dollars, plus a few extra."

Oh man. It got late before I knew it. And what a day it's been. "Thanks. And the girls were super cute. So fun to play with." Part of that is a big fat lie. "Molly is adorable."

"And Sara?" Noah asks, totally serious.

"She's . . . precocious?" I think that's the right word for her.

Noah snickers while John hands me a stack of cash. I slip it into the back pocket of my jeans. "That's one word for it. Noah, will you walk Kole across the street?"

"Yeah." Noah heads to the door. Eek. Me, alone, in the dark, with Noah. It's the thing my fever dreams consist of. I slip on my oversized black sweater, the kind I can wrap over my hands and bury myself in. It's perfect for the chilly air and trying to hide from the cute guy next to me.

"Goodnight, Mr. Pisano," I say, passing by.

"Night!" John says. He only looks slightly older than his son. Poor guy has it hard with those girls, but at least he's got Noah to help him.

"So, I'll have to be at basketball until like six tomorrow," Noah says, holding his front door open for me. "You guys watching *The Space Game* on Friday night?"

Does a bear shit in the woods? "Yeah, of course. We have it carefully charted out so that we've done our rewatch by the time it returns." Slow down, Kole. Remember that you gotta play it cool to be cool. "But we can find a way to get you caught up."

I step on the porch. The early October cold is really no big deal, but when summer is so recent in my memory, the chilly smell of oncoming winter makes the nights drag. Soon will come the snow, soon will come the mud. But, soon will come *The Space Game*'s new season, and that's worth the crappy weather.

"It's cool. I can pop by after practice if I'm not too tired. And a quick shower, naturally."

"Naturally." Oh my stars. Noah in the shower . . .

Pumpkins line the walkway, which Molly told me was her idea, and leaves from the maple branches hanging above us dance on the grass. The breeze picks up, scattering them into messy piles all over the lawn. The streets will soon be filled with their bodies, concrete covered in fire and morphed to crunchy, brown carcasses.

"How's the blog? Has Damian's little scheme been successful?" Noah asks, hands in his pockets. He takes the steps down the porch two at a time, not even grabbing the banister. He's positively giddy. "Figured Will would have told me if something else happened."

I could tell him about what happened today in the computer lab. He knows *Spacer* is my baby. I could tell him about Damian and Hailey, and their conditions, but he's just so chipper. Do I want to break his spirit? Especially when I'm partially the reason why he didn't make the team in the first place? At least that wrong has been set right. "No, nothing new there."

Another lie. How many more before I get caught in one of them?

"That's good. At least you can keep writing in peace?" He looks at me. I wonder if he knows that though I like writing, the idea of writing in peace when I've got a major audience is pretty much impossible. "For a little bit longer maybe?"

"Maybe." He's got to sense I'm brushing him off. "To be honest, the words just don't come. It's like they're plugged up in my head."

"I mean, you don't have to worry about anyone having found you yet." He watches his feet. "There's nothing in a post that's going to lead them to your house."

"That's true." Oh, great. He's offering sweet, reassuring words because he's kinda the best and I can't tell him that Damian's upped the game. I don't want to ruin this night. "Writing in peace just sounds like something I used to be able to do. Now the story doesn't seem to come so easy."

We cross the street, the leaves and rocks crunching under our steps. It's eerie; the same dread I had as a kid clamors up my neck, like when I'd ride home from Michaela's house too late after twilight and even the fireflies had called it a night. Those were some lonely moments, but with Noah next to me, the darkness doesn't seem so spooky. Instead, those pesky butterflies are back again, flitting about like they're about to be fed.

"Why not?"

"Have you looked at the comments?"

"Nah. Always best to avoid that unless you just want to be more pissed off than you were before."

I smile. "Yeah, I've learned that too. It's a whole lot of pissed-off people with nothing better to do."

"Plus provoking trolls is a little too alluring to me." At this point our legs are walking in matching strides. I smile, keeping it between the ground and me. "I might not be able to *not* set them straight when they're bitching about something, especially when I know you're right about it all."

Be still my heart. "I'm not so sure I'm always right about *Spacer* anymore."

"What do you mean?" he asks, stepping over the curb to my side of the street.

"It's just that apparently I don't know enough about space, or physics, or travel, or character development, or sentence structure, or whatever. I mean, that's according to the comments section."

"Screw the comments section."

That's an idea I can get behind. I put a finger to my chin like I'm deep in thought. "Hmmmm. That sounds right. Screw the comments section."

Or ignore them. God, I sound like my dad. That's what I do when I'm at an away game. Sucks hearing what some of the other guys say, or their stupid parents. They suck a fat one. You just gotta tune them out."

"That's good advice, actually." We head up the stairs to my porch. The lights downstairs are out; Mom and Dad must have gone to bed. Ten bucks says Will is playing *Fortnite* in the basement, which means Noah and I are the only ones out here paying any attention to what's going on outside.

"Want to sit?" I nod to the porch swing. It's bold, and I really should be logging in and checking on *Spacer*, but I've got Noah alone. In the dark. And, holy hell, if I don't just want to be a little indulgent right now.

He looks back at his house like maybe he should go back, but then he turns to me. Damn those chocolate-chip eyes. In the semi-dark they shouldn't still look this all-good. "Yeah, okay, for a few minutes." His voice is super husky when he answers, turning my thoughts to mush.

"Just a few." I sit, pulling my legs under me into crisscross applesauce. Noah begins to rock the swing back and forth. The creak of old, rusty hinges is the only sound scattering through the trees around us.

"What made your dad pick Crystal Lake?" I yawn at the end of the question, the movement of the swing nearly rocking me to sleep.

"Needed a change after my mom passed away. He said he couldn't handle the porch where her flowers grew, or driving by the school she taught at, or seeing the hospital every day on his way to work. Too many reminders of her everywhere." He leans forward, resting his elbows on his knees, and folds his hands together, swaying the bench with his feet.

"Makes sense."

"Have you ever lost someone close to you?" he asks.

I shake my head.

"Then you're one of the lucky ones."

"I am." I lean my head back on the bench. I *have* been lucky. I'm in a quiet, safe town where I can ride my bike anywhere I need to. But there are still yucky people here, no matter how beautiful their lawns, how nice their cars. And the thought of what happened earlier today still makes my head throb. There are nasty people lurking in dark corners online, but some of them have found my hiding place. Dread slithers up my spine.

If what Colin said is true, there's more at school. *The Space Game*'s ship wars have found Crystal Lake.

I take off my glasses and rub my eyes.

They'll find me next.

Time to change the subject. "How are your sisters getting along?"

A few seconds pass before he responds. "The worst nights are when they cry for her and there's nothing we can do to calm them. They just have to see it through until they're so tired they finally shut their eyes." Noah watches his feet while he speaks, his voice all throaty again. God. "Molly's still the worst. Sara does better."

I close my eyes. My heart, not just my head, aches for them. For him. There's got to be times when he too cries for her. I swallow down the lump that's forming before I speak. "That breaks my heart. I wish I had something helpful to say."

"No one ever does. It's just nice to sometimes not talk about it. Sometimes I'll go for a whole two hours playing basketball and I'll forget—not about her—but I'll forget that she's gone. For whatever brief period, it's like things are normal again."

"I get that. Nothing like a good distraction."

"Exactly." He turns to me this time. "I don't mind talking about it with you though."

"I don't mind hearing about it from you." I lean my head in his direction and he sits back. "You can talk to me about it whenever you need to." I smile. Was that too bold? Eh. If it was, I'm too tired to care.

He nods. "Thanks, Kole. I don't mean to get so, I don't know, sappy?"

"It's not sappy. It's real," I say. And it's adorable. And honest. "I like sappy Noah." I don't stop the words before they come out, and a rush of warmth heats my face. He glances at me, and I don't look away. He tucks in a corner of his mouth, and I follow suit.

"Think your parents are wondering where you are?" he asks, not breaking eye contact.

I shrug, my head still resting on the back of the bench swing. "I don't really care if they are." A quick glance behind me would tell me if they've come downstairs, but I only want to be looking at Noah. No one else needs to exist in this moment. "Think your dad is wondering where you are?"

"Nah. He doesn't keep tabs on me. Too busy with the girls and the house and work."

"Then I see no reason for us to leave this swing." That was a ballsy, word-vomit thing to say, but I'm glad I did when I see the smile he shoots me. It sends prickles to my toes and pink to my cheeks.

He leans back and lays his arm on the back of the bench. It's close enough to touch my head, and he yanks on my braid gently enough to send a chill across my scalp. "Should you get to *Spacer*?"

Out here, where the chill and the dark leaves just enough mystery, it's safe from the comments. From the nonsense in the Journalism room today. "Nah. Not right now."

"You know *Spacer*'s coming up at school, right? A bunch of cheerleaders were talking about it yesterday. And kids were drawing spaceships on their notebooks in Forensics. You heard about lunch?"

"Yeah." We're quiet for a few seconds. I'm so very aware. But this bench feels . . . immune from the drama. It feels safe.

Noah clears his throat and touches my hair again, right where it meets my ear. "What would Will say about you and me out here?"

"Please don't make me think about my brother right now. Not when there's this swing, and the dark, and the quiet, and the fireflies." And you, Noah-of-the-basketball-field.

I shut my eyes as he reaches for my braid; sparks shoot to my toes. He drags his fingers over the length as it trails down my neck, and when he gets to the bottom, he pulls me a little closer. The night smells of him, of fall, of the sky after the moon has said goodnight. When I open my eyes, moving away isn't an option.

His lips are cherry-chapstick soft, and I put my hand on his shoulder, pulling his body closer. *This is happening. I'm kissing Noah. It's really, truly happening.* When his mouth opens, mine does too. I don't stop him when he leans farther into me. I press my back against the pillow and swing my leg on his lap. Before I do a thing to stop it, he's practically on top of me. The kiss grows into something hungry, something more than soft.

This kiss, this boy, this night, this thing between us, it's just right—but someone could hear us out here.

"Wait." I pull back, and Noah moves his lips to my neck. I make a squeak.

Embarrassing. But, oh my stars, that's just the spot, apparently. I run a hand through his hair. It falls over his forehead and is just as soft as I thought it would be. I sink deeper into him, my hands on his biceps because how could I not?

I want to curl around him and make this moment ours. This is way better than the other boys I wasted kisses on; I want to adopt a dog with Noah, name it *Snapdragon*, and spoil it rotten. I want to write up plans for our dream house and put up a *Blessed* sign in our kitchen.

But . . . I have to get inside. To *Spacer*. To Colin's script.

To other, even more (or maybe less?) pressing things.

I push him off, a little harder this time, and he gets the message. "I—um, I need to get inside. I'm sorry—I am. Can I see you Friday? When we watch *The Space Game*? It's the episode when—"

"It's cool. Don't worry—I mean, I get it." He sits up, rubbing his hands over his face and through his hair. I nod, standing up and readjusting my everything. That was moving a little fast there, but it was definitely something. And I definitely liked it.

He glances over to his house, no lights on. He stands, and I follow him to the edge of the porch. "Night, Kole." He leans in for one more kiss, cheeks as pink as mine must be, and I accept like it's the last glass of water during a drought.

"Night, Noah," I say as he runs off my porch and into the dark, fall night.

This must be what it feels like to watch someone else's life. He's seriously the cutest guy I've ever laid eyes on . . . so why do I feel the tug to get upstairs and help Colin? Why is the thought of our agreement nagging at the back of my mind?

Because I made him a promise. I said I'd help. And . . . I'm enjoying talking to him. Working with him.

That's all there is to it.

I rush to my room, wash my face, brush my teeth, and lay on my bed to open up Colin's script. While my laptop hums to life on my pillow, I rest my head.

CHAPTER ELEVEN

The air in Creative Writing is colder than usual. I hug my black sweater closer to my chest, my arms folded across my midsection. I came in a few minutes late, had to update Michaela about Noah last night, and I haven't so much as caught Colin's eye. He didn't even flinch when I pulled out my chair, rather noisily, and took my seat. Fortunately, I was able to avoid Hailey and Damian too. Their presence doesn't help with the vibe in here.

I've been an awful sorta friend to Colin. When I woke up this morning, my computer had long since died, and I didn't get his paper to him. I can't even say what his script was about. The last thing I remember was his name loading when I shut my eyes.

His sweater on this lovely Wednesday is a deep gray, forming the Great Wall of Colin, and it scoops up at his neckline, forming an uber trendy collar. His hair is starting to get a little too long; it curls just a little at the ends and lightly touches the fabric at the nape of his neck. I lean a little closer.

When he leans back, almost in my space, he doesn't push back as far as normal. Seems like he wants to get comfortable, but not in the obnoxiously in-my-space way he usually does.

Frigid. That's what it is in here. I rub my hands together, blowing on them.

I think he's ignoring me.

". . . and that, Apples, is why we include an MLA header on everything we write." Mrs. Liu heads back to her desk to grab some papers, her voice drowning away now that her back is to me.

This is good—I can get Colin's attention. Own up to what I didn't do. I lean forward, my stomach pressed against my desk, and tap his back. "Hey."

He glances over his shoulder, but all I really catch are his glasses. No eye contact. "Hi, Kole."

Suspicions confirmed. He's pissed. I can't blame him; I'd be too if I were waiting on him to look at my paper. Deep breath, here goes. Apologies are for the strong. The brave. The Kole. "I'm sorry I didn't get to your script last night. I had to babysit, and I got to bed way too late. I was so tired that I fell asleep with my head on my computer." It's the truth, one hundred and fifty percent, even if it is absolutely ridiculous. And he doesn't need to know that I was also out late because I was hanging out with my new, utterly adorable neighbor and that we were one hundred percent making out on my porch swing.

He turns around, careful not to let Mrs. Liu catch him misbehaving. "It's cool. Don't worry about it."

"Do you feel good about what you wrote? I mean, without peer editing?"

"It'll be fine." He focuses on the notebook in his hand. "Seriously, don't worry about it. Doesn't really need an editor anyway."

"Okay . . ." I lean back. He doesn't seem too upset, and he didn't say he'd never want to switch with me again. But, if he feels like his paper is good, why is he giving me the brush-off? I lean forward, resting my chin in my hands.

I did what I had to. I apologized. I'll do better next time he shares something. I'll get it done early.

The clock says ten more minutes of class. Of avoiding Hailey's and Damian's eyes, though I feel the snakes in the grass, itching for me to make a move.

Michaela and I enter the hallway, hugging our bags and notebooks closer and preparing to cross the juggernaut that is the second story of the building. The movement of students usually gets a little cramped before the stairs, and the crowd inches forward at a snail's pace. It's hump day. That's gotta be why.

I pass by the lockers' end, just north of the boys' room and the water fountain with the water everyone knows actually tastes good. Usually the line is around the corner, but not at the moment. Michaela bumps along at my side. Pack mentality. No better way to get down the stairs, and through all of high school, really.

Entry to the cafeteria is no small feat; the line is already forming. I groan. Fifteen more minutes until the fries hit my mouth, and by then we'll be halfway through lunch.

"Let's snag that table." Michaela points to the north side, right by some girls talking very loudly about their dates to the Harvest Ball. It's a perfect spot. We'll stick to the perimeter today. It'll make it easier to slip out should I see Damian or Hailey, or overhear anyone badmouthing *Spacer*. Or Byron. Or Cedric, really, cause it's my show and that means all the characters. Sticking to the side means I can dodge out of here faster than the *Snapdragon* in light speed.

We toss our bags down and skip over to the line. No sign of Will in here, which means no sign of Noah yet. Wherever he is, I wonder if he thinks anything of our little porch hangout last night, or if he noticed that my lips are quite well moisturized at any given moment.

"Did you write any more last night?" Michaela asks.

"No. I fell asleep as soon as I opened up my computer. That's why Colin was pissed in class. I didn't get to read his script." I lean against the wall behind me and begin to study the bottom of my braid. "I liked his sweater today."

"Of course, you did. That's why I ship you guys. Team Kol-Col."

"Stop. I don't think it's like that. Or, if it ever was, he's probably erased me from his mind entirely since I left him hanging." I wrap the end of my hair around my finger. Colin is . . . cute, and annoyingly smart, but there's no *us*. I glance over to his usual table, and he's about halfway through his sandwich, probably talking to his speech and debate friends about entrance fees to Yale. Laughing about some joke on *Last Week Tonight*.

Michaela crosses her arms. "The vibe in class today was off. Too much shit going on with everyone—you two, the douche team in the back, plus did you hear about Lauren's score on the AP Language pre-test? Apparently she's grounded up until they take the actual test. That's like eight months. She was whining about it in Algebra this morning."

"I guess I missed that one. Too bad." In the distance, the crowd opens up. Will and Noah waltz in with their usual level of cool: packs slung over shoulders, hats flipped backward, the rest of the basketball team trailing after them. Not a care in the world about who's looking at them.

I wonder if Will knows about last night?

I'm not going to tell him. He'll probably get jealous again that I'm logging time with his best bro. They're quite the team, yeah, but last night Noah and I were quite the team. I guess I'm no longer benched.

And now I'm staring again. He's got a massive, rolled-up poster board under his arm, probably something for English 12. So cool. So casual. So Noah. The line in front of me moves, and I take a few steps forward. I stick my hands in my back pockets, my black sweater hanging loose over the gray shirt underneath.

Noah and Will make their way through the crowd, squeezing between groups and patting their buddies on the shoulders, finally snagging their usual table. They're met with a flourish of *heys* and fist pumps, and they toss their bags to the ground. I glance away. Staring might not be best. Especially when my mind wanders to what Noah's lips taste like again.

"Kole?" Michaela says.

"Sorry, Noah and Will just got here." I look at Michaela again. "Noah's just something else, isn't he?"

Michaela catches their eye. "What are they looking at?"

I look in their direction again. "Probs some book report or something. The bio fair isn't this week, right?" Noah unrolls whatever it is and shows it to Will. Will smiles, laughing as he reads whatever's on it. I turn back to the line, stepping forward. Ten students between me and the french fries. That's about 2.5 minutes and—

"Kole!" someone yells from an impossibly far distance. I turn. Will. He and a bunch of boys are staring at me. My stomach bounces. What's going on? Will motions for the other basketball players to stand. They hop onto the tables in some kind of choreographed move from *Hamilton* and kneel on the tabletops. Noah is the only one standing, his gorgeous hair hanging loose over his forehead, smack on top of the table across the cafeteria. His eyes lock on me. I catch their gooey goodness from here.

People around us pull out their phones, aiming the cameras at Noah.

At me.

Michaela grabs my arm. "Oh my god. Kole. What are they doing? They're going to get detentions."

"What the heck," I whisper. By now, every single student in here, and the teachers monitoring us, are looking at the basketball team. And they're looking at me. My mouth hangs open, like some kind of doof. I close it.

Noah opens up the massive poster board. It's bright orange—no missing it—with a poem written on it in fat bubble letters. I start to read, but there's no need. The entire team begins to chant the words.

Pumpkins, corn, and raisin spice
It would be awfully nice
If the cutest apple in the orchard
Ended my torture
And went to the Harvest Ball with me
So what do you say, Kole, are you free?

The cafeteria is silent. Those that aren't filming are staring at me, waiting.

Michaela squeezes my arm. "Say something. Everyone's looking at you."

I glance around. Noah is asking me to the dance in the most horrifically public way possible—not to mention the comma splice and lowercase *k*—oh, who cares? It's Noah asking me to the dance that I didn't want to go to in the first place . . . but I *am* going.

With Damian.

I sense the snake's eyes watching me.

I swallow. How do I say no to the guy I want to twirl with around the dance floor until my heels bleed? To the guy I want to fall asleep with on an old porch swing, the night drifting by as firefly twinkles fade out?

He tugs one corner of his mouth inward in a little, hopeful grin.

He's beautiful.

I have to say something.

I could lie. Tell him yes and save him from what's about to happen—but then Damian will strike. He'll announce who I am to the whole freakin' cafeteria.

Or I could do it myself. Tell them I'm *ToTheStars*.

I can't.

Not ever.

Or at least, not yet.

I cross my arms and close my eyes. This is going to break that beautiful boy, but there's no other way—I'm not sacrificing my work, no matter how cute his eyes or his forearms. "I can't." My voice shakes. It makes me want to vomit.

Noah's smile falls, his normally striking eyes grim and his brow confused. He lowers the poster a little and looks to Will, kneeling next to him. Will shakes his head at me. Michaela nudges me.

I have to end the silence. Make this go away. "It's just that—I—I—" I swallow. Again. Noah turns back to me. "I'm going with someone already."

Damian steps out of line far behind me, snaps his fingers above his head, and points at himself. He twirls in some kind of victory dance.

My stomach is in my toes. The whole school now knows I'm going with Damian's dumb ass.

Will cocks his head and puts his arm out. I can practically hear him. *What the hell, Kole?*

A few people snicker. At the tables in front, they laugh to one another. They point. They cover their faces. They aim their phones in my direction.

I don't look at them. I look at Noah. He nods and steps down from the table, rolling up the poster board. He, and Will, grab their things. The other basketball players come down from the tables too, just as confused, and the cafeteria morphs back into motion.

As they file out the double doors, Noah tosses the poster board into the trash can. It's loud enough to hear the clunk from here.

The walls press in on me, forcing my chest to tighten. I have to get out of here. Too many eyes staring. Too many thoughts, questions, assumptions—I feel them tumbling straight toward me as big black-and-white dominoes stack up around me. Too many phones are pointed at me, cementing my every move in forever. Red splotches build behind my eyes. A headache moves in behind my ears.

I can't do this. I run to the bathroom on the other side of the cafeteria, blazing by Colin, who's leaving with more of a scowl than I saw this morning.

Slam dunk, Kole.

After hitting up the bathroom, I text Mom. She calls me out without a fight. Picks me up within a half hour, and I throw my bike into the back of the Suburban, probably breaking one of the pedals.

I rip open the door to the back seat and jump in, spreading my legs out in front of me and slouching down farther than I thought possible. Normally Will takes the front seat, so now the distance between Mom and me is undeniably awkward. Now I'm wishing I hadn't thrown my phone in the back. That would give me something to look at so I could avoid her eyes.

I need to talk to her. But not about the cafeteria. About the con. And I'm kinda feeling like feck it all anyway. The silence beats as she puts the car in drive and slowly hits the acceleration.

"So, are we not going to say anything?" She pulls out of the roundabout in front of school. "You just made me come get you and you're not going to talk about whatever is going on?"

"My stomach hurts, okay? I told you that."

"And all this after a detention. You've seen my flowchart. You know acting out at school is one of the first steps to incarceration later in life."

"Ugh. Seriously," I mumble.

She continues. "Is there something more going on? Or is this just your anxiety again? Let's talk about meds if you think it's time. I can call the pediatrician. Or are you actually sick?"

"Mom! I don't want to talk about that. Something happened, but it's not serious. It's just dumb drama with dumber people." That happen to be ridiculously cute and now ridiculously mad at me. If I hadn't gotten sick in the bathroom, my stomach would be rolling again.

Noah will never talk to me ever again.

"Is it something in one of your classes? Dear god, please don't let it be another detention?" She angles down the rearview mirror farther than it should even be able to go, and I feel her eyes on me. I turn my head and stare out the window as houses whiz by.

"No. It's something else."

"I've made a reputation out of questioning witnesses. I'll get it out of you if you won't tell me." Her voice is heavy, coated in concern.

I roll my eyes. Yeah, I know. I have to get her to stop bothering me about today. Diversion time—another conversation I haven't been exactly excited about having. But at least it'll get her off the scent. "Okay, so you know how my thing is my show, right? And I won that contest?"

She waits five extra-long seconds before she responds. "Yes."

"Well, I got an email from someone at the Con-athon, which is the biggest convention for the show, and they want me to have my own panel. So they're asking me to be a guest there. It's the opportunity of a lifetime, but I already know you're going to say no."

Mom slows down at a stop sign and turns the car very, very slowly. Okay, maybe she's considering this. Or she's completely confused. Probably both.

"I'm not so sure about this. You know how I feel about that hobby of yours." She heaves a sigh. I catch her right eye twitch in the mirror. I pick at my sleeve. She clears her throat. "I'd need more details. Like, for example, what is a *con*." The word comes out with an overly hard *c*.

"It's a place where fans get together and geek out over their *thing*, whatever that is." I'll spell it out for her since she hasn't completely said no *yet*.

"Oh, so like a seminar."

Her tone changed there, to one of possibility. That's . . . unusual. "Except less socially acceptable." For some weird reason.

"They want you to do something there?"

Now that's a genuine question. It's not a brush-off. "Yeah, like speak on a panel. Face people." *Fans*. "Talk about my fanfic and the show."

She taps a finger on the steering wheel. "Let me ask you this, Kole, if you like this kind of thing, why are you so stressed about it?" That's her high-impact voice. The one that she uses when it's a loaded question.

All right, my move. I am stressed, but today wasn't about this. I'm not telling her that though. I'm not ready to just spill all my guts here in the car. "I'm not sure yet." Because other fans are scary. "It just is."

See Damian. Hailey. The comments section. The kids at school.

"I know your blog means a lot to you, so I'll mull this over. I'll take a look at the information, but your father and I will need to discuss it. And it's not going to even be a possibility if there's another detention email headed my way."

Did my mom just not close the door on the con? She's actually considering it?

The battle's not over, but this is a victory. I see the *Snapdragon* before me, blasters lit and aiming straight for the belts, but it's not Pippa at the helm. It's not Byron.

It's me.

"There's no detention coming," I say, a half smile sneaking onto my face. "I'll send you a link to it. It's a cool opportunity."

For a second, we lock eyes in the rearview mirror.

Maybe it's something for my resume . . .

I better not say that. Don't push it, Kole.

SPACER 3.11
Posted by: ToTheStars
Oct. 2, 2019. 1:32

Byron lunges for Santiago and they lock arms. The blade was a moment away from taking Benedick's life, and Byron's struggling to keep Santiago from sticking it in his chest.

Damn it all. Forget the Rocks. Santiago is a bastard, and Byron will rid the skies of his curse. In the second confusion takes, he slams the knife through Santiago's back, angled toward the lungs where Byron knows air will slip out of the wound.

"It's over, demon!" Byron yells into his ear.

Santiago cries out, his eyes wide as his voice fails. His body starts to fall, rigid and heavy, like a tree tumbling over, and Byron falls with him. He lands, knees next to Santiago's broken torso, the knife shoved in good and deep. It was a strike to kill, and Santiago sputters, his head flopping to one side, his face frozen in life's last instant.

For a moment, he looks like Carter Carlyle. But for a moment longer, he looks like Pippa.

Cathartic—that's what that scene is. It's going to have to do for now. My brain is fried. My phone is heavy with unread text messages. Michaela wants to know where I went. Will has no idea what the hell is going on. He's still at school, and I'm in my bedroom. His last message just read *DAMIAN. WTF Kole.* And honestly, I agree. What the fuck, Kole.

I don't have a good answer.

Dare I check Snapchat? Instagram? Twitter? I'm sure the video is up. I'm sure that they're not just laughing at me in the cafeteria; they're laughing at me online. Like the comments section. But this time, my face is a part of it. They all know who I am. I can't hide from this dumpster fire.

Worse, they're laughing at Noah for something he didn't know. For something he's got to still be wondering about.

I need a distraction even more so than *Spacer* right now.

Colin's script—that's what I can do. I click from my dashboard to Google Docs. There, in the *shared with me* section, is Colin Clarke's latest masterpiece.

```
Colin Clarke
Mrs. Liu
Creative Writing
01 October 2019


CREATIVE WRITING, TUESDAY, LESS THAN TWO
WEEKS BEFORE THE HARVEST BALL


Students file into a classroom and sit,
preparing their supplies for class to
begin. Teacher is at a desk, taking
attendance.


          BROODY KNOW-IT-ALL DUDE
   (turns around to the cute girl behind him,
      hoping he remembers to smile)
      Hey Kole. Did you get a chance
      to look at my poem last night?


          CUTE INTROVERT GIRL
   (grimaces at BROODY KNOW-IT-ALL DUDE)
      I did. It's going to need some
      work.
```

BROODY KNOW-IT-ALL DUDE
(scared she had to clean her eyeballs
with alcohol after she read his poem)
Will you help me? I need an A.
Desperately.

CUTE INTROVERT GIRL
I dunno, BROODY BOY. You're
kind of an ass.

BROODY KNOW-IT-ALL DUDE
(figuring he was going to get called on that
earlier, he attempts to make it right.
BROODY BOY scoots closer to INTROVERT GIRL
so the other students can't hear. He looks
from side to side before he speaks)
Here's the truth, INTROVERT
GIRL. I don't have a good
reason for half the stuff I
say. And I'm not that good at
words hence the constant SAT
practice. I truly, deeply, and
devoutly need your help.

CUTE INTROVERT GIRL
(waits an uncomfortably
long time to respond)
That's the most words you've
ever said to me without any
sarcasm.

BROODY KNOW-IT-ALL DUDE
(realizing he may have been a little
too much; that he may be receiving a
restraining order in the near future)

Look, words and feelings hardly
meet at the right moment for
me. But, there's one question
I need to ask you before they
fail me again. Will you go to
the Harvest Ball with me?

                CUTE INTROVERT GIRL
            (Your turn, Kole. Finish
                the script for me?)

I slam shut my computer and lay back on my bed.

Colin Clarke asked me to the dance.

Via homework.

That's so . . . *nerdy*.

So . . . *Colin*.

And so . . . private? Like, not in front of the whole freaking school . . .

And that's why he blew me off today. He was waiting on an answer that never came. And I didn't even hint at it in class. I rejected him without even knowing it.

My ceiling stares back at me, judging. *You must have done something really terrible in a past life*, it says. That's the only thing that can explain what the heck is going on in my life right now. Or maybe the world's decided that shitting on my life is pure enjoyment. Or maybe I'm being dramatic, but what the hell, World? Is this how you get your kicks? I rip off my glasses and put them on my bedside table. Squeezing the spot just at the top of my nose only relieves some of the pressure building in my sinuses.

Cricket jumps onto the bed and lays on my tummy. She begins to knead, her claws little pinpricks on my doughy center. She knows the mess I've made. And she judges, yes, but she also knows how to help.

"Our human problems must seem so silly to you. All you need is food, water, and a place to poop. Must be so simple to be a cat." I fold her up into my arms, and she purrs as loud as a spaceship.

I don't know how to answer Colin. He already knows the whole slimy truth about the dance. He was right there when this all went down. It's Noah I need to own up to first . . . I just don't know how to approach this whole shitstorm.

I shut my eyes. Everything has become so complicated, like flying through space during a meteor shower with the debris shield turned off.

2:30 p.m. isn't too early to go to bed, right?

CHAPTER TWELVE

Thud. Thud. Thud. "Get up, Nikole! Rise and shine! You've got some 'splaining to do!"

Tugging my sleep-crusted eyes open, I roll over and squeeze my pillow around my head. It's Will, the world's worst alarm clock.

I stuff the pillow over my face, avoiding my drool pool, but I know full well it's not going to make a difference. I was able to avoid talking to him for most of the week, but now it's Saturday morning. He's not going anywhere. "Go away, Will!"

"I'm coming in in three seconds—hair brushed or not!"

Feck. My room is a mess. There's nothing I need within grabbing distance. I don't care about my hair—I can't put on a bra in three seconds. I sit up and prop a pillow over my chest. I ruffle my hair out and rub my fingers under my eyes. I probably have black circles so far under my eyes they touch my chin.

He barges in, dressed for basketball, his nose still dark from the bruising, the area under his eyes tinged yellow. "You don't answer texts. Your lights are out when I get home. You forget to feed Cricket. You ignore me at home and at school. You don't come watch our show. Remember your fav?"

"Ugh." I look to the ceiling. No prayer will get me out of this.

"I half expected to find flies under the door feasting on your dead body. So tell me what the hell happened yesterday."

Oh god. I groan. I completely forgot about our viewing party last night; I passed out as soon as I got home, without a peep to anyone, especially Noah. I glance at my phone, on my bedside table, but it's dead. Any text messages are lost somewhere in the ether. Michaela is probably convinced I'm dead too. I've never gone so long without answering her texts. Will's stare is burning craters into my face. I've got to give him an answer. "I slept until you barged in here, doofus."

"So it would appear." He kicks the pile of clothes at his feet.

"Did Noah come last night?" I ask, glancing at the window. My stomach twists at the sight of his bedroom window, no sign of movement anywhere at the house. Even the girls must be sleeping in.

Will shakes his head. "Nope. Me and Michaela and a boatload of awkwardness."

"You really think it would have been better if we were there? After what happened?"

"Yeah, let's get to what the hell happened." He sits on the edge of my bed, balancing his basketball in between his hands. "Damian, huh? After *everything* over the last few days you're going to the dance with Damian Dickhead?"

"Will." I drag out the word like I used to do when I was young and he was being a dumbass. My voice hasn't changed, and neither has his ability to get me to spill the beans. "You know I don't want to go with Damian!"

He raises his hands to the ceiling. "Then what the hell? I thought for sure you were into Noah so I told him to ask you and then he did and you turned him down in front of the whole damn school. The guy is humiliated."

"I *am* into Noah! You don't know the whole story!" I reach for my glasses and put them on. All the better to face my brother with.

The room morphs into focus and I spy my bra draped over my purple armchair. Too far away to hide.

Dad's voice comes booming up the stairs. "Stop yelling, you two! You're not too old to wear the 'get-along shirt'!"

Oh god. If he makes us wear the shirt with one neck hole and two sleeves as a junior and senior I will absolutely die right here in my pajamas. But at least then I won't have to go to the dance.

Will yells in hushed tones, screaming with his eyes and his arms. "What the hell? Damian likes you too? And you agreed to go with that toolbox?"

"It's not like that. Some stuff went down." It comes spewing out of me in a manic regurgitation: the Journalism room. Mrs. Brittain. The quests they've given me. I wish it ended there, but it doesn't. "And it kinda involves . . . you."

"Ah, the fuck does he want with me?" Will asks, his voice steady and stern, all walls up. If at all possible, his whispers are more intense than before.

I clench my fists in front of his chest, tightening them until my knuckles pop. I'm mad at him for what happened with Noah, mad at Damian for his supreme douchebaggery, and mad at my dumbass self for logging in at school. But all of this, if it works out, will have been worth getting my site back. But I'm not going to tell him that Colin asked me to the dance. That would baffle him even more. Two guys interested in his sister? What sideways world is this?

"He wants me to go with him so he can find a way to talk to Daisy. He's pissed that you asked her first. He has a super crush on her, borderline stalker, so he's hoping that I can be his way in to talk to her. Like, maybe we could make that happen? Just satisfy his weird fixation and then you guys can have the rest of the dance together?"

Will clenches his lips, the veins in his neck popping out. "No way. Not for Damian."

"Please, Will. I just need this and it'll be over."

He waits, his eyes searching across mine. "So this guy wants to blackmail you into making your blog his fanboy wet dream, and now he wants to force a conversation with a girl that likely doesn't even know he exists? This isn't how things are supposed to happen, you know that right? You can't just manipulate your way into getting someone to like you."

"Of course I know that, dipshit," I say. He sneers at me, shaking his head. "And you can't just expect a story to be told your way. Daisy will quickly know that she should stay far away from him, because Damian will feck things up quickly, and then the night will be left to the both of you. I'll make sure of it. Promise."

"You had better. It's my Harvest Ball too." He breathes deep, channeling his rage like Dad always says to. "I'm not a dipshit."

"You're not. I'm just mad at everything." One of these days, I'm going to try that anger trick.

"You have to tell Noah," he says, running a hand through his tousled hair. "He's going to be at practice in a few."

"No! This isn't his problem. I'll get it sorted. I mean, it's just one dance I didn't want to go to in the first place. Is it that bad to suffer through one night? To help stupid Damian impress some girl he likes?"

"Yeah, it's that bad. You're playing into his BS."

I shrug. "I'll get it over with and get my site back. I'll talk to Noah on Monday. After what happened in the cafeteria, some time needs to blow over. But I'll make it all okay again."

I can fix this.

Pippa's words. Episode twelve, season one. She can fix anything.

I can channel her. I can be the girl who doesn't let the skies scare her.

Will sucks in his bottom lip. "Just don't try to do it at lunch. He's got detention for the next week."

"For what?"

Will chuckles, pointing at himself. "We all do for standing on the lunch tables. Because *someone could have been seriously hurt and then all of our parents would sue the school* and so on. We're lucky they're still letting us play next week."

"Seriously?" I close my eyes and lean back on the pillow. "I said no to Noah in front of everyone, and now he has detention? This is the worst garbage fire I've ever started!"

"You better tell him what's going on soon." Will looks at me, dragging a hand to the back of his head. "At least explain what happened, you know?"

I swallow. Noah deserves an explanation. The last thing I want him to think is that there are no feelings between us. There totally are. Ooey, gooey ones. "Yeah, I know. Just not right away."

Will gets up and walks to the door. "Don't wait too long. He's been asked to the dance like three times already."

Of course he has been asked. He's still got that new-guy shine.

And I care.

I do.

Don't I?

By the time I've showered and semi-cleaned up the trash heap that is my bedroom, my phone decides it's gotten its beauty sleep and buzzes back to life. I sit on my purple-and-green quilt and prop myself up against the massive lavender pillow leaning against the wall. It's best to be comfy for the storm.

After a few seconds, the texts come through. My phone ignites. Michaela texted eleven times before calling it a night. I can respond to her with some groveling. She'll get why I checked out early last night.

An unknown number slips into my texts. Two new messages.

Unknown

4:43 PM

Hey Kole. It's Noah. I got your number from my dad. Sorry about what happened. I didn't mean to put you on the spot. Was hoping for a different answer.

Anyway, have fun at the dance.

I open the text and type a quick response.

I'm sorry. I didn't mean for it to happen like this. I want to go with you more than I want anything in this stupid town.

My cheeks flush. That's not entirely true. My fingers stutter over the send button.

I also want to go with someone else, and he asked me too. But I saw it too late.

Should I have written my *no* in Colin's assignment? His phone would have beeped as I edited it. He would have been watching me type the words. And that would have hurt just as much.

Asteroids. One day you're flirting, and the next thing you're making out on a swing, and then you're stuck in a real-life love triangle. Only it's no fun in the real world, when real emotions twist your insides into knots and you realize you're hurting people.

I don't hit send on the text. Instead I look through my other notifications, passing Will, Noah, and Michaela. But there's nothing from Colin yet. Not a peep. I pinch the bridge of my nose. There's nothing I can say to him right now. It will have to wait until Monday.

The only thing that can solve this is *Spacer*. Time for the angstiest damn bit of text I've ever churned out. Beware, dear readers. While I'm at it, I'm going to send an email to customer service at Stumblr. See how easy it is to steal a blog, as Damian threatened. They've got to have some kind of major security in place.

And then I'll get to that poem I owe Hailey for the lit mag. I'll make it breathtaking and be one step closer to being done with this crapola. One step closer to being in charge of *Spacer* again.

The Monday morning sun is blanketed in clouds. Rain threatens, hidden deep in the puffs, but even more troublesome is my cramps. They shoot through me in their own lightning bolts, and the wind has been ripping my braid around my back since I left the garage. I've added a black jacket to my sweater, shirt, undershirt, and bra, because there's no moodier Kole than a cold one.

Creative Writing is coming like a comet, fast and unavoidable. I pump my legs and push hard on my pedals, jumping my bike up on the curb. Hailey will need *her* poem today. Colin will know that I know he asked me to the dance and I haven't done a thing about it. Damian will be leering at me, wondering when I'll touch base with him about making plans for this Saturday. Yep, class is about to split me right down the center. And my uterus is helping.

A group of girls, a couple of boys too, all dressed in black *Space Game* T-shirts, stand by the bike rack. I squeeze past them, careful not to disturb their conversation, and slide my bike into the rack.

My lock is buried too far down in my backpack, so it takes a second to dig out.

"That's the girl," one of them whispers. I swear I can hear her finger extend to point in my direction. I try not to look.

"That new kid is the cutest boy at Crystal Lake. Saying no to him is like saying yes to Cedric." They giggle, covering their mouths. The October wind races through the lawn, scattering the leaves spread over the crunchy grass.

I cringe. Someone just compared me to Pippa, so that's a bit of a good thing, but also, they're making fun of me. A-holes.

"Big mistake," one says. "Have you seen him at practice? I'd let him dribble on me."

Gross. I stand, trying not to hear anymore, but I can't keep my mouth quiet after a comment like that. "You guys should stick to *The Space Game*. At least there, no one can hear you scream." Okay, it wasn't a very good one, but maybe they'll think it's super clever and that they just don't get it. That's one of the advantages of being the quiet one; they never know if I'm super dumb or super smart.

The girls look at one another and back at me. "Oh, Kole. I'm sure Damian will be a much better choice." The tall one snickers. "Since he's Mr. Popular now."

"Bet the Curve-Breaker doesn't like being dethroned." She flicks her hair from her T-shirt. Pippa's forlorn look stares back at me. A character whose head I know well.

"It's *usurped*," I say, rolling my eyes. At least I can do words . . . and I think that's an SAT one. Crap. Is Colin rubbing off on me?

"Skank," one of them whispers.

I turn, my braid bouncing from shoulder to shoulder. Can't let them see me blinking back tears. Damn my body and its stupid reactions. It'd be easier to melt into the crowd if I could hide my hurt. I head across the green and to the staircase, clutching the straps of my backpack so tight my fingertips get cold.

"Kole Miller! Heard Damian's rented a stretch Hummer for the big night. Are the rumors true?" Barry McMillian hollers as I trod up the front stairs of the school. He's one of Crystal Prep's biggest bullies. He used to give me a hard time in PE when it would take me like twenty-six times to serve a volleyball properly. "Wonder what else he's planning?" He pushes his blond hair out of his eyes, his letter jacket nearly bursting at the seams.

"Get a haircut, Barry." Ad hominem and I don't care. I hang my head, wishing I hadn't said anything as he follows me.

I walk a bit faster. An escape plan is what I need. I glance to the side. Barry is literally right behind me. "What did you just say?"

"Go bug someone else." I pick up the pace, pushing through the crowded hallway. I could sneak into a classroom, but I don't know if I'm opening up a door that'll leave me alone with this asshole, or if there will be a teacher in there.

"Little miss google glasses knows my name. What an honor—and from someone starring in a video that's gotten like 32K shares on Twitter. I should ask for your autograph or something." He pulls my backpack, tugging me backward. I stop, inches from the girls' restroom by the gym. I can sneak in. I just have to duck backward. "How'd ya do it, Kole? How did you impress the star of the basketball team *and* Damian Wiles?"

"I need to get to class." I back up to the wall.

"It's cool. I just want to talk. Remember how we used to have PE together?" He punches my shoulder not so lightly. "Good times."

I flinch as the bell rings, shattering the calm of the hallway.

Kids reach for their backpacks, beginning the count down from four minutes to get to first period. This is my chance. Barry yanks his phone out of his back pocket. When his eyes settle on the cracked screen, I step a few tiles down and dash into the bathroom. The door closes before he can slip in after me.

Thank the stars. I'm safe. For now.

My chest heaves. There are a couple of girls standing at the sinks, applying makeup and fluffing their hair. "Hey, you're the girl from the video," one of them says, lipstick in hand. It's a god-awful shade of purple, but it looks pretty cool with her jet-black bob.

"Guess I'm going to get that a lot today."

"So what? Own that shit. The whole school is talking about you." She smushes her lips together and rubs the metallic purple around.

"It's better than a rumor about an STD, or something," the other girl says. She's fluffing her bleached hair and teasing it to oblivion. "It's about time we had something else to talk about. All I've heard about for the last three weeks is that stupid blog thing Damian started."

Pippa's voice echoes through my head. *Oh, feck me.*

I go to the mirror and take my braid out, pretending that redoing it is what I came in here for in the first place. "That stupid blog thing. Anyone figure out who's writing it yet?"

They shrug in unison. "Who cares? It's a good TV show and all, but he's taking it way too seriously."

I nod. They're not wrong. "Who do you guys ship?"

"You and Noah, obviously," the girl with the purple lips says. The other one heads into a stall, locking the door behind her. "It's kinda nice. The geek girl and the jock. Like something out of one of those classic '90s rom-coms."

OMG. "I mean who do you ship on *The Space Game*," I say, tying off the braid. That got awkward real quick. I really hope they don't notice the pink spreading across my face.

"Pipron. Liking Cedric would be like liking a brick or something. So boring. And the writers never did do a good enough job with his redemption arc, ya know? I'm Stormy, by the way," Purple Lips says.

I pull a few strands from my braid out, hoping it'll look perfectly messy. "Thank god! I mean, Stormy, it's about time I met someone who knows which side of the ship war is unsinkable." Wow. Look at me, talking like I'm some anon online. "Maybe the *Spacer* writer will do better with Cedric's arc. Wrap it up better than head-canon can."

"Hey! Cedric is hella cute!" the other girl calls. "And I like a bad boy. I mean, there's no good guys on that show anyway."

Stormy and I look at one another. I shake my head. "He's so freaking dumb. Remember that time he killed those Zorgs when they were unarmed? Lazy writing."

"So lazy. Plus his mere existence on the screen makes my sound go out. I swear it isn't a fluke."

I reach for my pink-lemonade chapstick, the brand I've been building since middle school, and the warning bell buzzes overhead. One minute to get to class. I'm gonna be so late. Who knows if Barry the Bastard is still lurking outside?

"Kole, you're Team Pipron? Dumb, but you should add it to the official tally." The girl in the stall flushes the toilet. "If you haven't already."

"Official tally?" Oh dang. *The bathroom by the gym. Spacer Port.*

"Check it. Show her, Ruby," Stormy says, nodding toward the stall in the corner.

"Yeah, um, please do." I swallow. My feet don't seem to care that this is one of those times when caution would be welcome. I get to the stall in two big steps and wait half a second. First of all, you only look in a public bathroom stall if you really, really have to go, and second of all, if I get worked up, this could get me in detention again. Or, more likely, back in my bed at 2:30.

On the walls, in thick, black Sharpie letters, two columns: *Pipron. Pipdric.* The tallies are almost nearly split, but there are a few more on the Pipdric side.

My heart falls. Pipron is the losing ship. What the hell kind of upside-down world is this? People are doing things with my show, with my life, that I don't approve of. And are they even watching the same show as I am? The love between Pippa and Byron is there. How do they not see it?

There's more covering the walls. Seven planets, all laid out exactly like the opening credits. Pictures of the *Snapdragon*, moon rocks, hearts, and someone's strangely accurate depictions of the main characters. Some dickwad drew a mustache on Byron. The eyes are all wrong, but I see what they were going for.

Above the toilet, someone wrote the *Spacer* URL. Someone added *sux* underneath it. Another someone added arrows leading to that and exclamation points.

Underneath, it reads, in fire-red letters, *Who is* ToTheStars, *Crystal Lake?*

There are a million names listed underneath, some with lines marked through them, some with a question mark. Michaela's on there with lots of question marks. Colin, even, though they forgot the *e* at the end of his last name. Amateurs.

None of the anti's are listed. No Hailey. No Raya. It had to be them that did this.

"Bye!" Ruby yells.

"Bye!" Stormy echoes. Within a second, I'm alone. Their footsteps echo down the now silent hallway. Good. Barry must have slunk back to his gopher hole.

I scan the wall. There's my name, smack-dab in the center of the massive list of students and tally marks. Three question marks follow it. I reach into my bag, fingers wrapping around my own black Sharpie and yanking it out into the open. I stare at it like it's a mosquito in amber.

Someone will find me out. It's going to happen sooner or later. But at least this buys me a little more time to dig myself out of this hole.

I whisper, "Bye Kole," as I put a thick line through my name. And, what the heck, let's take Colin out of this too. I add a thick line through his name, add the *e* at the end, and put the cap on the Sharpie.

No harm in hanging out in here a few more minutes. I'm already late anyway.

I sit.

My next *Spacer* entry will be an angry one, that's for sure. There's not enough data on my phone to be able to start it. If I leave now, snagging a pass and hiding my face as I approach, Mr. Reynaldo in American History shouldn't be too terrifying. What's scarier is knowing that all eyes will be on me when I walk through the classroom mid-lecture. A fate worse than death.

I swallow, gripping the straps of my bag. I have to go. One foot in front of the other. The walk through the bathroom and down the hall is long. It's quiet. It's lonely. I make it to the back of the classroom with only putting the pass on his desk. Reynaldo nods at me. I dodged a detention-sized bullet.

"Tell Noah he can ask me to the dance," the girl next to me whispers as soon as I sit down.

"We're here to learn about battles and shit, okay? Don't talk to me." I shoot her a look that I hope screams STFU and reach for my journal. I've already missed a lot of notes. Reynaldo is probably on page six by now.

She giggles. "Noah's so hot."

I clench my lips. *I will not respond.* He *is* hot. But he's so much more. Some lucky girl at this school is going to realize that soon and he won't give me a second look. I've got to find a way to talk to him.

Resting my head in my palm, I write the date on my paper. I'll have *Spacer* back soon. Then I won't have to worry about any of this dumb drama. I'll be *cute introvert girl* again.

I smile.

The girl next to me passes me a note. There's no avoiding the words.

I ship Nikmian even if no one else does.

Nikmian?

Nikole. Damian. Nikmian.

Mouth agape, I turn to her, whispering, "No!" That's the absolute worst ship name in the history of ships and actual real boats and everything even minutely related.

"Kole! Will that be another detention?" Reynaldo yells. I spin around, eyes on the PowerPoint. His eyes are bulging five minutes earlier than usual.

My eyes sting with moisture. If the school's given me a ship name, then things are very, very bad. I scribble notes from the PowerPoint in my journal, ripping my pristine paper in the process.

Shit. This is out of control. But there's no way in this chaotic galaxy that this dance with Damian will sink me.

I will *not* go down with this ship.

Hailey is already talking Mrs. Liu up when I get to Creative Writing. On the board, in big green bubble letters, is the due date for the lit mag submissions. Two days.

Well, Hailey will have something to submit. That's step one.

I set down my bag, no sign of Colin, Michaela, or Damian yet, and fish out the draft. Hailey will have to print it on her own lavender-scented paper this time. I drop it on her desk, facedown. She'll know what it is right away. If she needs an electronic copy, she'll have to type it out herself. That's right—revenge is a dish best served as a hard copy. Take that, Hailey.

"Don't forget to share it with me too," she says, glaring.

Fecking foiled. I scoff. "Whatever."

This needs to be done. I plop into my seat, my trusty notebook coming out of my backpack, followed by my orange pen. I set them on my desk, catching a peek at the spot where Colin wrote his phone number a few weeks ago.

He'd caught me off guard. I click my pen awake and draw a cute little border around the numbers. A few daisies and a couple of stars and it's even cuter than when it was just his messy boy handwriting.

I sit back and stare. I've got to talk to him too, except he never comes to class. I'm left that much closer to Mrs. Liu without the Great Wall of Colin standing between us. I narrowly avoid her eyes when she asks for readers for *Harrison Bergeron*, and I have no hidden place to snicker when she tells us our next assignment is to write a sci-fi story. That's the first asteroid I've narrowly missed today.

I *so* got this assignment.

Colin's in the hallway before Culinary. It's another dark sweater kind of day, paired with nice khakis and chucks. He must have come in late—not like him to miss a whole day, much less a class period. I pick up my feet and catch up to him, calling his name loud enough for him to hear through his earbuds. When I get closer, I yank on his sleeve and he pulls one out.

"Kole?" he says, dark brows lowered.

"Hey! When did you get here?" I shut my mouth. *Not to sound like I was looking for you or waiting for you or hoping to talk to you or anything.*

"At lunch. I was Skyping with a counselor from Yale."

Of course he adds *from Yale* at the end of that sentence. "Oh, I'm sure you're a shoo-in." And I also know that I'm a butt-kisser only when the occasion calls for it—like groveling. But no way am I on par with Damian for Colin's Butt-Kisser-of-the-Year.

Glancing around, I pick a spot next to the locker room and close to the drinking fountain with the crispest, coldest water, Counselor Falls. I motion for him to follow me out of the stampede of students headed to class. Kids always end up here when we want to get out of class. All you have to say is that you need to go see the counselor. People funnel by us, and some of them point. One even yells, "Where's Damian?" but Colin ignores them.

Deep breath. Okay, confidence, now's your time to shine. "I just need to say something to you. So, you know the other day when I said I was sorry I hadn't read your script?"

He bites the inside of his lip and glances around. He looks down his nose as his eyes settle on me. "Yeah?"

. . . And cue bravery. "Well, you forgot to revoke my reading privileges, and I read it."

"Whatever. It's too late for editing. They're turned in." He looks back to the crowd, almost stepping into it. "I put in the *no* for you. And, I didn't actually need help this time. So we don't need to talk about it."

I grab his arm, swallowing as he turns. "Okay, stop." That's not what I wanted to say, Colin. "I know you were in the cafeteria the other day. You saw what happened."

"I gotta get to class." He tries to take a step forward, but I step closer, blocking him from joining the other wildebeests.

I keep going. "So, you know I'm already going to the Harvest Ball with Damian."

"Weird choice," he says, shaking his head. "There's more to that, isn't there? I can tell something's up, and I'm not in on it. Does it have to do with his post about that site?"

Crappers. I double blink. "It's . . . legit. The dance thing." Gotta get him off the scent.

"Really, Kole?" He shakes his head, searing lasers into my face. "You don't want to tell me. I know he's gotten weird lately. But I can help. I know the guy well."

Colin's the only person in my inner circle who's not a part of this game. I need to keep it that way. Time for a good old subject change. "I know you guys aren't friends anymore. So, I know that you probably won't tell him if I—" The words that are about to come out of my mouth don't make sense, but somewhere in the last few weeks, Colin's crappy attitude and infrequent smiles became things I don't mind. "Let's work on today's assignment together. The specifics are in Google Classroom. Are you busy after school?" Sometimes the words that come out of this mouth are so bold that I think I'll need a shovel to dig myself out of the pile they leave me in. But I *do* want to hang with Colin.

"Okay." He scratches his head, and when he looks away, there's a tiny smile, like a crescent moon. "I have the NHS meeting after school, and then I'll be at the Bag O'Beans. We can write there."

A coffee shop. "Perfect." I match his little crescent with the moon's next phase. The Bag O'Beans is not far from campus, and I can work on my next blog entry till he gets there. That'll give my laptop about twenty minutes or so to gear up. "I'll see you then. And, we missed you in class today."

There's no *we*. I missed him.

He doesn't say anything else, just grins before he hides his face again. I smile back, watching like some kind of goon as he joins the rush to class.

Well, that's one apology down. Just have to get a hold of Noah now—

Wait.

I put a hand on the wall behind me.

Did I just ask Colin Clarke out?

October 7th, 2019

Dear *ToTheStars*:

Hello! It's Kasey with Galaxy Conventions again—just thought I'd check to see if you've had a chance to consider our request to come to the official Con-athon yet. We're hoping to have our guest list complete within the next week.

We'd love to have you—our guests are clamoring for more information on *Spacer*! Please let me know by the 25th if you'd like to join us!

Thank you,

Kasey Foster

Galaxy Conventions
Boston, MA

CHAPTER THIRTEEN

My hand shakes as I reach for my water and take a long sip. Kasey emailed. Again. Would be really nice to drop some of this ice down my shirt—I'm boiling in my own pot. Someone grinds coffee behind the counter of the Bag O'Beans, and a couple of girls laugh obnoxiously at the register. A baby fusses by the seat at the window, and random coffeehouse tunes float from the old speakers on the wall.

What do I say? I answer yes, and I'll have to form words around the cast of *The Space Game*. I'll have to answer fan questions and nod and grin when they say they like my work. What does one say to that? *Thanks, I do too?* Or, *Really, why?* These are serious considerations. I pick at the lemon bar in front of me. Some of those fans will love *Spacer*. Some of them won't.

And there will be no hiding it from Crystal Lake. I will have outed myself.

If I can actually go through with it all.

Yet another big *if*.

"Hogwash," I whisper, squishing part of the caramelized sugar down into the plate. How in the world do I summon the confidence to speak on a panel?

Colin's walking through the front door. I look up from my laptop, as heat rises to my face. Then it morphs into something different—something bubbly. I feel my eyes get a little wider. The corners of my mouth turn inward. This is . . . butterflies. How did I even muster up the confidence to invite Colin Clarke, Mr. Yale, future valedictorian, and all-around jerkface, to get coffee with me?

Maybe I can be brave. Sometimes. It's just buried under a whole lot of other things. But I guess that's what anxiety does.

I look up and wave. He nods when he sees me, his hair a bit in his eyes, his sweater not so nicely pressed anymore.

A little stress looks good on him. Something must have happened at the NHS meeting. He maneuvers his way through the tables as I sit up a little straighter and tidy the mess of napkins.

There's a tap on my shoulder. I turn around.

Abby Quinn. Another one of the anti's from middle school, but even she and Hailey are no longer friends. We had Earth Science together last year, and she would ignore me except for when she needed to look at someone's homework. She's also one of Will's biggest fangirls.

"Hi, Abby," I say. "Long time no talk." Does she not see that I'm about to be very busy blushing?

"Seriously? Now you're hanging out with Colin? Are you starting some kind of boyfriend collection or something, Kole?"

Asteroids. Gossips travels so fast at this school. "Very funny."

"I ship you and Damian. Two big geeks make for one happy dork couple. Your little dorklings will be quite adorkable."

"That was way too much dork in there, Abby." Let's turn this around. "Also, you don't know the half of it. I've got more boys' numbers in my phone, all hoping to be lucky enough to get to hang out with me." I pop a shoulder, the sarcasm thick.

"Liar. You're shooting for the stars with the Curve-Breaker,"

Abby whispers. The girls around her laugh. I turn away as Colin sits down. He glances at them but doesn't say anything. "I'm going to grab an Americano. You want one?"

"No, thanks. I'm good." I reach for my water, trying to maintain my composure. I'm not dating three guys. I haven't even gotten back to Noah. Probably blown any chance I had with him. And Damian is a big, fat load of nothing. "Want me to plug your computer in for you?"

"Sure, thanks." He turns and heads to the counter. I reach for his bag.

"Kole," I hear one of the girls whisper from behind me. "Kolllllllllllle."

I whip around, braid flailing, and whisper-yell, "Do you guys have anything better to do?" I glance at their computers, hoping to call them out for not working on homework.

Crap. My eyes widen. The page they're looking at: white text against a deep gray background. Stars that outline the top and fade away as the text scrolls down. *Spacer.* I whip around and minimize the email in front of me. If they get one hint of who I am, I can add them to the list of rotten Apples that know my identity.

I switch tabs to my inbox. There's one new message since Kasey's.

October 7th, 2019

Hello Kole,

I know we haven't had a chance to talk since the journalism room. Shame.

We need to make plans for this weekend. I'll be wearing

a white suit with gold accents. Mother said it'll bring out my eyes. Please dress to match.

Loving the new blog entries. It's fun to watch a real writer come up with ideas before she posts them. Keep up the Cedric work. It's really getting some good commentary.

Always here, always watching,

Damian

(Hope Noah's not too broken up about what happened in the cafeteria)

PS: Also, make sure Will's not really into Daisy, k?

PPS: And maybe make sure to find ways you can distract Will so I can talk to her.

Mother. Of. Pearl. I swallow. Hard.

Colin is heading back. I've got the Sanderson sisters cackling behind me. My phone buzzes. I glance at it—Will. He needs a house key. It's not my fault his dumb ass forgot it for the umpteenth time. He can go in through the loose window in the back like I've done a million times—I tell him I'm at coffee and stuff the phone under my thigh.

"So sci-fi this week?" Colin sits down, his drink sloshing a little over the rim and onto his hand. "Ow, shit." He sets the mug down and rubs the soft spot between his thumb and pointer finger. I glance around the table—there's a use for all these napkins.

"The great Colin Clarke swears?" I scoot around the side of the table. Close enough where I can hand him a few napkins and use the rest to wipe up the spill.

He dips the napkins in my cup of water I ordered before he got here and puts them to his hand. "Sorry. I need the caffeine."

"No. Don't be sorry. I don't mind. I've been known to drop a few F-bombs here and there. Sometimes they're the right way to say something, ya know?"

He nods. "Exactly."

A moment passes. "So, how do you feel about sci-fi?" I'm going to have to play like this is foreign territory. "World-building is a must, I hear."

"Honestly, I have no fucking idea. The only space stuff I've seen are the old Star Wars movies."

Attaboy. "That's a great start! The originals are classics, obviously, and so—"

He shakes his head. "No, not those. The ones that have the orange alien and that kid in the podracer who becomes Dark Vader."

Oh man. He doesn't mean the—

"And the cloned robots," he continues.

"Oh, Colin. The prequels." I cringe, but it turns into a smile pretty quickly. I officially, unapologetically get to tease Colin Clarke for the rest of existence. "You mean the shitty ones with all the CGI that came out at the turn of the millennium."

"Hey! I loved those." His eyes light up, the normally oh-so-straight lines around his mouth cracking into a semi-smile. His teeth are pearls, I swear on my reputation's grave. "When they went to that underwater world? Some of my best memories are playing that in the pool in fifth grade."

"Seriously?" Okay, can I completely fault him when my alarm clock is the theme song from *Wonder Pets*? I mean, I've got geek in my blood, but at least it's the right type. I sit up and rest my arms on the table, careful to avoid getting my sweater in the tiny spots of coffee. "Okay. I'm not sure how to break this to you, but a grievous wrong has been done to you. You need someone to tutor you in proper sci-fi."

"Now you sound like everyone at school."

"What do you mean?"

"Spaceships, planets, comets, time travel, cyborgs. That blog and ships, but not the kind that float in water, the kind about characters." He leans forward and takes his glasses off, resting them by my elbow. "The blog that I know you secretly like."

I smile. Yeah, I like it a lot. "I hear it's pretty good."

His face, without the glasses, is all angles and points. They come together at just the right spots, where the creases meet the freckles. I guess the sun, a long time ago, liked Colin's face too and left its mark.

I gotta stop looking. It's Colin. Enemy #1 since freshman year . . . and now . . . friend. Possibly . . . more?

What a plot twist.

I take my glasses off and set them on the other side of my laptop. Two can play at this game, but I can't forget who I'm talking to.

"And your eyes are twinkling again, just like every other time it's come up," he says, cracking a grin. His lips only open a little, but then he decides that maybe he doesn't mean to smile and all that's left are leafy-green irises with a ring of brown looking right back at me. When I look beyond him, the world is fuzzy. When I look back at him, it's still blurry—but not from the missing glasses. Something else.

"So I'm a fangirl. No big deal." First secret spilled for the afternoon.

"You don't need to apologize. It's kinda cute. Wish I had time for stuff like that, but if it's not about academics, or character build-ing, or organic chemistry, and finding ways to save the planet, then there's no time for it. The brochures all say junior year is the year Yale cares about the most." He takes a gulp from his steaming hot drink, and a couple of bubbles linger on his bottom lip. "Which means I have to care. And I do, I mean, I want to reverse climate change as much as everyone else."

"You're gonna save the planet?" I like that. Reminds me of how Pippa's father cured that disease in his backstory. I stare at Colin a little harder, my heart beating a little louder.

"That's the plan. No room for fun. Especially not as far as my parents are concerned."

Is it possible Colin faces the same crap I get from my mom at home? "You make time for the fun stuff. For escapism, Colin." I reach for my glasses and slip them across my face. I leave them a little farther down than I usually do. I mean, I can't just stick my finger right in the middle and push them farther up my nose in true geek-style in front of him. But Colin reaches for my face, and puts a finger right at the hinge. He doesn't pull away; his finger just kinda stays there, and he taps the thick black frame.

I stare. I swallow. I wish I had a drink.

"Those are mine. Funny how much our glasses look alike, huh?

I noticed that in class a few weeks ago." He's not moving his hand. It's practically on my face.

I fast blink, tucking in a corner of my mouth. Whoops. Grabbed the wrong ones. "But I can still see you in high def?"

"I'm nearsighted. Lucky enough to have an astigmatism in both eyes."

"Seriously?" I tuck a strand of hair that's fallen out of my braid behind my ear, the one that's not right next to his hand.

"Yeah. Guess it's my superpower. Crappy-Eyes Man."

Then I'm Crappy-Eyes Woman. "That's my exact problem too."

He smiles, like one of those uber-bright supernovas on the show, and tucks another strand of hair behind my ear in the most delicate move of the century. I swallow. I need water. Now. And someone's going to need to wipe me off the floor.

"So, can I have them back?" He pulls them from my face before I answer. I reach for my actual pair, on the other side of my computer, and then take a long sip of water.

"So, sci-fi?" he says.

"So sci-fi," I say. "It's really not intimidating; you just have to explain stuff enough so that Mrs. Liu won't—"

"Kole!"

That voice.

Will. I glance at the door, ripped from Colin's orbit. It's my brother, basketball jersey and all, in the Bag O'Beans. And Noah is right behind him, all backward baseball hat and cute, little curls falling out of it. They're coming at me, their own kind of asteroid field, and Noah sneaks a glance at who I'm with.

Will puts his hand out, expecting something this very instant.

"Can I have your house key, please?" He looks at Colin. "If I can interrupt."

"Yeah, of course. I just figured you'd bust open the back window." I reach into the pocket of my pants, stretching out a leg and kicking Colin's in the process.

He leans back, moving out of my atmosphere.

"Except Dad fixed that last weekend. Said he didn't want anyone creeping into his house." He narrows his eyes at Colin, who sits taller. "Especially people who have always been, up until this very moment and as far as I knew, *notorious fuckwads*. And that's an exact quote." He looks at me halfway through.

"Bullshit. Dad never said that." And, not fair. I only called Colin that once freshman year and it was in my journal. I glance at Noah, who's folded his arms over his chest. He looks at me, and all I see are chocolate eyes and perfect lips. I look back at Will. "Taking the big brother thing a little far here?"

He shakes his head and leans over the table toward me. "You've got a lot on your plate right now, Kole. Not sure this is where you need to be."

Yeah, I've got a lot going on. But I don't need Will here making it worse.

"We're studying. Chill out," Colin says, snarky-like. He leans back in his chair and folds his hands in front of him. "Take the act elsewhere."

"Hi, Will!" Abby yells from behind us. I'd forgotten she and her friends were here.

I glance to the side. Will doesn't look away from me.

"Things changed. Take the stupid-ass key, and go home, Will." I shove it into his hand. He grabs it and storms out of the coffee shop, nearly knocking over a few stools in the process. Noah follows him, no look back. No words. Nothing to me. When they leave, I see them talking through the window. They turn the corner.

I reach for my braid and pull the pieces apart. What a nasty pile of space junk I've flown into. My chance with Noah is melting away like the ice cubes in my water. Crumbling into the tiny bits left of my lemon bar.

"Sorry." I look at Colin, whose eyes are on me. "Will's just over-protective, that's all."

"Apparently he's an all-around douche-nozzle." Colin flips open his computer, firing it up.

"Can't disagree right now, but he has his moments," I mumble. It was a jerk move, sure, but there's more going on than Colin knows. What if Will won't help me with Daisy and Damian after this?

"You want to call it a day?" He logs in. "Or should we try to get something down?"

"No. It's fine. It's all fine," I say, wiggling my finger on the mouse to get my computer going again. If I say it enough, it'll be true, right?

"So, sci-fi?" he asks.

"So sci-fi," I say, reaching for the final bite of my lemon bar.

SPACER 3.12

Posted by: ToTheStars
Oct. 11, 2019. 8:12

Byron leans into the hatch, grabs Sebastian by the lapels, and shoves him against the bottom. He spits in Sebastian's face, a tiny bit of catharsis for everything this leech has put the *Snapdragon* through. "I will slide a knife into your heart someday, just like I did your father."

Grabbing the soup bowl, Byron tosses it over Sebastian's once perfect suit and throws the bowl into the hatch. It lands with a crack, soup and almost-chicken flying over Sebastian's face. Yeah, it's a bit much, but this man killed Byron's captain. Ain't nothing right in the stars about that.

With a slam of the hatch door and a beep of the locking mechanism, Byron stomps to the kitchen, grabs a spoon, and launches it at the bloody hatch. It ricochets off the door and slams into some crates, bent to a fraction of itself.

CHAPTER FOURTEEN

A date with Damian Wiles: a tableau.

A stretch limo with about two feet in between us. A white tux with gold accents, hair slicked back with bag balm, and a belt buckle bigger than last year's blue-ribbon apple pie. A hot-pink carnation in his pocket, a matching corsage tied around my wrist, tight enough to cut off circulation. Silence fills the air around us. Daisy Bringas will have to notice him tonight. This guy's a catch, and I feel like a cupcake. Half of my hair is braided around my head, the other half hanging down my back in loose curls. My rose-gold dress hugs my chest and poofs out at the waist, ending almost at my knees. It's pretty enough—Mom loved it when she picked it out—but I feel like a billboard in Vegas. I would have chosen navy or something that would allow me to blend into the wall, but navy wouldn't have matched my glorious date's outfit, as he reminded me in three different emails.

He insisted I wear contacts. And don't even get me started on the heels. They'll be off as soon as I can find a safe spot to stash them. I stretch out my fingers over the taffeta. My left hand will be blue in an hour.

This is not how I imagined my first dance of the school year to go: date-wise, clothing-wise, or transportation-wise.

The evening sky pours its orange-and-pink beams through

the clouds above, the sun settling into her favorite spot against the horizon. Before long she'll slip away, silent, and the night will grow cold. The fireflies will fade out, the dance in full swing. I'll be on Damian's arm, laughing.

I keep my eyes on the horizon. My phone is pressed right between my girls, digging into my ribs. Whoever invented strapless bras had their heart in the right place, but that's about it. All this thing does is pinch like a mofo.

I could text Michaela, but Damian's rules are strict: No friends at the ball. Nothing but making him seem like the best Apple in the bunch.

Michaela's with Will, Daisy, Noah, and his date. I tried to get them to ride in the limo with us, but Will scoffed at me and walked away. We're still in this *not really talking to each other* space since the coffee shop. I stretch out my fingers, the tips frigid. If it weren't for Damian, I'd be with them. Heck, I'd be here with Noah. But now I've yet to talk to them since the coffee shop.

Will Colin be there? He cranked out an awesome story the other day. Mine was good too, maybe even better, but it took a few run-throughs with Michaela and him. Too many other things were rattling around my brain.

I wiggle the ribbon around my wrist, coaxing the blood through. About two minutes until we're at the Apple Dumplin' Barn, the most popular orchard in Crystal Lake.

"A quick reminder. Showtime begins the second the door opens. We'll meet up with your brother as soon as we spot him. You're my in, so you get to distract him and the others while I chat with Daisy." Damian reaches over and touches my arm. I flinch, all the way to the door. "Make sense, *ma chérie?*"

"Whatever. Let's just get this stupid night over with." I cross my arms, pushing the phone farther against my ribs. I guess Damian's not going to be the only pain I'm dealing with tonight. I'll do what he wants, if it gets him to drop this whole charade. And if not . . . I haven't figured that part out yet.

The limo pulls into the circular dirt driveway, kicking up dust behind us. The orchard is stunning no matter the season: twinkle lights line the road, tree branches dangle over the pathway with skeleton fingers, their nails polished in reds and oranges, browns and yellows. Most leaves have fallen to the ground, but a few hang on, hoping for one last dance. The oversized barn doors are propped open, and kids lean against the walls, drinks in hand. "This Is America" radiates through the air, and the bodies inside bump and jive to the beat through the entrance way. A couple of girls I recognize from Algebra whisper sweet nothings in one corner, while a group of kids I've seen in the cafeteria a few times gather around the punch bowl. Shoot, even some of the gamers club have made it almost through the doorway. One thing catches me in a place I didn't expect: it actually looks like fun.

But . . . Damian. I glance at him. He's playing with his Apple watch. How long until he makes me laugh at a joke loud enough for his lady-love?

God. Poor Daisy Bringas, poor Daisy Buchanan. Both objects of affection for some guy who tries too hard to get their attention.

"All right, my love. You ready?" Damian puts a hand out to me as the Hummer slows to a stop. He opens his door and I take his hand.

Game on.

After five nauseating spins around the dance floor, one that got too-close-to-boobs close, Damian decides to grab some punch. The barn is probably hoping we'll think it's some kind of wine knockoff, but it's probably just watered-down Juicy Juice. It's a nice venue, but skimping on the punch is something I can pretty much count on at any of Crystal Lake's dances, regardless of how much money walks through its hallways.

"Have you texted them? Where are they?" Damian asks, punch in hand and eyes scanning the room. It's nearly 8:30, pitch-black outside, and still no sign of Will and the others.

"Like I have any idea? You've been making me dance," I mumble.

"Wait, *ma chérie*, look." Damian points.

There they are, walking through the barn doors. Noah looks perfect even with another girl I can't recognize yet on his arm, Michaela is even more stunning in a gown, and Will, well, he looks pretty sharp, but he's still on my shit-list until he apologizes for what happened at the Bag O'Beans to my face. I have to be the one to break the ice between us now.

Daisy hangs on Will's arm, and I have to all but grab Damian to get him from running over there. "Not yet," I mouth to him. I have to figure out how to play this first.

Damian stands up straight, wrapping his arm around my shoulder. I inch closer as he yells against my hair, pointing toward the other end of the dance floor. "See her? Right under the green exit sign. Time to wow her." That's Daisy all right—skintight dress, standing really close, like yucky close, to my brother. She looks gorgeous, but I have to go split them apart. Damian nudges me. "Got your A game, Pippa?"

I choke down bile—I can't do this yet. Make poor Daisy have

to hang out with this dude? And he just called me Pippa, which is taking it too far. I throw back the rest of the punch, screaming a battle cry through my head, like Aragorn before the gates of Mordor.

For *Spacer*.

"Wait, Damian, we dance first. Let them come to us. People don't like it when others are too eager . . . it's off-putting. I know Michaela will head over here as soon as she can." I pull him to the dance floor by the lapel and tug him way too close. I dance like there's nothing but me and the stars on this dance floor. Like there's no one to hear me screaming in my head. Like there's nothing more to this than me and this guy I really like out here. But it's all a big fat lie.

Pippa would never do this. Not long ago, I would never have done this.

By the time the next song begins, Michaela has found her way to us. My moves get smoother, the beat finding its way into my bones and emanating through my limbs. Will and Daisy join, grinding their way over to us, but Will doesn't really make eye contact with me. Where's Noah? Elsewhere, I guess. With a girl I couldn't recognize through eyes that throb more the longer I'm out here.

Damian grabs my face, looks me in the eyes, and says, "You're making me look good. She keeps looking at me."

Is she? I'll have to pay better attention. I dance harder. Faster. Wilder. I dance until sweat lines my forehead and makeup is smudged under my eyes, lining my fingers more each time I wipe it. My dress grows warmer as the crowd moves in. My contacts sting. Damian's gotten a little too bold with his hands more than once; I've had to pry them off, but, thank the stars, he's right—it's working. Daisy keeps glancing at me and Damian, and every once in a while, Damian flashes her a jack-o'-lantern grin.

I think she might actually be noticing him?

Spotlights circle the dance floor, and just as the crowd separates, I lock eyes with Noah. I spin to a stop, my chest heaving and heart pumping. Even if Damian would allow it, I couldn't apologize for the cafeteria now—for not being here with Noah. The sea of jiving bodies is impassable. Damian puts a hand on my hip. I glance away before the blush crawls to my cheeks.

All this for *Spacer*.

"Time to take a little break, *ma chérie*," Damian yells over the *thump thump* of the bass. Thankfully. I need a drink. And a trip to the bathroom. Then I can check my makeup mess and chuck these heels in the pile of banished footwear in the corner. He puts his hand way too low as he leads me out of the crowd. "Time to drain the lizard, you know?"

"No, I don't know, Damian." I don't hide the cringe this time. On the way to the bathroom, I grab a cup of water and down it. I toss it in the trash can in what may be the first time I've ever made it in.

"Find a way to get me to talk to her while I'm gone. See how she keeps checking me out? She's totally feeling it. Will's just a cover; it's so obvious. Girls think they're so clever." He laughs until the bathroom door is closed behind him.

God, he's from another planet. I slip into the girls' room, nudging past a few others. I flip my hair off my shoulders and fan my neck, hoping the sweat takes a quick reprieve. Once the makeup circles are tamed, I turn to the stalls and slip in. My business takes all of a minute, but halfway through, my bladder freezes up. More girls came in and one's voice sends a shudder through my bones—the kind I get when cold air hits my too-sensitive tooth.

"How does one even dance to something like Bazzi? He's got no soul. Let's request some Ariana."

Hailey is here, chatting with someone else. Another anti.

I close my eyes. *Please, gods above, let me pee again.* Worse time ever to have a shy bladder. I count to ten in my head.

"So, is Colin a good kisser?"

My eyes shoot open. *Motherfucker.*

Giggles. "Stop it! I'm not kissing him. Well, unless . . . I mean, we'll see where the night goes. I'm open to it."

I peek in the crack between the door and the stall.

Raya. Colin came to the dance with Raya. And I was too hopped up on the dance floor with Damian to notice he's here.

Okay. This sucks ass. They keep talking about Colin, and Hailey's date. Barry. The same Barry who tried to hunt me down in the hallway. How special. I stand, my bladder done for the night. I pull up my spanx, readjust my worthless strapless bra, and kick the flusher. I poof out my skirt, stick some toilet paper down my shirt to make things a little drier, and readjust my phone.

The voices resume once the flush is finished. "He likes Kole Miller."

Hailey sucks in her breath. "For real? I thought he was just entertaining her *pay attention to me schtick* in class."

"Nope. On Monday, let's think up something good to put in *Spacer* Port. Have you seen her out there? It's like she's never danced in her life."

Asteroids. The bathroom. And, my dancing?

"We have to get the okay from Damian first. It'll be cake; I know how to play him," Hailey adds.

But also . . . Colin likes me? That's the best thing I've ever heard.

I unlock the door, louder than necessary, and kick it open as a wave of anxiety courses through me. The door flies. I go to an empty sink, aware of their eyes locked on my back. I grit my teeth.

"This sweaty mess?" Hailey laughs, looking me up and down.

"Sounds like it's this chick." I wash my hands and before I can make it to the dryer and flick my wet fingers at Hailey. I glance at Raya, who is blushing and staring at her feet.

"Bitch!" Hailey says.

I hightail it out the door before she punches me. It takes a second for my eyes to adjust to the darkness in the barn again, and damn these stupid contacts; they're starting to hurt. I catch sight of Damian, locked in a dark corner with Daisy and a few other couples. Good. He found his moment. Will catches my eye over at the punch table. He's putting back a drink and just kind of waiting. He shrugs his shoulders at me, all nonchalant, before watching the dancers.

All right, well, this is what Damian wanted. Still, it seems too easy. He's got to have something more planned. I scan the crowd. Time to sneak away and find Michaela; I need a game plan for Monday.

"Hey, Kole."

I flip around. Colin.

"Hey," I say. Holy cinnamon rolls, Batman. A black suit. Silver bow tie. Black shirt. Pants a tad too short, shoes a tad too pointed, his hair perfectly coiffed. It lays at angles I could never find, even with my TI-84. And his glasses . . . I miss mine.

"You look amazing," he says, hands in his pockets. "That color is great."

"Thanks. You look . . . cute." I swallow, prying my eyes from his face. "You waiting for Raya?"

He shrugs.

"Good, then come outside with me." I don't really care what exactly he meant by that shrug. I just need some air before my face meets the floor. Raya and Hailey are going to make things even worse. I need some cold air to figure this out. I grab him by the elbow and drag him outside and through the twinkle light picnic tables, past the old wooden fence that lines the orchard, and into the trees. I glance back at the doors, see that Damian is still chatting up Daisy by the entrance, and keep walking. Chilly leaf corpses crunch under my bare feet, my heels long since discarded. It's even colder in the trees, even darker, but I stop at a spot that's not too far in.

"Kole, what's going on?" Colin says, coming to a stop about four trees in.

"I just need to breathe. Like, seriously. This night is too much." I run my hands up and down my arms, careful not to let branches grab my dress. Once, years ago, Will told me there were witches here, and a part of me still thinks that might be true.

"And this is going to help." Colin's voice is coated in disbelief. The music pumping through the air switches, the beat lowering and tempo slowing. The words are too muffled to be heard.

"Try not to sound so incredulous. I just need to get out," I say.

He smiles. He caught it. I just used my first SAT word in front of him. I match his smile, my first real one tonight.

Goose bumps jump from my skin, all the way down to my toes. This was a bad idea. But at least Damian and Noah and Will and Hailey are on the other side of the wall. And at least I'm in a place where the air doesn't feel like steamed clams.

Colin looks at me like I've grown three heads. "Are you aware that your eyes are beet red?"

I reach to rub them but stop. More makeup smudges will only make it worse. "It's the stupid contacts. Can it be time to call it a night yet?" I look up at the sky. "I think the stars are aligning in some weird pattern that bodes my doom."

He smiles and glances up at them. "You wouldn't be Kole Miller if you didn't find a hyperbolic way to express your thoughts."

"You wouldn't be Colin Clarke if you didn't use the word *hyperbolic*, smart-ass."

"An SAT word, my thirteenth one today. It's seared on my brain, along with incredulous." He takes off his glasses and offers them to me, the music from the barn building to something quiet, and slow. "You can borrow these. I can find my way around."

I almost grab them, but Damian sure as heck would notice if I came back with glasses. And Raya too. "Your date might not appreciate that."

"Yeah, maybe not. Then how about this." He reaches for one of my arms and twists it around my head, uncomfortably, until I realize he wants me to spin around. I spin so fast my hair flies off my shoulders, my skirt filling with autumn air and poofing out around me. By the time I'm done twirling, he's pulled me into his chest, one arm around my waist. The other holds my hand in his. I fan out my fingers, and he cups them against his chest. "A dance."

A super close, super private dance in the dark. With Colin. I nod, no time to overthink. I'm infinitely warmer than I was a second ago. We move our feet, rustling through the leaves, finding rhythm a couple of steps in. I turn my head into his neck. He smells like pine needles, and cologne, as he always does, but I don't mind, not even a little. It's not like class. It's just me and him and the skeleton branches around us, the moon watching with her Cheshire grin.

His breath is against my hair. The crisp air fills my lungs and brings me back to life. Now that the crowd is gone, I can think again.

So what about Damian and Noah. So what about Hailey and my stupid brother and this stupid game.

But, *Spacer*.

I feel the familiar wave closing in on my chest. It's still on the line, but only for a few more hours. For a tiny while I'm here, dancing away the night without anyone else's eyes but Colin Clarke's.

I move closer to his neck, and I think he moves into me too. Stars, this is too real—me and him and the trees and the dark, moving in unison through the galaxy.

The song fades out, and the DJ drones on about something I can't make out. I move my face closer to Colin's, hoping he'll catch the hint that maybe closer is where I want to be. I work my hand up his chest, feeling it rise under my palm, and reach his neck. His skin is chilly, the hair at the bottom of his neck so very soft. I put a finger on one of the perfect little curls.

He turns his face to me, swallowing. "Kole," he whispers.

I write moments like this all the time and, now that I hear my name in Colin's very real voice, it feels like maybe I could have my own love story someday. Not just something I find in my imagination and put down in a blog somewhere. A real romance.

His lips are very close to mine. Do they taste as nice as I think they will? I wonder what he's thinking, and if my name in his voice is enough to take away all the frustrations that have been written into this night. He leans closer to me, head angled, and I reach up to meet him.

"Kole!"

I jump away.

Colin brushes a hand behind his ear, putting back the curl I was touching.

I heave a sigh at the sky. I'm so fecking tired of hearing my name yelled. My face burns, but it's not from embarrassment. I look to the barn: Damian. Daisy's behind him, Hailey, Raya, a few other kids. Likely Will, which means likely Noah.

I guess Daisy got tired of talking to Damian. But why does it have to be now, at this very perfect moment?

"Oh, um, sorry, Damian," I say. Back to the act, anger and all.

But . . . am I sorry though? Colin's the rightest thing about this night.

"Why are you out here with him?" Damian yells, standing at the picnic tables.

I swallow. "Did something go wrong?" I thought he wanted time with Daisy? Isn't this a part of his grand scheme?

"We just needed some air, Damian." Colin fills his words with venom. He turns to me, whispering, "It's okay. Let's just go back in."

"Mind your effing business, Colin. And stay out of mine," Damian grunts.

I nod at Colin and we traipse through the dead leaves, making our way to the old wooden fence. I barely care this time when the branches reach out and rip at my dress, dragging their sharp edges on my arms and ripping little scratches into my skin. I try not to flinch when I step on a rock. That'll be another stupid bruise.

By the time we get to Daisy and Damian, Raya's latched onto Colin's side. He puts an arm haphazardly about her waist, and they start to walk into the barn along with other kids. He glances back at me, briefly. I turn to Damian.

"Shall we go to the dance, *ma chérie*?" Damian tries to act like he's flirting, but his eyes are lying. He's breathing heavy, tapping a foot, and loosening his collar. His lips are practically snarling.

Daisy looks me up and down. I stand by Damian, back to pretending he's my sugar daddy. But my eyes are lined with water, fingers trembling.

"Damian, if this chick's your date, why was she out here with the Curve-Breaker?" Daisy asks, pointing at Colin. The tiny crowd out here turns at our conversation. Colin and Raya turn back to us. That's Crystal Lake; the tiniest bit of drama and they're flies on shit. "I mean, you said you guys were getting serious, right?"

Will comes up behind Daisy and stands over her shoulder. He's looking at me so intensely that I think I might have grown colder. I glance at Colin, whose brow is so low, his stare so intense, that I feel like I might crumble under it. I glance at my feet, but I can feel Damian look at me with fire in his eyes before he speaks. "We are, right Kole? Like, hot and heavy?"

Add Colin to the list of people I'm lying to tonight. But I have to save this. "Kinda? I mean, Damian *is* the hottest guy at school. I'm so lucky." The words come out monotone. I try to look at him like he's a million bucks, but it's never been harder than in this moment. I blink back hot, angry tears. Fire blazes on my arms from little pink scratches.

I've always been a good storyteller, but I've never been a good liar. I suck in a breath. They're going to find out the truth.

"Damian, this doesn't seem right." Daisy grabs my arm, staring into me with flying-saucer eyes. "What's going on?"

"I—" How can I lie to her? I mean, I *have* been here with him all night. "Damian is the cutest guy in all of Crystal Lake, and he's the best dancer and the very best writer in Creative Writing," I mumble. I can feel Colin's disgusted look.

"Kole—" he starts, stopping when I shoot him a look. I shake my head slightly. Please let this stop, now.

"Gosh, Kole! You suck so hard at this!" Damian stomps his feet and then moves between Daisy and me. "Look, everything I've done has been for you, Daisy. I just wanted you to notice me. Right, Kole?"

"Right," I squeak. Finally, some truth.

He keeps his eyes on her, the crowd building around us. "It's just because I love you so much. It's just like one of those things you can tell, you know? I believe Jesus put you in my life just at this moment so that we can be together. I've even written you a ten-page ode. I'm emailing it to you right now." He whips out his phone and furiously begins to type.

Did he seriously just drop the J-word about a girl he barely knows? "Damian, you are such a creeper!" I say before I can stop. "Just because you like her doesn't mean you get to manipulate your way into a moment with her—and the other people you dragged into this? Me? My brother?"

Shit. I just kept talking, didn't I? I see Will put a hand to his head. Even he knows I need to shut up.

"Um . . ." Daisy backs away. She flicks her long dark hair off her shoulder, and Damian shoots me a look. She looks to her girlfriends and then back at me.

Damian glares.

"No, no, Daisy, it's—Damian is just—" I stop. God. Is this worth it? Continuing to lie to her? He's only going to get worse. I mean, imagine actually dating him? I have to save her. "He's just a big fat liar."

Damian is on fire, his eyes bulging out of his head.

"I'm going to destroy you and your dumb little story," he whispers, shaking his head.

I don't lower my voice. I get that he's mad. I get that I'm going against what I promised, but Daisy shouldn't be a part of this anymore. I'll figure the rest out in a minute. "You think that just because you like someone, or some*thing,* that means you own it." Shit. I'm veering into *The Space Game.* "Like Daisy here. You don't just get to manipulate your way to her. You, Damian, are just a fan of something that doesn't like you back and you can't handle it."

"Kole Miller, you're going to be ruined." Damian starts to raise his voice, but Daisy cuts him off.

"What the fuck is she talking about, Damian? You were just telling me about your Pokémon and now she's freaking out?" Daisy's face crinkles up.

Pokémon? I mean, weird flex, but if that's his game and she's into it, then cool.

"That's what makes us soul mates—I can tell we're perfect for each other," he squeals. "We have so much in common!"

Oh my god. Toxicity at its finest. "Daisy, if I were you, I'd get far away from this whole dumpster fire here." I swing my arms out in front of me, at the hot mess this night has become.

"Good advice. I don't know what you've got going on here, Damian, but you need to take out your trash." She looks me up and down, turns, and stomps into the barn, the sound of her heels disappearing into the music.

That wasn't cool. But I'd be weirded out by this situation too. Still. "Rude!" I yell after her as she blazes past Will.

"Kole, we need to go." Will's voice is low. He's pissed. "Now."

"Follow Daisy." A shiver rattles through me as Damian fumes. "Just please go."

He doesn't move.

"I got this." I'm not sure I do got this. I didn't keep up the game. And now I'm going to lose *Spacer*.

"Nah. I'll stay here." Will crosses his arms. "If you need me."

"Whatever." I stand up a little taller.

"You've literally ruined everything!" Damian yells.

"Damian," I say, ignoring what's now an even bigger crowd. "It seemed like she was into you until just now. Just be normal; you don't have to go all stalker on someone to get her to want to talk to you. Just be chill." I can try to be a supportive friend here—a last-ditch effort to salvage things.

"No, she won't, Kole! This is the fifth time I've tried to get her to go out with me and it's the closest I've gotten. And you didn't hold up your end of the bargain, not even close. Disappearing with Colin? Were you even trying to make this work?"

I glance at Colin, in the middle of the crowd. He starts to say something, but I don't wait. "I just wanted to give you two space. Things looked like they were progressing!"

"You were wrong. It's time, butterfly. I'm putting up my post." Damian begins to type into his phone. The little boop sounds are louder than the music. He lowers his voice. "I wonder how long it'll take this gossip to spread to everyone. Faster than a handsome Squidward meme I bet."

He's going to tell them. They'll laugh at me even more than they did after the promposal gone wrong. Everything will get worse. "No, please." My mouth tightens, and I bite my bottom lip. I force my eyes closed, my head spiraling. There's an end to this, but it's going to hurt. "Don't do this."

"It's over. You didn't hold up your end of this."

Okay, I'm officially and unapologetically pissed. I reach for his phone, but he pulls away, yanking free when I grab his elbow. Around us, the crowd starts to whisper in tiny spurts of words I barely make out. *Blog? Her? A nobody?*

They're figuring it out.

Damian, this little gremlin, this warped Rumpelstiltskin, thinks he can destroy everything I've worked for? The ground starts to spin beneath me, but my eyes lock on Damian's phone. I take the few steps closer, trying to get a glance. Blood pounds in my ears.

"All right, who wants to hear a truth?" Damian yells. The crowd collectively gasps, a few of them laughing.

Fiery tears blaze down my cheeks. Feck this all to the stars and back.

It's time for a truth.

Mine.

I become Byron Swift, Captain of the *Snapdragon*, and all-around intergalactic badass. Someone who doesn't take shit from the stars or the other sky rovers or even his own brother. Someone who, when the stars don't align just right, makes them bend into formation. I throw back my arm, fist raised, and, as hard as possible, launch my knuckles into Damian's left cheekbone. His phone flies from his hand, landing somewhere in the trees. Comets shoot up my arm and I clutch my wrist to my chest. "Take that, douche-wad!"

He falls back into the crowd, staggering, landing on his butt. He yells something about pain and broken and blood and payback, but I'm standing over him, silent. I put my knuckles to my lips. Holy balls, that hurts. Even my shoulder is throbbing. But, holy crap, did that feel so fecking good to see his face break.

"Kole!" It's Will. But I pull away when he tries to reach for me. I take a few steps back as kids try to help Damian up. They keep their eyes on me, except for a few.

I have to say something. "What are you all staring at? Go to your dance. Go, drink punch." I wave my hands at the doors, feeling the right words slip away. "Go laugh, and flirt, and whatever."

Damian stands. The crowd is silent. I hold my hands out, ignoring the throbbing pain radiating up my arm. I lock eyes with Colin for a split second. Noah's watching, but I don't give a shit. There's more. There's Hailey. There's Raya. There's most of the junior class. Faces I know and faces I want to forget.

"What the fuck is up with her?" someone asks rather loudly.

I breathe in so deep that my shoulders rise. It's time to end this. "What the fuck is up with me is that I've been under this a-hole's foot for weeks now. So take it all in, folks. Decide if he deserved every bit of that punch. Spoiler alert: he did." I have to take this situation by the balls. "I'm writing *Spacer*."

My chest may be heaving, tears may be lining my cheeks, but my voice didn't shake.

"I'm *ToTheStars*. The mystery is solved." I don't look away as they turn to one another, whispering.

I glance at Damian. I did it. I smashed his hold on me. And his nose too.

Instead of walking through the crowd, I storm into the orchard, my feet burning fire into the dead leaves.

I've got this.

I've *so* got this.

The trees wrap around me as I disappear into them. It's time for the whole fecking world to know *Spacer* is mine.

I whip out my phone. It's time to send that email.

October 12th, 2019

Hello Kasey,

I'm sorry to keep you waiting. I'll come to the convention.

Send me the details,

Kole Miller

ToTheStars

Sent from my iPhone

The email zips through the interwebs faster than I can hit undo. I had to send it. I just admitted to the whole school that *Spacer* is mine in a tattered prom dress, scratches up and down my arms, barefoot and freezing my ass off—and my voice didn't even shake. No quiver. So maybe I can handle a con? I don't know. I haven't thought that far ahead yet. I just know that I had to reply and I had to do it now before I let the wave wash over me and drown my courage.

I stand on the edge of the orchard. Cars zip past, and I keep to the trees. I just told the whole school the truth. I punched Damian. I almost kissed Colin. He knows who I am. And now I'm going to sit on a panel.

My stomach flips. *Yikes.*

"Kole!" Someone yells, but it's too dark to tell where the call is coming from. As a car gets closer, and the high beams cease their assault of my eyeballs, I recognize Mom's Suburban.

Will.

I rush out of the trees, flagging him down with the hand that's not throbbing. Thank the stars. He's a good brother—sometimes a bit much, but his heart tends to be in the right place. Especially if there's pizza.

"Get in," he yells, leaning over to open the door for me. I jump into the passenger seat and flip my hair off my shoulders. With Daisy missing, there's one extra seat. I buckle in, favoring my right hand. It's literally throbbing. "Quite the night, huh?"

"Can we please just go home? I really don't want to talk." But I have to say something. "Except that I'm sorry about Daisy. I didn't mean to ruin your date."

"Whatever." He shrugs. "I wasn't too into her. But, have I not taught you how to throw a proper punch? That was hard to watch. You're going to need ice." He chuckles. "But watching Damian's face break was pretty fucking awesome."

"It was fucking amazing! That little goblin will never mess with us again!" Michaela says from the back. "How's *Spacer*? Is it okay?"

I smile. "Yes. And that sure as heck was amazing." I'm too hopped up to look back at her or even worry about the coding club. If he even tries, I'll punch him again. I run a finger over my bruising knuckles. Even if this is gonna take a while to heal.

Will hits about fifty, skating around the road like he's soaring through the sky. I lean my head back and close my eyes. How do I face everyone on Monday? I've got one day to figure that out.

"Noah!" Someone giggles in the back seat. I turn around. It's him. And . . . Lauren, who is, apparently, no longer grounded. They're locked in some kind of an embrace. I couldn't tell who she was at the dance. Great choice, Noah. Michaela's stuffed against the window, trying her hardest to scoot away. She shoots me a look that screams WTF.

I close my eyes again. I'm going to have to pretend like they're not back there, flirting rather loudly, and making this night even more ridiculous. The road stretches out before us. If I keep quiet enough, I can pretend I'm floating through space, Pippa and Byron on either side of me, Captain Worley at the helm, and nothing but the dark before us.

"Pick a world, Kole." Pippa turns to me. "I'll take you wherever you want."

The seven planets are laid out before the massive window of the Snapdragon. *I choose the golden one. I point. "Aureus."*

"Quartermaster, get us there in under three turns of my wheel," Pippa commands Byron.

"Aye-aye," Byron says, fingers racing across the command table. The engines of the Snapdragon *deepen, their groan sounding through the skies.*

"When my mom died, Dad said he needed to get out. And that's what got us here, in Crystal Lake," Noah says, under his breath. "I like it here."

Now wait just a minute. This conversation sounds . . . familiar.

"Oh, I'm so sorry! Must be unbearable to be without her," Lauren whispers.

"I don't mind talking about it with you," Noah says. "Or being here."

My eyes shoot open. Noah is using the same lines he used on me. I whip around and glare at him. Lauren shoots me a death ray. *I* am intruding on *her* precious little moment.

"Really, Noah?" I say, ignoring her. "I think I know how you're hoping this will end." A big fat make-out session. Just like with me.

He clenches his mouth. "Hey, Kole, remember, you left me dateless in the cafeteria, no explanation. Don't get judgy on me."

"I had to. It's not my fault you asked me in front of the whole fecking school. Which, by the way, is the worst way to ask me, ever." Okay, that was kinda harsh, but I'm having A NIGHT. "You don't even know the whole story."

"Pretty sure we all do now." He reaches for Lauren's hand and she giggles.

OMG.

What a tool.

"Plus, hello, dancing with yet another guy when you were there with Damian? How many boyfriends does one girl need, Kole?" Lauren asks.

"Please. Do you have any idea that your Casanova here used those lines—" I cut myself off. I could tell her. Maybe I should, but he's talking about his mom, and, yeah, taking advantage of it, but maybe that's his twisted way of grieving?

"I mean, Colin Clarke? How the heck you got on his radar is beyond me." Lauren looks to Noah, laughing. He drops his shoulders, turns from us, and rests his elbow on the door. He's not even looking at Lauren.

"Hey guys? Look at the roadkill over there—I think it used to be a possum. I've never seen so much blood," Will says loudly.

Michaela turns to the window, two hands on the glass. "Where?"

Good. He's changing the subject. I flip back to the front seat.

Will reaches for the radio and turns the music up. I can't hear Lauren if she's still talking.

See, a good brother.

Can this night please be over?

CHAPTER FIFTEEN

The funny thing about having everyone's eyes on you is that you get to a point where you just don't care, and once you make that choice, you realize everything you do is laced with *feck it*. Especially if the others aren't laughing. And they aren't. Yet.

At least, that's how I'm hoping this works. I mean, the trick to walking through the hall without being self-conscious is to walk fast. That's the first thing I figured out. And I had my music in, so that helped.

Creative Writing is cold. I guess that's just how this class goes. I don't even care anymore. I slam my book bag on my desk (not intentional), and in comes Damian. His nose looks like an eggplant. I quickly glance away while I get my things out and stifle a chuckle. His face is full-on because of me. Victory is a powerful poison, shooting little boastful blasts through my head.

I won at Damian's game.

Taking my seat, I pull out my notebook and my gooey, multi-colored pens. I begin to draw a *Spacer* doodle in one corner as Michaela walks in. She glances at Damian and matches my chuckle.

Next comes Hailey, heels clicking. Hair bouncing. Eyes narrowed at me. She walks by, intentionally bumping my shoulder with her bag, and says, rather loudly, "Team *Nikmian*."

My mouth falls open. I shake my head as she takes her seat.

STILL THE WORLD'S WORST SHIP NAME. "Behind on current events? That's no longer a thing, Hailey."

"Still a great name. Still a great couple." She glances at Damian.

"Eff you all," he says, slumping lower in his chair.

I flip back to my seat. I've gotta deal with her. And, according to the whiteboard, the lit mag draft is what we're looking at today. *My* work with *her* name on it. Asteroids. There's still work ahead of me. I've gotta find a way to get to Hailey.

Colin throws his bag down and slides into his seat after a quick glance at me. I smile, but I'm not sure he caught it. I'm not sure how to play this yet—I didn't hear from him all weekend. Every time I considered texting, my thumbs just kinda sat there and didn't listen when I told them to get typing. I guess they were waiting on me to find the right words, but they never came.

"Apples! I'm passing around our gorgeous *Literary Magazine* draft. I want to hear your thoughts, but I think it's even more beautiful than last year." Mrs. Liu hands us each a copy, *The Apple Literary Magazine* in sprawling cursive characters on the front, but I stare, fingers toying with the cover. If I open this, I'll see Hailey's name at the top of my work.

At least I can look at the other entries. I flip through, quickly. It's mostly seniors, but Colin has one in here, and a few others from class.

"Would anyone like to read their piece?" Liu asks in her sugary-sweet voice.

No. No. Please.

Hailey's hand flies up. Naturally.

"Hailey! Come on up." Liu takes a seat while Hailey comes to the podium. She's got her copy in one arm. She sets it down, licks a delicate finger, and finds the page with *her* poem on it. She clears her throat, steals a glance at me, and begins to read like it's the Gettysburg Address, pausing at the end of every line and staring into our souls. My stomach rumbles about halfway through, and I sit up. I only steal one tiny glance at the back of Colin's head. His curls look dashing today.

Hailey's—my—poem ends. I look at Mrs. Liu while a few people clap. Liu's eyes are rimmed with water, one hand over her heart. She bought Hailey's bullshit, hook, line, and plagiarism.

I shoot my hand up. "I have a question, Hailey. What inspired you to write something so moving? I mean, that was exceptional."

She fast blinks. "Why, Kole, since you asked, it's something I've been working on since freshman year—I know every word like the Scripture, and I knew the lit mag was where it was meant to be. I couldn't be prouder." She glances at Liu. "The mag is the most indomitable publication at our school."

Indomitable. *Unbeatable.*

Unlike you, Hailey.

"Not better than the newspaper," Damian mumbles.

"No, I mean, how did you come up with these words? The way you put them together, syllable by syllable. It's in perfect tetrameter, right?" I cock my head, lining my voice with curiosity.

"Very astute, Kole!" Mrs. Liu chimes in.

"Well, yes, it is." Hailey adjusts her stance. "And the words—what can I say? They just came to me, almost like a dream. I felt like Plath."

"A dream. That makes sense." I nod. "If only we all dreamed like you, Hailey."

At this point, Colin turns to me, an eyebrow lifted. "What are you doing?" he whispers.

I shoot him a quick and effective side-eye.

"If only." Hailey closes her book and looks to Liu.

"Wait—" Where exactly am I going with this? They all turn, Hailey gazing daggers at me. "What was that last line again? You should be able to recall it, right, since you wrote it? The beat always helps with memorization. That line was the—"

"Pinnacle. The *pinnacle* of poetry," Colin finishes, staring intently at Hailey too. He jots something down in his notebook. Good for him, another SAT word.

"Right," I say. "Exactly."

Hailey shakes her head, her hair hardly moving, and shuffles her feet. "Oh, um, let me find it . . ." She riffles through the pages. In about fifteen seconds, the room has switched from quiet to awkward.

"Like Scripture?" I ask, my face cracking into a smile. "That's how well you know this work of art?"

"Yeah, um." Hailey keeps flipping. "It's . . ."

"You must have forgotten. No harm, Hailey. I'm sure you'll remember something you know so vividly soon." I shrug like it's no big deal. Michaela stifles a laugh.

"That's fine, Hailey. Thank you for sharing." Mrs. Liu takes her spot at the podium, watching as Hailey takes her seat. Hailey's face is red, her walk less sure than before. Mrs. Liu stares for longer than usual and then looks at me. She's got to sense that there's something more to this. I've never spoken up so much.

I bite my bottom lip. She's on to me. I should explain why I'm acting like this and tell her what happened with "Hailey's" entry. Then maybe she can change the lit mag draft before it's ready for its final print. But how does one just casually accuse someone of plagiarism, even if it is the truth?

There's only one way to do it.

I have to come clean—it's not like Hailey just found it on some random site online. Which means I have to tell Liu I gave it to her.

I draw a little flower on the inside of my wrist. I can set right what happened between Hailey and me now that the truth is out. And besides, according to the email I got from Stumblr, it's not so easy to hijack one of their sites, so the coding club is virtually no threat. I called their bluff. Which means both Damian and Hailey will have gone down, along with the RMS *Nikmian*.

Admitting what I did will take some courage. How much more of it can I possibly muster?

By the time lunch rolls around, I've caught approximately seventeen whispers about me. Sometimes it's just giggles and pointing fingers, sometimes it's people pointing at their *The Space Game* T-shirts, and when it's been at its worst, it's them yelling ship names. *Pipron. Pipdric.* You'd think people wouldn't come near me for fear of another punch-heard-round-the-dance, but they do.

Michaela and I make our way into the cafeteria. I do my best to avoid direct confrontation with anyone else, because I've gotten very good at that since toddlerhood, but when I walk through the double doors, my skin prickles. So many eyes are on me. It feels like the whole darn room.

The shirts. The *Piprons* on one side, the *Pipdrics* on another. Silence.

I recognize a few faces, but one sticks out more than the others. Damian. I'm pretty sure he's glued his eyeballs to my face.

"Byron is toxic!" someone yells. I can't make out who's speaking, but the few people who weren't looking at me sure are now.

"Cedric's a douchebag! He sucks balls!"

I glance at Michaela and flip around. I shake my head, slowly, desperately. Heat rushes to my cheeks.

"Pippa's a skank!"

"Kole Miller's a skank," someone responds. "Team Nikmian!"

Me. Damian.

"I can't be in here," I say, tears leaping front and center. My eyes may not be crying yet, but my palms are. This shippy load of shit is about to explode in my face. And if this is what it'll be like to face "fans" at a con, how the fuck am I going to pull myself together?

Something soft hits the back of my head. I turn back around. On the ground is a golden, delicious french fry.

"Kole! Sit with us!" A few kids wave at me. I swallow and look back at the crowd. I lock eyes with Damian, his hand still extended. This guy. Fanboy extraordinaire in a new *The Space Game* shirt. He threw a fry at me. Double waste.

"Kole!" A girl is standing, waving her hands at a seat next to her. They want me to sit with them. On the *Pipron* side.

"Go," Michaela whispers.

I make a beeline to their table. *Please, let them be my people.* I grab the straps of my backpack and practically sprint to the empty seat. *Remember: walking fast looks confident. Life lesson #1 today.*

I fake a smile, no teeth, and pull a leg over the bench. "Thanks."

Michaela slips in next to me, the chanting ship name fading into the hum of the usual chatter.

"You guys can sit with us. Always," one of the girls says, the logo on her T-shirt outlined in gold glitter. She clears off a few empty chip bags and a soda bottle, motioning for the others to tidy up. "Obviously we ship Byron and Pippa. Have since the second she walked onto the *Snapdragon*. Anyone else is blind. Or trolling."

A girl across from us chimes in. "Seriously. I mean all you have to do is slow down a second on the show and make it into a gif to see their chemistry." She flips up a page of her notebook where she's been working on a green-and-purple rendition of *Spacer*'s logo. "At least that's usually what I do after a new episode."

I nod. "Like the opposite of microaggressions or something. Micro heart eyes." It's not my cleverest, but these are strangers. That have read my blog. That like my blog. *Breathe. These are what they call . . . fans.*

"Endgame," Michaela adds, pulling out a sack lunch.

"Okay, but multi-shippers are cool too." A girl with a nose ring points to her shirt, which says *Pipronric.*

I giggle. "I don't think network TV will go for that anytime soon, but it would make for some gorgeous scenes." I think I'm going to like this spot in the cafeteria. A lot. And Pippa, Byron, and Cedric all together? Now I'm getting exciting ideas.

"How are you the one writing *Spacer?* I mean . . . the show . . . it's garbage, but you've made it better in your own little way," a girl on the other side of me says. "Like, better than dirtbag Andelman."

Andelman. The executive producer who's messed up the show since its inception: pushing shippers in one direction and then tossing them into a barbwire bed of heartache come mid-season. Throwing us bread crumbs during season finales so we'll come back for the next go-around. Laughing at our tears as he announces another new season is coming, all while knowing he crushed the show's biggest fans under his Farfetch boots.

"No kidding. All he does is bait us. And I don't know where my inspiration comes from. I guess it just appears. Social osmosis or something." Shit. That doesn't even make sense, but hopefully they won't notice. I grab my braid and twist the end. How am I going to answer these kinds of questions on a panel? Like, in the spur of the moment? And knowing there are even more eyes out there and my answers will be broadcast online? My stomach grumbles at an embarrassingly loud volume.

"Like, there has to be something, right? All the writers have some great tragedy in their lives, don't they?" one with a red mohawk asks. They chomp on an apple slice, studying me. "What's your great tragedy, Kole?"

Yikes. That's a hard question. I look from side to side. "I don't have good answers right now—or great tragedies, I guess. This whole everyone-knowing thing is still pretty new to me. So rather than con-level questions, let's start with names. Sound good?"

They nod. "Yes, queen."

That's a bit much. "I'm Kole." I'm pretty sure they knew that already, but hello, awkward.

"I'm Michaela." She glances around and gives them a little wave. Her eyes linger on one girl for a second longer than the others. "Uber fan and ready to die for my ship."

"As we all would," a girl says. She's got *Snapdragon* earrings dangling down to her chin. Where the heck do I get a pair of those? "I'm Bri. She/her works."

They go around: Alex, Andrea, Winston, Jason, Kalli, and Liv.

"So, queen," Alex says again, a tiny corner of their mouth smiling. "I'd kill Sebastian myself if Pippa would let me. Too bad she won't do it herself."

I fast blink. Normally I would read being called *queen* as condescending. I mean, I do have a big brother, and I'm used to Hailey, so jerkish nicknames are a norm, but I think they mean it.

I sit up straight, resisting the urge to scan the crowd for Will. "Yeah, well, relationships with big brothers can be complicated."

"Not when they kill your dad," Alex says, their face breaking into a smile finally. "But Byron's going to destroy him. That'll make it all worth it. Right?"

There are plans for that. But it's going to hurt first. It has to scar to make us care. "I better not reveal that spoiler." The heat spreading across my cheeks will probably tell them I've got something up my sleeve.

"And by the way," Liv, with the cute blonde bob, says, "we consider *Spacer* canon at this table. We like your version one thousand percent better." She takes a big sip from her hydro flask, and Michaela is literally staring. Can't blame her. Liv's beautiful. So's Michaela. Major love connection happening right here. I nudge Michaela, and she gets a goofy grin, the kind she usually reserves for Will.

"Thanks, Liv. That's the nicest thing anyone has ever said to me. Where the fuckity have your comments been, you guys? I've been drowning in hate for weeks." I scan the table.

"Okay, well, only a few of us were reading before Damian's post. And even then, not everyone is going to venture into the comments. Lurkers exist."

"Besides," Michaela interjects, "you turned off the comment notifications a bit ago, remember?"

Crap. I did. "They were nasty. I had to."

"And Noah told you to." Michaela shoves a fistful of Cheetos into her mouth. It was good advice, even if he's not at the top of my list right now.

My stomach grumbles. A couple of snickers rise above the din of the kids around us, and a few of my new best friends nudge each other.

"What?" I ask.

They look away.

"What?" I say, louder.

"It's just that . . . have you been to *Spacer* Port recently?"

"Yeah. It's bull-crap." Ugh. I'd almost forgotten about the mural in the bathroom.

"Hailey was in there right after last class. She made some additions," Kalli says. "I didn't see them, but I could practically smell the Sharpie searing into the stall. She definitely said something about Noah to whoever was with her."

"Have you done anything to piss her off lately?" Bri asks.

"Only every day," Michaela says, glancing at me. Her grin is wicked. "But today? Most assuredly."

"We have to go. Now." I stand up. What the feck is Hailey up to? The crew looks at me, mouths agape.

"You'll be back tomorrow, right?" Winston says.

"Maybe!" I start to run before I make sure Michaela is keeping up.

I'm huffing by the time we get to *Spacer* Port. It's pretty empty. That's a good sign. I open the door, make my way to the last stall, and come to a stop. It reeks of urine, hair spray, and Sharpie, but luckily, we're alone. Before I open the door, I take a deep breath. This may make things a whole lot worse. Whatever Hailey did . . . it's sending creepy skeleton fingers up my spine.

"Open it. Whatever crap is in there, we can handle it." Michaela nods, right next to me. "Do you like my pun? Also, how cute is Liv?"

I ignore her and crack the door open, the light from the window near the ceiling illuminating the stall like I'm Indy, standing before the Ark of the Covenant. The Sharpie mural is twice as big as before. Names are everywhere, strike-throughs and dots, hearts and cartoons. So many people must have been in here, adding names and striking them off like a massive crossword puzzle for the entire stinking school. There are even more doodles on the other walls— more stars and smiley faces, spaceships and planets.

My blood rushes to my head. The Cedric poll is still winning.

And, the most terrifying thing of all: all names are crossed out on the potential-*Spacer*-writer list. Only one is left, but it doesn't matter that I tried to cross it off. It's circled in bright red Sharpie, arrows pointing at it. No one could miss it, even if they weren't at the dance or didn't hear the gossip that's made its way through Snapchat and Instagram and Twitter.

Kole Miller.

Okay, that's no surprise. I swallow. There's more. The other wall shows new additions in the same red Sharpie: *Kolah. Kol-Col. Nikmian.*

Ship names.

Me and Noah. Me and Colin. And me and Damian.

There are no tally lines save for one: Hailey's. Under *Nikmian.*

This was her plan.

"She's making it about me, and now everyone knows," I mumble.

"It's always been personal. Because it's always been *our* show." Michaela's eyes are as big as flying saucers. "What's our play?"

I lick my lips. They sting, but I forgot my chapstick. They, and *this*, are only going to get worse. "I dunno. I need you to have a plan right now."

She shrugs. "Maybe we let it go. Something will happen next week and maybe we let everyone care more about that?"

"Let it pass?" Can I do that? Again? Let them try to beat me until I reach a boiling point and force my fist into Hailey's face? Or do I ask for help? Talking to Brittain did nothing. Would Liu be any different?

"Well, what's your plan, Kole? I got nothing." Michaela folds her arms.

"I'm tired of doing nothing. That's why I had to say something at the dance. That's why I didn't turn around in the cafeteria and run home." I put my hands on Michaela's elbows. "I need to take her down because I sure as fuck am not going down with any of these ships."

Michaela nods. "Except for the RMS *Kol-Col*."

"It's . . . it's . . . complicated with him." I have no idea where we stand. Besides, I can't think of Colin right now, though the image of him in his suit scratches at the back of my mind, begging to be let in.

"So, how do we do it?"

I exit the stall and turn to the sink, Michaela next to me. Scratching my head, I take off my glasses and clean them on my sweater. Culinary starts in ten minutes, and I'll have to avoid Hailey again. I close my eyes. I can't wait on this any longer. "I'm emailing Liu tonight. That's the first step: tell her what Hailey did. Show her that I own the document with *Hailey*'s entry in it. See if that will mean anything."

"That's good. She won't let plagiarism fly. But Kole . . ." Michaela says.

My eyes shoot open. "There will be consequences for me too since I let her do it."

"Exactly."

I grab Michaela's elbow. "How bad can they be? Detention? A call home?"

"Your mom." Michaela looks like she might barf. "She'll say no to the con."

"My mom." I might barf.

She'll destroy me.

I'll have to tell her that Hailey blackmailed me into having her name on my poetry. "She's going to kill me. She's never gonna let me go now."

Michaela cocks her head to the side, sucking on her bottom lip. That's her deep-thinking face. "Yeah, you should come clean. Like, just try telling her what happened and hope for the best? And Liu will have to do something about the mag."

"All I can do is pray that Mom will see why I did it. Why this all matters to me." I nod, thoughts settling. If Michaela thinks so, and the idea's nipping at my mind, I have to see it through. I'll send Liu an email. "And then we prep for the con. We watch hours of panels. I draft answers and I memorize them until my brain is hemorrhaging." I take the band out of my braid and redo it, fingers flying on a mission of their own.

"Okay, without the brain hemorrhage, this sounds pretty good."

"Agreed." We turn to each other and smile. I put a hand out for lip gloss. She gives it to me without a word. We so got this.

The next step is within our well-moisturized reach.

But a lot rests on my mother.

Asteroids.

October 14th, 2019

Hello Mrs. Liu,

I'm sorry to email you about this after the draft of the literary magazine has been printed, but Hailey's poem is not hers. It's mine. I know this will seem outrageous, but I've shared the document so that you can see who created it and the revision history. It's all me. I shouldn't have done it, and I'm sorry.

Please let me know if there's anything that can be done.

Kole Miller

PS: I'm sorry if I acted strange in class today on top of all this. I realized I couldn't let her pass my poem off as her own anymore, and my irritation got the best of me.

Sent from my iPhone

October 14th, 2019

Hi Kole,

Thank you for sharing this with me. I'll review the document and discuss it with administration. I appreciate your honesty and your apology.

Mrs. Liu

The Apple Irregular

An Apology

Posted by: Mrs. Lucianna Brittain

Oct. 17, 2019

Apples,

I received this correspondence from Mrs. Wiles, Damian's mother, a few days ago. She asked that I make it accessible to the student body ". . . so that Damian may find forgiveness and be spared from the fires of hell." It reads as follows:

To the students of Crystal Lake Prep:

After praying about it for several days, I'd like to apologize for my son's behavior. I had no idea what had been going on until he came home from the Harvest Ball in tears over losing a girl he has prayed for since he was old enough to ask Jesus for a wife. Despite my frequent shuttling of him around town and monitoring of his online exploits, I somehow managed to miss that he was holding a peer's website hostage, turning classmates against each other, and forcing someone to go to the dance with him. Rest assured, we will be reviewing the rules of dating as our Lord and Savior Jesus Christ laid forth, and he'll be taking a few classes on both social boundaries and proper etiquette according to the sacred word.

Respectfully,

The Wiles Family

John 3:16

CHAPTER SIXTEEN

At approximately 11:23 p.m. last night, Cricket stared at me and said telepathically that it's time to let what happened at the dance and in the coffee shop go. Even Damian's moved on, or at least his mother is making him. But, I reminded my orange fluff that one of my superpowers, along with holding a grudge, is the silent treatment. Still, she insisted I *get over it*.

The Egyptians didn't worship cats for nothing.

I put one bare foot on the first step into the basement. It's Friday night. There's a *Spacer* marathon going on. Will cackles about something, but I don't catch what. Michaela chimes in shortly thereafter, with Noah's throaty laugh rounding out the trio.

Things have been a little stressed between Will and me since the car ride. In the last week, I've refused to listen to him defend his friend twice. I ignored Noah when I saw him in the halls, even when I passed him after school and should have been looking forward to the smile we used to share.

A creaky floorboard gives away my presence. I cringe, nearly falling down the stairs.

"Is that you, Kole-cakes?" Will hollers. "Like a moth to a flame." He fake-whispers that second part.

I start down the steps again, like it's any other Friday night and this is totally, one hundred percent normal.

Michaela, Noah, and Will are splayed out on the beanbags, the lights low. Noah's got a bowl of popcorn, and a few bags of Twizzlers lie on the ground between them. The TV has the next episode in our lineup queued, ready for someone to hit play and send us to the stars.

"Hey guys," I say, biting the inside of my lip. I should have practiced something. The silent treatment would have been easier.

"About time you decided you were over all this shit. Now, whatever you do, don't smile, Kole," Will says, partially because he knows it pisses me off. It's also because he knows that there's only one sure way to get me *to* smile: tell me not to. He throws a piece of popcorn and it bounces down my Sox shirt and comes to rest right between my knockers. The three of them laugh like hyenas, and before I know it, I'm giggling too. That was a pretty good shot.

On the coffee table is a fresh bouquet of dark-plum dahlias, my favorite since I was a kid. I glance at Will. He remembered.

"I thought you'd like them," he says, handing me a glass of sparkling cider.

I nod. "I love them. Thank you." Crap. Is my stupid big brother my favorite person again?

"Hang on, don't get all mushy. At least, not yet." He turns to Noah.

"We have something for you," Michaela says, all giggly. She's been texting with Liv for a few days, and the smile hasn't left her face. "Even though it's my birthday week so technically you should be making me something."

"I will! But what the feck are you talking about?"

Noah stands up and pulls from underneath him a folded black T-shirt. He hands it to me. God, if this were two weeks ago, I'd be dying. I'd be melting into his chocolate-chip eyes. Except . . . I'm not. And that's . . . different.

I take the shirt and open it up. Across the front is *The Space Game* logo, outlined in silver glitter, with the *Snapdragon* buzzing by underneath it. It's one of my favorite Etsy shirts, but I've always been too scared to get it because when would I wear it? To sleep? That would be a travesty. Sacrilegious even. And I could never have worn it to school: if people linked it—and me—to *Spacer*, I'd have been doomed.

Which happened anyway, so I guess I'm in the clear.

"Flip it over," Noah says. I turn it around and hold it out. In the same font as the logo is the following:

I'm THE Kole Miller.
Yeah, I'm writing Spacer.
No, I don't care who you ship.
Get out of my atmosphere.

"Seriously, you guys?" Tears fill my lower lids. I try to blink them back, but they're stubborn, and not the weepy kind—the kind that mean this touches me deep down, where I don't let the stars shine—where my stories live. "It's . . . it's . . . perfect. You even got my favorite line on here—from when Pippa punches Calico Jack. How did you guys know?"

Will flashes his best basketball-star grin at me. "It was nothing."

"That line was my idea." Michaela stands up and gives me a hug. "We had to. Figured it would save you from about ninety-nine awkward conversations that are still headed your way."

"Especially since they just announced when the new season is returning," Will says. His hug comes next. And then, when he's done, Noah gives me a look. I go in for it, and the hug is nice. It's just that though . . . nice.

And I'm okay with that. Nice is . . . nice.

I step back, slipping the T-shirt over my old long-sleeved Red Sox shirt, before falling onto a beanbag between them. Will lets out a big burp, disgusting and juicy, and just like that, all is forgiven. I toss a pillow at him. Filthy animal.

"What's the next play? Sounds like Damian is gone for a little bit. We're just going to let all this roll over into next week's drama?" Noah asks.

"Nah." I reach for the remote. "Got one more player to take care of."

Will is never one to just let something go. "Want to TP their houses? I haven't done that since middle school. I'm down."

"Sounds fun, but that's not how to take down Hailey," I say, rather confidently I might add. "I need to make sure she answers for taking my work in Creative Writing. I'm going to go down for it too though."

"Shit." Will shakes his head. "What did you do?"

"I emailed Liu about what happened. She has to take the situation to the powers that be and they'll figure it out."

Will chuckles, turning his head to the screen. "Quite the shit-pie, Kole, but I trust you got this. Though an old-fashioned TP would be a hell of a lot more fun."

"I certainly hope I got this. And Michaela, I'll make you your fav." My heart is so happy that I'll even try something I'm rarely good at—baking. Cupcakes are her favorite. And I've got to bake the best dang bunch this side of the galaxy.

Michaela raises her head and looks to the ceiling. "I see cupcakes in my future!" she yells.

I hit play and "Previously on *The Space Game* . . ." rattles through the basement. A little bubble of excitement pops in my stomach because my show is still my show, shithead classmates and all. And, hey, I've got new friends now that share my thoughts, and they're way cooler than I ever thought anyone at Crystal Lake was. I take a big old gulp of my cider just as Noah leans toward me and nudges my arm. I only spill a little on my jeans.

"Yeah?" Maybe it's more questions about hyperspace. Or the funky cliffhanger that built up to this episode, or the fact that they recast that one character last episode because the actor tweeted racist comments about—

"Need help making cupcakes? I'm a good cook, believe it or not," he whispers.

My response is a thought I'd better keep to myself: if you were, you'd know that saying you're a good *baker* is accurate. "I'm good, thanks. And I'd hate for you to eat any eggshells."

He shrugs, flashing me that million-dollar grin yet again. "I'm down, if you are. I'm sure they're full of fiber."

"It's okay. I've got it." I smile, batting an eyelash or two. "Thanks though." He turns back to the TV and reaches for a handful of popcorn.

Now . . . I've got an idea. To quote the Grinch, an awful, wonderful idea. I reach for my phone in my back pocket. Time to break the other icy barrier between another *sorta* friend and me.

7:56 PM

Hey . . . soo . . . how are you?

Colin and I haven't spoken. I haven't tried; I've been too nervous about how he took the news at the dance, and he hasn't so much as turned around to scowl at me since Hailey passed my poem off as hers. But, sometimes before I fall asleep, I think about that dance in the orchard, how he twirled me around and breathed in my hair and whispered my name. I think about what would have happened if Damian hadn't found us. By the time I start drifting off to sleep, my chest aches.

My phone vibrates.

Probably Shouldn't Text Him
8:15 PM
Hey. I'm fine. What's up?

8:16 PM
Do you like cupcakes?

Probably Shouldn't Text Him
8:23 PM
Yeah. Is this you checking if I have a soul or something? Of course I like cupcakes. But not red velvet.

Yikes . . . no red velvet? Is that a deal breaker?

I shut my eyes and count to three.

I'll allow it.

Here goes everything. I glance to the side to make sure Noah's not watching. I may not want to bake with him, but I'll take his suggestion—a baking partner. Just not one that's shaped like him. One that's taller, more smolder-y. A tougher nut to crack.

8:25PM
Want to help me make some on Monday? At my house? It's for Michaela's birthday. I really need the help. :)

Probably Shouldn't Text Him

8:27 PM

Sure. I'll find a sub for the chess club practice tournament. 😉

Colin is talking to me. And he said yes. And he winky faced me. Again.

I shove my phone under the beanbag before I squee too loud and embarrass myself.

Oct. 19, 2019

Comments Section:

TeamByron {Yuma, AZ}: Can Pippa and Byron make it already

Anonymous94793 {HIDDEN}: there's no fucking way Captain Worley's actually going to just walk into a star station. There's rovers everywhere and Sebastian is always watching . . . this isn't going to end well, is it ToTheStars?

Farts4all {Camelot, NIR}: they're keeping wolves in this space station? animal cruelty much?

CartersAlive {Huntsville, AL}: spoiler alert: they all die

HairyGreenPickle {Uranus, ME}: I stan a legend KOLE MILLER

Anonymous37304 {HIDDEN}: they're not going to die!!! They haven't even kissed yet. But we could do without Benedick at this point

DookieMaster {Littleton, CO}: Benedick is a precious cinnamon roll that must be protected at all costs

Cedricismyboo {Crystal Lake, VT}: where the hell is Cedric? You can't just ignore one half of the ships. 1/2 of us will stop reading.

AdmiralSnackBar {Norwich, ENG}: Cedric needs to just find Aster already

GoGnomes {Crystal Lake, VT}: This is bogus. Pippa isn't the kind of person that would just go into Circe's throne room all willy-nilly. And Worley left the weapons on the *Snapdragon*? Not plausible. They're sky rovers for fuck's sake. PIRATES WOULD TAKE WEAPONS WITH THEM, KOLE.

Ding-a-lingBilly {Yourmomsbed, TX}: Who's Kole

GoGnomes {Crystal Lake, VT}: Someone who's writing this pitiful blog all wrong.

CrystalLakeSux {Crystal Lake, VT}: Not you're best work Kole.

DAMIANSMOMMY {Crystal Lake, VT}: I will pray for all your souls. Byron is a sinner, just so everyone knows #TeamCEDRIC

CHAPTER SEVENTEEN

I t turns out this *Space Game* T-shirt looks pretty good with a pair of skinny jeans and an eggplant sweater. The sparkles are even shinier this morning, perhaps brought on by the fact that tonight I'm going to be making cupcakes with el supremo nerdo, Colin, and I've had a hard time keeping the butterflies at bay. They've been fluttering around since I went ingredient shopping yesterday and overthought my choice of cupcake a lucky thirteen times.

American History has been exceptionally draining. Maybe it's because my head's stuck in the clouds—I mean, Pippa is scheduled to take down Circe this week—but I had to get out. I make my way down the hall by the lockers' end to Counselor Falls. There's five kids ahead of me, a couple on their phones. I lean against the wall, crossing my arms. StuCo already has signs up for the Winter Ball, right before break. I sneer. I won't be caught dead at another ball.

"Hey, you're the girl, right?" The dude in front of me is chewing his gum like a cow with its cud. "From Hailey LaFonte's Snapchat story?"

"Nope." Most likely.

"Liar. I put my vote up this morning. You'll be glad to know I voted for the Curve-Breaker. You guys just seem so perfect. Like, happy little dorks." He keeps chomping away. "I'll tell him in the MUN meeting on Friday."

"Happy little dorks?" I scoff. Who the heck is this guy? Talking to me like we're friends? And sneaking into the girls' room? Creeper. "As though I want everyone's input on my personal life?"

"Whoa, getting pretty high and mighty there, Kole? A personal life? This is high school. It's all fair game, even when you're insta-famous."

No, it really isn't. Or it shouldn't be. We move forward as a couple of girls get in line behind me. "I am *not* high and mighty. And who the heck asked you to weigh in on my love life?"

"Damian told everyone to cast their vote—said you needed dating advice."

Hang on. *He* announced to the whole school that I needed help with dating? Oh god. I'm sweating through my sweater. I mean, why's it called that if not to hide your sweat?

The anonymous love guru takes a drink and steps back. By now there are about ten kids behind us, giggling and gossiping. I bend down to take my drink, maybe splash some water over my forehead, but something pokes my shoulder and I whip around. "What? More thoughts for me?"

A girl this time. "Well, not about you anyway. I just wanted to say that I'm on Team Cedric and I think I speak for a lot of fans when I say that you're so obviously favoring Byron. We haven't even seen Cedric since they flew to Coracinus. What, do you expect us to keep him as head canon? I mean, feed us, please. We're here too."

"He'll be back. Maybe in a few chapters or so. They aren't even going to Viridis for another few weeks, so buckle up." I bend down and take a big drink. Can't I take a drink in peace?

"That's not good enough. Pippa needs to be thinking about him at least." She stomps her foot in some kind of tantrum. "You can't just erase her feelings for Cedric."

I close my eyes. Breathe. Shipping is as shipping does. "Please go watch *Stranger Things* or something. Stick to the mainstream."

"I've watched four times already. Don't you think Byron and his daddy issues are played out?" She flips her hair, rattling on about Cedric. "Byron is soooooooooo moody . . ."

"Pippa doesn't care about Cedric." I turn back to her. I need to get better at listening to my own advice. "Byron and Pippa are co-rovers, more in unison than—you know what? I can't do this. I need to get to class and learn about another big bad battle."

"Yes, she does. She likes Cedric. It's canon. They even kissed. Byron isn't."

"Shots fired!" the love guru says, hands around his mouth.

I nearly spit my words. "I plan to throw Cedric out the airlock very soon, so stay tuned!" I rip off my sweater and turn my back to her, pointing at the shirt. My middle finger itches, but I don't shoot her the bird. Gotta maintain some class.

"What a bitch," someone whispers. "Take a video."

When I turn back around, the Pipdric's look says one thing: she got the message. But they all need to get the message. I take a deep breath, ignoring the tremble in my legs. There's a time and a place for declarations of ship-dependence, and *Spacer* Port is it. "And the rest of you, what the fuck? Our shows are supposed to be fun. Entertainment, right? They aren't supposed to split us down the middle until we've made enemies of strangers and lost potential friendships of the very best kind—forged in fandom." I suck in my bottom lip. I mean, if anything can be learned from what went on with Hailey and Damian, it's that we can't let this stuff go too far.

Also, that was unexpectedly profound—where did it come from? "We're supposed to skip class and meet at this, the very best of water fountains, to talk crappy plot points and silly hair extensions, not eviscerate each other."

One by one, the heads nod. The hands come together. They applaud. My chest swells. I put my sweaty hands out to silence them. "So, put this on your stories. Your Instagrams and TikToks. Your whatevers. I, KOLE MILLER, DON'T CARE WHO YOU SHIP. Just ship it well."

I turn around, my thoughts spinning, and book it down the hall. I'm dizzy, my hair's a mess, and my palms are clammy.

I did it. I made it clear where I stand. The applause follows my footsteps. A smile encompasses my face. I swirl my sweater around the air.

Victory.

Eggs. Flour. Blue, green, purple, and pink food coloring. Baking powder and soda. Sugar. Icing mix. Salt. Vanilla. Cupcake wrappers, non-toxic star sprinkles, edible glitter sprinkles, vanilla extract. Butter, milk, buttermilk (that makes total sense). Mixing bowls. A mixer. A big Ziploc bag. Cupcake baking sheets. A stained old apron with *oh crêpe* across my chest. A frying pan. I wipe the sweat from my brow and push my braid off my shoulder. I think I have everything we're going to need, and it's a heck of a lot.

But no Colin.

"*Merow*," Cricket says. I glance at her fat butt, on the club chair in the living room, and she stares back. Probably wondering why I'm making all this racket.

"Don't worry, you're still my number one favorite thing in the galaxy. I've just learned to like Colin. And you're going to like him too."

I mean *tolerate*.

She meows.

Mom is working late on some big case tonight—she wasn't so happy that the friend coming over isn't Noah, but her eyes lit up like Fourth of July fireworks when I mentioned a few key words: *Yale*, overachiever, 4.7. Will and Dad are at a game until ten-ish, so tonight should be cake . . . or cupcakes, rather.

The doorbell rings, and my stomach lands somewhere near my feet. "Oh crêpe," I whisper, pushing my glasses up and fluffing out the top of my braid. It's 6:59. Colin's exactly one minute early. Well, if prompt isn't one of the best ways to describe him, I'm not sure what is. I make a dash for the door, apron and all, and open it far too quickly. One of Dad's all-too-familiar quotes rings through my head: *no one likes an eager beaver, Kole*. One of these days I'm going to listen.

"Hi," I say, a big old grin across my face. Gotta rein that in. Especially because he's not smiling. I mean, yeah, he's Colin, and he's right out of a Lands' End catalogue, so I shouldn't really expect him to smile.

"Hello." The furrowed brow has already made its appearance as he takes in my apron. He's got one hand behind his back. "That's a great apron."

I put a hand up, flashing a smile. "It's the first one I grabbed. Come in, I'll introduce you to my cat." Oh shit. I made it weird.

"I brought you this." He hands me a bouquet of soft orange peonies with several sprigs of goldenrod, bright and yellow, tied together with a pretty pink ribbon. "I hope you like them. My mom's a botanist—she grows them in our greenhouse. These are the ones I tend, Coral Charm. I've grown the plant from seed, and her blossoms represent good fortune." He stops abruptly, sucking in his bottom lip. "My mom loves them. They remind her of growing up in Spain."

"Spain? That's incredible." Is he Spanish? I think I'm so into that. And, a greenhouse? No wonder he usually smells woodsy, in that *I've been out chopping pine trees and carrying them over my shoulder* kind of way. "They're lovely. And I could certainly use some luck." Their fragrance is light and sweet, like when the smell of the early spring lilacs floats through the air. Goldenrods grow up and down the roads all over Vermont, so I've been seeing them for years, and they're gorgeous. Too bad they'll make me sneeze within thirty seconds if I stay this close. Minus the allergies, the flowers against his brown checkered button-up are perfectly fall and perfectly beautiful. "Thank you."

He hands them to me, and our fingers touch for a quick second. Not that I noticed.

I buzz past the living room, meaning to put the flowers in some water, and call back to him. "Come in! That's Cricket on the club chair. Don't mind her—she's fat and cranky." I grab a vase to plop the flowers into. They'll look great next to Mom's turkey decorations on the mantle. But . . . then I'll have to explain to my family where they came from and why a boy was here and why he brought me flowers. And Will's face when he finds out it was Colin . . . maybe I'll just put the flowers in my bedroom, on my bedside table.

In the other room, I catch his voice. "Hello, cat. I'm Colin."

Oh, my god. Adorable. It takes everything in me to not tell him that she already knows about him.

"You had a chess tournament tonight?"

"Yeah, Monday nights are practice rounds. Private lessons are on Tuesdays." He comes into the kitchen and leans on the counter, taking in the array of supplies on the island. "Holy crap. I may as well be at a match. This looks complicated."

Private chess lessons. Of course. Probably at the club, in smoking jackets, saying things like *checkmate, Jeeves.* "Yeah, um, it's a lot. Don't be intimidated. It's okay if we mess up. So hopefully less pressure."

He grits his teeth and rolls up the sleeves of his shirt.

"It's okay if we mess up. Right." He nods like he's giving himself permission to relax.

"You're not used to that, are you? Messing up?" I ask, reaching for my computer. I've got the instructions ready to go. I hope he knows there's no pressure. It's just me and the mix and no judgment. No competition.

He pauses, considering what's sure to be a thoughtful response. "Not in public, at least. I usually try something new ten times at home before I ever give it a go in front of others."

"Okay, that's a lot of pressure to put on yourself. Here, in my castle, it's okay to mess up. We're not in class, got it?" The oven beeps, preheated and ready to turn batter to nummy goodness.

He nods. "Got it. So where do we start?"

"With this." I yank an apron off Dad's hook. There are about six more underneath it. I just have to make sure to put them back in exactly the right order, one for every weekend in the summer. This one, Dad's favorite, says *I turn grills on* and has a picture of a barbeque on it. "I kinda think it's perfect."

He looks it up and down before sliding the loop over his head. "Great. A pun."

"Yeah, that's what I meant." *Not at all that you turn girls on.* Because that's the joke. He turns around and I tie it behind him, keeping my eyes on the strings, and not at all even in the very slightest on his butt. "There are thirteen steps to these bad boys. Shouldn't take more than a couple of hours."

I hit play on the YouTube tutorial. We watch in silence. These are infinitely complicated, but hopefully they'll be fun.

Maybe.

Colin is so intense that the computer may explode from his stare.

"So . . . galaxy cupcakes." There's a lilt to his voice. He eyes me as he turns, both arms prop_d on the table. What he said is not a comment . . . more of a question. And I'm busted. "Any particular reason?"

"Galaxy cupcakes. They're for Michaela," I repeat, swallowing, but I don't think that's why he asked. He knows the truth now. But now I have to own what happened. What's worse, I have to explain why I didn't tell him about *Spacer* in the first place. "They look good, right?"

"Definitely."

Come on, Kole. If he were mad, he wouldn't be here. If he thought this whole situation was too stupid, he wouldn't be here. I try to look away, but I'm drawn back to him. This is the guy who told me to read my story out loud in front of Hailey and Damian and Liu, to look at him when my voice started to break and it felt like my legs would give out. And when I did, he was as steady and sure as a buoy in the waves.

"You can tell me. It's okay," he says.

I suck in my bottom lip. "Because space is my thing." Gulp. "Or, *Spacer* is my thing. I should have told you. I was working really hard to make sure it was a secret, and then Damian was convinced that he should change that . . . and . . . you saw what happened." A hand flies to my glasses, pushing them farther up my nose. Did it get hot in here?

"I had a feeling it was you, you know. Writing the blog." He turns to me, crossing his arms in front of him.

"You did?" I ask. "How?"

"Because of the smile you get whenever *The Space Game* comes up. And the fact that I can see your writing style all over *Spacer*. I *have* been reading your work since freshman year, remember? Back before you were too busy hating me to swap drafts." He raises an eyebrow.

My cheeks turn what I'm sure is a lovely shade of pink. What a tease. But . . . also . . . Colin's been reading *Spacer* if he can see my work all over it. A big grin splits my face yet again. "Well, I got over it. The hating you thing."

"I'm glad you did," he responds quickly.

I look away after a couple of seconds. We've got cupcakes to make. "So, you start the batter. I'll start the icing. Sound good?"

"Sounds good." He moves to the other side of the island, reaching for the eggs. "Time to get cracking."

I smile, yet again. Colin made a pun.

By the time we get the first batch in the oven, a thunderstorm has started to build. The first raindrops tap a cadence against the window above the sink, steadily growing louder than the sound of my tunes. I put Dad's Elvis mix on super low, because Colin said that's his jam, and I'm focused on the cupcakes.

We haven't messed up yet. The icing is mid-mix, Mom's old mixer humming in my hand. Three batches will create the purple, green, and blue.

My phone lights up on the other side of the counter. I scoot behind Colin to reach for it and almost get icing on his sleeve. Yikes.

It's Mom. She won't be home until ten-ish, which is good because the little hand is nearing eight. I glance at Colin, spooning little proportionately-perfect plops of batter into the cupcake spots.

"Got it," he mumbles as a plop lands beautifully in the paper cup. "This isn't so bad. Maybe a little fun."

I glance at my side of the counter. I'm still on my second icing mix. Way behind him. At this rate, the cupcakes will be done before I've got the swirly icing complete. Back to the mixing. I hum along with the tune wafting through the air. *Are you lonesome tonight . . .* Dad's played this one so much I've known the words since the womb. Grabbing a bowl, I drag a spoon along the sides to get all the icing into the middle. "So, how many SAT words did you get today?"

At the same moment, Colin speaks too. "What's Damian got up his sleeve next? We're still not talking."

We stop ourselves and laugh. A nice little coincidence.

"So, uh, only three words today. Not my best. I was distracted." He plops down another perfectly blended bit of batter, eyes on the spoon the whole time. "Your turn."

I mix, but I'm stalling. I'm risking making the icing too liquidy. If I stop, it might be too chunky. Didn't realize that baking from scratch requires a degree in alchemy.

Okay, no more avoidance. "Damian's done. This time it's Hailey I've got to deal with."

"Hailey. I could tell something was going on there. Never seen you perk up in class like when she was reading from the lit mag."

"Yeah, there's more to that. She's Crystal Lake's own Medusa. She, and Damian, went after *Spacer*." I fill him in on what Damian and Hailey did to *Spacer*. How they held it against me while I catered to their demands. By the time I'm done, he's moved to my side of the island and begun tossing utensils into the sink. I should be helping more, but I'm sitting on the counter next to the sink, legs dangling and hoping that he doesn't think the story is so laughable that he runs out the door.

"Okay, so they blackmailed you. Damian made you go to the dance with him. And Hailey stole one of your poems, the one in the lit mag, hence the awkward read-aloud in class the other day. And that was to impress Liu?" He begins to run the sink.

"Exactly. Ten points for Mr. Smarty-pants." A flash of lightning claps in the distance.

"Very funny." He's got one eyebrow raised, a shy smirk on his face. Colin likes a good old-fashioned tease like the rest of us peasants.

I glance at the window. By the look of the clouds, a storm's set to strike.

"So what are we going to do about Hailey?"

We.

Colin is willing to help me. But he can't—if something goes south, he'll risk his flawless record. I can't have that happen. I have to do this myself. "You're sweet, Colin, but I have to do this on my own. I can't have you risk getting in trouble. I've already landed in detention once because of this situation."

He sucks in his bottom lip, nodding a breath later.

"As for Hailey, I emailed Liu. And now I'm baking and biding my time until I find out what's going to happen." I spread my hands out like I've created the galaxy around us. "So, yay, cupcakes. A welcome distraction."

Colin puts his glasses back on and turns the faucet off. "That's good. Liu'll do something. I mean, it is plagiarism, the worst possible thing you can do in a writing class."

I nod, but heat grows in my belly. That's the problem with plagiarism. Hailey won't be the only one in trouble. But there's nothing I can do about it now. I just have to deal.

There's one spatula, covered in batter, to my right. As soon as Colin's not looking, I'm grabbing a taste. I grab a few more bowls on my right side and set them carefully into the sink. They sink to the bottom of the suds as lightning zaps outside. I reach for my braid and twist it up a little before letting it fall back down my shoulder. The rain isn't letting up, and thunder is following the lightning with heavy footsteps. It's not dangerous, but if Dad were here, he'd have the generator fired up. And if Colin weren't here, I'd be in my room with a flashlight, a fat cat, and the jelly beans I hide under my bed.

I sneak a peek at him, his sleeves rolled up and his forearms in the sudsy water. Just a few weeks ago, at the coffee shop, I was wearing his glasses and he was touching my face, sending rocket ships to the moon with his fingertips. And more recently, we were wrapped around each other under the moon in the middle of an orchard, and I was touching his neck hoping for something that didn't come.

When, in this bizarre universe, did Colin Clarke and Kole Miller go from frenemies to a possibility?

I have to consider this. It's now on my list of overthinks for tonight.

A nasty bolt of lightning strikes close enough to rattle the windows, and I jump. He looks at me, a sparkle in his eyes, and smiles. He's going to be saying something snarky by the time the next bolt hits. I begin to count under my breath, *one one-thousand, two one-thousand . . .* and so on.

"Really, Kole? Scared of a little storm?" He dries his hands off on a rooster dish towel and leans against the counter, shoulder to shoulder with me.

"It's nothing." Lies.

"I can stay until your brother gets home if you want."

I nod. I do want that. But Will and Colin are oil and water. Them running into each other again? Shudder. I shake my head, glancing out the window again, but it's too hard to see anything with the rain blurring the view. I reach for my phone and keep it next to my leg. Colin turns to me, close enough to touch, as the lights flicker above. We look to the ceiling, but they're back on in an instant. I study his eyes, green and big, and notice little dark circles underneath them, before his skin is dotted with little, light freckles.

He takes a step forward, like he's going to get back to work, but I grab his arm.

"Are you tired? Your eyes are red," I ask, always nosy as feck. Even behind his glasses, I can tell they're lined in pink.

"I've stayed up pretty late the last week."

"Studying?"

He reaches around me for the spatula to my right. *Mine.* I put a hand out to stop him.

"I'm going to throw that in the sink," he says, trying again.

"No," I say, grabbing his arm again. "That sucker is mine."

"Why?" He gets this little wrinkle between his eyes when he furrows his brow.

I put a finger to my lips to silence him. "Have you been studying for the SAT late at night, Mr. Clarke?" I have to get him off the scent of that spatula.

"It isn't for another few months. I'm not worried. I've been practicing the vocab for two years. Taking the PSAT since I was a freshman." His voice is low and throaty.

"Are you bragging?" I cock my head, teasing him. That *is* wildly impressive. But I can't tell him that. It would spoil the fun. "What'd you score, show-off?"

"That is private." He leans into me, placing an arm on either side of my legs, and tries to grab the spatula. I beat him to it. Without thinking, I put it to my lips and lick the greenish-bluish batter across the top of it while his arms lock me against the countertop. And he's watching me; planets and stars above, he's staring. His eyes follow the movement of my mouth across the batter. And when I'm done, he puts a hand on the handle, right on top of mine.

"Private-shmivate. Like you wouldn't announce your score to the whole Creative Writing class, Mr. Valedictorian." My voice sounds like an old-fashioned movie star's.

He tucks in a corner of his lip in that jerkish smile of his—the kind he'd flash at me from the podium back before I'd ever given him more than a scowl. He's not looking at my eyes though; he's looking at my lips. "Oh really, Miss Best FanFic?"

I know this play. He's going to tease me about *Spacer*. Well there's one thing writing fan fiction has taught me—details. Micro-movements. I've been writing kiss scenes long enough to know that when someone looks at your lips, like he's doing now, they're coming in for something.

"How's it taste?" His voice is thick. "Good enough for Michaela?"

Another crack outside stops my answer, and I grab his arm. I clench, probably too tightly. The lights flicker, clinging to life, but they flutter out as death's scythe slashes the wires outside.

"Asteroids," I whisper, as we're bathed in darkness. He doesn't flinch. My turn. "What's your PSAT score, Colin?"

I turn the flashlight on my phone on and set it down, the light hitting the ceiling. Colin smells of pomade and laundry detergent, not at all like the stale smell of Liu's classroom.

"Freshman year, 1419. Sophomore year, 1430. This year, I'm anticipating a 1520."

"Oh, there you go. Unabashedly predicting a perfect score." I put my hand back on his arm.

"Did you just use an SAT word on me?" He takes the spatula, hand still over mine, and puts it to his mouth. He drags it across his tongue, getting the last bit of frosting. I blink in rapid succession. Staying focused on words is proving difficult. I should have a clever retort. I swallow, my mouth growing drier by the second. As soon as he lowers our hands, I toss the spatula into the sink.

He brushes the base of my braid, right where it falls over my shoulder, and breathes close to my ear. "Remember the orchard?"

I nod, next to his face, and close my eyes. He puts his hands on either side of my hips and brushes my knees. He inches closer, searching my face, probably for more frosting, and I'm nothing but gooey melted cupcake batter.

"What do you think would have happened out there if Damian hadn't found us?"

I swallow. Putting a hand on the back of his neck, I pull him to me. Time to get my hand in those too-long curls. I move my hand up the back of his head. His hair is softer than should be legal. The rain pounds the window as we lock foreheads.

He clears his throat. "My eyes are red because I've been up the last few nights reading a little something called *Spacer.*"

"My *Spacer*?" I squeak.

"Yes, from the very beginning. It's made me want to take a shuttle to the stars and explore the seven skies with your motley crew of space pirates."

Oh my stars. I put a hand on the counter, just to make sure I'm still grounded. "They're not mine, technically. They're—"

"Sure they are. I'll be the Byron to your Pippa, if you let me," he whispers.

The butterflies start their dance, fluttering up my throat. My stars, being his Pippa sounds like everything right in this universe, but can Colin define *fan fiction*? He knows every SAT word, but how much does he know about my strange little universe?

"How do you feel about conventions?" Not the best time to ask, but he's so close; I can taste the frosting on his lips. And I want to go in for it—to kiss Colin—I do. But something yanks at me—pulls me back to where my world meets his, and I'm not sure they mix.

He pulls back, glancing over my face. "I'd go if you're there."

"I'll be at one in a couple of weeks. I'm terrified." I haven't actually been to one yet, but all my research shows that they're unreal. Fun. Intense. Stressful. Exciting. All emotions rolled up into one big sweaty fangirl ball.

"Can't be worse than high school, right?" He puts his hand under my chin. "Can I ask you something?"

"Of course," I say, the lights above flickering and sputtering out.

"The other day, in the cafeteria at lunch—what were the other kids yelling?"

I shut my eyes. The ship names. "It was about the ships in the show."

"I remember some of those weird words from the debate a few weeks ago, and I've seen parts of them on *Spacer*. But that's not all they were yelling." He backs up and leans on the island, too far from me. We're officially not touching.

"The other ship names—the ones that people are talking about on the walls in the bathroom." I put a pointer finger on my thumb and start a fresh hangnail. How am I going to explain this part? That being friends, or whatever we are, means that he's part of a big old dumpster fire?

"Tell me what they meant." He looks up as the lights tremble on, like someone aimed a spotlight on me. "And what the hell is going on in the girls' bathroom? I heard kids talking about it."

I scratch at my skin, digging so deep it stings. I could tease him that he knows every SAT word but can't figure out ship names, but he's turned so serious that I don't dare. "It's not just about the ships on the show anymore." Gulp. "For some stupid reason, the anti's—my old friends—have decided that my personal life is open for their criticism too. It's not just about my blog anymore—they made it about my personal life. And that's what you heard about: them casting their votes in the most annoying way possible."

He tucks a strand of hair behind his ear and folds his arms over his chest. "The Damian thing was just the dance, right?"

I nod. It's coming.

"What about the other ones they're talking about?"

Okay, I can do this. It's better he knows now anyway, before I fall asleep thinking about how soft his hair is. Thinking that there is a *thing* between us. "One was Kolah. That's me and Noah. Will's friend. We had a brief moment, that's all. It's done." And that's all he needs to know.

He nods. "And the last one?"

"Kol-Col. You and me." I jump off the counter and step toward him, taking his hands.

He swallows, his eyes hard. "You live in a strange world, Kole Miller."

"I do. And it's only going to get stranger, but I like having you in it."

He puts a hand on my hair and looks at my braid, his eyes miles from me.

I keep going. "Until this spotlight fades, the others are going to be watching. Waiting to see what my next play is."

He puts a hand on my face. "I like what's happening. But I want it between you and me, not the whole school."

I swallow. I've got to be real with him. This has gone beyond my control. "Then you need to know that I'm speaking on a panel in a few weeks. I can't promise you that the school, or the internet, is going to lose interest anytime soon. I'm just me, in this situation, and I wouldn't mind if you were my copilot, but if rough waters are too much, then you need to abandon ship now."

He searches my face.

My phone alarm sends a blaring *beep* into the darkness. The cupcakes would be done, if the electricity were working.

"Let's see if we can fix these cupcakes first," he says, reaching for an oven mitt and pulling away from me.

Thank the stars for the dark. It means he can't see me bite my lip as he pulls away or put a hand to my brow and pinch where the tension likes to build. Can this ship float in stormy waters? I don't want to lose what's happening between us before it's even begun, but there are more waves coming. The plagiarism issue. The convention. The panel. It's a lot. And he may walk away.

I'm not sure I blame him.

SPACER 3.15

Posted by: ToTheStars
Oct. 22, 2019. 11:21

Pippa bends down and inches her face closer to Byron's. She kisses the spot right underneath his left eye, where the bruises lie purple and tender, and quickly turns to the next cheek. This time, he closes his eyes when her lips meet his skin, on the spot where the flesh is still soft and the tears will touch first. She lets them linger a second longer, and Byron catches the scent of the wildflowers on Malva, a whisper of sweetness.

Feck it all. His world is about to come together. He reaches for her shoulder, to keep her just there. No more kissing foreheads. No more cheeks. No more dancing around where he wants his lips.

He puts a hand around the wrist that just held his chin and pulls her to him. He cups her neck and she kneels, her hair grazing his fingers in petal-soft strands. And her lips, when they touch his mouth, feel like something too soft for a rover. Pillows with goose feathers. Rabbit fur blankets. Things he's only imagined. And when he pulls her further into him, he sees that that's all of Pippa. Something too damn good, and warm, and soft, for someone like him. A sky rover.

But still he kisses her because someday she may wake up and realize that he's no good for her. That he's something the stars will spit out when they realize they don't like how he tastes.

And she will do the same. Because she's smart.

She will realize, someday, that he's the man who took her *real* father from her.

CHAPTER EIGHTEEN

Thursday. The air on campus is downright heated, the ship wars boiling the student body to a crisp. The only reprieve was Michaela's cupcakes, and we devoured a few in between classes. Not five minutes ago, an announcement went over the loudspeaker to the whole school.

Nikole Miller and Hailey LaFonte to Principal Whitehead's office.

Now I walk to my death, one Converse after the other. This must be what an inmate feels like on their way to death row.

Okay, academic death.

Actually, it's not even that bad. I've come clean with Liu. But it may be for Hailey. I'm just going to explain what happened, and what my role was in it, and then everything will be just fine. Ratting out Damian has already been done. It's the truth. But why does telling the truth today feel harder than landing the *Snapdragon* on the planet Aureus during a solar storm?

Fine. It'll be fine.

The line at Counselor Falls is four students deep, since it's still a good eight minutes until the bell rings. A few students giggle when I walk past, but I've gotten good at staring straight ahead and staying true to my mission. Besides, my shirt says everything they need to know.

I glance at my phone. Michaela texted that she finished her makeup test. I type that I'll see her after school. When I glance up, something gaudy and metallic catches the light from the skylight above and nearly shoots a laser through my retina.

It's Damian's belt buckle. Of course. The plan: walk like I don't see him.

"Kole. What a pleasure," he says, stopping right before me. His lizard grin suggests he's happy to see me, but surely that's not it. "I wonder what Whitehead's got in store for you. Gotta be a suspension. Something for your record."

"Not a pleasure. Whatever I get won't be worse than the email your mom sent out." I try to keep walking, but he stops me, not saying anything as he takes in my sparkly *The Space Game* shirt. I've had to wear it two days this week. Just when I thought people were done asking me about the ships, they asked me again. I'll stop wearing it when they stop asking me about it. At this rate, never.

"Where's your new friends, Ms. Popular?" he asks, taking his sunglasses off and hanging them on the front of his gnarly Nirvana T-shirt.

"None of your beeswax." I angle to the side, but he stops me. Again. "Get the feck out of the way. I need to be somewhere."

"I'd hate to make you late for a date with Whitehead, but last night's entry was awful. You actually had Pippa and Byron kiss? You lose half your fans when you let your ship set sail. More when it's the wrong one." He leers. "Save the real writing for the pros. But I would imagine you already knew that, since you're on top of the world and all."

"Guess what, Damian? It's not too late to start your own blog. Get your own fans. If you dare," I say, eyes wide. "Then you can write the story however the hell you want. Shit, make Cedric and Pippa get married and start their own fleet. It'll be spectacular, and all yours. Fanboys will worship you. You may even find some *Star Wars* bottom-feeders to stan you. Every nerd boy's dream."

"Ugh. Who has time for that?" Damian says. "Not my bag, baby."

I glare.

"Heard you'll be at the Con-athon." He rubs his nose, almost like he's trying to keep it covered. How covert. "I'm considering a ticket myself. Mother said I can go if I turn on location services on my phone."

Mother? "Ew, *Psycho* much? And that's mere rumor," I lie. If I see him in the audience, it'll be the biggest mindfuck in the history of mindfucks. It's hard enough for me to try and pull this off—throw in this slimy eel dick and I'll be screwed.

The bell rings, echoing down the hall.

He grins. "I'll be watching. Waiting for another slipup, Nikole."

I push past him. It's going to take an atmospheric miracle to get through what's about to happen and make Con-athon come together.

The hallway in front of Whitehead's office is largely empty. He's not in his office yet. I have nothing but silence and the plaques in the hallway to keep me company. *Crystal Prep Alum Accepted into NASA Program. Local High Schooler Working On Dementia Cure at Tufts. Crystal Lake Apples Win State. CL Alum Publishes Award-Winning Exposé.*

A lot of accomplishments have come from this school. What will my legacy be? Will's sister. The girl who punched Damian Wiles. The one who brought the ship wars to school.

Ha. That'd be something for the yearbook.

"Good morning, Mrs. Baggs. I love your sweater!"

"Oh, Hailey. Always such a joy. Whitehead will be back shortly. You can wait in the hall."

Oh great. She's here. Sucking up to Whitehead's secretary—a pro move. I do everything to avoid eye contact, but I can't help but feel like she's staring at me. It's like a shark has caught the scent of blood on the current. Hailey grabs a chair two seats down from me and pulls out her phone. I catch her leaning toward me out of the corner of my eye. "If your shenanigans jeopardize my *Great British Baking Show* chances, then you've got an even bigger problem than what's going on right now, Kole."

I suck in my breath quickly, and it sounds like a laugh. Gotta muster up some courage. "I'm not scared of you, Hailey. You and Damian messed with my dreams *first*, like they're a game, and I won. As you're about to see." I blink quickly. It's big talk. I really fecking hope it's true.

"It *was* all a game. But it's over, Kole, so move on," Hailey says. "I don't even know what I'm doing here. I should have never spoken to you after middle school." She glares into me. "Unless you've done something *really* stupid."

"Oh, you're going to find out," I whisper. I'm not one to judge other's dreams, but how does that even work when you're American? "And you're not British—you're a Yankee. There's no baking show in your future."

"You know what, Kole? That's *my* show, so you should get what it means to me. It's not my fault *your* show got super lame and that we're not friends anymore because you got lame along with it." She bites her bottom lip, the hand on her phone trembling, the waterslide curl at the bottom of her hair shaking. Her makeup is a little less than perfect today. Maybe, just maybe, this little game she's helped create has been a lot on her too. I suck in my breath. I don't have compassion for her. She stole my blog, plagiarized my work, flaunted it in front of the entire class. She's going to crash and burn.

But still. We have something in common: our shows mean a hell of a lot to us, even if they aren't the same one anymore. "Okay, *The Space Game* isn't always the best, but we didn't all have to stop being friends over it," I say quickly, surprised to hear my own words. I guess I have harbored some resentment, but I didn't think either of us would ever say a word about it to each other again.

"Well, that's not gonna change." She moves a seat closer to me, staring me in the eye.

"I didn't say I wanted it to. But just because we stopped agreeing on the show ages ago doesn't mean you have to be a jerk to me just because we like different things now." I meet her stare, dead-on.

"Whatever happens, you won't win. You'll never have Mrs. Liu crying over your stupid little space blog, and you'll never have the admiration of anyone in Creative Writing. Fan fiction is for kids looking to read smut, plain and simple. That's not *real* writing. Spaceships, planets, love triangles? Get a fucking life." She points a finger, red nail polish and all, right in my face.

"Girls!"

We freeze. Liu and Whitehead are walking rather quickly toward us. Mr. Whitehead opens the door to his office and motions for us to enter. "Come on in, ladies. Looks like we should have been here about a moment before. Leave your bags and phones in the hall, please."

I stand up, pull down my shirt, and enter his office. I feel Hailey's dragon breath on my back as we both take one of the leather seats that surround his wooden desk, and Mrs. Liu goes around to Whitehead's side. She leans against the wall, her gaze thick on us.

Whitehead's office is a shrine to Crystal Lake Prep. Not only is it full of banners and pendants, but it's lined with pictures of our most accomplished teams: tennis, swimming, football, basketball, rugby. Ribbons hang from the shelves that line the back wall, and the windows to the front of the building have trophies teetering on the edges. He's got more articles hanging in here than I even knew existed. Makes sense at a school like Crystal Lake, where everything rests on how much of something you've won . . . or inherited.

"Now. Mrs. Liu has filled me in a little on what happened in her class. But what's this I see out there? An argument?" Whitehead is the kind of principal who walks the halls during passing periods and comes to all the games. He knows each student by name, but he's not lame enough to insist we call him a princi-PAL. For that reason, I've always appreciated him. I hope this stays true now. "I expect better of my Apples. Especially the upperclassmen."

"We're waiting on a few more people to join us, Mr. Whitehead," Liu says. "If you'd like to wait."

"No, thank you. I'd like to talk with them alone first." He opens a drawer and grabs a notepad and pen.

My mouth falls open. Who the feck would need to be here? Damian? His coding club friends? But . . . they never actually did anything.

"Great," Hailey moans. Guess she's dropping the nice act.

"As I'm sure you've guessed, we got an entanglement in the lit mag." Liu pulls a copy of it from her folder and opens to the page with my poem in it. A hot-pink sticky note marks the stolen poem. "This piece has been mis-authored."

Hailey's eyes grow wide and she sits up straight. She folds her arms over her chest. "What do you mean? I wrote that weeks ago. Kole, did you claim it as yours?"

My jaw drops, but I don't say a word. She's still lying.

"What I mean is that Kole has shared with me that this is her poem, and the revision history supports this. Kole wrote it. It's time-stamped and shows her revisions—but how it ended up as a submission from you in the lit mag is what remains a mystery."

Hailey's eyes grow wide, her cheeks red.

Whitehead reads over the poem. "This is good work . . . but claiming work as your own when it isn't is a major academic offense. It will get you kicked out of university. Hailey, I can't imagine that you, with your parents' numerous donations to our Creative Writing program, would be aware that this belongs to someone else."

"I have no idea what Mrs. Liu is talking about. It must be some kind of mistake. Did Kole fake the history?"

"Really, Hailey?" I tuck in a corner of my mouth, trying not to smile. Smiling right now would be very, very bad.

Save your receipts, baby. Victory tastes good.

"Kole, is there something you'd like to say?" Liu looks to me, blinking quickly. Whitehead turns and waits for my response. He taps his fountain pen on the top of his desk, awaiting some kind of statement from one of us.

The words come up in some kind of vocab vomit. Here goes. "Hailey made me give her my poem. I wanted to submit to the lit mag—I could use the prize money for a bus ride to Hollywood after Crystal Prep—but Hailey didn't like what happened in Creative Writing a few weeks ago. That Liu liked my story. And so she and Damian—"

"Damian?" Whitehead asks, cocking his head.

"Damian Wiles," Liu says.

"They found out about my blog, which is insanely popular." Those words come from a place of disbelief, like I'm still trying to convince myself that people find value in my work. "And they decided they were going to tell the whole school that it's mine if I didn't write my fanfic the way Damian wanted, and write a poem for Hailey so she could get the prize money, and go to the dance with Damian so he could impress a girl. It's like I'm on a series of quests and the final boss . . ." I glance around the room. Not the time for metaphors adults won't get. "And it all just came to an ugly head at the dance and that's why I—"

"That explains the drama in Journalism." Whitehead nods his head.

Thank the stars he stopped me before I said that I punched Damian. I zip it before I say anything more.

"Indeed," Liu says. "This explains a lot of the tension I'm seeing in class. The competition between a few of the juniors has been worse than at the start of the year, Mr. Whitehead."

"It happens in classes like this, where both the creative talent and the stakes are so high. But we can't let that get in the way of doing the right thing." He jots down a few notes on the notepad on his desk.

"Which is what? What should I have done?" I say. "Let them tell everyone about my work?"

"You came clean, for one," Liu says. "But what's the worst thing that can happen when your peers know you're writing something of merit?"

Not so easy when it's fan fiction. "They can be cruel. Social media would have destroyed me. But it doesn't even matter anymore because I don't care about what they think now. Too much happened and I'm dealing with it." I glance at Hailey. Her eyes are red. She's fuming.

"Had you come to us earlier, spoken to an adult, any adult about this, you would have remained consequence free. But here we are now with a joint-plagiarism offense. According to our student handbook, that's a stage-three offense. And a lit mag that has to be reprinted. That's time and money, ladies. Hailey, is there anything you'd like to add to this?"

She crinkles up her chin and the waterworks start. "Just that I've never wanted anything like I've wanted that prize money. I did what I thought I had to. I guess it just . . ."—by this time tears are streaming down her cheeks—". . . got carried away."

The loudspeaker on Whitehead's phone buzzes. "Mrs. Miller and Mrs. LaFonte are here."

My blood runs cold.

Mom.

Why couldn't they have called Dad? Ughhhh.

"Send them in," Whitehead says.

After ten of the longest seconds in my life, they enter the office and take seats on the sofa behind us.

I can't even look at my mom.

She's going to destroy me.

"Mrs. Liu, will you kindly inform these two of what we're dealing with here." Whitehead stands up and introduces himself to our moms. Guess he's not aware that we all know each other—that we all used to be friendly. Hailey reaches for a Kleenex and blows her noise after she kisses her grim-faced mother on the cheek. I sit here, arms crossed. I'm dead meat.

By the time Liu is done with the story, I've heard Mom shuffle her feet no less than three times. I can tell that she's jotting down notes, and by the sound of her *mm-hmms*, they're a dead giveaway that she's got something to say. Likely many somethings.

And I'm doomed. Fight or flight is kicking in. I can feel my legs trying to get up and run out of the room.

"I'm going to be recommending to the counselors, Mrs. Liu, and the vice principal that, as a consequence of her actions, Hailey drop Creative Writing. She may try again next year, but that will be contingent on her behavior in her grade-level writing course."

"She'll have to lose credit for first semester," Liu says. "As per the syllabus."

Hailey dabs her eyes, sucking in a snotty breath. "It's not fair!"

"Hailey, control yourself. I understand, Principal Whitehead," her mother says, putting a firm hand on Hailey's shoulder. "I'm in complete agreement with this consequence. This is unacceptable behavior."

Whitehead turns to me. "And as for you, Kole, I'm suggesting—"

My ears perk up, the wave of heat in my belly rising to my face. I don't want to drop. I want to stay in Honors Creative Writing. It's the only practice I get outside of *Spacer*, and I need the exposure. Hollywood may not want only space opera someday, so I have to dabble in other topics—

"Hang on, Mr. Whitehead. I have a few questions. You're telling me that my daughter gave in to the demands of two of her peers because she was scared? Kole struggles with anxiety. Can you blame her for fearing the repercussions of her peers when they found out who she is?"

My heart is about to jump out of my chest. "Okay, Mom, I think I see what you're doing, but must we talk about this very personal detail?"

She continues over me, "Can't you see why she'd have a hard time with this entire school knowing what she writes? She's what they call an *influencer*. She's even speaking at a con next week. In front of thousands."

I flip around. Asteroids. Not thousands. "I am?"

"You are." She looks back to Whitehead.

Holy crap. Mom is giving me the go-ahead.

She continues, "I know, very personally, how much her blog means to her. I see her every single night, for far too long, writing away the hours at the expense of her other classes and any extracurriculars. Dare I ask if you would give a consequence to one of your football players who stayed up all night practicing and then had his ability to play compromised by one of his peers? Would you bench him as a consequence and deny his dedication?"

Whitehead looks to an image of last year's football team.

I watch Mom. First she was humiliating me. And now . . . my mother is . . . defending me? Her glasses sit at the edge of her nose. She's got her defense lawyer face on. We're in a courtroom.

"Why, I imagine there would be some kind of consequence for that—"

"Hmmm. Interesting. Then why wasn't there five years ago, when the news of the college admissions scandal broke and we found out that a few of our own families were involved? I don't see that story lining your walls in here—how they bought their way into perfect SAT scores. Is that because you let the boy who was buying his way into UC Berkeley off scot-free? Even though he was faking his stats?"

Whitehead's face goes stony. He clears his throat. "I can't discuss other students in here. I'm sure you're aware of that, Mrs. Miller, but I was going to suggest a not-so-drastic consequence for Kole since she did come to us. The truth is always the right route, as I frequently repeat at our assemblies."

He's not wrong there.

Mom squints. "Let's hear it. And you better have a good justification for why my daughter should have any consequence in the first place when this is a clear case of bullying." Whitehead stumbles for a minute, and I can barely hear him when my mom adds, "Oh, and according to my son, you may want to ask Ms. LaFonte about the vandalism in the bathroom."

She shoots, and she scores. Hailey reaches for her hair and lets out a long, high-pitched scream. It makes my toenails want to run off my feet.

"Hailey!" her mother yells, reaching for her. "Dear! Are you all right?"

Whitehead calls for the nurse on his loudspeaker. "I need the health office in here now."

"Let's go." Mom puts her hand on my shoulder this time. I cannot believe that she's come to my defense. That she's standing up for my work.

This is . . . everything.

Mom worked magic. I only got lunch detention through the

end of next week. The car ride home was quiet, but as soon as we left the office, I gave her a major hug. Not gonna lie, I broke down a little when we got home, but it was in the silence of my room, the perfect place to let go.

It's much too cold to write outside, so I've cleared off my desk for tonight's writing session. Honestly, I'm too anxious to care about what happened with Hailey. Next week, Mom, Michaela, and I leave for the Con-athon. Mom's working hard on this whole *I care if you care* thing.

I click *new entry* on my blog, gearing up for tonight's writing session. Shouldn't take too long to write about Pippa sassing Circe, and it's strangely fitting for how I'm feeling right now.

If anyone asks me on the panel if I ever draw inspiration from real life, it'll be hard not to mention Hailey Buttface, but I can tease that some entries are right from my every day.

I take a swig from the glass of water on my bedside table. Despite all the reading up on cons that I've done since Kasey's email, actually being on a panel is a much bigger bag of stress than what's happened at school.

I glance at my phone. I'm being called out after American History next week for the con which means I'm missing Creative Writing, which means I won't be seeing Colin. He knows I'm going to the con.

Colin. A nerd. He gets straight As, he plays chess, and he gets excited about the Model United Nations club.

Kole. A geek. I obsess over minutiae in my show, can beat anyone at pop-culture trivia night, and can fangirl squee better than anyone.

I take off my glasses and rub my eyes. I want a reason to text him. To see him.

Knock knock. "Are you turning the light out soon?" Mom says.

"Yes," I say. If soon is in three hours.

"Can I come in?"

I put my glasses on and grit my teeth. Here it comes, the look of stress she gets when she considers the strange, geeky land we'll be walking through together next weekend.

"Okay," I say as she opens the door.

I flip around and cross my legs, shoving my last few jelly beans under my pillow. I really don't want to talk dietary decisions tonight. Or ever, really.

She sits on my bed, crossing her legs and bracing her wineglass for impact. "I want to talk about next weekend. I'll leave you and Michaela alone for most of it, but I do want to see some things with you. Maybe we can all grab dinner at the Boston Public Market?"

The market? Too touristy. "Okay, I guess, but, I'm going for the con. It's a really, really big deal, Mom. It's pretty much my version of heaven." And I'll stay with her some of the time, but not in the exhibit hall. And I really don't need my mother at my signing, or when Caden Rodgers signs my neck with red lipstick. Or when I meet Nina and tears are streaming down my face.

She nods, slowly. "I'd like to be in the front row for your panel. I want to see why this is so important to you. So important that you did what you did."

I glance at my *Spacer* poster. "Mom. Whenever I talk about *Spacer,* your eyes glaze over. You can't wait to get back to the dishes, or Will's game, or your Chardonnay." My eyes burn. That's one of the most honest things I've ever said to her, so why do I feel so guilty?

She goes silent for the longest thirty seconds of my life. "You think those things are more important to me than your mental health?"

"Well, why wouldn't I? I'm constantly being reminded not to eat this or that. Or that writing fanfic isn't a legit hobby in your eyes, but basketball is. Like, of course, I couldn't come to you. You've never shown any interest."

She's silent well beyond comfortable this time, like forty-five seconds. Cricket rolls over on the bed, stretching out her nubby orange limbs.

"But it's everything I want in this world," I mumble.

"What is it exactly that you want from this hobby, Kole?" she finally asks.

I bite my bottom lip. Time to be out with it. To put the words into the universe and hope it's listening. "I want to go to Hollywood. I want to write for TV. And I think my fanfic is prep for that. And people like it. So maybe I have a shot?"

I can't tell if she nods or blinks more. But whatever it is, it's some kind of acceptance. "I can wrap my head around that, but I might need some time. Or some more wine." She smiles.

I smile too. "You're definitely going to need it next weekend." Time for some truth in here. "Here's what you need to know about a convention and about *Spacer*. I've been working on this for a long time, and I've done it without your approval, or your respect, or even your interest. Why does this change at the con? You're going to be more mystified by my life. And wait until you see the other fans, or the cosplayers." I look at the ceiling, blinking back steamy tears. She's going to have to reserve judgment, and that's going to be next to impossible.

"I'm bracing myself for some oddities." She speaks slowly, thinking through each word.

Oddities? That's one way to look at it, but she'll be the fish out of water, not me. "Geeks aren't predictable, they aren't boring, and they certainly aren't *normal*, whatever that means. That's the beautiful thing about them, and why I'm one. We just don't fit in a boring world, and we don't apologize for it. You need to prepare yourself for that."

She takes a long gulp of her wine, blinking quickly when she's done. "I'm willing to give your world a chance, if you'll let me."

I take a deep breath. She *is* my mom. Our relationship is worth a chance. "No judgment, about me or anyone else there, okay?"

"Okay," she says, standing. "I won't make you hug me, but I'm going into next weekend with an open mind."

I smile. "It's going to be a trip, that's for sure."

She runs a hand through her hair, the same color as mine but cut just at her shoulders. "I should tell you that I've been reading *Spacer*. I don't really understand all of it, but I can see why people like it. And, I'm excited for you." She smiles, and I see something in it that I haven't seen in a good long while. "There's hard work in those entries. I can see it in the storyline. In the sentence structure. In the word choice. In all of it."

"Seriously?" I ask, my eyes so wide they're drying up.

"Seriously." She nods. There's something in her grin that I haven't seen in a good long while. Pride. "I've always been in your corner, honey, I think I just thought you were going to be on a different path. But this, your writing, is what you love. And I'll walk down the path you choose, even if I have got a lot of reading ahead of me."

"Thanks, Mom." Can the universe be working in my favor again?

I stand and I hug her, nearly spilling her wine in the process.

SPACER 3.16

Posted by: ToTheStars
Oct. 31, 2019. 9:33

Carter pushes open the heavy wooden door, hair askew, glasses ready to read, hands ready to create, and stares at Pippa. He wasn't expecting his daughter to be in his lab.

"Tell me about the drawing," Pippa commands.

He stands in the entryway, his body dwarfed by the massive rolling balcony above. It willows down to two separate walkways leading to walls upon walls of bookshelves filled with stories that Pippa got lost in as a child. The deep mahogany wood sucks the light from the circular window above into its crevices as shadows creep into the room and call for lamplight.

Pippa takes a deep breath and lays the picture Katherine drew before him. "You know more. You want me to be great, like you. You want me to learn about your potions and fancy ideas. To cure disease and make space travel easier. To help you jump through time and stop death. But how can I learn from someone who won't fill in the blanks for me? Tell me how I began. Tell me about my mother."

CHAPTER NINETEEN

My heart is beating a million times a minute. I've followed the constellations. I've landed in geek heaven. The Con-athon is my eternal home.

Before me is the most beautiful thing I've seen in my seventeen years on planet Earth: a massive model of the *Snapdragon* painted and lit to perfection. Every minute detail—from when she was scratched on her undercarriage in episode six, to the scratches from the too-tiny tunnel in episode thirteen. It even has the old-fashioned script written on her side: *Snapdragon*.

Never in my wildest nightmares have I seen a convention hall so freaking big. A significant portion of it is dedicated to vendors selling more swag than my geeky little heart can fathom, and it's not even all related to *The Space Game*. It's *Star Trek*, *Battlestar Galactica*, *Star Wars*. Those are just the big ones. And the crowd—Ewoks, Star-Lords, Borgs, Captain Reynolds, Zeldas, Eren Jaegers, Ringwraiths. Those are just what I recognize. The only thing they share is the stardust of stories, imagined and brought to life in the hearts of geeks all over the planet.

Michaela and I take two steps closer to the model of the *Snapdragon*. Its bulk takes up a good chunk of the open space, with its massive hull and tail down its spine, sprawling front window, and long, angled wings.

I've written so many scenes in this hull, and here she is, practically breathing. I put my hand on one of her wings, as I've done many times in my head when pretending to be Pippa wasn't enough—when putting myself on this starship was the only thing that would quiet the thoughts sputtering through my mind. When dreaming the *Snapdragon* would come to my roof, toss down a rope ladder, and whisk me to somewhere only the stars have seen.

The lights on the side flicker as though the starship truly is gliding through space, Gertrude at the wheel and Captain Worley standing behind her. Byron and Benedick at the helm, on their way to meet Pippa. This is extraordinary.

I glance past the massive ship, past the huge platform on the other side of the hall and see the word *Spacer* on a banner above a black-clothed table.

That's it. That's my spot.

I look back at the *Snapdragon*.

A piece of her *is* mine.

A piece of her is *me*.

"Take us to Viridis," I whisper, blinking back the line of water that's found my eyes again. Pippa's final line in the season finale seems the most fitting thing to say to this beautiful hunk of metal.

"Ten minutes, ladies," Kasey hollers.

There's an ache in my chest, like I'm running to a finish line that's nowhere in sight. I think I've figured out why. This place is about to be filled with people who know who I am. Who want to talk to me. People with expectations.

And there's something else. My mom is here. My BFF is here. But there's one more person I want next to me. My plus-three nerd.

I reach for my braid and rub my lips together. Right now, I'm just Kole, but when Kasey takes me to my signing table, I'll become Kole Miller, author of *Spacer*. And then everything changes.

Then everyone knows who I am. And I wish Colin was here to see it.

Breathe.

I've got to get it together. I reach for Michaela and grab her arm.

"Ow," she says, staring as hard at the model. "I've never seen anything so glorious. I want to have its cyborg babies."

"And you will do that. I believe in you." I turn to her, tears in my eyes. Thank god Mom is sticking to the back, taking in all the cosplayers.

The massive platform ahead of us is for the cast of *Spacer*. Their pictures hang above the seats: Ben, Nina, Caden, Bill, Maria, Adam, and Freddie. Or, as I know them: Cedric, Pippa, Byron, Carter, Katherine, Benedick, and Sebastian.

"They'll be here in another few hours," Kasey says in her bubbly way. "Take this. It's your access pass. It'll get you in and out of the con however you see fit. You're free to roam, but some guests prefer to do that in costume so they're unnoticed." She hands me a laminated badge with my picture and name on it.

"Thank you," I squeak, accepting her offering.

"I know it's a lot. Especially when it's your first con. But just be you—that's all you've ever been, right?" She grabs my hands and smiles. "All you can do is share your experience, that's it."

"Okay. Thank you." My eyes water more as heat builds in my chest. It's not tears—no sadness here. It's bubbly, fangirl excitement.

"Follow me." She rips through the crowd and we try to keep up, Mom trailing not far behind.

I'm about to be sharing the same air as the cast of my show. I'm about to be seeing them in street clothes, with the accents they've worked so hard to forget. Discovering what their eyebrows look like in real life, and whether or not they let their hair go gray in between seasons. I'm about to be seeing the world I've escaped into for the last three years. I'm about to be the closest I'll ever get to the world of *The Space Game*.

But does seeing them like this take away the magic? I shake my head. If it does, I'll write it back in. Better.

"Your table." Kasey waves her arms over it. "The cast will arrive in another few hours, but don't worry, as soon as the fans are done getting their signatures, they'll be at your booth. We've sold about a hundred autograph tickets, so you'll be busy. More will buy when they see you here too."

"Yeah, okay." I'm not worried about how many are sold; that has literally nothing to do with why I'm here. I'm here to meet fans, to look them in the eye and tell them I'm writing for them.

Mom comes up behind me and takes in my name and the glossy papers before us. "Wow, Kole, this is exceptional."

"Thanks," I say, not sure if that's approval or not.

My stomach bubbles rather loudly. It better not be gas. Not now.

"Oh honey, do you need some Tums?" Mom riffles through her purse as another wave of nausea passes over me. "I know how your nerves get. Mine get like that before a big case too."

It's just anxiety. I can do this. I shut my eyes for a second and put a hand out as she finds the bottle. "Oh, my god, yes. Thanks Mom."

"Of course." She takes off the top and plops two pink pills in my hand.

I toss them into my mouth. She's always prepared, my mom. "I'm lucky you're here." I shoot her a smile, step around to the other

side of the table, and stand before the banner with the *Spacer* logo
Michaela made for me. There's my name, in big comic-book letters.
Written by Kole Miller.

"It's beautiful." I swallow the knot in my throat.

Michaela grabs my arm and squees. I turn to her and bounce
a couple of times before I give my own fangirl squee.

If only Colin could see this too.

"Don't worry, Sean will be here in case anyone gets out of line."
Kasey nods to a guy by the black backdrop. He's got even more
muscles than Caden Rodgers, and a face that'll scare away the most
terrifying of fans. "It doesn't happen often, but some fanboys get a
little grabby during a picture and such. So, it's twenty-five dollars
per photo op, and you'll pocket most of that. I've had some glossy
Spacer entries printed in case anyone wants you to sign an entry
and they forgot to bring something, which happens."

"Sounds like you've thought of everything."

Kasey looks to her watch. "The cast will be here soon. Panel is
at two. You good? Want to roam the hall before everyone bombards
you?"

My eyes shoot to the vendors. "Yes."

"I'll stay here. Keep your spot warm," Mom says. "And I'm going
to read some of these pretty entries here. See what these fans are
loving so much." She reaches for the pile and thumbs through it.

Holy carp. There was no condescending tone. She genuinely
sounded interested in my work. There might be hope for us in this
galaxy after all.

"Perfect!" Michaela yells, grabbing my arm.

We run to a booth faster than light speed.

"I just want you to know that I read your blog all the time. I've never missed a new entry—though there was that one time a few weeks ago where you skipped a post. I still love *Spacer*, but I definitely cried a little that night. And Team Pipron forever. I'll ship them until I'm a ghost," a fan, Annabelle, says. She's got on a *Spacer* T-shirt and hat. A tote bag full of swag rests under her arm. "Seriously, I'd die for them. Or kill for them. Whatever it comes to."

I nod, but the *Spacer* Port at school flashes through my brain. Brian drawing a line through Byron's name on my notebook. The cafeteria yelling about the ship wars. People pointing at me. Whispering. Laughing. "I get it. Just don't let the ships take the fun out of *The Space Game*, okay? Promise me."

She furrows her brow, signature Byron move, and cocks her head. "Okay. Just as long as my ship doesn't sink. Ever."

"Unsinkable ships burn slowly. Remember, okay? Though I know how hard we get swept away by them." Deep thoughts, by Kole Miller. She hands me an image of Pippa and her father, Carter, on the platform before he dies. I smile. The moment I knew I was trash for this show.

My signature is a little rocky, but I'm getting in a groove. Ten more of these and I'll have it perfected. I may even add a star or two. I hand it to Annabelle.

"Yes!" she yelps, hugging the picture to her chest.

I'm eighteen signatures and pictures in, and this is what I've put together from being nice to Piprons and Pipdrics alike: shipping is serious business for a shit ton of people, but it shouldn't be so serious that we forget how to treat each other like humans. I've talked with fans about the meta-universe, about insta-love and plot armor and glaring CGI mistakes, but the ships are the one thing we can't seem to agree on, and it splits us down the center.

Ship wars. Invisible lines drawn in chalk by writers and actors somewhere in Hollywood, but we fans rewrite them in permanent marker. We refuse to switch sides. And when we make it personal, it's too far.

"Thank you, Annabelle. I can't tell you how much it means to me that you enjoy *Spacer*." It's true. I hope it sounds genuine. I'm not sure . . . I think I'm doing this right.

"Can I take a selfie with you?" she asks.

"We can do a photo op over here." I get up and go to the green screen. Kasey gives me a thumbs-up. If fans want a pic, we gotta charge. She said it's something I have to get comfortable saying if I want to make any dough.

I grin awkwardly through a picture, eyeing the line that wraps around part of the hall. There are far more people in line at the cast table, as to be expected, but Kasey was right. A lot of them do head here right after getting the cast's signatures.

The con announced when the cast came out some time ago, but I can't see them from where I am. I mean . . . Caden freaking Rodgers is on the other side and I can't even see him. This is fangirl waterboarding. It's agonizing.

The Space Game's panel is in another fifteen minutes. Until then, I'm giving it my best over here and giving a big hug to each fan who passes my table. And their words about *Spacer* . . . they're glorious. If the nerves in my stomach weren't going haywire, I'd probably have more tears in my eyes.

Annabelle walks away with her new picture, squealing with her

Katie Kingman

group of buddies. It's a beauty seeing all these little chunks of fans with their garb. A few even have self-made *Spacer* T-shirts on. That's positively unreal. I go back to my chair, stealing a quick glance at Mom. She's on her phone, probably texting Will, and Michaela is flipping through her new *Unwritten* graphic novels.

"So *the* Kole Miller, huh? I've heard a lot about you, and I'm not impressed. You only get half the story right, half the time."

I glance up. A snake in the convention hall. Fecking Damian stares into my face, searing his gaze into my skin and wearing a fancy *Jesus Ships Pipdric* shirt.

"Can I sign something for you?" I give him my cheeriest, sweetest smile, but my blood runs cold.

"I've got some suggestions." He hands me a list of thoughts, in handwriting that's about a millimeter tall. "Let's let bygones be bygones. Forget the dance and all that shiz. All I ask is that you tell the story right. Get the science right. Get the characters right. Get the ships right. Is that too much?"

"You can go now." I swallow. Can he not leave me alone? I'm writing my story. Not his.

"It isn't if you want the verse's respect." He puts his hands on the table and leans forward.

I look at the line. "There's twenty people behind you. I'm not worried about respect."

He twitches. "Come on, Kole. We're old pals by now."

"Can I sign something for you?" I ask, louder.

"Yeah, make it out to *GoGnomes*."

The troll from the comments section. "*GoGnomes*?"

"That's me." His voice is thick with accusation, his eyes staring

316

into me. "Can you really be sure I don't have a keylogger on your site? Would be easy. Coding club does it all the time."

"You haven't. You'd have done something stupider by now." He's only trying to scare me. I lift one eyebrow, forcing the smuggest grin I've ever assembled. "It's hard work to tell a good story. Even harder to force a happy ending, huh?" I take the sheet of paper he gave me and begin to rip it into tiny slivers of itself. "Great thoughts. Save them for Reddit."

Damian's face grows red. "Was it the Curve-Breaker? Did he tell you what I was up to?"

I lose the grin. *Colin.*

"I bet he wanted to get in your pants more than he wanted to read your craptastic writing. Tell me he got some at least?"

I fast blink. Damian had said Colin didn't know about this. And there's no way—not with what Colin has said about writers. With what's happening between us. He wouldn't. Damian is full of it—a master manipulator. But I know better. I won't be taken for another ride. "Listen, if you don't have anything for me to sign, then you'll need to buy one of these." I move to the side, fingers shaking as I reach for an entry. I may not believe him, but he's still a guy in front of me with a vendetta. "They're from just a few weeks ago when—"

"Shut up, Kole. Tell me the truth. I'm sick of your crappy stories. Should have deleted them long ago." He swipes away the shiny copies of *Spacer entries*, hitting my hand in the process. A few fall to the ground.

I stand, raising my voice. "We're done here. You need to go or I will punch you again. Harder this time. It'll be worth the broken bones."

"Do it." Damian narrows his eyes.

"This man bothering you, Kole?" a deep voice says over my shoulder.

Sean. Security. Perfect.

"Yes, he is. Escort him out, please." I keep my eyes on Damian.

"I was just trying to get her to tell me one of her stories." Damian puts his hands up, but Sean goes around the table and grabs him by a wrist. He pulls him to the side, radioing for more security. "She's overreacting. Drama is what she does best, right? And she was threatening me!"

Sean grabs him by the neck of his shirt and pulls him into the crowd. "You won't be back this weekend, kid."

"What the fuck was that?" It's Michaela, her hand over her mouth. "How did he get here?"

"Kole?" Mom says, a pile of my blog entries under her arm. "What's going on here?"

"It's nothing. It's over with," I answer, my hands trembling. "Just an asshole. But he's gone now."

The loudspeaker cracks to life. "Five minutes until *The Space Game* panel in Hall C."

I look to Michaela as Damian disappears into the crowd. "It's time!" I turn to the line, but it's evaporated. Undoubtedly headed to the panel.

"Mom, I have to get to the panel. Can I meet you in a bit?"

Mom nods, reaching out for a hug. "Of course. You two have fun. I'm going to get caught up on the earlier entries. I may understand only about half of the terminology, but the story took quite a turn two days ago. Good stuff, Kole."

A smile splits my face. "Yes, it did that. Just wait until the next entry." I hug her back and run after Michaela and through the crowd.

Time to ignite fangirl mode.

We make it into the hall, huffing and puffing, but the only empty seats left are on the outskirts of the last few rows, three right in one spot. We dive into them, just beating a few middle-aged fans dressed as Benedick and Byron. They caught every amazing detail, down to their space boots. The lights fade just as they start to throw us some serious shade.

"It's actually happening. This is unreal." Michaela sits forward and pushes her pink hair off her shoulders.

I glance to the seat next to me. There's only one person who could make this moment more perfect, but he's back in Vermont.

The theme song blasts through the room, the massive screens along the side illuminating with the opening credits. The audience hoots and hollers, exploding with applause. I jump right in, forgetting any sense of decorum. This is my happy place.

I sit up straighter than I have since I first learned how. The moderator comes out and introduces herself. Lana is a blogger with respectable shipping thoughts, so this panel should go well. She flips her dark hair off her shoulders and takes the mic in one hand. "Who's ready for the cast of *The Space Game!*"

I scream. Michaela screams. We all scream, a high-pitched fan-ish cry loud enough to be heard on the moon. Lana introduces them one by one, and by the time she's done, I'm shaking.

Seth Andelman, the executive producer.

Ben, Nina, Caden, Bill, Maria, Adam, and Freddie.

Cedric, Pippa, Byron, Carter, Katherine, Benedick, and Sebastian.

The key players are here, breathing the same air as I am. I try to keep my own breathing normal, but it's getting heavier. I place a hand over my heart. All the beautiful, flawed antiheroes I've written into my life for the last three years are sitting before me. The embodiment of what it means to imagine, to create, to make the seed of a story into a grain of reality and they're in the same room as me.

The tension in my chest doesn't fade. I'm hanging on to every word like it's the last dehydrated strawberry in the *Snapdragon*. Lana starts with a few questions, mostly to Seth, before she turns to the cast. They tease about what we can expect this season: higher stakes, more kissing, new characters. Nina, in the most adorable sundress, talks about her worst blooper last season. And Caden, gorgeous, glorious Caden, whose voice doesn't sound at all like it does on the show, talks about all the hate Byron gets. His answers are divine. That's my Caden: an intellectual.

"So, Seth, when it comes to inspiration for the show, what's your go-to?" Lana asks.

"Hmmm . . . that's a good one. I talk to my husband a lot. He's great to bounce ideas off. I look at some fanart." The crowd likes that answer. "I watch my old *Babylon 5* DVDs. It can come from anywhere really, but mostly I consider who these characters are and where their personalities would take them."

"So when—" Lana starts.

"He's lying. He reads *Spacer*," Freddie interjects. "We were just discussing the scene with Sebastian in the hatch in the hull. Said I should channel that *defiance* this season."

Michaela grabs my arm. I put my hands on my mouth. *No, he does not.*

"Only on occasion, but I like to keep my ideas relatively free from outside influences." Seth leans back and tosses his hands in the air. "There are some good ideas out there, what can I say?"

"He's lying." Nina laughs, tossing her beautiful dark hair over her shoulder. "We discuss every entry."

"Okay, but only *Spacer*. No other fan site." Seth shrugs, guilt all over his face.

Nina reads my blog. Freddie. Seth. My blog deep in the interwebs. My mouth falls open. The crowd cracks up. Caden pats Seth's back, then leaves a hand on his shoulder. It's freaking adorable.

Caden clears his throat, answering in the Caden voice. "It's true. We all read it."

I'm dead. A puddle of goo on a sticky, stained floor. At least I died at a con surrounded by a geek platoon.

"Okay, okay, I've been known to peruse." Seth puts his hands up. "I like some of the thoughts."

"You know that there's a *Spacer* panel in a few hours, right?" Lana asks the panel.

Nina drinks her water, hiding one of her perfect smiles. "You should go, Seth. Take notes."

Oh my stars. She's going to get herself fired.

"So we know who's writing it now? That's common knowledge?" Maria asks. So far we've only seen Katherine, her character, in flashbacks, but they've teased that we'll be seeing Pippa's mother very soon.

"Yep. She's a junior in high school—"

"Kole Miller!" Michaela stands up and yells. I grab her hand and yank her back down. "And she's right here!" She points to me.

What do I do? Do I resurrect myself? Do I use my hearthstone to get back home? Do I faint like a screaming goat? I glance around me. Everyone has turned.

I stand. I have to. There's no other chance at this.

The cast and Lana search the audience for where the sound is coming from.

"Say something," Michaela whispers.

"I'm here. Kole Miller. I'm writing *Spacer*," I say at the top of my lungs.

"Come up here, Kole," Bill says. He's Pippa's father, the first person in a line of many to die on the show. I swallow down the lump in my throat. "I mean, if we're being honest, the blog does come up at every con we go to."

They nod furiously. Sweat lines my back. *I'm doing this. I'm really doing this.*

I scoot through the row, careful not to bump the bags and knees of those around me. "Sorry, sorry, sorry." A few fans pat my back or put a congratulatory hand on my shoulder as I get to the edge. These are my people. I am their chosen one, and they clap.

When I get to the aisle, a security man takes me to the front. Seth motions for me to join them on the stage. I take the stairs carefully, clutching the banister like the ground is moving under my flats. *Don't think of the crowd. Don't think of the cast. Pretend they're the characters. You've been talking to them for years. You know them better than most.* I swallow.

The lights are pointed on me, blinding me to everything but the stage. The cast of my show. They come to me in a huddle, arms and smiles and hellos. I see into their actual eyes for the first time, no screen drawing a barrier between us. They each take a turn hugging me. Nina's is warm and tight, like the kind of hug girlfriends share.

I can barely move my limbs when she knocks my glasses off and they fall under the table.

I move to grab them, but Caden comes in for a hug, and the world is on fire. His arms wrap around me, his chest pushes up against mine, my face grazes his, and my nose lands in his hair. It smells like waterfalls and rainbows, and the pot of gold at the end. Unicorns too, I imagine. My heart eyes are as big as the *Snapdragon*, my every nerve on fire. Even my feet are overheating.

"So, Kole," Seth begins once they all sit. "You write a pretty good story. Any suggestions for us this season?"

Caden takes his mic and hands it to me. I accept with shaky fingers, one hand on my braid. Oh my stars. My fingers are touching his fingerprints.

This is my chance. I get to speak for the fans. "I . . . have many, um, but, like, this isn't my panel. So, storywise? I guess I'll talk about those later today. But as a writer, here are a few that are just kinda coming to me—maybe stop baiting us? It's time for Benedick to go back to Coracinus and tell Frankie he loves him, I mean, obviously. Maybe you need to give Byron and Pippa more than lingering looks? And, um, please be building toward something with Sebastian and Aster. You can't get mad at us for shipping obsessions and explosions when you're the one lighting the fire, right?"

Seth nods at that, slowly, his eyes on the table. The crowd ignites. I glance toward the fans, losing feeling in my body. *They're staring at me. Agreeing with me.*

This is going . . . okay?

I must give them more. Here goes.

"Stop killing our favs—especially the people of color. Always keep the angst level at a steady squee o'meter. That's what I shoot for.

But don't forget about the other pieces of Pippa's life—give us more on her parents. Her time at the academy. More about Benedick and Byron's childhoods. Less on galactic war. We've seen it so many times before. Stick to the vengeful uncle plotline and let our favs breathe. Or let them smile, for feck's sake. Like, more than once a season."

The crowd claps so loud it hurts my ears. I look at the people to my right. Adam and Caden are giving me the thumbs-up. Phew. The space-pirate brothers like my idea. Thank the stars they aren't shoving me off the stage. I look back to Seth.

"All right, Kole Miller. How about this? How about we swap contact info and discuss some of these ideas? Can't get too specific onstage here—wouldn't want to spoil anything, like where we're headed with Cedric and Aster." He looks to the audience and wiggles his eyebrows. The crowd goes wild. "Since I do happen to like some of your thoughts, let's talk. See what can work. And if it does . . . maybe we find a spot in the writer's room for you for season five. Maybe." He stares into my soul. He's speaking the words of my dreams. Maybe, as it turns out, my bus to Hollywood was *Spacer*. It was my late nights writing. My blood, sweat, tears, and angst.

"Seriously?" I squawk. "That would be stellar. Like, interstellar." I gasp in a geeky half-laugh, half-smile way. And I will work for it, every day, until my fingertips bleed.

"Let's chat," he says, reaching into his back pocket and handing me a business card. I stick it in the pocket of my sweater. "I mean no promises, but I'm open to a conversation."

"Does that confirm a renewal, Seth?" Lana yells. "I mean, you did just say season five!"

He puts his hands up in a faux *I dunno* move. All I hear is screaming. The crowd loves it.

Someone behind me yanks on my shoulder. It's Ben, who plays Cedric, and he's brought me a chair.

"Thanks," I whisper. He nods for me to sit, flashing me one of those million-dollar smiles. Asteroids. He's a space puppy. I hereby take back all my yucky thoughts on Cedric as of now. But Cedric still isn't endgame. Not in my universe.

I sit for the rest of the panel between Freddie and Seth. Forget a happy place—I never needed one of those. I needed a geeky place, and this is it.

CHAPTER TWENTY

I stand behind a faux wall, just myself and a brand new, badass *Space Game* T-shirt that's low cut enough to show off where Caden signed my collarbone in crimson lipstick. Today has been unbelievable. I take a swig from a room-temperature bottle of water. The chattering of fans on the other side has grown louder over the last few minutes, drowning out the theme music. I've popped my knuckles so many times that there's no more feeling in my fingers. Still, I keep bending them, hoping for a satisfying crack.

I can do this runs through my head because if I say it enough, it'll be true. Right?

I shut my eyes. The rise and fall of my chest needs to be steady. *Focus.* I'll be okay once I sit down. Once the flood washes over me and I find my stride. Just like in Creative Writing when I read aloud. Just like what happened at the panel a few hours ago. I'll find Michaela and Mom in the audience. I can look at them, as blurry as they'll be.

The cacophony of movement on the other side of the wall sings with the clanging of chairs and chattering of fans. I wipe my brow, puffing out my braid for the tenth time. I was going to wear my hair down, but without my glasses, sticking to something familiar is the only way I'm going to get through this. They've got to be on a table in the other room, lonely and lost like I am. I texted Michaela to see if she could grab them, but she hasn't responded. And it's too late to go back myself. Mom's been somewhere in the front row for the last twenty minutes, reading the tail end of my season-two entries on her phone and carrying around my swag.

Dare I say it, she might be a fan. A noob, but a fan. I pop my knuckles. I'll take it.

The other side of the wall goes quiet as Kasey gathers the attention of the crowd. The lights in the hall dim. All eyes must be settling on the stage. Kasey runs through a list of *Spacer*'s finest moments while fans cheer and heat rushes to my face. I smile, memories of things I wrote filtering through my head, a highlight reel of my imagination. Things I wrote in the quiet of my room, in the bubbles of my bathtub, in the bathroom on occasion. Things I didn't realize others were loving.

Things straight from my brain. Which is all I'm going to have in there.

All right thoughts, we got this.

"And without waiting another moment, let's welcome Kole Miller, author of *Spacer,* onto the stage!"

I keep my eyes on my feet as I step up the little staircase at the back of the platform. Just like Pippa, landing on Aureus. Deep breath. Go.

The spotlights are pointed on me, blinding me enough to hide the crowd, save for the front row. There are a lot of people, a rather noisy bunch, but they're a blurry mess of camera flashes and sparkles, bright cosplay colors and props. The blur makes it a little easier to get to my seat and set my water down. To wave and smile like this is the most natural thing in the galaxy.

"Welcome, Kole!" Kasey yells, coming around and giving me a big hug like we haven't already seen each other a few times today.

"Hello!" I say into the microphone all cheery-like. It greets me with a loud ringing before the screech fizzles out. "Thanks for coming to my panel." And *smile*. "I'm Kole." Which they know. Heat rises to my cheeks, but there's nothing I can do but wait for it to fade out.

"So, Kole, you've got a few fans in here. About a hundred I'd say." Kasey extends her arms. The crowd roars.

I smile wider, biting my bottom lip to keep it from splitting my face.

"Thank you, all of you. I'm dumbfounded." Oh, an SAT word. The nerves in my head are starting to fade to black, and I'm relaxing enough to cross my legs. These are just a ton of fans like myself before me, with nothing but my site between us. That's the only difference—I started draining my thoughts into a massive project . . . and they like it. I've nothing to fear.

"We'd like to start with some questions we generated behind the scenes before we take some from the audience. In about forty-five minutes, Kole's agreed to read from this week's *Spacer* entry. I hope she won't be mad I'm saying this, but she teased that we'll be meeting Katherine very soon and get a lot of answers about the love triangle that destroyed Carter and Santiago's relationship. Maybe we'll get some foreshadowing today since they just left for Viridis?"

I wiggle my eyebrows. "Maybe? Let's just say that if it's true, *my* version of those answers will be coming soon. But before, we've got some hefty feels to get through. I mean, Sebastian is being held captive in the hull. I'm sure you're aware that Byron's not too happy about this."

"Oh, yes! More broody feels from Byron. Hey!" Kasey motions to the crowd. "Did you all hear that Seth Andelman just invited Kole to talk through some ideas with him for next season? He's even going to let her sit in the writers' room and pitch a few ideas, if they work with where they're headed after this season."

"Yes, after many nondisclosure agreements," I slip in. I give a snarky laugh. "And if they tell *my* story *right*." That was uber sarcastic, and the crowd goes wild.

"That promise all but confirms we'll be renewed!"

And the crowd goes wild. Again. Uproariously. God, I hope she's right. Kasey calms them down, and I answer usual convention-type questions. I've seen them asked on panels during San Diego Comic Cons and Fan Expos before—all part of my prep for this very moment. Where do I get my ideas, what scenes would I rewrite from the show, what characters would I bring back from the dead . . . I try not to use too many filler words to keep Kasey and the crowd in suspense but dangle a few bits of specifics out there. And the audience takes the bait every time. When I read from this week's *Spacer* entry, they squeal. They gasp. They laugh and they clap. I could get used to this. And hey, that whole eyes-on-me thing?

It's working out.

"All right, Kole, ready to take on some eager fans?"

GoGnomes, the nastiest reader I've encountered, has been taken care of. Now that I know it was Damian, the rest of those faceless commenters don't seem nearly so scary. They're just kids. Like me. There have got to be a few more in this crowd, but Kasey won't let them get out of line. And if I've proven myself something over the last few weeks, it's that they're everywhere, and I can handle them. I'll use my *sparkling* wit. My zero-bullshit o'meter. "Yes. I'm ready! And remember, I've been one of you from the get-go, so be nice. We're all fans here."

The first guy comes to the mic. I can barely make him out. I put a hand to my brow, but shading my eyes from the light won't make a difference. I better clear this up before anyone wonders what the feck I'm doing. "I'm sorry, guys, I left my glasses at the other panel and I'm having a hard time seeing past the lights," I say, blinking several times. It's not going to work. It never does. But I can answer questions. Don't need eyes to do that.

"Hi Kole, my question is this: who would you eff, marry, kill on *The Space Game*?"

"Oh geez. Okay, first of all, sorry, Mom." I glance to where I think she is, in the front row next to Michaela, but it's pretty blurry. It's probably a good thing I can't totally see her. She's got to be mortified. Okay, here goes. "Eff. Marry. Kill. Hmmm . . ." Like I haven't thought about this all the time. "I say eff Byron, marry Pippa, and kill Katherine—she's going to be the worst. I'd pick Santiago if Byron hadn't done it already." Whoops, I spoiled a detail about Katherine. Just call me Tom Holland.

The guy takes a seat, seeming to like that answer. Okay, first one down. Next, a girl goes to the mic.

"I just have a comment really, not so much a question. I just want to say that I'm a really big fan, and thank you for doing our ship justice," the girl says. I can tell she's cosplaying Captain Worley since she's dressed in an old military uniform. "If it weren't for you, I'm not sure I'd still be watching."

"Okay, that's phenomenally adorable. Thank you. I'll keep writing. I'm not sure I can promise I won't let you guys down, but I'll do my best. And I like your outfit." And I love her.

She sits back down, and another person takes the mic. "Yeah, hi, Kole. I was wondering if you'd ever try killing someone off?"

Oh, that's a good one. How do I answer without giving too

much away? "If I had my choice, I'd have killed Calico Jack long before Pippa did. I know a lot of readers want Sebastian dead, I see it in the comments, but I'm not sure I can go there. It would kill any chance Pippa has to right the wrong that happened between Carter and Santiago."

The audience applauds; a few people even hoot and holler.

Oh, look! I got this. I can answer their questions without pissing them all off.

"That's not what I meant. Kill your fav. He's problematic. The show would be better without Byron Swift." A couple people groan. One person claps loudly in the front row. Fanboy sits down.

I cock an eyebrow, grit my teeth, and feel my face growing stern. Crap. That's going to become a reaction gif; I just know it. "Not happening. Byron's brave, and rash, and, on occasion, jealous and mean and vindictive, but he's as flawed and as tortured as any good hero. Especially one who just lost their father figure. Unless the showrunners make it so, I'm not killing my fav." I take a sip of my water. "And not simply to end the ship wars, if that's what this is actually about."

More clapping. I'm pretty sure I hear Michaela screaming.

Boom. I *so* got this.

"Next, please," Kasey says.

The next fan clears his throat, taking a second to adjust the microphone stand. I take another a sip of water. Okay, I was sassy, but not so sassy the audience didn't agree with me. Not so sassy that Kasey threw me a *wrap it up* hand signal like we discussed. Not so sassy—

The fan speaks. "I have a question, but it's not so much about *Spacer*, though I might be the newest fan in the room."

That voice.

I choke on my water a little, putting one hand to my mouth and thumping on my chest with the other. "I'm okay," I say as soon as I can function. I blink back the water that's filling my eyes. "Nasty thing, water, when it's not sure where to go."

The crowd giggles, confused. Someone drops something in the back.

"I was wondering what you're doing for dinner tonight, Kole Miller?" That blurry, too-tall fan. It's my nerd.

Colin.

I put a hand to my neck and smile so hard I don't even bite my lip.

Kasey covers her mic and leans toward the table. "What's going on? Do I roll with it?"

I nod, eyes on the blurry figure. "Let it happen." The audience is still. The phones flash, snapping away. The static of the mic buzzes. "So, your question is about my dinner plans?"

"It's one. But there are details. I have notes in my pocket." He reaches for something and unfolds it. "Let me try being honest, if the audience will indulge me." He pauses; they clap. "Here's the truth, Kole. Since freshman English, there's only been one girl I've thought about. She's talented, beautiful, smart. I look around and I see that she's got the galaxy in the palm of her hand—and all I can do is bring her a couple of peonies and hope that maybe someday she'll give me a chance."

He pauses again. I can't speak. My mouth hangs open, growing drier by the second.

Colin is here. At my panel. I cross my hands over my heart.

"I want to read her words every night, like I have this last week.

Spacer is a masterpiece. But too recently, I've seen salt on her cheeks when I know the moon is in her voice. I want to get lost in it, to sit behind her while she realizes the universe is hers. And I want to stand with her when the noise is too much. To silence the voices that would absorb hers."

"Colin," I whisper. The mic catches it. My stars, he's here saying words I didn't know I wanted to hear. My chest fills with warmth.

He's publicly acknowledging his affections, and I . . . don't seem to mind? It was different with Noah. Noah did it at school, when he didn't know what was on the line. Colin is doing it in front of a thousand eyes that accept me. That appreciate fan fiction. That are unabashedly *my* fans. And I think I'm okay with that.

"So, my first question is, will you go to dinner with me?" he asks.

The crowd is silent until someone yells, "Say yes!"

I nod, but my voice is lost. I want to say that *every night for the seeable future, I will have dinner with you, Colin Clarke.*

"My second question is one I've asked before, in the middle of an orchard surrounded by the skies you live in. Please don't say no."

I double blink, my eyes stinging. I'm pretty sure I've lost any ability to say no.

"Would you like to borrow my glasses?" There's laughter in his voice. He's enjoying this.

"Yes," I say, much too loudly. My voice is back with a vengeance. "I really would. So very much. To both of your questions." I put my hands to my face and drag them along the bottoms of my eyes, part from embarrassment and part from absolute, over-the-moon glee.

Who is this boy I was too busy hating for the last few years? I was too blinded, too caught up in my own head to see that he's the thorny-on-the-outside, buttery-and-sweet-in-the-middle, perfect-for-me boy. And he can most definitely take me to dinner tonight. But we split the bill.

He moves through the crowd, shoves something under his arm, comes to the bottom of the stage, and puts a hand out. I grab it and yank him up here. The crowd laughs, part sighing, part clapping. All eyes are on us, I'm sure, so it's kinda nice that they're a big blur. They can't hear us, but I can feel their eyes on us.

"You're unreal," I whisper, hardly hiding a goofy grin. The mic can't catch my words from here. "And I've never been happier to see you."

"I had to come. I had to see this." He motions around him like it's the Emerald City, smiling. "So this is your thing?"

"I think so," I say, pushing my hair behind an ear. "And I'm really enjoying it."

"You're doing beautifully. Here. They've always looked better on you." He takes off his glasses and some of his hair falls around his face. He puts them across my nose and comes into focus, his eyes shadowed, dark-and-slightly-curled hair falling over his forehead. I take him in: cheekbones carved by the gods before they sprinkled freckles across his nose. Eyes I'd willingly drown in. He's adorable, and I'm seeing him clearly for the first time.

A perfect match, the geek and the nerd.

I look around the room, now clear, and see that the crowd has started to talk amongst themselves. They stopped the phone-camera flashes for now.

"Oh, hey, I brought this." He takes the document under his arm—the lit mag—and flips to my poem. "I talked to Liu. She's reprinting the whole mag with your name in it. And you're getting major money. The new editions go out next week."

I grab the copy. There's my name under my poem. My words, officially published. "But the blowback—Hailey won't rest. She'll find some way to—"

"They kicked her out. The syllabus says no plagiarism. This falls into that category. I think she learned her lesson."

My heart jumps. "So it's done—Damian's neutered. Kicked from the con. Hailey's condemned to grade-level English. The boss geeks have been destroyed."

"What? Boss?" he asks, entirely confused.

"Ah, Kole?" Kasey asks. I motion for her to give me one more minute.

"Don't worry about it. It's not an SAT word," I whisper to him, grabbing his hand and leading him around to the other side of the table so we can see the audience. Kasey's watching, her heart-eyes locked on us.

"Sorry. I'm back." The audience hushes. I lean down and speak into the microphone. "So, guys, this is my nerd, Colin. He's everything I didn't know I wanted." I stare at him, googly eyes and butterfly wings and shmoopy gushes. This boy melted a girl whose heart lived in the constellations.

He waves at the crowd without so much as a glance at them, looks right at my lips, and leans in. Before I can inhale, his hand is in my hair, mine around his neck, and he's kissing me. I feel it all the way down to my toes—and don't pull away when the audience erupts in applause. Being wrapped in him is something I would have never, ever imagined when he was at Liu's podium, or leaning back into my desk space, or racing to beat me to the stupid printer. I kiss him back in a way that will leave a bruise (I'll apologize later), and when we break apart, he keeps my bottom lip in between his teeth for a millisecond longer. I suck in a shallow breath. Someone is going to have to tell my parents to bury me with Colin Clarke's teeth-print on my lips.

I pull back. We're in front of a crowd. And . . . my mother's here. That's embarrassing. First, I smile at Colin, and then the audience. There will be room for kissing tonight. Lots of it.

My universe is coming together. I've got my site. I destroyed the jerks at school. I found my fans. I'm on my way to the writer's room. I'm kissing a beautiful boy in front of a packed room.

Michaela and Mom are in the front row, my glasses tucked into Mom's shirt. It doesn't look like she disapproves of what just happened *too* much. Michaela's knuckles are white from grasping her hands so tightly. "Time for a golden retriever!" she yells.

I give her a thumbs-up. I should have listened to her a long time ago.

"I ship it!" Kasey yells into her mic. The crowd goes bonkers.

Colin puts his arm around my waist.

Me too, Kasey. Me too.

Acknowledgments

A book is something a whole lot of people have a hand in, but one person sits down and types, or so I've found to be true.

Thank you to my husband, Matt; your utmost support and excitement for each step of the journey to publication inspire me to choose better words, write stronger sentences, and form heavier paragraphs. Thank you for pushing me and giving me my own green lights at the end of the dock: Charlotte and Ben. I never would have ventured into the world of writing if I hadn't been given two of the most precious plot twists. Charlotte and Ben, you are the reason why I'll never give up on the beauty of language and the thoughts of the world. Why I'll always see Frederick as the most important mouse in the fence—and may you find a little bit of him in you one day.

Thank you to my very first cheerleaders: my mother, Lesley; my brother, John; my sisters, Brindy, Allison, and Sherry; my Aunt Ayn; and my cousins, Abby and Spencer. I know the minutes ticked away while I talked about my books and writing over the years, but your open ears and encouragement kept me going long past when the neighbors turned out their lights. Thank you for not squashing my dream and for helping me to find it. Dad and Nana and Grandpa and Gram: you're not here to see this, but somehow I know that you know about this little geeky book, and I know that you're not at all surprised this wacky story fell out of my head. I don't know how I know all this, but I do. And I hope you're proud.

To Mr. Peterson: if I hadn't walked into your classroom freshman year and seen the words *do I dare disturb the universe?* across the whiteboard, then I never would have realized that yes, I really, really do dare. And if you hadn't seen something in the short story I wrote and read it aloud for the class, I likely would never have found Kole's voice within me. It may have taken me a while to find out what universe to disturb, but once I did, I couldn't stop. Thank you for believing in the quiet girl in the corner.

Thank you to Marie Rutkoski: if I hadn't stumbled upon *The Winner's Curse* in that tattered old bookshop in Denver, I never would have thought, *hey, I need to try this.* Boy, do you know how to craft a killer ship or what?

It would be an absolute mistake to not mention my Horizon family in my acknowledgments. From my early readers and cheer-leaders—Christi Britt, Joshua Garrett, Pamela Wagner, Davina Baird, Lori Hernandez—to every student who walked through the doors of my classroom—you played a part in this novel. No, you're not a character. No, I haven't picked any names on purpose. But what is in these pages is your spark, your drive, your *grit* (it's true!), and the subtle pieces of you that leave a mark on a teacher's heart. Find yourself in these words if you're so inclined, but may you also find the confidence in yourself that Kole eventually finds in herself. That is my wish for you when you walk out of my classroom, and what I'm always too emotional to tell you on the last day of the school year. Honestly, it's better you just leave. I have an ugly-cry face. (I'm not joking when I say that I see a spark in ALL OF YOU. Now go find it too in this big old world and then shoot me an email. Proofread it first.)

I owe a debt to the writing community on Twitter. There's ab-solutely no way I would have gotten here without Alexa Donne's Author Mentor Match and the support, friendship, and excitement that Rachel Somer displayed when she chose me as a mentee. Rachel, if you hadn't seen something in my first manuscript, then DWTS would never have been born. There aren't enough thank-yous in this world for you. Likewise, my agent, Rachel Brooks. You saw yourself in Kole. You cheered for her and you cheered for me. One of the luckiest days of my life was when you found me in the slush.

Kelsy Thompson and Mari Kesselring, my editors—you saw things in Kole and in this messy story that needed to see the light. You both pushed this novel, and I'm inexplicably proud of how it's turned out. Thank you. Thank you. Thank you.

So many other writers cheered on Kole—I think we can all find ourselves in the story of the quiet girl in the back of the room, right? I have some of the best critique partners out there: Katy Brooke and Cassie Miller, you got this story here. Thank you from the bottom of my heart. Thank you to Team Peppermint: Jade M. Loren, Heba ElSherief, Lauren Blackwood, and Suzanne Mattaboni. Your excitement fueled so much of this story! And the writers who supported me in the Pitch Wars community—Rachel Lynn Solomon, Tobie Easton, and Jennieke Cohen—the feedback and the answers you gave me made me believe in the potential of this concept. Thank you for taking this fledgling writer and helping her jump out of the nest.

And, dear readers, if I'm lucky enough to meet you in real life and you're feeling particularly courageous, ask me about my ships. I've got a lot to say. I promise to be nice, even if we disagree. I may even tell you which one inspired this book.

Maybe.

About the Author

Katie Kingman lives in Phoenix, Arizona, with her husband, two children, and cats. She spends her days teaching British Literature, Creative Writing, and a film class. Since she was young, she's been an avid reader; she used to sleep with *Jurassic Park*, *The Lost World*, and the *Star Wars* extended universe books under her pillow. She's wanted to be a writer since her English teacher read her short story out loud during freshman year. It was mortifying, but things worked out fine.